Pierre Chaignon

The Sacrifice of the Mass

worthily celebrated

Pierre Chaignon

The Sacrifice of the Mass
worthily celebrated

ISBN/EAN: 9783337299712

Printed in Europe, USA, Canada, Australia, Japan

Cover: Foto ©Andreas Hilbeck / pixelio.de

More available books at **www.hansebooks.com**

THE SACRIFICE OF THE MASS
WORTHILY CELEBRATED.

THE

SACRIFICE OF THE MASS

WORTHILY CELEBRATED.

From the French of the

REVEREND FATHER CHAIGNON, S.J.

By

RIGHT REVEREND L. DE GOESBRIAND, D.D.,

Bishop of Burlington, Vt.

———

NEW YORK, CINCINNATI, CHICAGO :

BENZIGER BROTHERS,

Printers to the Holy Apostolic See.

1897

PREFACE.

THIS admirable work of Father Chaignon, S.J., hardly needs an introduction. It was written by one who devoted his priestly life to the sanctification of the secular clergy. He rightly thought that the safest road to success in this work was to induce them to celebrate the sacrifice of the Mass in a holy and becoming manner. This conviction led him to write "Le Prêtre à l'Autel." It is divided into two parts: 1. Due preparation for the holy sacrifice of the Mass. In this part he speaks of the nature of the sacrifice, the holiness it demands of the celebrant, its advantages for the priest. 2. Fervor of the priest in the celebration of Mass. Father Chaignon, in this part of his work, follows the priest through the preludes of the Mass, its different parts, and the communion, explaining every prayer and ceremony in a learned and devout manner. The translator considers this book so admirable that he feels inclined to say to every priest on earth: "Tolle, lege."

CONTENTS.

PART I.

DUE PREPARATION FOR THE CELEBRATION OF THE HOLY MYSTERIES.

CHAPTER I.

Excellence of the Sacrifice of Our Altars, . . . 10

CHAPTER II.

Holiness Required for the Daily Celebration of the Sacrifice of Our Altars, ... 38

CHAPTER III.

Virtues Particularly Required for the Celebration of the Holy Mysteries 53

CHAPTER IV.

Powerful Means of Sanctification Offered to Priests in the Celebration of the Holy Mysteries, . . 88

CHAPTER V.

Preparation for the Holy Sacrifice, ... 116

PART II.

FERVOR WHICH SHOULD ACCOMPANY, THANKSGIVING WHICH SHOULD FOLLOW, THE CELEBRATION OF THE HOLY MYSTERIES.

CHAPTER I.

The Preludes of the Sacrifice, ... 134

CHAPTER II.

PAGE

The Beginning of the Sacrifice, or the Offertory, . 151

CHAPTER III.

The Preface, ... 169

CHAPTER IV.

First Part of the Canon; that which Precedes and Accompanies the Consecration, ... 177

CHAPTER V.

Second Part of the Canon—from the Consecration to the " Pater," 211

CHAPTER VI.

Proximate Preparation for Communion, . . . 234

CHAPTER VII.

Communion and Last Prayers of Holy Mass, . . 258

CHAPTER VIII.

Thanksgiving After Mass, ... 268

THE SACRIFICE OF THE MASS WORTHILY CELEBRATED.

PART I.

DUE PREPARATION FOR THE CELEBRATION OF THE HOLY MYSTERIES.

THE remote preparation for the worthy celebration of Mass consists in studying the excellence of this sacrifice, considering the necessity of a holy life for the worthy offering of it, bestowing special thought on the special virtues which this sublime function demands of the priest, and the powerful aids afforded him in this action for the attainment of an eminent degree of perfection. The proximate preparation consists in exercises of piety, whose object is to excite in the soul sentiments conformable to this angelical function.

CHAPTER I.

EXCELLENCE OF THE SACRIFICE OF OUR ALTARS.

WHAT is its nature? What are its effects? An answer to these questions will give us an idea of its supreme excellence.

1. When we say that the sacrifice of the Mass is the same for which the world sighed during four thousand years, the same which was foretold by the prophets, prefigured by all the ceremonies of the Old Law, offered near Jerusalem on Calvary, and which being offered once only was fully sufficient " to perfect forever them that are sanctified," [1] we acknowledge with all tradition that the Catholic Church has nothing more august— "cum augustius habeat Ecclesia Catholica nihil " [2]—and that no function of greater dignity can be imagined than that of the priest under the law of grace—"quâ nullâ major excogitari potest." [3] Hugh of St. Victor, speaking of this ministry, exclaims: " Magna dignitas, mira potestas, excelsum et expanendum officium." [4]

If, in fact, this sacrifice be the same as that of the cross, it must have the same priest, the same victim, the same ends, the same efficacy, the same value; and

[1] Heb. x. 14.   [2] Com. Melodun., an. 1579, titulo 10.
[3] Conc. Milan, an. 1573.   [4] Tom. iii.

if so, can we imagine anything either more dignified or more acceptable to God? Can there be anything more useful, not only to its ministers, but to the whole world? What an inexhaustible source of consolation for the priest and of blessing for the whole world there must be in this sacrifice! This thought was undoubtedly present to the mind of Jeremias when he said to the Lord: "Inebriabo animam sacerdotum pinguedine, et populus meus bonis meis adimplebitur." [1] Now, the Church has decreed in the Council of Trent that these two sacrifices are one and the same, and that there is no difference between them save in the manner in which they are offered: "Solâ offerendi ratione diversa." [2] In each of the two a *God*-priest offers to God a God-*Victim*. Everything is divine upon the altar as upon the cross.

1. *The same priest.*—"Oh, no," says St. John Chrysostom, "these wonderful works which we see on the altar are not due to the power of man—non sunt humanæ virtutis hæc opera." "We priests are simply the instruments and ministers of the veritable sacrifice—nos ministrorum tantum tenemus locum. The Lord Himself is He who sanctifies the material gifts offered for the sacrifice, and who makes them a source of sanctification for us—ipse est qui sanctificat et immutat." "When, therefore," he adds, "you see the sacred minister lifting up to heaven the holy offering, think not

[1] Jer. xxxi. 14.   [2] Conc. Trid. Sess. XXII., c. 2.

that he whom you behold is the real priest; but, rising above visible objects, consider the hand of Jesus Christ stretched out invisibly. Through Him everything is done." "Cum sacerdotem videris offerentem, ne ut sacerdotem esse potes, sed Christi manum invisibiliter extensam."[1] The words of St. Ambrose are equally formal: "Idem est hoc nostrum sacrificium cum eo quod Christus obtulit; pontifex enim noster ille est qui hostiam mundantem nos obtulit."[2] None else save the Word Incarnate has ever presented to God a victim of itself capable of purifying the souls of men. According to the Council of Trent, He who offered Himself upon the cross offers Himself now also through the ministry of the priests—"Idem nunc offerens sacerdotum ministerio, qui se ipsum tunc in cruce obtulit."[3] But what does He offer? The most insignificant gift presented by His divine hand would unquestionably be most agreeable to His Father. Were His offering to be none but that of a lamb, like the sacrifice of Abel, or of bread and wine, like that of Melchisedech, the dignity of this adorable Priest would not fail to impart an infinite value to His sacrifice. But a gift ought to be worthy both of him who offers it and of him who receives the offering. Since, therefore, this great High Priest is a God who offers sacri-

---

[1] Hom. 60 ad Pop. Antioch.
[2] Inter opera S. Ambr. in Ep. ad Heb. 10.
[3] Sess. XXII., c. 2, circa medium.

fice to God at the altar, it follows that a God-man was the only victim worthy of so great a sacrifice. It is therefore Jesus Christ whom Jesus Christ immolates.

2. *The same victim.*—When the Saviour, celebrating the first of all Masses, and instituting the priesthood for all time to come, imparted to us the power to do what He had just done Himself, we know what victim it was which He held in His holy and venerable hands, and which He put into our own. " This is my body," He said, " the same which shall be given for you"—" quod pro vobis tradetur." " This is my blood, the same which shall be shed for you"—" qui pro vobis fundetur." It was not therefore one body, one blood on Calvary, and another body, another blood upon the altar. They were the same. Was it not the life-giving Victim of the cross that reconciled us with God? Now, the Council of Trent teaches us that the same Victim also is immolated every day by the priest; and hence it draws this inference, which we ought to consider with attention—that the dread mystery is the most holy and divine of all the works which can be performed by Christians : " Necessario fatemur, nullum aliud opus adeo sanctum ac divinum a Christi fidelibus tractari posse, quam hoc ipsum tremendum mysterium, quo vivifica illa hostia, quâ Deo Patri reconciliati sumus, in altari per sacerdotes quotidie immolatur." [1] The same council

[1] Sess. XXII., Decret. de observand. et evitand. in celebrat. missæ.

had previously declared that "una eademque est hostia, idem nunc offerens."

Behold, therefore, divinity in the *priest* who sacrifices. Whenever we celebrate, Jesus Christ celebrates with us and through us.[1] Behold also divinity in the *victim* which is sacrificed! It is always Jesus Christ, "hostia mundans nos" (St. Ambrose), "hostia vivifica" (Council of Trent), "super sacram mensam Christus occisus jacet" (St. Chrysostom).

Where, therefore, is the difference between the sacrifice of the Mass and that of Calvary? It simply consists in the manner of the oblation of the one and the other—"sola offerendi ratione diversa." On Calvary the blood was poured out; Jesus offered to God His natural death, which was the separation of His soul from His body. On the altar, Jesus Christ, impassible and glorious, offers Himself in a mystical and unbloody manner. Upon the cross He offered His actual death; upon the altar He offers the death already suffered. He offered Himself upon the cross for a sacrifice of redemption, by which He merited all the graces which He wished to grant men until the last day. He offers Himself in our churches as a sacrifice of commemoration and application of His merits. He therein applies to us the merits of His death, and places under our eyes its living and touching representation. There is no

[1] The same ministry which Jesus Christ exercised visibly upon the cross, He exercises invisibly upon the altar. (Mgr. Gousset.)

virtue in the sacrifice of the Mass, except that which emanates from the cross. The cross is the source, the altar is the channel of grace. There is nothing so excellent as our sacrifice considered in its essence, viz., the priest and the victim. The same should be said of its effects.

II. As the Mass is the sacrifice of Calvary represented, applied, perpetuated through ages of time, it must have objects as noble as those of the bloody oblation, and means as efficacious for their accomplishment—"In qualibet missa invenitur omnis fructus quem Christus operatus est in cruce." [1] Was there anything wanting to the sacrifice of the cross for the fulfilment of all the designs of God's glory and for the satisfaction of all the needs of humanity? Oh! what virtue there was in the voice of that adorable blood which trickled down from all the wounds of Jesus and implored mercy for sinners! What power of salvation in the mediation of a God dying, and accepting for the attainment of our happiness a punishment of excessive confusion and anguish! Now, St. John Chrysostom assures us that an equal power is annexed to the sacrifice of the Mass: "Tantum valet celebratio missæ quantum valet mors Christi in cruce."

The Mass is pre-eminently an act of homage. [2] It is

---

[1] S. Thom. in cap. 6, Is. lect. 6.

[2] "To assist at the sacrifice of the true God is to assist at the most holy and august act of religion. Hence it is that in the most ancient

the act of man rendering to God the worship in spirit and in truth which is due to His infinite perfections. It accomplishes all the ends of religion.   We find herein everything which connects the creature with the Creator, and unites heaven to earth; viz., *adoration, thanksgiving, prayer, expiation.*   These are four obligations from which all others flow.   If these are well fulfilled in the sacrifice of our altars, united to the many mysteries which are therein represented, the Mass becomes an abridgment, a summary, and the centre of all religion.   The Jewish sacrifices, called by St. Paul "infirma et egena elementa," had no value or efficacy except inasmuch as they expressed faith in the One which they prefigured; that is, in the Sacrifice of Calvary which is continued in our churches.   This alone renders the divine perfections all the honor which is due to them.   It is the veritable *holocaust,* or sacrifice of adoration, which alone returns thanks to the Sovereign Benefactor in a manner proportionate to His blessings. It is truly *eucharistic,* and thereby is all-powerful to induce the Almighty God to pour down His choicest blessings upon us, and to appease His anger, however great.   In this sacrifice we have the most excellent *prayer,* the most certain propitiation.

liturgies this sacrifice is' called *the* act.   So, too, is it called even in our days ; for, according to the remark of a learned cardinal of our time, these words of the Canon, ' infra actionem,' signify nothing else than ' infra sacrificium.' It seems as if the Church would thereby admonish us that sacrifice should be the great act of our life." (Bourdaloue. Sermon for the Monday in the fourth week of Lent.)

1. *The Mass is a holocaust.*—Our first obligation is to adore God, to acknowledge Him as the principle whence all good flows, as the Sovereign Lord to whom everything belongs, as the last end of every creature. " Ego sum qui sum—Ego sum Alpha et Omega, principium et finis. Ego sum Dominus; mea sunt omnia." The formal acknowledgment we make of our absolute dependence, of our profound misery, of our nothingness in presence of His infinite power and greatness, is the very essence of adoration.

But how shall we be able to acquit ourselves worthily of this duty? What homage will we offer to God which will be equal to those which are due to Him? "Were I," said Isaias, "to gather up in one heap all the woods of Libanus, and to burn as a holocaust on that altar all the animals which dwell in its immense forests, this would not be enough"—"non sufficit."[1] Let us add with the prophet, Were I to humble myself in the dust, were I to annihilate before God all the creatures which now exist, together with those which will ever exist, what glory would accrue to Him from the humiliation of nothingness? For such, indeed, I am in Thy sight. "Substantia mea tanquam nihilum ante te."[2] As I am, such are all the nations of the universe. "Omnes gentes quasi non sint, sic sunt coram eo."[3] But when I go up to the altar; when I offer to God the adorations, the humiliations of His well-beloved Son, through Jesus

---

[1] Is. xl. 16.   [2] Ps. xxxviii. 6.   [3] Is. xl. 17.

Christ, with Jesus Christ, in Jesus Christ, I render to Him a glory which is absolutely infinite—"per ipsum et cum ipso, et in ipso, est tibi . . . omnis honor et gloria."[1]

It is indeed impossible to conceive how the Divine Majesty could receive an honor greater than this. In the ancient sacrifices, the victim standing trembling at the foot of the altar, ready to be immolated by the knife of the priest, was a vivid expression of the state of man under the hand of God, who can take away his life as He wishes, and holds the sword of death lifted up above his head to immolate him to His greatness and justice. It was the acknowledgment that every excellence of creatures is nothing, and should be accounted as nothing, when compared with His excellence. When in the offering of the holocaust the whole victim was burnt up in His presence, it was to acknowledge that His greatness deserves to be honored by the most absolute annihilation, that He is self-sufficient, and has no need of our gifts. "Deus meus es tu, quoniam bonorum meorum non eges."[2] But when the Victim which we immolate is Jesus Christ, then we truly render to Him the greatest possible glory; and what else could He desire besides? Every other expression of honor disappears when compared with that which He receives at the altar. How great Thou art, O Lord, in whose presence the humanity of Our Redeemer, all adorable as it is, acknowledges itself unworthy of Thy presence, con-

---

[1] Miss. in can.   [2] Ps. xv. 2.

ceals itself under symbols of death, under an atom! How deserving Thou art of veneration and holy fear, in whose presence the God-man, our High Pontiff, falls down annihilated, lost in respect at the sight of Thy ineffable perfections! Who shall understand all the submission which is due to Thee, O Lord, before whose feet, every day and on countless altars, a divine person dies mystically in sign of dependence, and in order to honor Thy sovereign dominion over all creatures! There is in the deep consideration of this thought an inexhaustible source of pure joy for the good priest, and he never allows a day to pass without celebrating Mass with all the piety of which he is capable.

It is related of a pious person that in the ecstasy of her love she expressed to God her regret not to be able, by every word and breath, to create thousands of worlds peopled with seraphim, who should have no occupation but that of praising and blessing God eternally. This desire would surely have procured much glory for God could it have been realized; and yet it is certain that a priest does infinitely more by the offering of one Mass. For however perfect and numerous we may suppose creatures to be, there shall always exist an immeasurable distance between God and them, and hence their homages can have no proportion to the majesty which receives them. But in the Mass, He who adores is as great as the object of adoration, as infinite in all kinds of perfection as He who is adored.

We need not fear, when we celebrate, that God will reproach us as He did His people Israel: "Si pater ego sum, ubi est honor meus?"[1]   Might we not answer Him with respectful confidence: Behold Thy altar, O my God, and look upon the face of Thy Christ? "Respice in faciem Christi tui." Is He not our Saviour and the Restorer of Thy glory? Through the sacrifice which He offers for us, and which we offer Thee through Him, Thou receivest adequate honor and praise. "Secundum nomen tuum, sic et laus tua."[2]   Neither let us fear that while we present to Him the sacred Host, and hold it in our hands, He might say to us, as He did to Israel: "Munus non suscipiam de manu vestra."[3]   Let us rather imagine that we hear Him say exultingly that His name is great and venerated amongst the Gentiles since the day that a spotless Victim has been offered to the glory of His name, in every place from the rising of the sun till the going down thereof. "Magnum est nomen meum in gentibus, et in omni loco sacrificatur, et offertur nomini meo oblatio munda!"[4]

The most pure oblation which we present to the Lord seems to have, all things considered, something more glorious to God than the sacrifice of the cross; although, as we stated, it derives all its excellence from the same. In the Mass, Jesus Christ is in a manner more deeply abased. Upon the cross He was "not a

---

[1] Malach. i. 6.

[2] Ps. xlvii. 11.

[3] Malach. i. 10.

[4] Malach. i. 11.

man, but a worm of the earth"—"Ego sum vermis et non homo." [1]   On the altar He seems to be less than a worm, for He gives here no sign of life.   He allows nothing to appear on the altar that would remind us of His humanity.   On Calvary He was passible and mortal.   Whilst in that state, He, by consenting to die for the glory of His Father, did but follow His destiny; for to His Father He owed a life granted to Him for no other purpose than its sacrifice.   But now He has fully accomplished the designs of that eternal Father. He has, at a great price, purchased immortality and the right to sit at His Father's right hand; and yet He divests Himself of that glorious state wherein He entered by His Resurrection; He again conceals Himself under humble appearances; He descends on the altar for no other end than to renew there the memory of His death. Here this divine Lamb suffers Himself to be mystically immolated as by a sharp-edged sword by the power of the sacramental words.   Do not these strange humiliations give immense force to His words, in St. John— "Ego honorifico patrem"? [2]

Other considerations there are which seem to enhance, if possible, the merit of the mystical immolation of the Saviour above His bloody sacrifice.   The sacrifice of the cross was offered only once; that of the altar is offered without interruption.   God never beholds the crimes of men without seeing, at the same time, in some

[1] Ps. xxi. 7.   [2] John viii. 49.

part of the world, the great act of reparation offered to His outraged glory. The sacrifice of the cross was offered only in Jerusalem; this is offered everywhere. The earth with all its extent seems to be nothing but an immense sanctuary, wherein the ever-living Lamb is immolated upon thousands of altars. The sacrifice of the cross was accomplished in the space of a few hours; the one which we offer has already a duration of over eighteen hundred years, and will endure as long as the Church exists—until the consummation of the world. Jesus Christ on the cross was in the state of man suffering; His state on the altar is entirely incomprehensible. He immolates Himself, and yet He does not suffer; He is distributed, and yet not divided; He is consumed, and yet not destroyed; He is such as He reigns in heaven, and such as He died on Calvary. He is on the altar as in heaven, but without glory; and as He was on Calvary, but without suffering. You wish to know how wonderful is the Holocaust? The heart of Jesus is its altar; His love is the flame; His humanity the victim. God is the end of this sacrifice, and the price of the same is His kingdom which He promises to us. Eternal Majesty! how great the glory that accrues to Thee from this sacrifice! What an idea it gives us of Thy grandeur! Thy holiness, Thy power, Thy justice, but, above all, Thy mercy shine therein in all their splendor.

2. The Mass is a *eucharistic sacrifice, or a sacrifice*

of thanksgiving.—God Himself cannot absolve us from the debt of gratitude imposed upon us by His blessings; for He being our necessary end, we must indispensably return to Him the glory of all the blessings received from His liberality. "In omnibus gratias agite, hæc est enim voluntas Dei in Christo Jesu." [1] St. Augustine considers this duty the most essential part of the worship which God expects of us—"Cultus Dei in hoc maxime constitutus est, ut anima ei non sit ingrata." [2] The Mass has the twofold advantage of kindling in our souls the beautiful sentiment of gratitude toward God, and of enabling us to fulfil worthily the duties which it imposes.

We cannot, first of all, refuse to acknowledge the intentions of the Saviour in leaving us this memorial of all that He did for our happiness, this abridgment of all the wonders of His love, in which we find anew each of the mysteries through which He worked out our salvation, and, above all, His passion and death, which were as full of blessings for us as they were of reproaches and suffering for Him—"tam beatæ passionis." Could He explain Himself more clearly than He did in the institution of the holy sacrifice? That which He then said He desires us to repeat every day. How can we help being moved when we consider the language He used to teach us to what extent He desires us to remember Him and the miracles of His good-

---

[1] I. Thess. v. 18.   [2] De spiritu et litteræ.

ness? " Hæc quotiescumque feceritis, in mei memoriam facietis."   " This do in commemoration of Me; remember My sufferings; do not forget Me."

A father loved his son excessively, and to save him from the capital punishment which this guilty son had deserved he offers himself instead, is accepted, and dies for him.   Before leaving him, however, before passing from his arms to the hands of the executioners, desiring to leave his son a last token of tenderness and make him understand what he expects in return, he merely says to him: " My son, remember your father; forget not his love nor the pledge which he gives you of it at this moment."   What energy in that language, simple as it is!   What does it suggest to the heart of a son in the circumstances in which it is spoken?   This is but an imperfect image of the incomprehensible charity of Jesus Christ for us.   Whilst renewing every day on our altars the ineffable mystery of His immolation, He repeats to us what He said to His apostles when taking leave of them on the eve of His death: " Do this in commemoration of Me.   In order to save you from hell, I have resigned Myself to the most horrible death, and I have waited impatiently for the moment in which I would be permitted to plunge Myself into this baptism of blood.   See to what state My love for you has reduced Me!   Remember Me.   Remember the death I suffered for you, every time you assist at Mass or offer it yourselves.   Understand what you then see and what you do.   If you are obedient to these injunctions, I shall have nothing more to ask of you; for you will then love and be faithful to Me, so as even to die for Me, if necessary."   At what moment is it that this generous Friend addresses to us this recommendation?   At the very moment of the consecration, when we behold with our eyes the most striking representation of what passed on Calvary.

When we pronounce separately over the bread and the wine the sacred words which operate the mystery of transubstantiation, our tongue becomes, as it were, the sword which immolates the Victim.   Do we not see with eyes of faith His blood running down in streams and His head bowing under the deadly blow?   When we hold in our hands the sacred Host, elevated between heaven and earth, can we forget Jesus Christ on the cross, interposing Himself between the wrath of His Father and the iniquities of the world?   See, then, how appropriate the words which follow immediately the two elevations: " Unde et memores nos servi tui."   All hearts should be penetrated with this grateful remembrance; but, above all, the hearts of the priests, who in this instance, as in every other, have the greater share in the favors of heaven.   But the faithful also should be grateful; for it is principally here that God treats them as His well-beloved people, and that He prepares them for sovereign happiness through this great means of sanctification—" Sed et plebs tua sancta."

Not, however, at the elevation alone, but during the whole celebration of Mass, are the faithful excited to remember the blessings of the Lord, and occupied in returning Him thanks. " Deo gratias." " Gratias agimus tibi propter magnam gloriam tuam." " Gratias agamus Domino Deo nostro." " Vere dignum et justum est, . . . nos tibi semper, et ubique gratias agere. . . ." Mark the words " semper et ubique;" for there is not a moment of our life, not a spot in the universe, where we do not receive in abundance the blessings of our good God. And is it not in the sanctuary, and at the hour of the sacrifice, that it is most becoming to bless His goodness?

Not in his own private name does the priest cause his offering to ascend from the visible altar on earth to the invisible altar of heaven. The Church has made him her ambassador and commissioned him to offer up to God the tribute of universal gratitude. Let him not fear to succumb to the weight of his mission; let him not ask, like David, what he could offer to the Lord that would be proportionate to the multitude and greatness of the blessings received by the whole human family whom he represents—" Quid retribuam Domino?" Since he has it in his power to offer the chalice of salvation and the Victim of Calvary, he is fully able to fulfil this obligation—infinite though it really is. One Mass alone suffices to repay Almighty God superabundantly for everything due to His goodness—for the graces and blessings He poured down so liberally upon the sacred humanity of Jesus Christ, upon His incomparable Mother, upon all the angels and saints, and upon every creature, animate or inanimate. Through the Incarnation, God has given us Him who is God like Himself; through the offering which the priest presents to Him on the altar, in his own name and that of his brethren, God receives of us as much as we have received of Him. A more magnificent expression of gratitude we could not present to Him, because Himself could not give us a richer present. In Jesus Christ He has given us everything; in Jesus Christ we return Him everything. "Cum illo omnia nobis donavit." [1]

All graces come to us from God through Jesus Christ; all, says St. Thomas, should return to God through the same channel. It is therefore through Jesus Christ and through His sacrifice that we should return them to their source, so that our great Saviour may, in everything and everywhere, be Mediator between God and men, both in the effusion of grace and in the return which is made therefor through our gratitude.

3. The Mass is a *sacrifice of propitiation*. If the liberality of the Lord imposes upon us immense obligations, we should not forget that we are amenable to His justice also. Can we think of this without trembling? Here again, however, let us tranquillize ourselves. We have in the Mass a sacrifice capable of appeasing the

---

[1] Rom. viii. 32.

wrath of Heaven, however great may have been the crimes by which we have deserved it. The blood of Jesus Christ is offered on the altar, as it was poured out on the cross, "in remissionem peccatorum." This divine blood had power to purify consciences when it was shed on Calvary—"sanguis Christi . . . emundabit conscientiam nostram."[1] It has not lost any of its efficacy since; for to-day, as on the day of His death, Jesus performs for us the office of Mediator, and is Himself our reconciliation—"ipse est propitiatio pro peccatis nostris."[2] He continues on the altar the work of our reconciliation; "quoties hujus hostiæ commemoratio celebratur, opus nostræ redemptionis exercetur."[3] The Mass, therefore, is not a mere representation of the mystery of the cross. In it our redemption is not merely commemorated, it is therein operated in a new manner; in it the office of Redeemer continues to be *exercised*—"opus . . . exercetur;" and this is signified by the priest when he says during the canon that the faithful offer with him to God this sacrifice of praise "pro redemptione animarum suarum." Souls are therefore redeemed through the Mass, delivered from the captivity of the devil and from sin. In what manner this is done, we shall explain later on. For this reason does the Council of Trent pronounce anathema against any one who would dare deny that the sacrifice of the Mass is really *propitiatory*: "Si quis dixerit missæ

[1] Heb. ix. 14.   [2] I. John ii. 2.   [3] Miss. Dom. ix., post Pent.

sacrificium tantum esse laudis, et gratiarum actionis, non autem propitiatorium, anathema sit." [1]   There continues to be in the blood of our victim a voice, a cry for grace, which penetrates the heart of God and inclines it to treat us with clemency, notwithstanding our heinous and numerous prevarications—and no wonder.   When it was shed on Calvary by the hands of wicked men, it had power enough to appease the anger of God and to change His projects of vengeance into designs of mercy and love.   Will it have less efficacy when presented by ministers of His own choice, consecrated for this very end, clothed with His authority, and who immolate Jesus Christ in union with Jesus Christ Himself?

We have in this the explanation of a mystery of divine patience which should produce deeper impressions than it does, if we but considered it more attentively. Have we ever thought to explain how it is that the torrent of iniquities which since the¯ supper in the Cenacle has already traversed so many ages, and which in our own knows not any bounds, has not forced the thrice-holy God to destroy the earth under the strokes of His justice?   Can it be presumed that the human race had more and greater abominations to answer for when it was buried under the waters of the deluge, than it has now?   Who does not understand that the crimes of the new people, which is incomparably more enlight-

____
[1] Sess. XXII., can. 3.

ened, more favored by heaven, have in them a character of malice and ingratitude which did not exist in the same degree in the crimes of the ancient world? What is, then, the hidden power which withholds His avenging arm? Why is it that God "overlooketh the sins of men for the sake of repentance"?[1] It is because, in the midst of wicked men, He beholds His Son debased, annihilated, in His presence, thus atoning for our prevarications, and begging pardon for us.

Moses of yore was able alone to arrest the anger of the Lord, and such was the power of his mediation that it reduced, as it were, this angry Master to the state of a suppliant—"dimitte me, ut irascatur furor meus."[2] And yet Moses was only one just man; and all that he offered was his prayer. Jesus, on the altar, opposes a penitent God to an offended God; He offers to Him for sinners His tears, His blood, His death. Here is the secret of a merciful patience which has not yet been wearied by our crimes. Jesus reproduces Himself continually upon thousands of altars, so as to be present in every spot which is threatened with divine vengeance. When entering into the world, He had said to His Father: "Ecce venio"—hither I come to disarm Thy justice; and now every day, when He comes anew amongst guilty men, He repeats in the silence of our sanctuaries: "Behold, O My Father, behold I come. I have already atoned for all their iniquities in the Gar-

----

[1] Wisd. xi. 24.   [2] Exod. xxxii. 10.

den of Olives, in the pretorium, and on Calvary. I now come to offer more atonement. Thou beholdest Me still in the state of a victim, and this victim is sacrificed for sinners. Behold the abyss of reproaches into which I plunged, the tortures which I suffered, the death which I endured for their sake. They are the children of My sorrow; on the cross I begot them. O My Father, consider not their sins, or consider them in connection with the reparation to Thy glory I offer for them! They rise up against Thee; but I humble, I annihilate Myself before Thee. They reject Thy paternal authority; I, however, in their stead make Myself obedient unto death. Wilt Thou forget that if they are men who offend Thee, I, who honor Thee, am Thy Son, and God as Thou art? Will the voice of their offences cry out louder than the voice of My merits?"

Behold, unquestionably, the rampart which protects our city and provinces, which has kept back the avenging fire destined to destroy the earth. This truth is particularly palpable in our days. For sixty years past, society, like an edifice which has been undermined, has threatened destruction; yet it still remains firm in spite of many warning shocks. What can be its stay? The adorable sacrifice. The priest at the altar, says St. Eucherius, is the pillar which sustains the world, staggering under the weight of its crimes—"nutantis orbis statum sustinens." [1]

---

[1] Hom. III., ex editis cum Theodoro-Studitâ.

The Council of Trent teaches us in what manner our reconciliation with God, which is the principal result of Our Saviour's redemption, is applied to souls through the Mass: " Hujus oblatione, placatus Dominus, gratiam et donum pœnitentiæ concedens, crimina et peccata etiam ingentia dimittit." [1]   The sacrifice of the Mass is, then, for us in reality a means of justification, not as Baptism and sacramental absolution, which produce immediately, in well-disposed sinners, justifying grace; but it moreover sanctifies men by obtaining for them those actual graces which excite and aid them to properly utilize the means of reconciliation instituted by the goodness of God—"gratiam et donum pœnitentiæ concedens." This accounts for so many blessed changes whose cause is often unknown. An Italian author, quoted in a work entitled " The Priest Sanctified Through the Celebration of Holy Mass," relates many instances of conversions, evidently due to devotion towards the sacrifice of the altar, practised by souls that had gone astray.   He avers that he had heard the general confession of many sinners who, being on the point of death, detested their sins with all the signs of perfect Christian contrition.   He then was wont to ask them from which good works they fancied they had obtained the grace of a happy death after having led so criminal a life.   They answered that God had perhaps been moved with compassion towards them on account

[1] Sess. XXII., c. 2.

of their special devotion to the Mass, at which they had frequently assisted with piety. How far the virtue of atonement of the holy sacrifice extends, we cannot tell. Jesus Christ, the Victim of the Mass, the substitute for sinners, in delivering them from eternal punishment by the application of His merits could deliver them also from the temporal punishment due to sins already pardoned.[1] In these satisfactions we participate with more or less abundance, according to the greater or less fervor with which we offer the sacrifice or assist at its celebration. Of these satisfactions the souls in purgatory also experience the efficacy.

4. The Mass is a *sacrifice of impetration.* Prayer, which is the fourth of our duties to God, contains in itself the three others already mentioned. It accomplishes an act of adoration by the annihilation of man before God, whose sovereign dominion and infinite perfections he honors. It is an act of thanksgiving; for the blessings which we pray for remind us of those already received, and this remembrance quickens our gratitude. It is a sacrifice of expiation, because it is a reparation for our heinous neglect to serve so loving a Father, and for the offences wherewith we repaid His

---

[1] Amongst the acts which dispose us to offer the divine sacrifice, one of the most important consists in exciting ourselves to sorrow for our sins, and especially for the venial sins which we have not yet detested, so that every obstacle having been removed, we may receive the full application of the merits of our adorable Victim, and satisfy in this manner the justice of God. (Le Prêtre Sanctifié par la Celebration de la Messe.)

benefits. The Mass consequently is the great prayer
of the Catholic Church, and this prayer, free and un-
trammelled, is ever full of efficacy from whatever stand-
point we may consider it: whether it be Jesus Christ
praying with us and for us, or whether it be those
who pray uniting themselves to this divine Suppliant.

As to Jesus Christ, we know that He is always
heard, and this is a consequence of the regard due to
His dignity.   He was heard on the cross in the bloody
sacrifice He made of Himself to His Father—" exaudi-
tus est pro sua reverentia." [1]   He deserves full as well
to be heard from the altar on which He continues this
oblation, although made in an unbloody manner.   Not
indeed with words and with a loud cry, as of old on
Calvary, does He now intercede for us—" cum clamore
valido et lacrymis offerens;" [2]   but He does so by a
state of humiliation, which is at least equally capable
of touching the heart of God.   We see Him in our
sanctuaries seemingly incapable of action, of move-
ment; it is a victim which has received the death-
blow, and which gives not a sign of life.   He offers as
a prayer for us His blood, His tears, His wounds, and
the abyss of humiliations into which He is plunged.
His silence itself speaks more eloquently than the
voice of the blood of Abel. [3]   " Cum in altari Christus

[1] Heb. v. 7.   [2] Heb. v. 7.
[3] Sanguinis aspersionem melius loquentem quam Abel.—Heb. xii. 24.

immolatur, clamat idem Redemptor ad Patrem, corpo-
raliter suas cicatrices ostendens."[1]

Considered in ourselves, the prayer which we offer
during the Mass is not a purely human prayer; it is
wholly permeated and filled with the sanctity of Jesus
Christ. It becomes entirely divine, having become one
and the same prayer with the prayer of the Son of God.
Therefore the priest at the altar sets no bounds to his
requests. He asks for deliverance from all evils, past,
present, and to come; for the possession of all goods;
for peace in this present life, and salvation in eternity.

Let us sum up and draw the consequences. The
sacrifice of the Mass, in itself and in its effects, is
really that which is most august, most useful to the
world, most agreeable to the eyes of the Divine Majesty; and were there no other function annexed to the
Catholic priesthood than that of offering the body and
blood of Our Lord Jesus Christ, it would still continue to be the treasure of heaven and earth. Let us
recall the beautiful words of St. Lawrence Justinian:

"Sacrâ Missæ oblatione nulla major, nulla utilior,
nulla oculis divinæ majestatis est gratior: quæ Deo honorem, angelis contubernium, exulis cœlum, religioni
cultum . . . gentibus fidem, lætitiam mundo, credentibus gaudium, . . . virtuti robur, hominibus pacem
conciliat. . . . Offertur æterno Patri Nati assumpta
humanitas; quatenus agnoscat ipse quem genuit quem-

[1] S. Laur. Just., Serm. de Euch., n. 27.

que pro salute hominum misit in terram; ut interventione ipsius delinquentibus veniam, lapsis manum, et justificatis præbeat vitam; in cujus oblationis hora, quantum fas est credere, aperiuntur cœli, mirantur angeli, sancti laudant exultant justi, captivi visitantur, compediti solvuntur, infernus luget, sanctaque in spiritu lætatur Ecclesia." [1]

What, then, does a priest do at the altar? The author of " The Following of Christ" will answer : " Deum honorat." He procures for God the greatest glory which can be offered to Him, either in this world or the next, in time or in eternity. He honors Him infinitely, and with that honor which His infinite perfections demand. "Angelos lætificat." He gladdens the whole of the heavenly court. "The angels and the saints exult," says St. John Chrysostom, "at being mentioned in the celebration of these ineffable mysteries." For them it is an increase of bliss to see that the earth associates itself so worthily to their praises, their love and gratitude. "Ecclesiam ædificat." Through the priest as sacrificer, the Church receives the most powerful aids to render her victorious in her combats, to strengthen her in peace, to preserve and animate the zeal of her Pontiffs, to augment and sustain the vigilance of her pastors, to protect the purity of her virgins, and to sanctify all her children. "Vivas adjuvat." It helps the living through the graces which it obtains for the conversion

[1] Serm. de Euch., ibid.

of sinners and the perseverance of the just. "Defunctis requiem præstat." Is not the blood of Jesus Christ the most refreshing dew which can fall upon the suffering souls of purgatory, tried amidst flames by the anger of the Lord? Oh! tell of the chains which can be broken, of the tears that can be wiped out, of the unfortunates who can be consoled by one Mass piously said! "Sese omnium honorum participem facit";—"omnium," for we refer to spiritual and temporal blessings. At Mass, especially, we are filled with every heavenly blessing and grace—"omni benedictione cœlesti et gratiâ repleamur."

Some of these blessings are imparted to us in virtue of the proper and direct efficacy of the sacrifice—or, according to the language of the school, "ex opere operato"; the others in reward of the holy dispositions with which we offer, or assist at it. It is therefore a great loss for heaven, for earth, for purgatory, for the whole world, and for myself, when, through negligence or indifference, I fail to offer the holy sacrifice. This I should seriously deplore had I been guilty of such negligence but once in my life.

CHAPTER II.

HOLINESS REQUIRED FOR THE DAILY CELEBRATION OF THE SACRIFICE OF OUR ALTARS.

WE find in the Books of Exodus and Leviticus, wherein the duties of the ancient priesthood are minutely described, that the Lord said to Moses: " Sacerdotes qui accedunt ad Dominum, sanctificentur, ne percutiat eos." [1] " Sanctificabor in iis qui appropinquant mihi." [2] " Sancti erunt Deo suo, et non polluent nomen ejus: incensum enim Domini, et panes Dei sui offerunt, et ideo sancti erunt." [3] The Hebrew text is still more forcible, as it might be translated " sanctitas erunt." Of this obligation to lead a pure and holy life, a life much more perfect than that of the laity, the priests of the Old Law were frequently reminded in the Scriptures. But wherefore? Let us consider it thoroughly. " Accedunt ad Dominum." They offer Him incense, place the loaves on the altar—" incensum et panes offerunt"; and in consequence of a ministry so divine—" et ideo"; and in order to fulfil it with due reverence, in order not to dishonor God in the exercise of functions intended only to glorify Him, " et non polluent nomen ejus"; in

[1] Exod. xix. 22.　　　[2] Lev. x. 3.　　　[3] Lev. xxi. 6.

order that they may not find death in the sanctuary, by failing to respect Him who dwells therein—" ne percutiat eas"; they are required to be holy—" sancti erunt."

From this is derived an argument whose force no subtlety can escape. If it is true that holiness of life should be proportionate to the rank which one occupies in the house of God and to the sacred duties he fulfils therein; if in the Church on earth, as in the Church in heaven, love should be more ardent and active and exuberant as it approaches nearer and nearer to Him who calls Himself a "consuming fire,"[1] what should be the innocence, the charity, the holiness of the minister of the New Law? O priest, how close is your relation to God during the celebration of the sacrifice! Since your voice, swift as thought, passing the nine choirs of angels, ascends to the very throne of God, to take thence the Word Incarnate, sitting at the right hand of the Father, to reduce Him anew to the state of a victim; since you have Him then before your eyes and in your hands; and since after a moment He shall be substantially united to your body and soul in His twofold nature, divine and human—can it be said there is any distance left between you and the Divine Majesty?

I. In His quality of priest we have the honor to represent Him. He appeareth not; we alone are seen, but in reality we are nothing more than His organs. To Him we lend our tongue and our hands, says a holy

---

[1] Deut. iv. 24.

doctor, but all is done by Him conjointly with the Father and the Holy Ghost—" Pater et Filius et Spiritus Sanctus omnia facit : sacerdos et manus et linguam præbet." We are simply the instruments which He uses; His is the principal action—" instrumentum principalis agentis." [1] " Sacerdos quidem minister est Dei ; utens verbo Dei, per jussionem et institutionem Dei ; Deus autem ibi principalis est auctor et invisibilis ope rator." [2] Now, to worthily represent Jesus Christ we should bear a certain amount of resemblance to our original. It would be intolerable presumption for a man of very little or no virtue to dare set himself up as the representative of the Holy of holies. It would not be asking too much to have the purity of an angel in order to hold the place and perform the functions of Him whom St. Paul portrayed to us when he said : " Talis decebat ut nobis esset pontifex, sanctus, innocens, impollutus, segregatus a peccatoribus, et excelsior cœlis factus !" [3]

The priest, being a universal mediator with Jesus Christ in the oblation of the sacrifice, stands at the altar between God and human nature; this is the noble and sublime thought of St. John Chrysostom : " Medius stat sacerdos inter Deum et naturam humanam." What is his duty in this position? He pours upon the earth the graces and benedictions he sought and obtained in the bosom of God Himself; he offers to

---

[1] St. Thomas.　　　[2] Imit., lib. iv., c. 4.　　　[3] Heb. vii. 26.

heaven, and places before the Divine Majesty the new requests which he received on earth—"illinc venientia dona ad nos deferens et nostras petitiones illuc referens." [1] Consequently, his charity should be immense; that his heart, expanding, should assume, as far as possible, the dimensions of the heart of Jesus, becoming as extensive as the world, since it must contain all the world's acts of homage, all its wants, all its gratitude. This love of the priest ought to extend beyond the confines of this world: it should embrace the Church suffering, which is not of this world, it should soar beyond the clouds of heaven, since all the members of the Church triumphant entrust to him the duty of returning their thanks to Him who so munificently rewards them.

Yet this will not suffice for the priest. He must moreover enter into the spirit of this mediation, he must become thoroughly imbued with its views, in order to make it the guide of his sentiments. He offers the sacrifice of *holocaust;* how great, then, should be his zeal for the honor and glory of God! How profound his respect for His infinite greatness! What submission to His sovereign dominion! How ardent his desire to bring all hearts to submission to Him! Should he not keenly resent the offences offered to so good a Father by so many ungrateful children who have rebelled against Him? "Opprobria exprobran-

[1] Hom. V. in Joan.

tium tibi ceciderunt super me." [1]   How painful for the good priest to see Him so little known, adored, and loved!   " Pater juste, mundus te non cognovit." [2]

The sacrifice which he offers is the *eucharistic* sacrifice, or the sacrifice of thanksgiving; and he offers it, as Jesus Christ did, in the name of every creature. He ought therefore to be filled with gratitude towards the universal Benefactor.

The priest's sacrifice is the sacrifice of *expiation*.   It is therefore just that he should do penance with the Saviour for so many guilty and hardened souls, who do not even think of bewailing their crimes.   " Sacerdotum est pro populo Deum propitiare planctu, precibus, pœnitentiis." [3]   He himself should be free from sin, since he asks pardon for his sinful brethren.

Finally, he offers with Jesus Christ to God the great prayer, the sacrifice of *impetration*, which is all-powerful with God.   He should therefore be a man of prayer, fully aware of the evils which afflict the Church, alive to the spiritual necessities of souls, according to the example of Him who would bear "our infirmities and carry our sorrows"—"vere languores nostros ipse tulit." [4]   Does not this reciprocation of views, of intentions, adorations, thanksgivings, prayers, and expiations, supposed to exist between Jesus Christ and ourselves through the celebration of Mass, lead us to infer that we are united to Him in all things and in all

[1] Ps. lxviii. 10.   [2] John xvii. 25.   [3] Cor. à Lap.   [4] Is. liii. 4.

places? It certainly requires that we should be His faithful representatives in the *ensemble* of our life, that He may be known in our person, as St. Ambrose expressed it: "Luceat imago Christi in operibus nostris et factis, et tota ejus species exprimatur in nobis."[1] Hence, when the Lamb of God is about to give Himself to us in holy communion, the Church wishes us to address to Him this request: "Fac me tuis semper inhærere mandatis, et a te nunquam seperari permittas" —make me always adhere to Thy commandments, and never suffer me to be separated from Thee. Hence, good priests have at all times endeavored to live the life of Jesus Christ, or, rather, to let Him live in them, directing their thoughts, governing their affections, regulating their actions. "Jam non nostram, sed Christi vitam, sed Christum ipsum vivimus." Oh, how great ought to be our holiness, that we may worthily represent the Incarnate Word in His quality of priest!

II. If we consider Him as victim, we touch Him, we exercise over Him a sort of authority, we take His body for our meat and His blood for our drink. Behold three immeasurable proofs of His love for us, three new motives for purifying and sanctifying ourselves more and more, raising ourselves to a still more eminent degree of perfection. "Qui justus est, justificetur adhuc, et sanctus, sanctificetur adhuc."[2]

1. We touch Him; for behold in this mystery a

---

[1] Lib. de Isaac et Anim., c. viii. 4.   [2] Apoc. xxii. 11.

great subject of admiration! This same Word of God who, according to St. Augustine, found but two thrones worthy of Him—viz., Divinity in the bosom of His Father, and Virginity in the womb of His Mother: "Sola Verbo digna sedes aut in Patre divinitas, aut in matre virginitas"—this sovereign Arbiter of our destinies who, at the end of time, shall come in all His glory to judge peoples and nations; this Lord of hosts puts Himself to-day in our hands. We bear Him who holds the earth in the palm of His hand. "O miraculum! O Dei benignitatem!" exclaims St. John Chrysostom, "qui cum Patre sensum sedet, in illo ipso temporis articulo hominum manibus pertractatur!" [1] What purity of life, what deep religion, should we not expect of a man so wonderfully favored by Almighty God? Is it asking too much that members honored by this divine contact should be as pure as the rays of the sun? "Quantum ab eo integritatem exigimus! Quantum religionem! Quo solari radio non oportet splendidiorem esse manum carnem hanc dividentem, os quod igne spirituali repletur, lingua, quæ tremendo nimis sanguine rubescit?" O priest, thy mouth is the mouth of Jesus Christ! says St. Anselm—"os tuum os Christi est." Consecrated as it is every day through the very consecration of His body, reddened by His blood, should it not be used only in speaking holy words? —"si quis loquitur quasi sermones Dei?" St. Augus-

[1] Lib. III., de Sacerd., c. iv.

tine seems unable to restrain his ardor when he speaks on this subject: "O sacrum et cœleste mysterium, quod per nos Pater et Filius et Spiritus Sanctus operatur! Uno eodemque momente idem Deus qui præsidet in cœlis, in manibus vestris est in sacramento altaris. O venerabilis sanctitudo manuum! O felix exercitum! O vere mundi gaudium! Christus tractat Christum, id est, sacerdos Dei Filium. . . . Super hoc tam insigni privilegio stupet cœlum, miratur terra, veretur homo, contremiscit diabolus, et veneratur quam plurimum angelica celsitudo!" [1]

If such great innocence is required of us to touch a God-Victim, how deep should not be our humility at beholding the absolute Maker of the universe as it were docile to our bidding! Every day He obeys with alacrity and untiring constancy. Nor is it only the Virgin Immaculate, His Mother, whom He obeys; but He obeys even sinful men, who deserve not to live in His presence. At the voice of those men He comes down upon the altar, places Himself in their power, that they may dispose of Him as they please. He permits them to immolate Him for the glory of His Father and the salvation of the world. But surely, he who immolates a victim must have over it the right of life and death! And who can have this power over Jesus Christ save Jesus Christ Himself? "Ego pono animam meam . . . nemo tollit eam a me, sed ego

[1] In Psal. ex Molina, tract. I., c. v.

pono eam a meipso." [1] This power of Jesus Christ would seem untransferable, yet He has communicated it to His priests, and has given them an express commandment to exercise it: " Hoc facite in meam commemorationem." " This being the reality," says Bourdaloue, " there is not outside of God a holiness sufficiently eminent to correspond to the honor of so high a ministry."

3. We do more than touch and immolate the adorable Victim. " O res mirabilis! Manducat Dominum pauper, servus et humilis! O sacrum convivium in quo Christus sumitur." Every day we participate in this heavenly banquet; the Eucharist is our daily bread. From us, and after us, the faithful receive it; such is the order established by the Saviour—" ut sumant et deut cæteris." Take, O priest, and then give! But consider again the obligation for us to be holy, and to advance continually in the ways of perfection! " O quam mundæ debent esse manus, quam purum os, quam sanctum corpus, quam immaculatum cor erit sacerdotis, ad quem toties ingreditur auctor puritatis!" [2] The hearts of Christians who communicate every day are the palaces of this Prince; these, having been erected to be His dwelling, ought to be in every way suitable to their object. When Jesus Christ gives Himself to the laity in the Sacrament of His Love, He, as it were, closes His eyes to their lack of great and

<hr>

[1] John x. 17, 18.   [2] Imit., lib. IV., c. xi.

excellent virtues. This man has recollected and prepared himself; he has been purified through repentance
and sorrow, or has had recourse to the Sacrament of
Penance; he has made the best possible preparation to
receive the adorable Guest who condescends to visit
him. The Lord forgives him for not offering a more
perfect reception; his soul is only a temporary dwelling for the divine King. But the soul of the priest is
His palace, His habitual abiding-place. He demands
of him, therefore, a lively faith, an extensive charity, a
firm, unshaken hope, a royal magnificence in all the virtues which should adorn it.[1]

All the preceding considerations explain why the
Church is so solicitous and watchful that she may send
none but holy priests to the altar, and that they may

---

[1] The celebration of Mass is unquestionably something greater, and
demands greater holiness than simple communion. The writer of the
book " Idée du Sacerdoce" proves it solidly. St. Gregory supposes it
in a letter to St. Augustine, the Apostle of England, wherein he decides
that in a given case one might communicate, but should not celebrate
Mass—" a perceptione sacri mysterii prohiberi non debere, sed ab immo-
latione abstinere."

Theologians, however, permit a priest to celebrate oftener than they
allow a layman to communicate, the dispositions of both being otherwise equal. Their reason is that the layman approaches the holy table in
his own private capacity, and for his own sake ; but the priest goes up to
the altar in the interest of the whole world and in the name of the Church
which sends him. As she expects invaluable blessings from the sacrifice which he offers, she covers up in a manner with her own holiness
the imperfections of her minister, whom she in this manner renders acceptable to God. " Cum ipsius Ecclesiæ nomine pro populis oraturi
deputantur, certam ab ecclesiæ ipsa recipiunt puritatem, vi cujus Deo
acceptiones efficiuntur."—Collet. de Euch., c. 7.

always treat mysteries so sacred with all the respect which is due to them. Sometimes by the mouth of her doctors, the Church teaches us that the soul of the priest should be pure and bright as the sun : " Solaribus radiis puriorem esse aportet animum sacerdotis . . . luminis instar universum orbem illustrantis splendescere debet ";[1] that his innocence and perfection should be so great that, if taken up amidst the angels in heaven, he would not be found out of place amongst them : " Necesse est sacerdotem sic esse purorem, ut in ipsis cœlis collocatus inter cœlestes virtutes medius staret";[2] that having been preferred to angels for this glorious ministry, he should lead a life more angelic than human : " Potius angelicam quam humanam debet conversationem habere;" that being commissioned to represent Jesus Christ, to act in His name, and with His almighty power, he should approach the altar as if he were Jesus Christ Himself. He should there conduct himself with the modesty and fervor of those pure spirits who stand in heaven before the throne of God, and acquit himself of all that is prescribed with the recollection and piety of a saint. " Accedat . . . ut Christus, assistat ut angelus, ministret ut sanctus."[3] In her councils the Church holds the same language, she is always inspired with the same thought ; and she tells the priest who celebrates that he must perform

---

[1] St. Chrys., de Sacerd., lib. VI.   [2] Ibid., lib. III.
[3] S. Laur. Just., Serm. de Euch.

this sublime function with all the care, all the dili-
gence, all the holiness, both interior and exterior, of
which he is capable: " Satis apparet omnem operam et
diligentiam in eo ponendam esse, ut quanta maxima
fieri potest, interiori cordis munditia et puritate, atque
exteriori devotionis et pietatis specie peragatur." [1]

To the language of words the Church adds the language of actions and figures. She leads into the sacred vestry the minister whom she is about to send to
God as her ambassador in the name of all creatures.
In this place, as in the vestibule of heaven, she prepares him to appear before the face of the Infinite Majesty. Will he be able to stand in the presence of God,
to enter within the mysterious cloud like Moses, to
treat with the Lord Himself concerning the salvation
of his people? He knows that the heavens themselves
are not sufficiently pure in His presence. " Sto attoni-
tus et considero quia cœli non sunt mundi in conspectu tuo.[2] Quis ascendet in montem Domini, aut
quis stabit in loco sancto ejus?" [3] The Church wishes
him to be deeply impressed with the sentiment of his
misery, being fully convinced that humility alone finds
grace with God. She bids him wash his hands, and
then with the profoundest respect to vest himself in the
insignia of his priestly office. These mysterious ornaments were blessed by her, and the prayers which she

---

[1] Conc. Trid., Sess. XXII.   [2] Imit., lib. iii., c. 14.
[3] Ps. xxiii. 3.

commands him to recite whilst vesting are so many lessons which she gives him.   He ought, according to her intention, to divest himself of all that might have remained in him of the old man and of his earthly inclinations, in order to assume the spirit of Jesus, the new man, all of whose thoughts are most exalted and affections most holy.   She endeavors to make him the living image of her heavenly Spouse, such as He appeared when He gave Himself up to death for her, and purchased her at the price of His blood.   In the amice which she places on his shoulders, she recognizes the veil of ignominy which was thrown over the face of the Saviour in derision of His title of prophet. In the girdle he sees the scourges wherewith He was beaten at the pillar; and in the maniple and stole, the chains wherewith He was loaded and the fetters with which He was bound.   She clothes his whole person, as it were, with innocence by giving him the white robe which is its emblem, and with charity by giving him the chasuble, its symbol.[1]   Finally, having sanctified her priest externally, and thereby taught him to sanctify the interior—the soul—she permits him to advance towards the altar.   Behold him now as he approaches; angels accompany him, heaven contemplates him.   But he has hardly reached the foot of the holy mountain when the Church stops him, to remind him anew of the majesty and sanctity of the throne before which he

[1] Accipe vestem sacerdotalem per quam charitas intelligitur.—(Pont.)

stands. She bids him once more pause and fathom the depth of his miseries.

Again behold him prostrate — overwhelmed, as it were, with the weight of his unworthiness. How great his terror, his alarm, at the thought of what he is about to do! He asks of his soul why it is sad, and the cause is well known to him. He supplicates his Saviour and Judge to separate him from sinners, and to give him entrance to the society of the just—"de gente non sancta." Were he to offer this sacrifice and not be holy, would he not be giving a just cause for tears to the heavenly spirits who surround the altar? But to humble one's self before God is to appease Him; the prayer of the humble has ever been pleasing to Him.[1] The priest then makes the avowal of his faith—he laments, he strikes his breast. He must now implore the intercession of Mary, the Virgin of virgins. Pure as she was, we wonder that the Son of God condescended to dwell in her bosom. Yet the priest is about to receive the same Son of Mary. Besides the aid of the Virgin, he must implore also the assistance of St. Michael, St. John the Baptist, the holy Apostles Peter and Paul, the first priests of the New Testament, of all the saints in heaven—yea, of the simple faithful who surround him; for he needs the prayers of the whole Church on this vitally important occasion, when all the interests of the Church as well as his own are

[1] Judith ix. 16.

concerned.   With this aid he is encouraged to ascend the formidable steps of the altar; he must supplicate God to be merciful to him—"ostende nobis, Domine, misericordiam tuam"—and this supplication he continues to offer until he has arrived at the middle of the altar. "Aufer a nobis, quæsumus, Domine, iniquitates nostras."   He must comfort himself with the thought of his vocation and of the divine commandment.   He begs of God, who called him to the priesthood, to direct him through the great action which he commences, directed by the same light and truth which led his steps to the sanctuary: "Emitte lucem tuam et veritatem tuam; ipsa me deduxerunt, et adduxerunt in montem sanctam tuam et in tabernacula tua."   All this amounts to saying with the faithful soul in "The Following of Christ": "Nisi tu juberes, quis accedere attentaret?" [1] The pious author had reason to add: "Cum tremore et reverentia ad hoc opus est accedendum." [2]   "Omnia," says Abelly, "in illo mysterio inveniemus summa, excelsa, sancta, ac prossus divina, proindeque omni cultu, reverentia, et honore dignissima." [3]

[1] Lib. IV., c. i.   [2] Lib. IV., c. v.   [3] Sacerd. Christ., c. vii.

CHAPTER III.

VIRTUES PARTICULARLY REQUIRED FOR THE CELEBRA-
TION OF THE HOLY MYSTERIES.

THE vestments which the Church wishes her ministers to use in the discharge of their functions at the
altar are emblems well suited to express their meaning,
and at the same time urgent exhortations to innocence
of life, piety, fervor—and, in a word, to the virtue of justice, which comprises in itself all perfection, and is the
true livery of our priesthood. "Sacerdotes tui indu-
antur justitiam." [1] "Eluceat in eis totius forma justi-
tiæ." [2] There are, however, three virtues which appear
to be more indispensable than the others to the priest
who celebrates: viz., a lively faith, a deep religious
feeling, an eminent purity.

I. *A lively faith.*—Faith is to the just what the soul
is to the man; it is his life, according to the expression of St. Paul, who simply quotes the prophet: "Justus autem ex fide vivit." [3] It is the life of his intelligence, by the infusion of light and truth; it is the very
life of his heart, by the introduction of charity; it is
the life of his works, by the sanctification of his com-
monest actions; whilst at the same time it enables him

---

[1] Ps. cxxxi. 9.   [2] Pontific.   [3] Rom. i. 17; Habac. ii. 4.

to undertake and accomplish the most noble and difficult works.   With this treasure, nothing is wanting to
the priest; without it, he is destitute of everything.

"I imagine," says Father Berthier, "that I am on
the summit of a high mountain, and that from this
point I behold immense countries.   The heavens appear to me to be of prodigious extent and ravishing
beauty.   The objects of earth appear like mere specks.
This very high mountain is lively faith.   It reveals
Thee, O my God, as much as Thou canst be compre-
hended by a human intellect!   I perceive Thy immensity, Thy greatness, Thy eternal, infinite being!   I
see at Thy right hand Jesus Christ, my Saviour, all resplendent with glory, condescending to show Thee in
my behalf His sacred wounds, to appease Thy justice.
I unite myself to Thy Holy Spirit, the source of all
light and of all love.   O God! how beautiful I now
find the prayer which I recite every day when ascending to Thy altar: 'Emitte lucem tuam et veritatem
tuam; ipsa me deduxerunt et adduxerunt in montem
sanctam tuam.'   This mountain is the mountain of
faith, whence I discover the eternal splendors, whereon
I learn what Thou art, what I am, what I ought to be,
what I cannot be without Thee.   From the summit of
this mountain I look on the earth, and I see nothing on
it but mere atoms, continually clashing, shattering, and
destroying each other." [1]

[1] Reflex. Spirit., vol. iv.

Is it not principally at the altar that we have need of this deep feeling of the greatness of God and the nothingness of all creatures in His presence? of this living remembrance of the Saviour's mysteries, which renders them as present to us, and impresses us just as deeply as if they were being enacted before our very eyes?

Faith teaches us to believe what we see not; and lively faith affords us an understanding of what we believe. Faith, according to St. Augustine, is the eye of the heart. If this eye be gifted with clear perception, if its vision is strong enough to pierce the clouds and to behold God in His infinite perfections, which we so rightly and royally honor in the Mass; if it understand Jesus Christ and His infinite mercy—then, indeed, the heart will expand with feelings of love and piety.

Father de la Colombière, taking up the well-known word of St. Augustine, "arma et fac quod vis," changed the first word "arma" into "crede"—"crede et fac quod vis"—and with this modified maxim he thought he had provided the faithful with an excellent method of preparing themselves to worthily partake of the holy table. "Believe," he used to say, "but with a lively faith, all that religion teaches you concerning Him whom you are about to receive, concerning the action you are going to perform, and it will be less necessary to excite your piety than to look after its moderation and direction." The same, in our opinion, may be said of the priest who is to offer the sacrifice. The degree of his faith shall be that of his fervor, whether before, during, or after the celebration of the holy mysteries.

Before Mass.—Let him realize the responsibility which the Church places on his shoulders, the mission she confides to him when sending him to the altar, and the infinite perfections of Him whom heaven and earth and purgatory intend to praise and supplicate through his ministry. Let him be well convinced of the consequences which one Mass may have for the whole world and for himself; he will then search his reins and his heart, he will purify his conscience more and more, and neglect no kind of preparation. You will not then see him listen to idle conversation in the vestry before clothing himself with the insignia of his glorious but dreadful dignity. He will then be too much impressed with the awful sanctity of the action he is about to commence.

During the Mass.—Represent to yourself a good priest leaving his oratory after a fervent meditation to ascend to the altar. He is another Moses going up the mountain to converse with God as a friend converses with a friend. When he enters the sanctuary, one would say that an angel appears. How recollected he is as he advances toward the altar! How solemn and modest his countenance when he ascends its steps! He already experiences the action of the Holy Spirit, and

that his prayer was heard when he said : " Emitte lucem tuam." This supernal light illumines his intelligence and gives him the full comprehension of what he says and does. With the aid of this heavenly light, which reveals to him otherwise hidden things, he penetrates the depths of the sacred mysteries; everything expands before him—all speaks to his heart.

After the Mass.—Faith shows him the treasure which he possesses, his influence with a Saviour who has given Himself to him without reserve. He turns to good account those precious moments which are worth a whole lifetime, and his ardent gratitude draws down new and abundant blessings upon himself, upon his people, and upon all the faithful.

We should better appreciate the gift of a lively faith at the altar, were we to reflect on the deplorable state of, and the dangers which surround, the priest who is destitute of it. He boldly rushes into the flames which surround the throne of God without for a moment considering that he may be devoured by them. His boldness increases with his blindness. Impunity gives him confidence. He knows not that there are secret punishments more to be dreaded than that instantaneous death which struck down the rash Oza and the indiscreet Bethsamites. He has eyes, but he sees not; his mind cannot be void of thought, nor his heart of affections, but would he not often have cause to blush if it were known with what phantoms his disordered imagination was occupied when the pious of his congregation thought him all absorbed in God and in the exercise of his sublime ministry? The treasures of heaven are open to him; the price of the world's redemption is in his hands; all creatures stand in awe-struck expectation of what he is about to do, or in admiration and astonishment of what he has already done; he alone, unmoved, untouched, frigid as ice, lets fall from his languid lips the most sublime words of the sacred liturgy. He goes and comes, moves before the tabernacle, opens it, closes it, with quite as much indifference as if no respect whatever were due to the incomprehensible majesty of Him who dwells therein. The presence of the Lamb, ever living, yet always immolated, makes on him no impression. He does not even give a thought to the subject. He beholds, he touches, elevates, lowers Him who with one hand poises the earth, as if he were attending only to the most commonplace things. One would naturally be led to think that it is mere bread he is about to eat, that it is mere wine he is going to drink. Immersed though he is in an ocean of love, says St. Augustine, he experiences not the least feeling of love: " Immersus amore, amorem non sentit." And whither does this blindness lead him? From routine to sacrilege, the distance is very short. Of that we have a remarkable instance in Holy Writ.

The first time the Levites and priests—children of Aaron—were admitted to the service of the tabernacle erected in the desert, the mere sight of this monument of the covenant of God with His people, the pillar of smoke and fire which preceded it, the magnificence and splendor of the ceremonies, the majesty of the Lord which filled that mysterious place—everything made a most striking impression on those men called to such a high ministry. There was no need to say to them: " Pavete ad sanctuarium meum, ego Dominus!" [1] How great was their zeal to fulfil all the prescriptions of the law! But by degrees they became familiar with the sacred objects of the veneration of God's people. The daily repetition of the same functions insensibly effaced their sacred character in the minds of these ministers. With want of respect in the service of the altar and of the tabernacle came lack of vigilance, till finally, by rapid and lamentable strides, they plunged into the most horrible profanations. " Fili hominis, fode parietem." [2]

Is not this a faithful picture of what has happened to more than one priest of the new law? Let us go back in spirit to the time of our priestly ordination. The remembrance of it will be no less beneficial to us because of the remorseful feelings thereby awakened than of the happiness it may recall. The imposition of hands, by raising us to the rank of the prophets, wrought within us a wonderful transformation. " Insiliet in te spiritus Domini, et prophetabis cum eis, et mutaberis

---

[1] Lev. xxvi. 2.   [2] Ezech. viii. 8.

in virum alium." [1]   What idea did we then form to ourselves of the divers functions of the priesthood?   What
was our idea of that particular function which we justly
considered far more elevated and superhuman than all
others?   Nothing, in our estimation, could be compared
to the holy sacrifice.   A glance at the sacred vestments
sufficed to excite in our souls mingled feelings of joy
and fear.   In the preparation for holy Mass, as also in
all the circumstances accompanying it, everything
seemed to us full of mystery, everything seemed to
nourish our piety.   The least fault or inadvertence
filled us with confusion and sorrow.   Oh, how attentive,
fervent, awe-inspired we were the first time we consecrated the sacred Host!   How great was our delight
when we for the first time beheld the sacred Victim in
our hands, when we offered it for our salvation and for
that of the whole world!   What energy, what courage
we derived therefrom to sustain us in all our undertakings and trials!   But to-day, if we interrogate our conscience, if we ask ourselves, with the prophet, How is
the gold become dim? [2] what was the first cause of our
misfortunes, wherefore and whitherto have we fallen—
what will it answer us?   We have neglected to keep
the sacred fire always burning upon the altar of our
heart. [3]   In losing the spirit of recollection, which always kept us under the empire of faith, we have lost

[1] I. Kings x. 6.   [2] Lam. iv. 1.
[3] Ignis in altari semper ardebit.—Lev. vi. 12.

with it that wise timidity, that inestimable sensitiveness of conscience which the mere appearance of sin sufficed to alarm. Fervor disappeared, and tepidity took its place. To the life of the spirit the life of the senses has succeeded, and we have come to this, that we experience no anxiety concerning the enormous and ever-increasing disproportion which exists between our conduct and the holiness required for the worthy discharge of our sublime offices. Alas! perhaps our transgressions even pass unobserved whenever they bear not on their face the evident character of grievous sin! Oh, if we would but raise the mask which conceals—perhaps even from ourselves—the sad secrets of our heart—what should we find? "Fili hominis, fode parietem." We who had been planted by the running waters which flow from the Saviour's fountains; we who had been destined to bear abundant fruit without ever marring the beauty of our foliage; we who could so easily have secured the blessing of the Lord upon all our labors, and prospered in all our undertakings [1] for the glory of God and the salvation of souls, have become sapless, withered, useless trees. "Ecce ego lignum aridum!" [2]

II. *Profound religious conviction.*—When one is illumined by the light of a lively faith, he cannot prize anything outside the Almighty and Eternal God. He does not then content himself with saying simply: *God*

---

[1] Ps. i. 3, 4. [2] Is. lvi. 3.

is great; he exclaims boldly: *God alone is !* [1]—so much does he consider as nothingness all that the world most admires.   This knowledge of the divine perfections, which the Scripture calls consummate wisdom—" nosse te consummata justitia est" [2]—inspires us with a sovereign respect for God and for everything that appertains to His worship.   It imprints upon our souls such a feeling of profound veneration for Him that we would be disposed actually to annihilate ourselves, if possible, in order to honor a greatness and holiness so absolutely infinite.

It has been observed in all true servants of God that the more they are enlightened from above, the more do they delight in considering themselves and all things else as nothingness in the presence of the Sovereign Majesty.   That is the reason why they so despise the world and all the seductions it presents to those who aspire not to higher things.   Hence that incredible joy which they experience when, after figuring to themselves millions of creatures thousands of times more perfect than those which actually exist, after oft-repeated multiplications and comparisons of those imaginary creatures, so numerous and so perfect, with the great God who exceedeth our knowledge, [3] they see all, in the twinkling of an eye, recede to their centre, which is nothingness, as soon as the immensity of the Almighty

[1] Videte quod ego sim solus.—Deut. xxxii. 39.   [2] Wisd. xv. 3.
[3] Ecce, Deus magnus vincens scientiam nostram.—Job xxxvi. 26.

looms up. Hence, also, that religious awe with which they draw nigh unto Him "whom the angels praise, the dominations adore, and before whom the powers of heaven tremble." [1]

The priest being the man of God, charged with the interests of His glory, is destined to do on earth what the angel does in heaven. As the blessed spirits, lost in veneration before the throne of the universal King, unceasingly sing His praises, and emulate one another in repeating their sublime *Sanctus*,—so, says Father Olier, the Lord, desiring to be worshipped in a similar manner upon earth, and seeing that the majority of men would not keep themselves sufficiently disengaged from worldly pursuits to devote themselves to this perpetual adoration, has instituted the priesthood to offer it in their stead.

The good priest is ever imbued with the profoundest love for God and the most ardent desire of procuring His glory. But it is especially towards the Holy Eucharist that his pious affection shows itself most ardent and zealous. It is in this wonderful mystery, as we have previously observed, that our divine Lord has humbled Himself most profoundly for our sake. Gratitude, therefore, demands that our love and veneration towards Him should be correspondingly greater than in other mysteries; and in this the Church and God Him-

---

[1] Quem laudant angeli, adorant dominationes, tremunt potestates.— Pref. Missæ.

self have given us the example. The Church displays greater zeal in honoring her divine Spouse in those mysteries in which He has been pleased to undergo greater humiliations. For instance, when she speaks of His Incarnation, it is on bended knee; and she bestows on His cross all the tokens of veneration that she can imagine. God likewise glorifies His only-begotten Son in proportion as this well-beloved Son humbles Himself for the glory of His Father. Thus, the abasements of the Nativity were glorified by angelic concerts; the humiliations of the stable, by the visit of the Magi; those of His Baptism, by the opening of heaven, the voice of the Father proclaiming Him His well-beloved Son, and the Holy Ghost in the shape of a dove overshadowing Him. For the same reason, the heavenly spirits have been commanded to adore Him under the Eucharistic veils. Some holy doctors of the Church have seen them in great numbers around our altars offering Him their homage of most perfect adoration; and the Church on earth, following the example of the heavenly hosts, commissions her ministers, who are *her* angels, to fulfil the same duties towards our God hidden in the obscurity of our sanctuaries. Is it not His love for us that reduced Him to that state so completely veiling all His greatness and glory? "Priests," said Alain de Solminiac, "being officers of the crown, are under particular obligations not only to honor their divine King, but also to make Him honored as He deserves."

When the minister of Jesus Christ is under the guiding influence of lively faith, he manifests in his whole exterior such modesty, gravity, and ever-abiding sense of God's holy presence that his very appearance becomes an homage to God and a salutary instruction to all who see him. People are influenced more by example than by precept. The sight of a holy priest prostrate before the tabernacle, motionless, and, as it were, annihilated in the presence of the Lord, has, not unfrequently, been the means designed by a merciful Providence to re-animate lukewarm Christians, to convert sinners, and even to convince unbelievers by awakening in their souls a spirit of reflection, study, and prayer.

A zealous priest of the Society of Jesus was once sent from Rome by his superiors to preach the Lenten course in a town of Apulia. On arriving at his destination a deputation of the inhabitants called on him and bluntly informed him that he had put himself to useless inconvenience in travelling thither; that they already had an excellent and popular preacher, whom doubtless they all would go to hear. The good missionary, without manifesting any dissatisfaction whatever, went quietly to the church to offer the holy sacrifice before setting out on his homeward journey. So great were his piety, his recollection, and devotion, during the celebration of the divine mysteries, that he appeared to the congregation more like an angel come down from heaven than a priest sent them from Rome. Their dis-

5

position towards him immediately changed; they begged him to stay and preach his mission, which he did with prodigious success.

St. Vincent de Paul said his Mass with such unction and fervor that all could see that his heart spoke through his lips. His modesty, the serenity of his countenance, his whole exterior appearance were calculated to impress the least susceptible of his audience. They observed in his person something so exceptionally noble and at the same time so humble that often some of them were heard to whisper to others: "How well that priest says Mass!"

On the other hand, it would be impossible to calculate the evil done to religion by inattentive, indevout, worldly looking priests, who, while celebrating, seem intent only on accomplishing their task in the shortest possible time, seemingly indifferent as to whether they offer God homage or insult. Seeing them, one would be tempted to ask, with Tertullian: "Sacrificat an insultat?"[1] Let us suppose that St. Basil and the other

---

[1] According to the Council of Trent, this want of gravity and respect in a ministry so divine can hardly be free from impiety (Sess. XXII.).

Father John of Avila, being present at a Mass celebrated, to all appearance, with sacrilegious irreverence, felt so deeply grieved that, leaving his place in the sanctuary, and going up quietly to the altar as if to arrange something, he turned to the celebrant, who was about to touch the sacred Host, and whispered: "Do not treat Him so ill; He does not deserve it." The admonition was happily well received. It opened the eyes of that thoughtless priest, who immediately after Mass cast himself at the feet of the father, and subsequently chose him as spiritual director.

ministers who served him at the altar in the church of Cesarea had been wont to celebrate Mass in a trivial, unbecoming manner, instead of that imposing solemnity which fills us with an awe-inspiring sense of God's presence in our sanctuaries; could they have so terrified the Emperor Valens as to make him turn pallid and tremble when he advanced toward the altar to present an offering which none would receive at his hands, because he was guilty of heresy?

We have read of a heretic who, after many conferences with a saintly and learned religious, had resolved to embrace the true faith; but having observed priests offer the holy sacrifice without respect or devotion, he was so scandalized by their irreverence that he could not be convinced of the truth of Catholic doctrines, or that those priests themselves believed them, and he completely abandoned the idea of entering the true Church.

One of the most infallible means of preventing that routine indifference which too great familiarity with sacred things so often superinduces, of escaping the abysses of evil which it leads to, as well as of fostering in our souls that feeling of religious awe so essential to the most sublime and sacred of all ministries, is to habituate ourselves to an exact observance of the holy rubrics, and to perform as perfectly as possible each one of the prescribed ceremonies. This is of the highest practical importance.

Father Tronson, in an instruction on this subject, aptly remarks with what care and in what express terms Almighty God Himself had, under the Old Law, ordered and regulated, even to the minutest detail, everything concerning His public and exterior worship.[1] And with what terrible severity He had punished all violations of those regulations, he furnishes three remarkable instances. The two sons of Aaron, Nadab and Abiu, are devoured by fire because, contrary to the ceremonial law, they put in their censers a fire other than that prescribed. Oza is punished with instantaneous death for having unlawfully touched the Ark of the Covenant, though under circumstances which seemed to render his doing so excusable, if not imperative. Ophni and Phinees, with their father Heli, who by his silence encouraged their sacrilegious temerity, were also punished in a dreadful manner for their transgression of the divine ordinance. Who will believe that God exacts less respect for our adorable mysteries than He did for those of the Old Testament, which were but feeble representations, dimly defined shadows of what is accomplished on our altars? Lend a respectful ear to what the holy Council of Trent says: " Si quis dixerit receptos et approbatos Ecclesiæ Catholicæ ritus, in . . . sacramentorum administratione adhiberi consuetos, aut

---

[1] Custodi . . . cerimonias atque judicia, quæ ego mando tibi hodie ut facias.—Deut. vii. 11. Observa, et cave ne quando obliviscaris Domini Dei tui, et negligas . . . cerimonias, quas ego præcipio tibi hodie.— Deut. viii. 11. Custodi cerimonias ejus, . . . ut beni sit tibi.—Deut. x. 13.

contemni, aut sine peccato a ministris pro libito omitti, aut in novos alios per quemcunque ecclesiarum pastorem mutari posse, anathema sit." [1]   Anathema is the greatest punishment which the Church can inflict. Against whom, in this instance, does she pronounce it? Not against those who change, neglect, or omit at their pleasure the rites which she has approved and adopted; but against those who simply say that every pastor can change them, that they can be neglected or omitted without sin.   Now, if the Church thus vigorously deals with whosoever speaks lightly of her sacred rites and ceremonies, will she spare those who in action disregard them?   In vain would we endeavor to palliate our neglect by pretending that we do not intend to disregard the rubrics.   Have we not just reason for alarm, when we reflect on the above-cited decree of the Church, and realize that we do not take pains to observe them religiously?

Shall we reply that in promulgating that decree the Church had in mind the rubrics which immediately concern the administration of the sacraments?   Assuredly, the sacrifice of the altar contains in itself the most venerable and holy of all the sacraments.   Speaking of the Mass, the same Council elsewhere says: " Si quis dixerit, cærimonias, vestes et externa signa, quibus in missarum celebratione Ecclesia Catholica utitur, non esse officia pietatis, anathema sit." [2]   A council held at

[1] Sess. VII., can. 13.   [2] Sess. XXII., can. 7.

Rome in 1725, under Benedict XIII., expresses itself on this subject in the following terms: "Ritus qui . . . in minimis etiam sine peccato negligi, omitti, vel mutari non possunt, . . . peculiari studio ac diligentia serventur."

Whatever relates to the order of the Mass, "from the time the priest arrives at the foot of the altar, until he has left it, is obligatory. The genuflections to the ground, the inclinations of the head and of the body, the signs of the cross, the words prescribed by the rubrics—all are obligatory." [1] "Communis sententia docet rubricas esse leges præceptivas, quæ obligant sub mortali ex genere suo." [2]

Practically, the whole is reduced to two points—exactness and devotion. Exactness consists in performing the ceremonies in the time and manner prescribed. Since they are all ordained, let us not omit or slight one of them; for we have no right to divide our obedience. Let us endeavor to merit the praise which St. Jerome bestowed on Nepotian: "Erat solicitus si interet altare, si parietes absque fuligine, si pavimenta tersa, si janitor creber in porta, vela semper in ostiis, si sacrarium mundum, si vasa luculenta, et in omnes

---

[1] Supplement des Conférences d'Angers, pp. 42, 43.

[2] Bened. XIV., de Miss. Sacrif., lib. II., cap. xiii., n. 3.

In regard to the prayers which the priest is directed to say when vesting for the celebration of holy Mass, St. Liguori says it is commonly thought that to omit them would be a sin, though not a mortal sin.—Theol. Mor., lib. VI., n. 410, dub. 3.

cærimonias pia solicitudo disposita, non minus, non majus negligebat officium. " [1]

Let us also observe the time and the manner, for these are regulated and prescribed as well as the ceremonies. If we do not harmonize them with the words to which they relate, they become meaningless and fail to accomplish the end for which they were instituted. For instance, the Church commands me to incline my head when I pronounce the name of Jesus, as a mark of veneration for that adorable name. If I should make that prescribed inclination either too soon or too late, whilst I pronounce some other word, the action ceases to be a religious ceremony—it signifies nothing. I am likewise commanded, at the offertory, to hold the paten in my hands, to raise my eyes heavenward whilst saying, " Suscipe Sancte Pater," to look at the Host while pronouncing the words, " Hanc immaculatam Hostiam ;" but if, through negligence or precipitation, I begin the prayer, " Suscipe," whilst uncovering the chalice ; if whilst saying, " Hanc immaculatam Hostiam," I look not at the Host, but elsewhere, I do not attain the end which the Church intended in prescribing these ceremonies. As the time, so also the manner, has been ordained. We should not be satisfied with a slight inclination of the head when a profound inclination is the rubrical direction, and so of the rest.

Finally, let us not be satisfied with merely external

[1] Epist. ad Heliodor.

propriety, but let us give spirit and life to those cor-
poreal forms.   Hence it is incumbent on us to ascer-
tain the sense of the rubrics, to be guided by their
spirit, so that the observance of them may be a faithful
expression of our sentiments.

The Church has instituted ceremonies alike for priests
and people.   For priests, in order to prepare them for
the mysterious and divine offices which they must fulfil,
to excite in them a lively faith, and fill them with veneration for what they see, touch, and do at the holy altar.
For the people, in order to inspire them with that awe
and love which are due these sublime mysteries, and to
lift up their souls by means of sensible signs to the
consideration of the great truths of faith.   "Quo et
majestas sancti sacrificii commendaretur, et mentes
fidelium, per hæc visibilia religionis et pietatis signa,
ad rerum altissimarum, quæ in hoc sacrificio latent,
contemplationem excitarentur." [1]

Make it a practice to previously look up what there
may be special for the Mass of the day by carefully
consulting the ordo; to read once a year in the missal
the rubrics of the Mass; in the breviary, those for the
divine office; and in the ritual, those for the administration of the sacraments.   By so doing, you will preserve yourself from a great many faults, and ease your
conscience of a great load of responsibility against the
dread account we shall all have to render to God.

[1] Conc. Trid., Sess. XXII., c. 5.

III. *Eminent purity.*—If we assign this virtue only the third place in order among those virtues which are imperatively required of the priest for the worthy and daily celebration of the holy mysteries, it is simply because it clearly springs from the spirit of faith and religion, just as the effect from its cause. For, after all that has been said in the preceding chapter, it is easy to understand that there is no virtue more indispensable for a priest than purity of life.

We have seen what doctors of the Church and the Church herself teach regarding the perfection required of him who offers the holy sacrifice. But purity of conscience, or exemption from sin, is, after all, purely negative holiness. That should be the starting-point. The Victim which we immolate is infinitely pure; the invisible Sacrificer whom we represent is purity Itself, and the Author of all purity; we hold intimate communication with Him before whom even the angels are not spotless; therefore, however great the innocence we bring to the altar, it will never be commensurate with the sublime functions which we there exercise.

A great tenderness of conscience, a lively horror for everything displeasing to God, an unremitting watchfulness to check every inordinate inclination, a constant fidelity to the salutary practice of making fervent acts of repentance to purify one's self of the slightest imperfection before going to the altar, have always been considered the best indications of true fervor in priests.

And whence this holy anxiety which, after all, is their best safeguard? Unquestionably it springs primarily from their love for God, but it comes also from fear lest they insensibly fall from negligence to tepidity, and from tepidity, not only to unfruitful communions—which would doubtless be an enormous evil—but, worst of all, to the sacrilegious profanation of holy things. But we shall not confine ourselves to the expression of only our own views on so momentous a subject.

How does it happen, asks Cardinal Bona, that of so many priests who celebrate every day, so few derive from holy communion the fruit which it ought to produce?—"Cur tanta Christi demissio superbiæ spiritum non elidit? Cur tanta ejus mansuetudo iram non compescit? . . ." And he answers: "Hæc prima tanti mali causa est quia aliud comedimus, aliud esurimus; comedimus panem angelorum, et immundorum animalium siliquas esurimus; . . . purganda anima à delectationibus carnis et sensuum, à tepiditate." [1]

St. Gregory the Great eloquently describes the deplorable state of priests who celebrate merely through habit, without recollection, without any examination of conscience, and with hearts actually attached to venial sin: "Qui quotidie non exharrit quod delinquit, etsi minima sint peccata quæ congerit, paulatim anima repletur, atque merito ei auferunt fructum saturitatis. Hac repletione nos evacuare Paulus insinuans ait:

[1] De Sacrif. Miss., c. vi., n. 7.

'Probet seipsum homo.' . . . Quid enim est hoc loco probare seipsum, nisi, evacuatâ peccatorum nequitiâ se probatum ad Dominicam mensam et purum exhibere? De repletis etiam subdit: 'Qui enim manducat et bibit indigne, judicium sibi manducat et bibit.' Qui ergo quotidie delinquimus, quotidie ad pœnitentiæ lamenta curramus." [1]

St. Bonaventure coincides with St. Gregory, and comments as follows on these words of the Apostle, " Probet seipsum": " Non sola mortalia vitanda sunt, sed venialia per negligentia multiplicata, et etiam per inconsiderationem et distractionem dissolutæ vitæ et malæ consuetudinis; licet enim non occidant animam, reddunt tamen hominem tepidum, gravem ac obnubilatum, nisi dicti pulveres et stipulæ venalium, per afflatum spiritus et flammam caritatis ventilentur et consumantur. Ideo cave ne nimis tepidus et inordinatus accedas, et inconsideratus; quia indigne sumis, si non accedas reverenter, circumspecte et considerate. Unde Apostolus: 'Judicium sibi manducat et bibit,' quod apertius insinuat cum subdit, dicens: 'Ideo inter nos multi imbecilles,' scilicet per fidei inconstantiam, 'et infirmi,' id est, gravi peccato sauciati, 'et dormiunt multi,' scilicet per torporem et disidiam." [2]

We have then two holy doctors applying the awful words of St. Paul, " judicium sibi manducat et bibit," to persons who are guilty of only venial sins—but of

---

[1] In I. Reg., lib. II., c. i., in vers. 5. [2] De Præpar. ad Miss., c. v.

venial sins which, through negligence, bad habits, and want of interior recollection, will eventually lead to the commission of greater transgressions.

"Jesus Christ," says Bossuet, "clearly shows how great is our obligation to purify ourselves of our daily faults when He says to St. Peter: '*If I wash thee not, thou shalt have no part with Me*'; for indifference concerning these slight imperfections may create a dangerous coldness between Jesus Christ and the soul, and ultimately lead to mortal sin." [1]

"Besides the *proving of ourselves* necessary to avoid eating our own condemnation, there is another preparation which is also essential in order that we may partake of that heavenly bread with more profit to our souls. If this preparation is not made, the Bread of Angels overloads the soul, which, if it be not already dead, will accumulate an amount of unwholesome humor which is a pretty sure indication of proximate relapse. The frequent reception of the Holy Eucharist is therefore to be feared by those to whom it does not bring increased spiritual obesity and vigor." [2]

The following words of Père Berthier are equally well calculated to inspire us with that salutary fear which, while not excluding confidence, yet banishes negligence and tepidity: "I fear lest that adorable Victim, so often in my hands, may one day rise up against

---

[1] Bossuet, Medit. sur la Céne, 10th day.

[2] Ibid., Medit. sur la Céne, 48th day.

me and seal my reprobation. To incur that awful fate, it is not necessary that I should fall into shameful crimes, or absolutely discard the principles of religion in my actions, or give public scandal to the Church of God. An easy, tepid, worldly life; motives purely human permeating all his actions; a heart forgetful of God in prayer; complete engrossment with worldly affairs, with enterprises suggested by interest or ambition; an almost continual neglect of Christian mortification; hard-heartedness towards the poor; extreme sensibility concerning the esteem of men; finally, much self-love and little love for God suffice to precipitate a priest to the very bottom of the abyss. . . . O Jesus Christ, immolated in the Holy Eucharist, far from me be the evils which threaten the profanation of Thy altar!" [1]

The preceding quotations amount to saying that tepidity can lead to sacrilege, just as frequent relapse into venial sin leads to mortal sin. Such, too, is the teaching of all the doctors who comment on these texts of Holy Scripture: "Qui spernit modica, paulatim decidet. [2] "Væ . . . qui spernis, nonne et ipse sperneris?" [3] "Qui in modico iniquus est, et in majori iniquus est." [4]

From the preceding reflections we may rightly infer that priests ought to be extremely solicitous to have frequent recourse to the Sacrament of Penance. It is to

---

[1] Reflect. Spirit., c. x., I. Cor.   [2] Ecclus. xix. 1.
[3] Is. xxxiii. 1.   [4] Luke xvi. 10.

them as easy of access and much more efficacious than was for Aaron that large brazen vase placed at the entrance of the tabernacle and in which the high-priest washed himself before entering into the Holy of holies. The pious laity confess their sins once a week in order to communicate once or twice; but there are priests who say Mass every day, and confess only once a month or two months. Do they sufficiently reflect on the many graces to be derived from the frequent use of the Sacrament of Penance? " Omnibus fere piis persuasum est quidquid hoc tempore sanctitatis, pietatis et religionis in Ecclesia . . . conservatum est, id magna exparte confessioni tribuendum." [1]

"When we approach the Sacrament of Penance with a lively faith, and particularly when we make a practice of frequent confession, we experience much more strength and determination to resist our evil inclinations and bad habits; we have much more energy to combat exterior temptations; we overcome with far greater facility our affection for sensible things; we acquire a much stronger relish for the possession of heavenly goods; and we possess that peace to which St. Paul alludes, and which he could describe only by saying that it 'surpasseth all understanding.'" [2]

Think of all the virtues which are practised in making a good confession! First of all, there is filial fear, so often recommended to us by the Holy Ghost: " Be-

[1] Catech. Counc. Trent.   [2] P. Berthier, Reflect. Spir., tom. v., p. 201.

atus homo qui semper est pavidus" — a fear which should extend to sins already confessed and expiated, " De propitiato peccato noli esse sine metu,"[1] and which is itself a powerful motive for hope, " Est ipse timor firmissima quædam et efficax materia spei."[2] By confession we profess our faith in the promises of God, our confidence in His mercy, our detestation of sin, our renouncement of self, and we especially practise humility, which makes a priest kneel at the feet of his fellow-priest, acknowledge his faults, and receive that fraternal correction which is always painful to our pride, that direction and advice which directors and guides need as well as the faithful, if they would save themselves from spiritual shipwreck. " Consilii expers similis est navigio rectore carenti, quod quibuslibet ventorum flatibus committitur."

But, independently of these advantages and of many others, can we remain unconcerned when we consider the loss we incur by depriving ourselves of a great number of indulgences which are nearly all applicable to the poor suffering souls, and which we could gain by confessing once every eight days? It would be easy for me every morning to take one or more souls from the flames of purgatory and place them amidst the de lights of heaven, thus procuring for God the pleasure of crowning with glory one or more of His elect; I could

---

[1] Prov. xxviii. 14.   [2] Ecclus. v. 5.

[3] S. Bern., Serm. xv., in Ps. xc.

thereby acquire for myself new claims upon the mercy of the Lord and upon the gratitude of these souls, whose influence by such translation would become so powerful; and to obtain these inestimable favors, all I have to do is to examine my conscience, to excite myself to sincere contrition, to undergo some slight inconvenience and spend some little time in going to see my confessor. Shall I be so foolish and heartless as not to do it? Yet I too often neglect it! Oh, how impenetrable is the veil which tepidity pulls over our eyes!

It is to be feared, some might say, that the too frequent reception of this sacrament may degenerate into a habit, and that a remedy so excellent may be turned into poison. We must certainly admit that routine can sully our consciences in the very act which should purify them. It is a shoal which ought be avoided at any cost, but without dashing into another equally dangerous. "Rest assured," says Father Nouet, "that as a general thing it is better to go often to confession than to absent one's self therefrom on the plea that there is danger in approaching the sacrament with routine insensibility or negligence, which would destroy the fruit of so holy an action. If you experience any disinclination to go to confession, surmount it courageously. It is often but an illusion of which the spirit of darkness is the author, or it may be the effect of secret pride, or a punishment for lukewarmness, or the result of pusillanimity. But, whatever may be the cause of it, to neglect confession is always a great evil, and a serious obstacle to salvation." As to the rest, we will assuredly avoid the danger of making useless confessions if faith, fostered by interior recollection and prayer, keep continually before our mind the thought of God's holy presence, which can hardly fail to inspire us with sentiments of fear and love. And with hearts full of the fear and love of God, we can easily acquire the confusion and sorrow which dispose us for a fruitful confession.

We shall close this chapter with extracts from authors justly held in high estimation. We cannot fail to find in them principles and counsels calculated to guide us in a practice which will decide the eternal happiness or misery of a great number of priests.

Cardinal Bona, and with him the author of "Triplex Expositio Totius Missæ," distinguishes between the confession which is absolutely necessary, and that which is simply useful.

"Formidabilis est, et non sine horrore audienda Apostoli comminatio dicentis: 'Quicumque manducaverit panem hunc vel biberit calicem Domini indigne, reus erit corporis et sanguinis Domini.' Quare celebrare volenti revocandum est in memoriam ejusdem præceptum: 'Probet autem seipsum homo, et sic de pane illo edat et de calice bibat; qui enim manducat et bibit indigne, judicium sibi manducat et bibit.' Et quidem probatio omnino necessaria est, ut nullus sibi conscius mortiferæ labis ad sacrificandum præsumat
6

accedere, non præmissâ sacramentali confessione, quantumvis sibi contritus videatur; alioquin panem vitæ in mortem et condemnationem accipiet.

"Ut vero ex hoc divino convivio, quod sanctis animabus inexplicabiles prabet delicias, meus abundantius reficiatur, non solum à mortalibus, sed etiam à venialibus culpis, et ab omni terreno affectu eam expugnare oportet, et puram ac vacuam Deo exhibere, gratiæ suæ donis implendam et exornandam. Hac de causâ boni sacerdotes . . . vel quotidie,[1] vel alternis diebus, vel bis saltem in hebdomada, animo vere contrito ad confessionem solent accedere, omnesque malorum radices evellere canantur, atque omnem vel levissimam maculam abstergere."

He then gives directions as to the manner of confessing:

"In ipsâ autem confessione vitanda prolixitas et nimia diligentia in levioribus culpis recensendis; satius est enim intime de iis dolere, et per devotam cordis ad Deum conversationem eas expiare, quam in iis, ad instar historiæ, sine proposito emendationis, sicut ut plurimum contingit, enarrandis immorari. . . . Cavendus item multorum error, qui se prolixe de iis accusant quæ peccata non sunt, ut de pravis habitibus et passionibus, et de circumstantiis impertinentibus; quod sint su-

[1] St. Francis Borgia went to confession regularly every morning and evening. The first religious of St. Dominic confessed every day, and often more than once a day; yet, according to St. Antonine, most of them led angelic lives—rivalling the angels in innocence and purity.

perbi, viacundi, . . . et alia ejusdem generis multa; de quibus et aliis ad confessionem pertinentibus suadeo, ut omnino legatur tractatus S. Bonaventuræ de modo confitendi et puritate conscientiæ."

The most important point, however, is to excite ourselves to contrition, without which no sin is remitted. The pious Cardinal in the following passage indicates many motives for contrition:

"Quandoquidem hujus sacramenti pars essentialis, eaque præcipua est dolor et contritio ob admissa facinora, huic maxime insistes, præmissa brevi consideratione alicujus motivi ejusdem contritionis, qualia hæc sunt: 1. Gravitas peccatorum quibus offenditur Deus, cujus bonitas infinita nec levissime quidem lædenda foret etiam ob salutem totius mundi. 2. Atrocissima damna, quæ tam in istâ quam in alterâ vitâ ex peccato oriuntur. 3. Inscrutabilitas judiciorum Dei sæpe ingratos deserentis et tepidos evomentis. 4. Brevitas et incertitudo temporis gratiæ, quo potest offensa Dei expiari. 5. Memoria æternitatis ejusque interminabilis durationis. 6. Inæstimabilis dignatio Dei, qui tanta passus est, ut te à peccatis liberaret. 7. Magnitudo beneficiorum tibi a Domino collatorum pro quibus turpissimum est non te gratum bene vivendo exhibere. 8. Sublimitas æterni præmii et facilitas mediorum ad illud acquirendum. 9. Infinita amabilitas Dei infinito obsequio propter se dignissimi, quia ipse est summum bonum, qui te amore incomprehensibili prosequitur.

" Hæc motiva si attente consideraveris, facile poteris
summum in te contritionem excitare. Sic autem dis-
positus ad pedes confessarii accedes, quasi ad laværum
sanguinis Jesu Christi, in quo te ab omnibus inquina-
mentis tuis dealbandum fore confides. Duos ibi sacerdotes adesse putabis, visibilem unum, alterum invisibilem qui penetralia cordis intuetur. Idéo humillimé,
quasi filius prodigus resipiscens, benedictionem petes
et gratiam bené confitendi, præmissaque generali confessione, actum contritionis renovabis. Tum magna
interiori et exteriori reverentia, quanta judici solet à
reo exhiberi, peccata tua sacerdoti ; qui Christum judi-
cem repræsentat, confiteberis nudé, sinceré, humiliter,
non ex habitu et consuetudine. . . . Dum vero sacerdos profert verba, absolutionis, iterum actum contritionis elicies, teque a Christo, sicut filium prodigum,
osculo excipi, novâ 'stolâ ornari, amplexa constringi
putabis. . . . Quare gratias si ages, dicens cum pro-
pheta : 'nunc cœpi,' et incipies ab illâ horâ vitam
sanctius instituere."

Among the rules prescribed by Father Nouet for the
frequent and fruitful reception of this sacrament, we
note especially the following :

" 1. Before your confession, spend a reasonable time
in preparation. Place yourself with great respect in
the presence of God, and realizing the need you have of
His help, pray to the Holy Ghost to enkindle in your
heart the fire of His love, and to excite therein a lively

sorrow for your sins. · Beseech the Son of God to grant you light to know your sins and words to confess them with humility. Ask God the Father for the gift of strength to do penance, and repair the injury you have offered Him. Implore the help of the Blessed Virgin and of your guardian angel, who is the witness of your actions, and then examine yourself carefully on the faults you may have committed since your last confession. He who faithfully examines his conscience every day, who constantly watches over himself, and seeks God in truth, must necessarily be so afflicted at having offended Him that he needs not spend a long time to discover his sins. His principal concern should be to excite in his heart as perfect a sorrow as he can.

" 2. In accusing yourself of your sins, use simple, precise, and plain language, desiring simply to make known your faults such as they are before God, who sees your heart and who is to be your judge. The confusion you may experience will be beneficial as a satisfaction for your transgressions, and will obtain for you many heavenly blessings. In the confession of venial sins, avoid all embarrassment, prolixity, and superfluity. Be satisfied with selecting four or five of those which cause you greatest concern, and which would be more prejudicial to your soul if you neglected to apply to them the proper remedy. Be particularly careful to correct yourself of sins contrary to obedience, fraternal charity, and the reverence which at prayer you owe to God.

" 3. When your confession is ended, enter in spirit into the wounds of your Saviour. There you will find a remedy for the wounds of your own soul; there you will find strength to overcome your perverse nature and those weaknesses which so often lead to your downfall. Listen attentively, and with sentiments of deep humility, to the advice of your confessor, accepting cheerfully the penance which he imposes on you. Resolve to add thereto some voluntary mortifications to satisfy the justice of God and escape the pains of purgatory. The best possible proof of the good fruit produced by this sacrament is habitual hatred of sin after confession and whenever occasion demands it."

Father Judde points out many defects which insinuate themselves into what are called devotional confessions; that is, confessions in which there is a moral certainty that the penitent has but venial sins to confess :

" 1. People confess through habit, and without fully realizing what they are doing. We should never approach the confessional till after fervent prayer, and never after distracting visits, occupations, or conversations in which everything but God has been discussed.

" 2. Contrition is wanting. If the venial sins confessed were committed deliberately, the penitent must endeavor to have a well-defined contrition for them, and this is quite possible. But, if they are indeliberate weaknesses, it is not necessary that the sorrow and firm purpose should relate immediately to them; it will suffice that they be referred to neglect in using the means which would have helped to prevent them, or at least to diminish their number."

" 3. Some people are in the habit of confessing the slightest faults, which are often involuntary, and for which they have no real contrition. It would be much more profitable to occupy ourselves with faults which call more imperatively for correction and amendment."

" 4. After confession, people return too quickly to their worldly occupations and distracting amusements. Great is the favor which they have received, and great should be their precaution and care against the danger of losing it. Therefore, after confession, thanksgiving, generous sentiments, resolutions of amendment are in order."

CHAPTER IV.

FOR the faithful in general, holiness consists in two things : to die and to live—to put off the old man and put on the new. " Expoliantes vos veterem hominem, . . . et induentes novum." [1] But besides these, the priest is called upon to communicate to others the supernatural and divine life which he derives from Jesus Christ. For he is not holy as he ought to be unless he is also *sanctifier*. In his case, to become holy means to die, to live, and to vivify. These three degrees of sacerdotal perfection we can easily acquire if we turn to account the teachings, examples, and powerful graces which Our Lord offers us at the altar.

I. We are worthy ministers of the Eucharist only in so far as we are imitators of Christ concealed under the sacramental veils. Where shall we find a model more attractive and amiable?

1. Model of mortification. Our first duty is to die to the world and to our own natural inclinations.

The Mass is the memorial of the passion of Jesus

[1] Coloss. iii. 9.

Christ. His death is here mystically represented by the separate consecration of the bread and of the wine. The ornaments are all marked with the sign of the cross, which is used in all ceremonies and benedictions. But above all, the silence, the meekness, the patience of the adorable Victim—everything at the altar—vividly remind us of the ignominious and sorrowful scenes of Calvary. Moreover, outrages ceased not to be offered to Jesus Christ with the termination of His mortal life. We know what indignities have been reserved for Him hidden under the eucharistic veils. Alas! does He not find in our churches a renewal of the cruel trials of Calvary? Does not His heart experience the same sorrow at the sight of the crimes daily committed by men, whilst He offers Himself to the Eternal Father as a victim of propitiation? Does He not find also coldness, indifference, abandonment—and that, too, on the part of those very persons who were the recipients of his greatest favors and on whose fidelity He had therefore the strongest claims. On the cross He was loaded with opprobrium by the Jews; on the altar He is overwhelmed with it by the heretics and the impious. But in this example of the Saviour, who not only devotes Himself to torments and to death, but who also, as it were, prolongs and perpetuates His passion by leaving Himself in the hands of men, there is a wonderful power to make us love mortification, or at least to render the practice of it more agreeable.

Jesus Christ foresaw everything. Therefore, when through love for men He constituted Himself a prisoner in the Holy Eucharist, the persecutions of the future were as clearly present to Him as those which He was actually undergoing. His tender love for us triumphed over every feeling of repugnance. He accepted the twofold chalice. Oh, that thought alone—which everything connected with the celebration of the sacred Mysteries so vividly recalls—ought to suffice to inspire the priest with unbounded generosity and courage! Thou hast, O Lord! constituted Thyself my Victim; shall I refuse to be Thine? When instituting the Sacrament of the Altar, and pre-ordaining me to be its privileged minister, Thou didst well know how many tribulations Thou wouldst have to undergo from that moment to this. Thou hadst ever present to Thee those numberless impieties, those horrible sacrileges, committed against Thee in Thy holy sacraments during this long interval of nearly nineteen hundred years. Thou didst distinctly foresee how many Judases Thou wouldst encounter on Thy way, how many times on multiplied Calvaries Thy thirst wouldst be sated with vinegar and gall; yet that terrifying prospect could not allay the fervor of Thy love, nor prevent Thee accomplishing this prodigy of charity in my behalf. Will it now be said that I have nothing but a lukewarm heart to offer Thee in return for all Thou hast done for me? For love of me Thou hast sacrificed consolations, glory, life itself; shall I hesitate to sacrifice for Thee my love of ease, my sensitive emotions? For the love of me Thou hast consented to be spit upon, to be trampled under foot, to be crucified; Thou hast abandoned Thyself to the fury of Thy enemies, to be rejected, insulted, vilified by many even of Thy own disciples—and all this Thou endurest till the consummation of the world; and shall I complain of remaining in obscurity during the few days of my sojourn on earth? Shall I permit a slight insult or contradiction to irritate me to such an extent as completely to upset my mind? Shall I continue to be proud, impatient, excitable, exacting? Such a contrast should not be tolerated.

No person on earth should be such a perfect image of Jesus Christ as the priest; because the priest is His minister, His visible representative who continues His work; therefore, none should suffer as much as the priest. But if he faithfully meditates on the Eucharist, and is docile to the inspirations he may derive therefrom, he will view sufferings—whatever may be their nature and origin—in the light martyrs, nourished by this heavenly food, looked upon the prison, the gibbet, and the stake.[1] He will then learn to die to himself,

[1] The pious Baron de Renti, in one of his ecstasies of love, said : "As the grain of wheat, in order to become my eucharistic food, had to be put into the ground, to be decomposed, to be crushed under the millstone, kneaded in water, and baked at the fire ; so I, also, in order to become the bread of Jesus Christ, must be buried in the earth, rot in abjection, be crushed, annihilated by calumny and persecution, kneaded in the water of affliction, and roasted at the fire of sorrow and tribulation."

according to the admonition which the Church gives him in the ceremony of his ordination: "Imitamini quod tractatis, quatenus mortis dominicæ mysterium celebrantes, mortificare membra vestra à vitiis et concupiscentiis omnibus procuretis." [1]   Happy indeed would be the death which would make him live a most saintly sacerdotal life!

2. What is the life of Jesus Christ in the Most Blessed Sacrament?   It is a life entirely inspired and directed by divine wisdom.   Human wisdom understands nothing of that profound obscurity wherein the Sovereign Majesty conceals Itself, or of that silence, solitude, and unspeakable union of contemplation and action.   For in the Holy Eucharist Jesus seems to do nothing, and He does all; from the humble sanctuary in which He resides He governs the universe.   Glorifying God by continual adoration and humiliation, sanctifying men by pouring down upon them the blessings of His love, such is the whole life of Jesus Christ in the tabernacle and on the holy altar.   That life is but the continual exercise of all virtues practised to infinite perfection.   How great the meekness and patience of this Lamb of God!   He suffers Himself to be approached, handled, insulted!   He rejects no one. Little and great, ignorant and learned, just and sinful —all find ready access to Him.   How great His humility!   He puts off all that might reveal His glory;

[1] Pontif.

He hides His Godship; He veils even His humanity. What He is appears not—or, rather, He appears to be nothing. He is as if He were not. How admirable His obedience! He is the King of kings, the Lord of lords; yet to what extent does He practise subjection! Every hour of the day finds Him, in some part of the world, in the hands of His ministers, who expose Him to the adoration of the faithful or shut Him up in a tabernacle—in fact, dispose of Him as they please. But this life of our divine Lord in the Eucharist is, above all, a life of interior recollection, of silence, of disengagement. How intimate His union with God! For nearly nineteen hundred years His prayer has not been a moment interrupted, and to this continuous prayer the world is indebted for all the happiness it enjoys. Behold the true model of sacerdotal life!

To live as a priest should, and worthily bear that beautiful name, the spirit of God must be the principle and the rule of our thoughts, the motive-power of our actions; being guided in all things by the maxims of faith, and putting away from us that prudence of the flesh which is veritable death—"Prudentia carnis mors est." [1] How this wisdom is death is explained by the great Apostle: "Quoniam . . . inimica est Deo." It separates us from God, who is the source of life, inducing us always to prefer the creature to the Creator; imparting to us no zeal or activity except for accumu-

[1] Rom. viii. 6.

lating what the world calls a fortune—as if he had not already acquired the best fortune who has left all to follow Jesus Christ. " Ecce nos reliquimus omnia, et secuti sumus te." [1]

The example of the Saviour in the Most Holy Sacrament, whilst teaching us this sublime wisdom which is folly to the world, inspires us also with that charity, pure and courageous, which labors for God alone, rises above every human consideration, beholds obstacles without fear, and confidently advances towards its only object, which is the will of God. This example, in which divine power and meekness are so admirably blended, attracts and at the same time directs us in the ways of that interior life, entirely hidden in God, which ought to be the soul of the apostolic life. The silence, calmness, and peace which reign about the tabernacle eloquently teach us that the Lord is not to be sought amidst agitation and trouble, and that we must first of all possess our own souls in peace before we can successfully attend to other service for God or to the spiritual welfare of our neighbor.

Let the priest but obey the instructions which he receives every day at the altar, and his lively sense of God's presence and his love of prayer will become habitual. To him St. Paul would have no need to repeat what he has unprofitably told so many others: " Attende tibi. . . . Attende lectioni. . . . Noli negligere

[1] Matt. xix. 27.

gratiam quæ in te est. . . . Hæc meditare, in his esto." [1] He will not suffer his soul to flow like water through the outlets of the senses, or to gather up in the outside world a thousand images and troublesome recollections to disturb him in the exercise of prayer. He will be prudent and circumspect in all his ways, discreet in his words, watchful over all the impulses of his heart, submissive to the decrees of Providence, obedient to those who have authority over him. The Apostle St. Paul desires that we should be adorned with every virtue,[2] and the Church teaches that "ministras ecclesiæ fide et opere debere esse perfectos."[3] Perfect we shall surely become if we endeavor to imitate the divine Model given us in the tabernacle. It is thus that, having taught us to put off the old man ourselves, Jesus Christ, in the great mystery of His love, teaches us to put on the new man, to live of His life, and then enables us to vivify souls by communicating His spirit to them.

3. The greatest misfortune that could happen the world would be the extinction of holy zeal in that privileged tribe to whom, as the Council of Milan says, God has confided the happiness of all peoples. "O magna et inclyta Dei instrumenta, sacerdotes, a quibus omnium populorum pendet beatitudo!" But what misfortune for the priest himself were he destitute of a virtue which appertains to the very essence of the priesthood!

---

[1] I. Tim. iv. 13–16.   [2] I. Tim. iii. 2.   [3] Pontif.

"Curam fratrum nostrorum genere, summa vitæ nostræ." [1]   "Si officium vis exercere presbyteri, aliorum salutem fac lucrum animæ tuæ." [2]   For my own sake I am a Christian; for the sake of others I am a priest.   "Omnis . . . pontifex . . . pro hominibus constituitur." [3]

Nothing will give me greater consolation at the hour of death than the remembrance of hardships undergone and sufferings endured for the salvation of souls.   On the contrary, nothing can be more dreadful than to fall into the hands of the living God [4] without being able to offer my Judge good works sufficient to "cover the multitude of my sins." [5]   The priest who is destitute of devotedness and zeal is a stranger to the love of God and of his neighbor; on what, then, can he ground his hope of sharing the blessed inheritance of the elect in the kingdom of charity?   He does not love God, since he does not labor for the interests of His glory; he does not respond to the most ardent of His desires by co-operating to the sanctification and happiness of God's children, and he nullifies the designs of God in calling him to the sacred ministry.   Was it not for the sake of saving souls that God made him His ambassador, set him up as the light of the world, the salt of the earth, a master and teacher of people, a fisher of men?   He does not love his neighbor.   Can one love with an iron

---

[1] S. Chrys., Serm. 9 in Gen.   [2] S. Hier., Epist. xiii.

[3] Heb. v. 1.   [4] Heb. x. 31.   [5] I. Pet. iv. 8.

heart? Such a heart must the priest have who is indifferent to the sad state of so many unfortunate souls who live lives of crime and suffering, who are ignorant of all that is most necessary for them to know, or else who use their knowledge but to make them more guilty and wretched—for, alas! whither do such blind people go? on the brink of what abyss are those sinners sleeping? "Tot accidimus, quot ad mortem ire quotidie tepidi et tacentes videmus."[1] Therefore, when we speak of sacerdotal zeal, the subject is one of vital importance; it is a matter of life or death for the priest. But this zeal we shall not lack if we study carefully and are solicitous to follow the example which Our Saviour gives us in the Sacrament of the Altar. Therein we shall find both the most powerful stimulus to our zeal and the safest rule for its practical direction.

In the first place, the example of Our Lord in this sacrament enkindles our zeal, inasmuch as it strikingly reminds us of all Jesus did and does, every day and every moment, for the salvation of souls. The Mass is the memorial of all the mysteries of His life, and especially of the touching mystery of His death. Now, in the life and death of Christ everything was directed to the one end—to procure the glory of God by the salvation of souls. These souls Jesus Christ came on earth to seek through so many humiliations, privations, and sufferings. It was the thought of their happiness that

[1] S. Greg.

7

comforted Him, that sustained Him, in the agony of Gethsemani and through the tortures of Calvary.

But He is still, in the Eucharist, the great zealot of souls. By daily offering Himself to His Father, through the ministry of the priests, He continues amongst us, with the same burning charity, the work of redemption which He commenced at the moment of the incarnation. It is love of souls which draws Him down on thousands of altars, as it made Him enter the womb of Mary and there offer His first sacrifice. The object of His eucharistic life is the same as that of His mortal life. He continues to dispel our illusions, to direct our inclinations, to save us. For upward of eighteen hundred years He has been to the Church, in this sacrament—so justly called the mystery of His love—what the sun is in nature, diffusing everywhere light, fecundity, and life.

In His tabernacle He waits for sinners, inviting them to unload in His merciful embrace the anguish of their troubled consciences. He offers them His merits, His influence and mediation with the Father. As during the days of His mortal life, He has now but one overmastering desire: namely, to close the abyss of hell and open wide the gates of heaven by enkindling in all hearts that sacred fire which He came on earth to kindle: "Ignem veni mittere in terram, et quid volo nisi ut accendatur?" [1] He spends Himself wholly and in-

---

[1] Luke xii. 49.

cessantly for souls. Finally, foreseeing that His example would not sufficiently inflame our zeal, He superadds the most pressing exhortation at the very moment of His mystical immolation; for He then commands us to remember His passion when He puts Himself as a victim in our hands, and not to forget Calvary when we stand at the altar. "Hæc quotiescumque feceritis, in mei memoriam facietis."

By reminding us, at that solemn moment, of what He suffered for souls, does He not pathetically admonish us to be solicitous for their salvation? Is it possible to celebrate Mass with that recollection which so sacred an action imperatively requires, without at the same time hearing in the very depths of our hearts the reverberations of the awful words which so deeply moved the heart of Peter, and which in all succeeding ages inspired devoted pastors and apostolic men? "Lovest thou Me? Lovest thou Me more than these? Feed My lambs; feed My sheep." Take care of souls. Wilt thou suffer thy brethren to perish, for whom thou knowest that I died? Tell Me not of thy love, if thou carest so little for the happiness of those whom I love so tenderly, and whose salvation I purchased at so high a price. Hence St. Cyril of Alexandria says: "Ex hoc loco agnoscunt fidei magistri non aliter se summo pastori gratos fore, quam si omni studio caveant ut rationales oves recte curentur." And St. Laurence Justinian: "Nihil tam Deo gratum acceptumque est, quam pro viribus operam dare ut homines reddantur meliores." St. Gregory: "Ille apud Deum in amore major, qui ad ejus amorem plurimos trabit." St. John Chrysostom: "Si immensas pecunias eroges, plus tamen efficies, si unam converteris animam: . . . hoc maximum amicitiæ erga Christum argumentum."

Reverend Father Olier wrote as follows to a person who could not understand the father's solicitude for his sanctification: "You are astonished at what I do, and what I would willingly do and suffer for the sake of your soul. You apparently ignore or at least forget that every morning, after the consecration of the chalice, I see bubbling up between my hands the adorable blood which has been shed for your salvation."

Jesus Christ, in the holy sacrament, regulates and directs our zeal whilst stimulating it by word and example. Think of the purity of His motives! Does He seek His own interests whilst striving to procure the glory of His Father? Is there any mixture of self in all that He undertakes to make the Father known, loved, and glorified? In His ministrations to the souls of men, does He regard flesh and blood, distinctions of rank, character, or fortune? How kind and condescending in the means He employs to withdraw them from sin and subject them to grace! How gently He insinuates Himself into the hearts of men! He makes Himself all to all, in order to win them to virtue and to happiness. Does He extinguish the smoking flax?

Does He reject sinners, even the greatest? If He does not at once admit them to His table, at least He suffers them in His presence. How many have come and outraged Him at the very foot of His altar! and the only way He punished their sacrilegious audacity was to pray for them and repeatedly tender them His friendship. How constantly unalterable His love for men, notwithstanding their ingratitude and hardness of heart! O priests, study this model, and the love of Jesus Christ for souls will be transfused from His heart into yours! And especially you, pastors of souls, study Jesus in the sacrament of His love. You will then assuredly love those sheep the Son of God loved so tenderly; you will then entertain towards the flock committed to your care the sentiments of St. Paul concerning those whom he had begotten to the faith: "Ego autem libentissime impendam, et superimpendar ipse pro animabus vestris; licet plus vas diligens, minus diligar." [1] You will then cheerfully undertake any labor, make any sacrifice, overcome every reluctance, whenever there is question of saving souls; and in order to co-operate thereto, you will always rely more on meekness than on authority, more on patience than on hasty zeal; and to the exertions of a love as active as a flame you will add the constancy of a love as invincible as death—"fortis ut mors dilectio." [2] Be thoroughly convinced that the success of apostolic labors is

[1] II. Cor. xii. 15.　　　　　[2] Cant. viii. 6.

in proportion with the sufferings of the apostle; and the contradictions and difficulties continually springing up, far from allaying your zeal, will, on the contrary, arouse your courage and strengthen your confidence. Do not anticipate the moment of grace; but, if you can, hasten its coming by your prayers and tears, and never despair of the conversion of sinners. Continue to pray and to hope, though still apparently unheard. "Omnia sperat." If necessary, go after the lost sheep to the very gates of hell. If sinners resist, if they even outrage you, let your compassion for them augment in proportion to the injury they do you. "Tantum quisque portat, quantum amat." [1]

It is thus that the Son of God, renewing every day and perpetuating upon our altars His mystical immolation, teaching us by His example to die, to live, and to communicate to souls that supernatural life which we have received of Him, smooths for us the path of sacerdotal perfection in every degree. Let us add that if we are so disposed we cannot fail to make rapid progress in the way of sanctity, for He offers us at the altar graces which might well be called all-powerful.

II. To us priests our kind and generous Master has addressed Himself thus condescendingly: "Jam non dicam vos servos, sed amicos." [1] Therefore, what injustice, what blasphemous insolence on our part, were we to say to Him, in the language of the wicked servant of

[1] S. Chrys.   [2] John xv. 15.

the Gospel: "Homo austerus es: tollis quod non posuisti, et metis quod non seminasti." [1] No, God does not gather where He has not sown. If He exacts of us an extraordinary sanctity, He makes it easy for us to attain it by the many and powerful graces which He prepares and reserves for us in the inexhaustible treasury of His mercy. To speak of the Mass only—oh, if Christ dwelt in our hearts by faith according to the desire of St. Paul: "Det vobis . . . Christum habitare per fidem in cordibus vestris;" [2] if our love for God were such as to enable us to comprehend with all the saints the wonderful extent of the Saviour's charity towards us—"Ut possitis comprehendere cum omnibus sanctis quæ sit latitudo, et longitudo, et sublimitas, et profundum" [3]—our souls would indeed be filled with consolation at the thought of the immense resources offered us in the Mass to consummate the great work of our sanctification!

God is ever lavish of His gifts; but never does He lavish them so prodigally upon us as when we perform, with all the care and devotion of which we are capable, the sublime function of sacrificer. It is then that He pours into our hearts that good measure, pressed down, shaken together, and running over, to borrow the words of Jesus Christ Himself: "Mensuram bonam, et confertam, et coagitatam, et supereffluentem." [4] At the altar we receive a sacrament, and we offer a sacrifice.

[1] Luke xix. 21. [2] Eph. iii. 16, 17. [3] Eph. iii. 18. [4] Luke vi. 38.

Our acts of thanksgiving eternally continued would be insufficient to adequately acknowledge all the graces and favors contained in either separately and singly. How, then, shall we competently express our gratitude for the treasures of grace contained in the union of sacrifice and sacrament?

1. At the altar we receive a sacrament; but one, of all sacraments, the most holy, the most fruitful, the most sanctifying—that which contains really and substantially the Author of all holiness. My God, is it possible to communicate—to communicate every day—without attaining the highest perfection, and becoming a great saint! What is there of goodness in the Source of all good, what is there of beauty in the Source of all beauty, that is not communicated to the soul by this nutriment of the elect? And where shall we find the principle and germ of the most perfect innocence, if not in the eucharistic wine?—" Quid bonum ejus, et quid pulchrum ejus, nisi frumentum electorum, et vinum germinans virgines?" [1]

Communion means God enriching us with Himself; for in giving Himself to us He sets no bounds to His liberality: all that He has, all that He is, becomes ours. After receiving from Him a gift of such magnificence, our domain extends, as it were, over the immensity of His riches and the infinity of His perfections. O impenetrable depth of the mystery of His

[1] Zach. ix. 17.

love! when I have eaten the living bread that came down from heaven—Jesus is mine, He is all mine; His divinity, His humanity, are mine. If I know how to listen to Him, when He takes possession of the sanctuary of my soul, I shall hear Him say to me, as He said to the blind man whom He met on the way to Jericho: "What wilt thou that I do to thee?" What dost thou desire? Speak out! When I came down upon earth by becoming incarnate in the womb of Mary, it was for the whole world's sake; but to-day I give Myself to thee. "Quid tibi vis faciam?" [1] O priest, wilt thou always remain sick, when God offers to heal thee of thy infirmities? Wilt thou continue poor, when He places at thy disposal the inexhaustible treasures of His omnipotence and of His incomprehensible love? The graces, merits, virtues of Jesus Christ are all yours in the holy communion. "Audeo dicere quod Deus, cum sit omnipotens, plus dare non potuit; cum sit sapientissimus, plus dare nescivit; cum sit ditissimus, plus dare non habuit." [2] "O ineffabilis dignitas conditoris! O stupor indicibilis charitatis! Quis non contremiscat? Quis non cum exultatione miretur?" [3]

All His *graces* are yours. In the other sacraments and by the various other means of sharing heavenly favors, you drink as from the stream; in the Holy Eucharist you possess the Fountain itself, and this inex-

[1] Luke xviii. 41.   [2] S. Aug., Tract. 84, in Joan.
[3] S. Laur. Just., de Euchar.

haustible Fountain supplies the whole Church and all ages that water which springs up into life everlasting. The light which enlightens, the power which sustains, the unction which consoles, the fear which chains down the passions, the hope which animates us, the various graces which God employs for the sanctification of His elect, have but one and the same principle, which is the adorable heart of Jesus; and this heart, which is the treasure of heaven and earth, is given to us in the holy communion.

His *merits* are yours. After holy communion you have the right to say to the Lord: "Thou art mine;" and you can add, if you choose: "And all Thy merits belong to me." For it is principally in this mystery that there is instituted between the Son of God and the soul which receives Him that blessed community of goods and of life, compared by Christ Himself to that which faith reveals to us between the Eternal Word and the Frst Person of the Blessed Trinity—"Vivo propter Patrem, et qui manducat me, et ipse vivet propter me."[1] As the Father, without suffering any loss or diminution of His infinite being, communicates it entire to the Son, who is His Word, so in the Holy Eucharist the Incarnate Word preserves His humanity and divinity whilst unreservedly communicating both to the soul that receives Him. Blessed soul, who in consequence of this union can in a manner say to the

---

[1] John vi. 58.

Saviour what Himself said to His Father: "Omnia . . . tua mea sunt !" [1]

Indifferent servant that I have been, I view with alarm the approach of evening, when the laborers will be called and the wages will be in proportion to the work done. Small, alas! is the amount of good which I have accomplished, and even that little has been marred by many defects. How much time lost during my life! And where can I find in that life anything that would entitle me to the kingdom of the blest? Have confidence, O my soul! Thy claims to the possession of heaven are grounded on the infinite merits of Jesus Christ, which are thine when thou hast received Him in holy communion, and which, if thou wilt, thou canst appropriate to thyself.

Finally, His *virtues* are yours. At the blessed moment when Jesus is in you as the Father is in Him— "Ego in eis, et tu in me" [2]—communicating to you the glory which the Father has given Him—"Ego claritatem quam dedisti mihi, dedi eis" [3]—fear not to appear in the presence of the thrice-holy God. For there, if I may so express myself, you are all resplendent with the virtues of His Son. Lift up your head with a saintly pride, and say with confidence: However lowly I may be, O Lord! however humiliating the remembrance of my countless sins, I am no longer unworthy that Thou shouldst incline towards me the majesty of Thy counte-

[1] John xvii. 10.   [2] John xvii. 23.   [3] John xvii. 22.

nance.   O God! look upon the face of Thy Christ.   Is there anything that Thou lovest, and perceivest not in me?   Doth justice please Thee?   Behold my soul resplendent with justice and sanctity, united as it is with the soul of Jesus Christ!   Innocence, meekness, humility, zeal for Thy glory, charity, are the qualities Thou seekest in the hearts of men; and all these my heart offers Thee at this precious moment.   Surely, these virtues, and a thousand others, are within my soul, since I possess the infinitely perfect heart of Thy Son. O Beauty ever ancient and ever new! henceforth I shall never complain that I cannot love Thee as much as Thou deservest, since it has been given me to love Thee through the infinitely loving heart of the God-Man.   I shall no longer bewail my inability to adequately adore Thy greatness, acknowledge Thy good-ness, or atone for my transgressions, since I can now offer Thee the adoration, the gratitude, and the penitence of Jesus Christ.   Will what in Him is sovereignly pleasing to Thee not be in me equally pleasing to Thee?

Furthermore, after communion you can—not for a few moments only, or, as it were, by borrowing another's garb—adorn your soul with the royal mantle of Jesus Christ's virtue.   Place no obstacle to the designs of His love, and these divine virtues will flow from His adorable heart into yours.   They will habitually adorn your soul; they will make you another Himself; and they will make you the worthy object of His Father's complacency.

Why should we fear excessively at the recollection of our extreme weakness? God has provided us with a support which will render us at will immovable, and He points it out to us at the altar in the "corn" of the elect and in the eucharistic wine—"frumento et vino stabilivi eum." [1]

Doubtless our ministry is surrounded by difficulties. We continually meet with unexpected, embarrassing occurrences; everywhere there are snares to be avoided, obstacles to be surmounted, enemies to be encountered. But what need we fear, when the Lord is our light and our salvation? "Dominus illuminatio mea et salus mea, quem timebo?" [2] Have we really any reason to be alarmed, when He condescends to be the protector of our life? "Dominus protector vitæ meæ, a quo trepidabo?" [3] Is not God more powerful to save us than the flesh, the world, and the devil are to destroy?

No doubt, also, our ministry is laborious, its cares are exhausting, the duties annexed to it gradually wear us out. We therefore stand in need of substantial aliment to recruit our strength and sustain in our soul that apostolic vigor which is essential to the accomplishment of our duties. Eagles and lions do not feed upon worms—"non pascitur leo vermibus." But where shall we find that supernatural strength and en-

---

[1] Gen. xxvii. 37.   [2] Ps. xxvi. 1.   [3] Ibid.

ergy which our labors and our trials demand, if not at the table prepared for us by Jesus Christ? The bread which we eat there is in truth the bread of the strong. Is not this the bread which imparted to martyrs that heroic constancy which wore out the patience of their tormentors? St. Augustine said of St. Laurence: "Illâ carne saginatus, illo calice ebrius, tormenta non sensit."

No doubt, in fine, our ministry has its share of bitterness, of distastes, sorrows, and contradictions. But here also Jesus Christ has admirably provided for our wants. Many are the holy delights which a pure soul experiences at His table. There especially she tastes how sweet is the Lord; and there, inebriated with the purest joys, she loses all remembrance of earthly pains and of earthly joys. "Suavitatem hujus sacramenti nullus exprimere sufficit, per quod spiritualis dulcedo in suo fonte gustatur." [1]

Many, then, and powerful are the means of sanctification which the priest finds in the daily participation of the Sacrament of the Altar. Therefore, the fault is entirely our own if we do not return from the altar in the state described by St. John Chrysostom: "Tanquam leones ignem spirantes, facti diabolo terribiles." [2] "Non est defectus in cibo, sed in sumente." [3] Let us no longer impede the tender outpourings of the heart

---

[1] S. Thom., opusc. 57.   [2] Homil. 61, ad Pop.

[3] Bona, cap. vi. n. 7.

of Jesus.   Let us not suffer anything to remain in our hearts which may interfere with His freedom of action, and we shall soon be ready to exclaim with the Royal Prophet : " Calix meus inebrians quam præclarus est !" [1] Thus far we have spoken of the effects of the sacrament we receive in the celebration of the holy mysteries.

2. As to the sacrifice which we offer at the altar, we have already stated, with the Council of Trent, that it is the same as that of the cross.   Its value is infinite, its efficacy all-powerful, whether to appease the anger of God, however great, or to obtain from His bounty all graces and blessings, notwithstanding our personal unworthiness.   One Mass alone would suffice to sanctify and save thousands of worlds.   Let us hear St. Laurence Justinian : " Nullus profecto valet humano explicare eloquio, quam locuples fructus, quanta ex ejus oblatione . . . spiritualia exuberent dona.   Reconciliatur quippe peccator Deo, justus autem justificatur adhuc, lætificantur angeli, cumulantur merita, facinora remittuntur, augentur virtutes, resecantur vitia, diaboli machinamenta superantur, sanantur ægri, eriguntur lapsi, debiles refocillantur . . . defuncti fideles liberantur." [2] These are the general effects of the holy sacrifice ; but what we too often forget is the very special, the immense, share which we as priests, elevated to the unique position of celebrant, personally have in its fruits.

[1] Ps. xxii. 5,   [2] Serm. de Euchar.

What a wonderful thing! We are delegated before the throne of God, in the name of the universal Church, to offer the homage and plead the cause of every creature! We go up to the altar as ambassadors of heaven, of earth, and of that other world which we call purgatory! It would seem that, being charged with a mission so vast and of such universal importance, we should be required to forget our own private interests; for a public man ought to devote himself exclusively to the public welfare. But that sacrifice of self-interest is not required of the priest in the first, noblest, and sublimest of all his functions. He is not only permitted, but also commanded, to think of himself, his own needs, his own poverty, before pleading in behalf of his brethren. The sacrifice which is offered for the world in general is offered in a particular manner for him who celebrates. It is, therefore, for the remission of our own innumerable sins, offences, and negligences that we primarily offer to God the superabundant satisfactions of the immolated Saviour. The first drops of His precious blood are applied to our own souls to cleanse and purify them of every spot, stain, or defilement which may still remain even after we have done our endeavors to be pure. "Suscipe, sancte Pater, . . . pro innumerabilibus peccatis, et offensionibus, et negligentiis meis." Having first implored the divine clemency for myself, I shall then plead for it in behalf of all those who are present, and of all the faithful, living and dead.

" Sed et pro omnibus circumstantibus, sed et pro omnibus fidelibus Christianis, vivis atque defunctis, ut mihi et illis proficiat ad salutem, in vitam æternam." Note the words, "mihi et illis." Salvation and life everlasting for me; these are what the tears, the wounds, and the death of Jesus Christ will, before all else, demand for myself. Afterwards, all who belong to Him by faith will have a share in the treasure of His merits. Such is the order prescribed by the Church.

We find the same order all through the Mass. Always the first in the worship which is given to God, the priest is also the first in all blessings and favors granted in return. Towards the end of the Mass we say to the Most Holy Trinity: " Præsta ut sacrificium, quod oculis tuæ majestatis indignus obtuli, tibi sit acceptabile, mihique et omnibus, pro quibus illud obtuli, sit, te miserante, propitiable." Thus we here say, "mihi et omnibus propitiable," just as we said at the offertory, " mihi et illis proficiat."

But here is something still more astonishing, something which ought more profoundly to move our hearts —perhaps the grandest thing faith can offer for the consolation of the priesthood. Let us consider with particular attention the formula which we use, on the authority of Jesus Christ, to operate the miracle of transubstantiating wine into His blood. At that solemn and awful moment the priest says and does what Jesus Christ said and did in the institution of the divine sac-

8

rifice. Let us assist in spirit at this first of all Masses, and represent to ourselves the apostles at table, ranged about their good Master. To them, and through them to all the inheritors of their sacerdotal character, He addresses those wonderful words, which a priest should never repeat but with feelings of the profoundest gratitude: "Take and eat, this is My blood—qui pro vobis et pro multis effundetur in remissionem peccatorum." We distinctly hear Him say: "Pro vobis et pro multis." Here, then, are two classes of persons, perfectly distinct, whom Our Lord had vividly in mind during His passion, and for whom He continues to offer His blood on the altar. "Pro vobis;" for you, My apostles, the leaders of My people; for you, My ministers of all times and of all places, by whose labors I intend to bring all men to the knowledge of My name; for you, first of all, do I immolate Myself on the altar; and after you, for all those who through your apostolic labors will believe in Me and become members of My body by entering into My Church. I exclude none from participation in the abundant redemption I accomplish; but you, My priests, are the primary and especial objects of My predilection—"Pro vobis et pro multis."[1] In the admirable discourse after the Last Supper, every word of which breathes the most ardent charity, our loving Saviour prayed—we had almost said nominally prayed—for each of us as His represen-

[1] See Father Le Brun: Manuel d'un jeune prêtre, f. i., p. 114.

tatives: "Pater sancte, serva eos; . . . non pro eis autem rogo tantum, sed et pro eis qui credituri sunt per verbum eorum." [1] That, however, did not satisfy the immense love of His Sacred Heart for His priests; so He willed, moreover, that we should be the first to experience the salutary effects of that great cry for mercy which the voice of His blood spilt on Calvary sent up to heaven—a cry which He repeats every day in our silent sanctuaries. Let us, then, candidly admit that, with the daily celebration of Mass, sacerdotal sanctity and perfection are as easily acquired as they are absolutely indispensable to us.

[1] John xvii. 11, 20.

CHAPTER V.

PREPARATION FOR THE HOLY SACRIFICE.

To us it seems superfluous to prove the necessity of that preparation; it follows evidently from all the preceding reflections. Let us merely point out a terrible danger to which negligence in this respect might expose us. In our sacred mysteries there is nothing for the senses to feed upon. If we are not extremely careful to prepare ourselves for their celebration by enkindling in our souls that spirit of faith strong enough to pierce the clouds and to impart to us in a manner—as it did to Moses—the privilege of seeing the invisible —"invisibilem tanquam videns sustinuit," [1] force of habit, together with our unfortunate inclination to do inattentively what we do frequently, will soon lead us to perform the holiest and sublimest action under the sun as if it were the most commonplace. Then we shall carry our tepidity with us to the altar, and we shall richly deserve the reproach of the Prophet: "Seminastis multum, et intulistis parum; comedistis, et non estis satiati; bibistis, et non estis inebriati; operuistis vos, et non estis calefacti." [2] "You have sown

---

[1] Heb. xi. 27. [2] Agg. i. 6.

much and gathered little." What a rich harvest of merits you ought to have gathered from the celebration of so many Masses—and what fruit have you actually reaped from them? You have eaten the bread of angels; and it has not appeased your hunger, so you have sought other delights. You have drunk from the torrent of pure and eternal joys; but they have not quenched your thirst, and you still sigh for the vain joys of earth. You have placed within your bosom the sacred fire which at all times has inflamed the hearts of good priests, but yours has remained cold and languid. "Quam ob causam, dicit Dominus exercituum?" Is this a heavenly or is it an infernal miracle? What is the cause of it? It is this; for the Holy Ghost Himself has revealed it to us: "Quia domus mea deserta est."[1] The house of the Lord is a desert. Your soul, wherein He would fain dwell, resembles a land that has been deserted, and is open to all passers-by. It has forgotten the presence of God; it has not been purified; it is not fittingly adorned to be the abiding-place of the Most Holy God and to merit His favors. Wherefore, says St. Paul, you prevent the full realization of the designs of His love towards you; you remain subject to your imperfections, to your spiritual infirmities; you continue the victim of a sloth which might easily lead to incurable lethargy. "Ideo inter vos multi infirmi et imbecilles, et dormiunt multi."[2] It is in this sense, as

---

[1] Agg. i. 9.　　　　[2] I. Cor. xi. 30.

we have already seen, that St. Bonaventure interprets the text of the great Apostle.

Cardinal Bona, too, applies it in the same sense. Let us quote his remarkable words :

" Pervulgatum apud sanctas Patres axioma est, quod talem se animæ exhibet Deus, qualem se illa præparat Deo.   Ideo Christus in Eucharistia aliis quidem est fructus vitæ, panis angelorum, manna absconditum, paradisus deliciarum, ignis consumens, et tertium cœlum, in quo audiuntur arcana verba quæ non licet homini loqui.   Aliis vero est panis insipidus, omni carens dulcedine et vitali operatione, et nauseat anima eorum super cibo isto ; quia nimirum mors est malis, vita bonis ; et sicut quisque erga Deum affectus est, talem ipsum erga se experitur.   Pauci sunt qui admirabilis hujus sacri convivii in se sentiunt effectus, quia pauci sunt qui se ad illos recipiendos rite disponant ; qui serio cogitent se ad sancta sanctorum accedere, ad altare Dei, ad Deum ipsum.   Ideo multi infirmi sunt et imbecilles ; et dormiunt multi.   Mortem olim summo sacerdoti minabatur Deus, si ausus fuisset introire in sancta sanctorum sine strepitu tintinnabulorum, non radians gemmis, non fulgens auro, omnium virtutum varietate circumamictus.   Quam ergo pœnam merebitur novæ legis sacerdos, qui non ad arcam typicam, sed ad Deum ipsum accedit, ut Filium ejus Dominum Jesum Christum immolet, tangat, comedat, nisi id faciat ea sollicitudine, attentione et apparatu, qui dignus sit tali convivio, dignus Deo? Instante itaque celebratione totis viribus curare debet ut in arâ cordis ignem divini amoris succendat, actusque eliciat diversarum virtutum, qui heroici sint, et tanto sacrificio, quantum fieri poterat, convenientes." [1]

We must therefore prepare ourselves for the celebration of the holy sacrifice. But how? Jesus Christ Himself will be our Model and Instructor.

The whole life of the Saviour was but a preparation for His immolation on Calvary. That was ever present to His mind. Therefore did He, at the very first moment of His entrance into this world, make a full oblation of Himself to the Father as a preparation for the great sacrifice on the cross. After the example of Christ, the good priest's whole life is a preparation for the worthy offering of the sacrifice of the altar. He justly thinks that this preparation should precede, not merely begin with, the Mass. Not only the recitation of the holy office, so intimately connected with the Mass; not only the examination of conscience with which he ended the preceding day, and the prayers with which he begins this; but all his actions, studies, labors, trials—all are directed to the one great end: to say Mass well. In his life everything is either a thanksgiving for the holy sacrifices already offered or a preparation for those to be offered. "I have said Mass to-day, I ought to say it to-morrow"—such is the

----

[1] De Miss. celebrat., cap. v.

thought which is ever present to his mind. In it he finds a powerful motive for unremitting watchfulness over himself, and for a more fervent desire to please God. He cherishes in his heart a secret and habitual attraction for the altar, like to that instinct which brings back the sparrow and the turtle-dove to the place they have chosen for their dwelling. "Passer invenit sibi domum et turtur nidum sibi, . . . altaria tua, Domine virtutum."[1] Oh! let us think on the Mass; and if we cannot be always occupied with it, at least let us call it to mind towards the end of the day, before we close our eyes in sleep. It is so good to retire to rest with this thought: "To-morrow, to-morrow, I am again to sit down at the table of the King." "Etiam cras cum rege pransurus sum."[2] In the morning, as soon as we awake, let us turn our mind and heart to the consideration of the great, the all-important action which we are about to perform.

St. Charles Borromeo made a rule from which, notwithstanding his multiplied occupations, he rarely deviated. It was, not to attend to any other matters till after the celebration of Mass. Whether we imitate him in this respect, and adopt the practice of employing the interval between the meditation and the Mass in reading the Scriptures or some other pious book, or in reciting part of the office, or whether during that time necessity obliges us to attend to some matters for-

---

[1] Ps. lxxxiii. 4.   [2] Esther v. 12.

eign to the sublime sacrifice, let us at least never completely forget it; and before going up to the altar let us by all means set apart some precious moment to reflect with astonishment on *the immensity of the power* we are about to exercise, *the infinite dignity of Him* whom we are called to represent, and *the supreme importance of the offices* we are about to perform. We shall find the perfect model for this preparation in the Sacred Heart of Jesus, animated, burning with love for God and man as it was on the eve of the great day on which He died for the salvation of the world. Let us hearken to St. John the Apostle, and reflect well on what he says: "Sciens Jesus quia omnia dedit ei Pater in manus, et quia à Deo exivit, et ad Deum vadit, surgit à cœnâ, . . . et cœpit lavare pedes discipulorum." [1] In these words we have an inexhaustible mine for salutary reflection before we approach the altar to celebrate the august sacrifice. Let us meditate on these beautiful words.

First preparation of Our Saviour for His immolation on Calvary—His knowledge of the power conferred on Him by the Father. All was put into His hands. He can dispose of all, and He knows it. "Sciens quia omnia dedit ei Pater in manus." O you who are the minister of Jesus Christ, know also and understand, especially when you are going to offer the holy sacrifice, how awful is the power conferred on you! At that mo-

[1] John xiii. 3–5.

ment to you also can be applied to a great extent what St. John said of Jesus Christ: "Omnia dedit ei Pater in manus." All the treasures of heaven and earth will soon be placed in your hands, and will enable you to realize the desires of the Church triumphant, to provide for the wants of the Church militant, and to alleviate the ills of the Church suffering. In a few moments you will have at your disposal a Victim of infinite value. You will be at liberty to make of His merits such use or application as you deem most advisable for the glory of God, the sanctification of souls, the salvation of the world. O priest, how great will be thy power when God Himself will be subject to thy dominion! How many chains thou canst rend asunder, how many tears thou canst dry up, how many thou canst make happy, when the treasures of mercy will be thrown open to thee, and thou canst freely draw therefrom! Prepare, then, to avail thyself of the boundless favor thou hast with God through the spotless Victim thou art to present Him for thyself, for the souls entrusted to thy care, and for the whole world. Let thy only fear be to ask or to expect too little. Heaven will soon give thee far more than thou canst demand.

Second preparation of Jesus Christ—knowledge of His own eminent dignity. "Sciens quia à Deo exivit." He is God of God, Light of light, true God of true God, come forth from the bosom of His Father, equal to Him in all things. Jesus knows what He is, and

He will be worthy of Himself in the dolorous immolation for which He is preparing. And thou who enjoyest the privilege of renewing and continuing His sacrifice, dost thou desire to prepare thyself worthily to perform a function which would make the very angels tremble? Be vividly impressed with this thought: In a few moments I shall be the representative, the instrument of the world's Redeemer. To this great and unique sacrifice I am going to lend my voice, my hands, my ministry. A little while, and I shall be the visible sovereign priest, showing to the world Jesus Christ; for He will be in me speaking, acting, reversing the laws of nature, operating the most astounding prodigies. If fully impressed with this truth, it will be easy for the priest to regulate his features, his bearing, his whole exterior in accordance with the gravity and modesty of the Son of God, so as to delight heaven with his interior dispositions and edify the faithful by his exterior deportment, inspiring them with the veneration due to mysteries so holy. Therefore, when about to celebrate, let everything in thee be so pure, so devout, so worthy of the adorable Priest whose vicegerent thou art, that He whose eye discovers the most secret things may say of thee: "Hic est Filius meus dilectus, in quo mihi complacui."[1] Be well versed in the letter and spirit of all the ceremonies; apply thyself to perform them with so much grace, to enliven them with such faith, inte-

---

[1] Matt. iii. 17.

rior recollection, and piety that God may thereby be honored, the faithful edified, and the Saviour recognized in the person of His minister.

Third preparation of Jesus Christ—knowledge of the all-important interests entrusted to His charge—"ad Deum vadit." No cloud obscures His vision of the Father's infinite perfections with all their dazzling splendor. To God alone He tended. To God's glory everything in Him was directed. His words, His actions, His sufferings, His life, His death—all were for God. "Ad Deum vadit." He knew what adoration, thanksgiving, and satisfaction were due to the Father. He knew that He must offer Himself to the Father as Head of the whole Church, and offer Him also the whole Church in the person of her humiliated, immolated, annihilated Chief. He knew that He was to adore God for her, to thank Him in her name, to atone in her stead, and to pray in her behalf. All that we, too, should know and remember when preparing to celebrate. It is to the self-same God—that God so great, so glorious, so powerful, so tender in His mercy, so rigorous in His justice, so magnificent in His rewards, so terrible in His punishments; to that God who could not be adequately honored except by a God-Adorer and a God-Victim, we, as deputies of the universal Church, are going to offer the same sacrifice for the same ends. Now, should not these ends, so exalted and so important—these four sublime intentions—absorb all our thoughts, completely engross our minds and elevate our souls?

A priest penetrated with these salutary reflections will easily be led into the sentiments of Jesus Christ, who, in order to perfect His preparation and to teach us how we ought to perfect ours, rises from table—"surgit à cœnâ"—and, not satisfied with humbling Himself before His Father, falls down at the feet of His disciples, and of Judas—"cœpit lavare pedes discipulorum."[1] Here is a lesson of purity and innocence. Oh, shall we ever be pure enough, innocent enough, to approach this *altar of God*, the sight of which makes saints tremble? Ah! if the priests of the Old Law had to perform so many ablutions and undergo so many purifications to prepare themselves for their ministry—though they offered to the Lord but material loaves and vile animals—how great should be the holiness of the priest of the New Law who offers the sacrifice of a God-Victim? However good may be the testimony of our conscience, we should endeavor to purify it still more; we should wash it cleaner and cleaner with our tears; we should efface by sincere repentance even the slightest traces of defilement. We are about to celebrate mysteries which heavenly spirits hardly dare to contemplate. "Quod angeli videntes horrescunt, neque libere audent intueri propter emicantem inde splendorem."[2]

---

[1] John xiii. 5.   [2] S. Chrys., de Sacerd.

What an admirable model of humility and charity we find in Him! A model of *humility.* A God makes Himself the servant of men, casts Himself down at their feet, renders them services the most menial and apparently the most unbecoming His sovereign majesty. It is an exhortation to us that, even if we should have taken every possible precaution to prepare ourselves for the worthy celebration of the holy sacrifice, we ought still to strive to supply the essential deficiency of our best endeavors by the profoundest humility. Nowhere are we so great as at the altar, and nowhere can we procure so much glory for God. Let us therefore follow the advice of the Holy Ghost: "Quanto magnus es, humilia te in omnibus, et coram Deo invenies gratiam: quoniam magna potentia Dei solius, et ab humilibus honoratur." [1] A model of *charity.* Jesus washing the feet of His apostles who will soon abandon Him, and of the traitor who is going to sell Him and deliver Him up to His executioners, teaches us not merely to suspend for a short time before celebrating, but to stifle forever in our hearts every feeling of aversion or of dislike or of bitterness towards those who in any way may have offended us.

Besides these general preparations, which may be made during the meditation, especially when it immediately precedes holy Mass, there are particular preparations which each may prescribe for himself according

[1] Ecclus iii. 20, 21.

to the wants of his soul and the relish he experiences in them. Nay, it is sometimes necessary to change our method when we perceive that we no longer derive the same profit from the system hitherto pursued, and that the soul needs to be roused by something new.

Of the various formulas of prayer and direction of intention before Mass—which can be easily had anywhere—we will only say that we too often neglect to use them advantageously, and that, instead of enkindling in us the spirit that inspired the saints who composed them for their own use, we not infrequently lose precious time with vague thoughts which can neither purify nor warm our hearts. We shall here reproduce what De Lantage, in his "Instructions Ecclesiastiques," lays down as an excellent rule for guidance in this matter. He was the intimate friend of one of those men of God whose extraordinary virtues and piety make them the honor of the priesthood. One day, in a conversation regarding our sublime power of consecrating and immolating the body of Jesus Christ, our author requested his saintly friend to tell him candidly how he was wont to prepare himself for this most sacred of all actions. We here give substantially the good priest's reply:

"For many years," said he, "I have been so absorbed in the contemplation of this ecstatic mystery that it is ever present to my mind during my religious exercises. I am thoroughly convinced that this practice will never become wearisome to me, because I know from experience that the more I consider what the Mass is, and what a happy intercourse it establishes between God and us, the more I am seized with admiration and love for the beauties and excellencies I discover therein. This habitual disposition is the groundwork of my preparation.

" From the early morning I begin that preparation during my meditation, and whilst it lasts I am already in spirit at the altar; for as the first object of meditation is to adore, praise, and thank God, I understand that I cannot attain it but by offering Him the adorable Victim. Bound as I am to appeal to Him for mercy on account of my sins, as well as those of the whole world—since the priest is a universal mediator—I have no means of propitiating Him in any degree comparable to the oblation I make Him of the blood of His own divine Son, shed upon the cross and offered upon the altar 'in remissionem peccatorum.' Moreover, as I pray in order to obtain from God the graces I stand in need of, I clearly see that my prayer would be cold, timid, and impotent if I do not offer it by that holy Victim who is at once the centre of my devotion and the mainstay of all my confidence.

" After this first exercise of the day and first preparation for the holy sacrifice, I continue as much as possible in a state of interior recollection, observing strict silence, after the example of St. Charles and other holy priests, and avoiding all useless conversation. I recite some part of my office, always thinking of the Mass according to the spirit and desire of Holy Church; and if, before celebrating, I have to perform some other priestly function, I endeavor to do it so that it may help to prepare me for Mass.

"Finally, when the hour so desirable, but also so awful, has come to approach the altar, I do my utmost, with the help of God's grace, to offer the holy sacrifice with attention, devotion, and a well-regulated exterior. To my mind, these dispositions are indispensable:

"1. *Interior recollection.* Should not our whole soul be absorbed in the contemplation of this abridgment of all sacred mysteries? Can a priest whilst celebrating allow even the slightest distraction to enter his mind? What strict vigilance should he not exercise over all his senses, and particularly over his eyes? 'Oculis Christum spectaturis nihil aliud dignatus est aspicere.' [1]

"2. *Devotion.* Where or when shall I have devotion if I am destitute of it at the altar? Fearing, therefore, lest I be wanting in this essential disposition, I implore the holy priests already crowned in heaven, the angels, and especially Mary, 'vas insigne devotionis,' to offer to God their heavenly fervor to make up for the weakness of mine. I beseech the Holy Ghost to unite me to Jesus Christ, our High Priest and immaculate

[1] S. Hier., de S. Joan. Bapt.

9

Victim, who on the altar burns with love, ardently desiring the glory of God and the salvation of the world.

" 3. *A well-regulated exterior.* This disposition requires three things: religious exactness in performing the prescribed ceremonies in a becoming and dignified manner; distinct and devout pronunciation of all the words of the Mass; modesty in our hearing and movements, indicative of our union with God and our conviction of His divine Presence."

St. Charles advises priests who are about to celebrate to observe the following rules:

1st. " Ut propter erroris casum, qui in omni missæ parte gravis, in canone gravior, in consecratione gravissimus est, missam legant, nec memoriter dicant.

2d. " Ut antequam celebrent, se recolligant." A few minutes suffice if we made our meditation in the morning, and were afterwards careful to avoid distraction.

3d. " Ut, anté, missam perlegant, et singulas partes ita præparatas et notatas habeant, ut celebrantes neque errent, neque hæreant." Nothing is more disagreeable to the people who assist at Mass than to see the priest stopped, embarrassed, turning over and over the leaves of the missal without being able to find what he wants.

4th. " Ut sacris vestibus induti cum nemine colloquantur, neque loquentibus aures præbeant."

5th. " Si parochi sint, metu cujusquam gratiane, mis-

sam non anticipent aut differant, sed illam horâ eâ celebrent quæ populo magis accommodata est.

6th. " Ut celebratio fiat non quasi ex consuetudine,
sed magna cum attentione et devotione, sedate, tran-
quille, leniter."

Thus prepared, and with a heart full of the most
beautiful sentiments, which gather new strength from
the prayers we are invited to recite before Mass, the
good priest, having already become all divine—to borrow an expression of St. Bonaventure [1]—seeing and attending to nought but God, proceeds to robe in the sacred vestments. In them he sees but symbols whose
mysterious signification he well understands; and his
fervid faith renders still more fruitful in grace the prayers which accompany an action so seemingly commonplace. He bows respectfully to the image of the crucified Redeemer, whose remembrance he carries in his
heart to the altar. May it be ever present to his mind
whilst he commemorates a mystery in which the Son
of God has manifested towards us a love so incomprehensible! Standing thus under the protection of the
cross, sustained by the graces which flow therefrom, advance, O minister of Jesus Christ! advance confidently
towards the sanctuary where the people await the Desired of nations. The angels behold thee, all heaven is
attentive; let the sacrifice begin!

[1] " Abstractus et divinus factus, nihil aliud videat, nihil aliud sentiat
quam Deum."—De Præp. ad Miss.

PART II.

"GREAT fervor," says Peter de Blois, "is required in the oblation of a sacrifice which contains all the mysteries of our redemption—Magnus ignis devotionis et dilectionis exigetur, quia ibi est tota nostra salus." This pious author adds: "Certe indevotissimus est sacerdos, qui ibi non conteritur, ubi Filius Altissimi ante Patris oculos immolatur. Sané sacerdos devotus et prudens, dum mensæ divinæ assistit, nihil cogitat nisi Christum Jesum et hunc crucifixum."[1]

According to the judgment and practice of the most fervent priests, the best manner of celebrating Mass consists in attending to the sense of the prayers and ceremonies; in following Jesus Christ step by step through the whole course of His passion; and in combining these two methods, devoting one's self more to the consideration of the one or the other, according to the pious inclination of the soul or the spiritual advantages we derive therefrom. We suppose, however, that attention to the words and ceremonies will always be

[1] Serm. 56, ad Sacerdotes.

considered as of the first importance; for devotion, it is well understood, will always accompany strict conformity with the spirit and desire of Holy Church, who has prescribed with such religious care the various formulas of prayer and the sacred ceremonies of the Mass.

We shall go over, as quickly as possible, the different preludes and the essential parts of the sacrifice, .dwelling preferably on whatever is best calculated to nourish our piety. From the more extensive development we shall give to certain prayers, each one can readily understand how he may develop all the others, and unfold their divers significations.[1]

[1] Nothing is better calculated to awaken in our souls fervid emotions during the celebration of Mass than to meditate successively, according to St. Ignatius' second manner of prayer, on the principal prayers of the holy sacrifice ; for instance, on the prayers which accompany the separate oblations of the bread and of the wine—"Suscipe," "Offerimus;" those of the Canon—"Te igitur," "Communicantes," etc.; and those which immediately precede the communion. St. Ignatius' second manner of praying consists in reciting some vocal prayer, pausing to reflect on each word as long as the soul finds in it relish and devotion. In this second part our reflections will often be but a simple reduction to practice of that method.

CHAPTER I.

THEY begin with the arrival of the priest at the foot of the altar, end at the offertory, and contain within a limited compass all that can most efficaciously dispose the soul for the great act of celebration: viz., the psalms, which arouse it and excite its attention; the humble acknowledgment of our faults, which purifies it; the sighs, with which it bewails its misery and which attract the compassion of divine mercy; a sacred canticle, which exalts it; a prayer or *collect*, which unites it with God all the more intimately because offered in the spirit of charity in the name of the whole Church; finally, the reading of pious lessons, which instruct, enlighten, and animate it.

I. The Mass begins just as did that career of humiliation and suffering which Christ inaugurated at His departure from the Cenacle, and which culminated on Calvary. The priest at the foot of the altar is Jesus Christ in the Garden of Olives.

Behold the God-Man prostrate before His Father, in whose sight He appears covered with the leprosy of the world's sins! "Non est species ei, neque decor; et vidimus eum, . . . despectum; . . . et quasi absconditus vultus ejus; . . . et putavimus eum quasi leprosum." [1]   Behold Him humbled, confounded, crushed, as it were, beneath the accumulated weight of the innumerable crimes of mankind which He mercifully condescended to take upon Himself!   These crimes He detests and bewails.   He bears the load of shame and humiliation and anguish as if He Himself were the criminal.   He seems about to recoil with horror at the sight of that dreadful chalice; yet He will drink it to the dregs, because it is the price of our redemption.   If He thrice asks that it might pass away from Him, He also thrice accepts it out of compassion for our misery.   He generously volunteers as Victim for all men, to undergo all the humiliations and sufferings which we have deserved.   "Holy God, just God, deluge My soul with bitterness; make it sorrowful even unto death; let Thy revenge fall upon Thy Son, but do Thou spare sinful man."   Such is the cry of His tears and His blood—for His blood already flows in this cruel agony.

Behold the priest.   Hardly has he come in sight of this *altar of God*, whereon he is to renew the sacrifice of Calvary, when his soul is troubled, as Jesus was when He entered the Garden.   Has he heard the threatening voice which arrested Moses at the foot of Mount Horeb? —"Ne appropies, inquit, huc: solve calceamentum de pedibus tuis; locus enim in quo stas terra sancta est." [2] He finds it necessary to encourage himself thrice be-

---

[1] Is. liii. 2–4.   [2] Exod. iii. 5.

fore drawing nigh unto a God whose goodness is the comfort of pure souls and the joy of fervent hearts; as His sanctity is the terror of the lukewarm and of those who have forsaken the ways of innocence. "Introibo ad altare Dei." He beseeches the Lord to take his cause in hand, to separate him from the ungodly; for holiness is indispensable to worthily perform the divine function for which he is preparing. He asks God to exercise justice against him, against that multitude of strange and criminal thoughts and inordinate inclinations which wage an incessant warfare against him. He implores God's aid against that "old man," *deceitful* and *cunning*, who strives to involve the "new man" in his natural corruption. "Ab homine iniquo et doloso erue me." "Art Thou not, O God! the strength of him whom Thou hast made Thy minister? 'Tu es, Deus, fortitudo mea.' Why shouldst Thou repel him? Why shouldst Thou suffer him to remain mournful and sad, whilst his enemy pursues and oppresses him?"

This psalm is an admirable expression of fear and confidence, and the good priest, whilst reciting it, lets these two sentiments penetrate his innermost soul. The angels of the sanctuary applaud, and with him bow their heads in adoration when he repeats that grand doxology which terminates all the sacred canticles, "Gloria Patri," etc., and which seems to have its most perfect application at the beginning of the Mass. Glory, then, to the Father, and to the Son, and to the Holy

Ghost. It is the glory of the Father to receive the adorations of His incarnate and immolated Son. It is the glory of the Son to be Himself His Father's Victim and the salvation of the world. It is the glory of the Holy Ghost to be the sword which immolates that Victim, the fire which consumes Him as a holocaust. It is the glory of the Holy Trinity that all the efforts of the devil to destroy man have only resulted in uniting man more perfectly to God through Jesus Christ Our Lord.

The celebrant has already prepared himself for his sublime office by the habitual sanctity of his life, the fervor of his prayers, the remembrance of those virtues which God particularly requires of him as His representative. He was, moreover, reminded of these virtues by the sacred vestments which he put on. But there is need, besides, of a public preparation, in which all the faithful participate; for they, too, are about to exercise a kind of priesthood by uniting with the priest in offering the Victim and offering themselves with Him. Such is the object of that sublime dialogue which the Church prescribes between the priest and the faithful at the foot of the altar; and this preparation will end by the energetic and oft-repeated supplication for divine mercy at the " Kyrie Eleison."

The predominant feeling of every heart is then one of compunction and religious fear, but always tempered with heavenly hope. It might be said that the Lord

re-echoes in the chamber of every soul the oracle which
He once pronounced by the mouth of His Prophet:
" Ad quem respiciam, nisi ad pauperculum et contri-
tum spiritu, et trementem sermones meos?" [1]   All humble themselves, all strike their breasts, confessing that
they have sinned, sinned exceedingly and inexcusably—
" peccavi nimis, . . . meâ culpâ."   First the priest, and
after him the faithful, acknowledge their guilt in presence of the Almighty God, who loves to manifest His
power and greatness by sparing the weak and compassionating the unfortunate; in presence of the Virgin,
who knew no sin, and who on that account is all the
more compassionate towards poor sinners; in presence
of St. Michael, who displayed so much zeal in avenging
the outrage offered to God by the first and greatest of
all transgressors; in presence of St. John the Baptist,
sanctified in his mother's womb, and worthy because of
his innocence to be the particular friend of Jesus; in
presence of the Apostles Peter and Paul, both once sinners, but both also penitents; and, finally, in presence
of all the saints, who are now glorious in heaven only
because they triumphed over sin.   All confess in the
presence of God, and in face of the Church universal
of heaven and earth, that they have sinned—alas!
sinned exceedingly and in every way by the abuse of all
their senses and faculties — " cogitatione, verbo, et
opere."   The priest then implores the mercy of the

<hr>

[1] Is. lxvi. 2.

Lord in behalf of the faithful, and the faithful in behalf of the priest—"misereatur vestri, misereatur tui." This is a touching concert of sighs and groans, far different from that celestial harmony to which, later on, we will ask to blend our voices. Then we shall joyously sing the glory of the thrice-holy God; now we bewail our ingratitude and our audacity in presuming to offend His divine Majesty.[1]

O priest! omit not a word, slight not a sign, which the Church has prescribed with so much wisdom. Reflect, particularly during this first part of the holy sacrifice, that you, too, are a public penitent, charged to answer for all sinners, to reconcile them to God through the merits of the blood of His own divine Son, and to atone for their iniquities as well as for your own. Humble, confound yourself in presence of His sovereign Majesty by the general acknowledgment of your sins and those of all the people. "Confiteor." Unite your contrition to that of Jesus agonizing; and, bent as you are under the weight of so many sins, implore grace for all impenitent hearts, that God may be pleased to convert them. Beg pardon, also, for yourself—for you, too, stand in great need of it. If your soul, purified in the blood of the Lamb, has not the

---

[1] "Sacerdos et minister dicunt Confiteor, et orationem Misereatur, quia sacerdos et minister, seu populus pro quo minister loquitur, mutua ejusmodi confessione et oratione assecuturos sese confidunt levium peccatorum remissionem, quo puriori mente Deo Sacrificium offerunt."—Ben. XIV., de Miss. Sacrif. l. 1, c. iii., n. 5.

whiteness of the undefiled, the untrodden snow, how could you dare ascend to the altar and enter the Holy of holies? This is the thought which should occupy your whole mind during the immediate preparation for Mass. "Take away from us our iniquities, we beseech Thee, O Lord, that we may be worthy to enter with pure minds into the Holy of holies—Aufer a nobis, quæsumus, Domine, iniquitates nostras, ut ad Sancta Sanctorum puris mereamur mentibus introire." In order to more surely obtain that your least imperfections also may be obliterated, have recourse to the intercession of the saints; but particularly honor and invoke those whose precious relics you venerate in respectfully kissing the sepulchre which contains them. "Oramus te, Domine, per merita Sanctorum tuorum, quorum reliquiæ hic sunt, et omnium sanctorum, ut indulgere digneris omnia peccata mea." [1]

II. At the foot of the altar you lamented your unworthiness, you humbled yourself with Jesus Christ penitent, you besought the Lord to show you mercy, you implored indulgence, absolution, and pardon for

---

[1] " Sacerdos postquam adstantes ad preces Deo fundendas excitavit dicens : Oremus, gradus altaris conscendens recitat orationes : Aufer a nobis, et: Oramus te, et tunc primum osculatur altare, quod aliquoties in missæ cursu itidem osculatur. Hoc osculum salutatio quædam est, ut notat Pouget, qui propositam quæstionem Cur sacerdos ascendens ad altare hoc osculatur, idemque faciat quoties ab eo recedit, ita solvit: Hoc salutationis genus est. Osculatur sacerdos altare quia typus est Christi, eoque osculo profitetur adhærere se Christo, cui sicut membra Capiti, connexi sunt sancti, quorum reliquiæ ibi servantur."—Ben. XIV., ibid., c. iii., n. 7.

all sinners; and as a pledge of that forgiveness you have addressed to the people the salutation of peace—"Dominus vobiscum." [1] Behold you now at the altar.

At the *introit* honor the first entrance of Jesus Christ into the world, coming to redeem mankind and to restore to wandering humanity that happiness which God in creating us destined for us. Do not forget that all mankind deputes you to offer to God its gratitude for so great a blessing. Again invoke the Saviour of our souls, the Repairer of all our evils, and emulate by the fervor of your desires the impatient yearnings of the patriarchs and prophets. "Rorate, cœli, desuper, et nubes pluant Justum." [2] You shall be heard. Jesus will come. He will soon be before your eyes, in your hands. But, alas! He has already come so often, and though His heart's desire was to load us with blessings, the lukewarmness of ours forced Him to shut up the treasury of His graces, or to sparingly communicate them to us. Let us acknowledge our blindness and beware of its consequences. "Terra sæpe venientem super se bibens imbrem, . . . proferens spinas ac tribu-

---

[1] Eight times during the Mass does the priest wish the faithful that Jesus Christ be with them ; and the people return the priest the same salutation. This is an excellent means of reviving the attention of all by reminding them that in order to offer Jesus Christ properly they should have Him in their hearts, be animated with His spirit, and filled with His love. "Quoties dices: Dominus vobiscum optabis intimo affectu Ecclesiæ Dei et toti mundo omnem Dei benedictionem, per quam singulis animabus id quo maxime indigent, conferatur."—Bona de Sacrif. Miss., c. v.   [2] Is. xlv. 8.

los, reproba est, et maledicto proxima."[1] In order to
preserve ourselves from this extreme misfortune, and
be delivered from an infirmity which leads to death, let
us have recourse to Him whose property it is always
to have compassion on the wretched and to forgive.
"Deus cui proprium est misereri semper et parcere."
Let us implore His tender compassion, and with the
afflicted of Judea address to Him that prayer, so touching, so simple, so respectful, and so much the more efficacious, because it confides entirely in His infinite
goodness—"Kyrie Eleison."

At this moment, says Bossuet, you might represent
to yourself all mankind prostrate with you before the
majesty of the Lord, imploring clemency from that
merciful God whose only object in coming into this
world was to exercise mercy. Nine times successively
priest and people send up to heaven this cry of sorrow
and distress, and in this oft-repeated supplication we
well recognize the language of a heart whose desires are
vehement and whose hopes are well founded.[2] Hence,
after this outburst of fervor, this outpouring of confidence, the soul is filled with a joy so irrepressible that

---

[1] Heb. vi. 7, 8.

[2] "Misericordia petitur dicendo : Kyrie Eleison ; ter quidem pro persona Patris, ter autem pro persona Filii, cum dicitur Christe Eleison, et
ter pro persona Spiritus Sancti cum subditur Kyrie Eleison ; contra tri-
plicem miseriam ignorantiæ, culpæ et pœnæ ; vel ad significandum
quod omnes personæ sunt in se invicem."—S. Thom., in 3 part., q. 83,
art. 4.

"Kyrie Eleison ad singulas tres personas mente in cœlum erectus

it must needs proclaim it in that beautiful canticle, the first words of which have been wafted to earth by heavenly choirs.

III. "Gloria in excelsis Deo." Angels on earth, blend your voices in harmony with the celestial choirs to celebrate the great mystery of reconciliation and peace which was begun in the womb of Mary, manifested in Bethlehem, accomplished on Calvary, renewed on the altar. God has re-entered into possession of all the glory which sin robbed Him of. Nay, He is more glorified than He had been offended, and man has recovered more through Jesus Christ than he had lost through Adam.

Glory to God, peace to men. It is in the sacrifice about to be offered that this alliance of justice and peace becomes manifest through the reparation of the outrages offered to God by sin, and the abolition of the sentence which His justice had pronounced against guilty man. In this sacrifice God finds His glory. "Gloria in excelsis Deo," in the obedience of His Son, which induces Him to forget our rebellions; in the humiliations, voluntary and profound, which atone for our pride. In this sacrifice man finds peace—"et in terra pax hominibus"—by his union with God which it re-establishes, and by the eternal possession of heaven

diriges, petens remissionem peccatorum cordis, oris et operis, pro te et aliis ; et quia novies repetitur, quot sunt angelorum chori, ipsorum vocibus tuam conjunges, et cor ad illos elevabis."—Bona. de Sacrif. Miss., c. v., art. 5.

which the Mass secures for him.   One condition, however, is required to attain that end: man must offer
this sacrifice with at least *incipient good will*, or the desire of drawing nigh unto God; that, consequently, he
must become, by corresponding to the graces derived
from this sacrifice, truly and absolutely *the man of good
will*, determined to detest, to avoid, to atone for sin;
that he be a man subject in all things to the sovereign
will of the Lord, the test and criterion of all good will
—"bonæ voluntatis."

It is this good will, this desire to please Thee, O my
God, that puts Thy praise upon our lips—"Laudamus
te."   We praise Thee, O Lord, on account of Thyself
and of Thy infinite perfections.   We praise Thy unspotted sanctity, Thy beauty ever ancient and ever new,
Thy wisdom profounder than abysses, Thy justice more
elevated than mountains, Thy mercy more extensive
than the earth and the heavens.

"Benedicimus te."   We bless Thee, and we bless
Him also who cometh in Thy name to be our Priest
and our Victim.   We bless Thee for all, O Lord, whose
paternal providence embraces all.   We bless Thee for
adversity as well as for prosperity, since both proceed
from Thy love.   We bless Thee for the crosses by
which Thou triest us, as well as for the consolations by
which Thou sustainest our weakness.

"Adoramus te."   We adore Thee as do the blessed
spirits whose language we borrow; and soon shall we

adore Thee with Thy incarnate, immolated Word, Thy sole worthy Adorer. We offer our adorations to Thee, O Father of mercies! who hast so loved the world as to give Thy own Son for it; to Thee, generous Son, who hast so loved us as to die for our sake; to Thee, Spirit of Charity, principle of that love, sacred fire that consumest our Victim.

"Glorificamus te." Glory, honor, empire, and power to God, who sitteth on the throne of His eternity, and to the Lamb who immolates Himself upon the altar to recall the dead to life! We now glorify Thee by our canticles; we desire to glorify Thee continually by our works; and we hope to glorify Thee eternally with the glory Thou receivest from Thy elect.

"Gratias agimus tibi propter magnam gloriam tuam." Thou gloriest in doing good to us. Thy great glory is our great happiness—Jesus Christ, the Source of all our felicity. We return Thee thanks for having given us Jesus, since in Him and through Him Thou hast given us all good.[1] O Lord! O God! O Sovereign King! Thy greatness does not make Thee forget Thy

---

[1] We might say simply : "We thank Thee for Thy great mercy which glorifies Thee so much ;" but the Church, inflamed with love for God who has loved her so much, and being more occupied at that moment with the glory of her Sovereign Benefactor than with the immense advantages that have accrued to us from His bounty, wishes that we should say to Him in an outburst of pure and generous charity : "We give Thee thanks for Thy great glory, which shines with a splendor so mild and beautiful in the mystery of our redemption." The glory of Him whom we love is, as it were, our own glory. His happiness is ours.

mercy. Thou thinkest of us in the midst of Thy glory, and, though infinitely happy, Thou dost not forget our miseries. "Qui sedes ad dexteram Patris, miserere nobis."

There is something heavenly in the sublime simplicity of this canticle—one of the oldest and most impressive which the Church employs. Everything in it breathes of joy, admiration, hope, and the most ardent love. This is especially true of the last words: "Tu solus sanctus, tu solus Dominus, tu solus altissimus, Jesu Christe." Do they not seem to proceed from the mouth of the holy priest like so many sparks of that divine fire which glows in his heart?[1]

IV. After praise comes supplication. By paying to God the tribute of our homage we dispose Him to favorably receive our requests. Now, then, is the favorable time to offer our petitions, and with them those of the whole Church, to the throne of eternal mercy. *Pray, brethren,* we say to the faithful—"Oremus;" for they should join us and ask for themselves what we demand for them and for ourselves. But it is the duty of the priest, as mediator between God and the people,

---

[1] "Ad 'Gloria in excelsis' nonaberis quomodo peccator in terrâ alienâ canticum Angelorum canere præsumas; tum alias affectus adjunges laudis, adorationis, gratiarum actionis, fidei, spei, amoris, zeli gloriæ Dei, petitionis et obsecrationis, juxta sensum verborum. Hæc autem verba: Tu solus sanctus, tu solus Dominus, tu solus altissimus, Jesu Christe, tensiori affectu caritatis et reverentiæ ergo Christum Dominum pronuntiabis, desiderans ut ab omnibus ametur, honoretur, glorificetur."
—Bona, ibid.

to *collect* all the prayers and vows of the faithful and offer them to the Lord. His duty, also, is to give life and fervor to public prayer, supplying by the ardor of his own whatever may be deficient in that of the people. What a humiliation for him before the angels of God should there be in the congregation some simple soul whose prayers are more fervent than the celebrant's! Standing erect between heaven and earth, with arms outstretched, as if to uphold the interests of the entire world, speak, O minister of the Lord! supplicate in the name of all, plead the cause of the universe; and however great may be the number of your requests, however unworthy you may be of a hearing, nevertheless pray with confidence, for you re-echo a name most powerful in the ears and heart of God—"per Dominum nostrum Jesum Christum Filium tuum." [1]

V. As supplication followed praise, instruction will

---

[1] "Expendat sacerdos verba orationum, quæ magni ponderis sunt; et recogitet quod per illa specialem misericordiam seu beneficium petit à Deo Patre, per merita Jesu Christi, et per intercessionem illius sancti cujus festum celebratur.

"Quando dicit: Per Dominum, ... ferventius illa verba recitare debet, et majorem quasi vim facere Deo Patri, ut postulata concedat per Dominum nostrum; quasi diceret: fiat, fiat, Pater clementissime, per Jesum Christum Filium tuum, in cujus nomine petentibus nihil negare soles." (Tripl. Exposit.)

"Ad solum Patrem omnes fere collectæ directæ sunt, paucæ ad Filium, nulla ad Spiritum Sanctum. Non quia Is donum est, et a dono donum non petitur, ut nonnulli cum Durando in suo Rationali philosophantur; sed quia missa representatio est ejus oblationis qua Christus se Patri obtulit, ac propterea ad ipsum Patrem liturgicæ præcationes diriguntur."—Bona.

now succeed to prayer.   The object of all our petitions
should be to obtain grace to accomplish the will of the
Lord.   That will He will now make known to us; for,
says St. Augustine, it is He who speaks to us when we
read the Scriptures or hear them read, just as it is we
who speak to Him when we pray.   Let us therefore listen to Him if we would have Him listen to us.   Let us
submit our minds and our hearts to His teachings and
make them the rule of our lives.   A pious ecclesiastic
used to say that he every day heard two excellent sermons.   In the epistle he heard the voice of the apostles
and of the prophets; and in the gospel that of Jesus
Christ.   Is there any knowledge worth the having that
cannot be acquired in the school of such eminent teach-
ers? [1]

The priest, however, is not merely a disciple of God
like the individual faithful.   He is God's ambassador
to men, the interpreter and preacher of His law—a
dread function especially to him who has not always
respected that holy law so inimical to every defilement
—"lex Domini immaculata."   Need we wonder that he
trembles at the recollection of his faults when he is
about to perform this ministry.   He fears lest the Lord
should say to him, in the words of the Prophet: "Why
dost thou declare My justices, and take My covenant in

[1] "Sequitur instructio populi in fide, per doctrinam prophetarum et
apostolorum in epistola, per verba Christi in Evangelio, per articulos
fidei in symbolo ; quæ omnia . . . ut nos purgent, et præparent, præ-
mittuntur."—Bona, de Sacrif. Miss., c. v., n. 6.

thy mouth? Seeing thou hast hated discipline, and hast cast My words behind thee." " Quare tu enarras justitias meas?"[1] He is terrified as was Isaias when he received a similar mission. He desires to speak, but dares not: " Væ mihi, quia tacui, quia vir pollutus labiis ego sum."[2] " Cleanse my heart and my lips, O Almighty God! who didst cleanse the lips of the prophet Isaias with a burning coal. . . . The Lord be in my heart and on my lips, that I may worthily and in a becoming manner announce His holy gospel."[3]

Before announcing the word of God we make the sign of the cross on the book which contains it, on our forehead, lips, and heart. What profit us these exterior signs unless we endeavor to understand what they signify? The sign of the cross traced on the book teaches us that the cross is the pulpit whence Jesus Christ has most energetically taught the austere truths of the Gospel, and that every successful and true preacher must be crucified to the world. We next sign our forehead, desiring that through the merits of the cross our minds may be enlightened by that light which radiates from every word of that inspired book. We sign our mouth

---

[1] Ps. xlix. 16.   [2] Is. vi. 5.

[3] " Vetustissima consuetudo est, ut cum Evangelium legitur, populus stet, ut significet paratum se esse ad ea Domini perficienda mandata, quæ leguntur in Evangelio. . . . Et religiosi equestrium ordinum, cum in missâ legitur Evangelium, vel manum gladio admovent, vel etiam ipsum é vaginâ educunt, ut se pro Christi fide paratos esse declarent ipsum profundere sanguinem."—Ben. XIV., c. vii., n. 14. Bona, Rerum Liturgicarum, lib. ii., c. vii., n. 3.

in order to render it less unworthy to utter words which, according to St. Augustine, deserve no less respect than the very body of the Son of God. Finally, we sign our hearts in order to engrave deeply on our soul the lineaments of the "new man," who was created in justice and veritable holiness, and to obtain grace to esteem, to relish, and to practise the maxims of the Gospel.[1] After the reading of the gospel we religiously kiss the sacred deposit of the science of heaven, in order to blot out, by an act of love, the last vestiges of our past infidelities. "Per Evangelica dicta deleantur nostra delicta."

After the gospel and the sermon, which is generally an explanation of it, it is very appropriate that both the priest and the faithful should make a common profession of faith by the recitation, or the singing, of the Creed, and thus fittingly terminate all preparations for the holy sacrifice. Whilst reciting it let us earnestly pray to God to grant us the precious gift of a lively faith, for with it we shall participate abundantly in the fruits of the mystery of redemption.

Hitherto we have been only preparing for the sacrifice, of which the Offertory or oblation is the first part.

---

[1] "Innocentius III., et post eum Gavantus, dicunt sacerdotem signo crucis Evangeliorum librum signare, quasi dicat : ' Hic crucifixi liber est.' Seipsum vero signat in fronte, juxta id quod ait Augustinus in Psalm. cxli.: Usque adeo de cruce non erubesco, ut non in occulto habeam crucem Christi, sed in fronte portem ; tum in ore et pectore, juxta illud apostoli ad Rom., cap. x: ' Corde creditur ad justitiam, ore autem confessio fit ad salutem.' "—Ben. XIV., de Miss. Sacrif., lib. ii., c. vii., n. 12.

CHAPTER II.

THE BEGINNING OF THE SACRIFICE, OR THE OFFERTORY.

THIS first part of the sacrifice proper contains the Offertory, or offering made to God of the matter of the sacrifice, the mixing of wine and water, the washing of the fingers, with the prayers, " Suscipe, Sancte Pater;" " Deus, qui humanæ substantiæ;" " Offerimus tibi;" " In spiritu humilitatis;" " Veni, Sanctificator;" " Lavabo inter innocentes;" " Suscipe, Sancta Trinitas;" and ends by the " Orate fratres."

In the preparatory prayers, lessons, and ceremonies which we have treated in the preceding chapter, in the different actions of the priest, now ascending to the altar, now stopping at the middle, now passing from one side to the other, we may have been reminded of Jesus Christ during His passion going from Annas to Caiphas, from Caiphas to the pretorium of Pilate, from Pilate to the palace of Herod, and everywhere the recipient of ingratitude and outrage for His love, patience, and kindness. When we uncover the chalice for the Offertory our soul should be filled with tender emotion at the thought of our dear Saviour, so magnanimous and at the same time

so meek, suffering Himself to be stripped of His garments and presenting His divine members to be torn
by scourges. For our sakes He abandons Himself to
all the rigor of His Father's justice. It is the same
Victim which we ourselves offer to God, notwithstanding our great unworthiness—" Quam ego indignus famulus tuus offero tibi;" a pure and spotless Host—
"immaculatam Hostiam," which is not yet upon the
altar, but soon shall be.[1] It is to the same God we
offer it—to that great God whose holiness, omnipotence,
life, and eternity cannot be fully and adequately honored
save by a victim who possesses the same infinite perfections—" Suscipe, Sancte Pater, æterne Deus." Receive it, *Holy Father*, for thus it was that the Saviour
addressed Thee in the prayer which He offered in the
interval between the sacrifice of the cenacle and that of
Calvary. *God Almighty*, who alone hast power to remit
our sins and to operate all the miracles which will soon
attract to this sanctuary the astonished regard of the
whole heavenly court. *Eternal God*, upon whom alone
all creatures depend, deriving their existence from Thee
who alone hast life by Thyself. Receive this offering
at the hands of Thy servant, however unworthy he is to
represent that Pontiff, holy, innocent, separated from

[1] " In hâc oratione hostiam quæ est super patenam, etsi nondum con-
secratam, vocat immaculatam, . ∴ . quod quidem nemo miretur ; neque
enim ea verba ad panem referenda, sed ad corpus Christi, quod futuræ
consecrationis vi sub ipsius speciem panis subibit."—Ben. XIV., ibid.,
c. ix., n. 2.

sinners, raised higher than the heavens. O Thou, who art my *living and true God,* the sole source of life, the . principle of all truth, by the merits of so holy a Victim grant me the pardon of my innumerable sins, offences, negligences, and culpable omissions. I offer it to Thee both for my open violations of Thy law and for the tepidity which prevented my more perfect observance thereof; for the evil I have done and the good I have left undone; for the countless imperfections which have marred my best deeds—"pro innumerabilibus peccatis, et offensionibus, et negligentiis meis."[1] May it obtain mercy for him to whom Thou hast committed a ministry so disproportionate to his weakness, and who in Thy sight must bear not only the crushing weight of his own sins, but also the heavy burden of the sins of his brethren. May it draw down Thy blessing upon all those who surround Thy altar, upon all the faithful, living and dead. Grant that the blood of this immaculate Victim may not through our fault become an infertile seed, but

---

[1] "1. Peccata, intelligo culpas proprie sic dictas. 2. Offensiones, cupæ minus proprie dictæ, seu involuntariæ, in quas scilicet offendere fragilitatem nostram in tot tamque variis vitæ hujus casibus pronum est, ferme ut per viam salebrosam incidenti frequenter offendere seu impingere vel nolenti accidit. 3. Negligentiæ, ea, quæ ad rationem quidem peccati omissionis non pertingunt, sed in actiones nostras irrepere easque, si minus vitiare omnino, tamen imperfectas minusque acceptas Deo reddere solent; suntque profecto innumeræ, sive intentionis puritatem et intentionem spectes, sive modos omnes quibus actiones nostras ornari ac perfici in Dei conspectu decet, pro mensurâ luminis et gratiæ nobis à Domino communicatæ."—Exercitia Spiritualia à Patre Roothaan annotata.

that it may bring forth fruits of grace and salvation. May it be for all the principle and pledge of that blessed life which consists in knowing and loving Thee eternally—"ut mihi et illis proficiat ad salutem in vitam æternam."

I. Having made the signof the cross over the corporal, we deposit thereon the Host which we have just offered, and which in a few moments will become the body of Jesus Christ. This short ceremony, seemingly unimportant, and which the indevout priest performs inattentively, is well calculated to draw tears from him who has received of God those enlightened eyes of the mind which St. Paul so ardently desired for his disciples.[1] To him, it is the divine Lamb, Our Lord Jesus Christ, giving Himself up to the executioners, stretching His adorable body on the cross to be immolated.[2] This is an excellent and appropriate time to offer to God, without reserve and in union with our divine Saviour, ourselves and all that we call ours—our body, our life, our goods, to use them only according to His holy will; our soul and all its faculties, that He may be pleased to direct us by His Spirit, and transform us into the resemblance of His divine Son, as He is about to trans-

[1] Det vobis spiritum sapientiæ, . . . illuminatos oculos cordis.—Eph. i. 17, 18.

[2] " Illud signum crucis significat hostiam super crucem poni, ubi Christus Jesus æterno Patri ipse se obtulit, ut nos a peccatis redimeret."—Ben. XIV., lib. ii., c. x., n. 2.

form the bread and wine into the body and blood of that same well-beloved Son.[1]

Let us offer ourselves also to Jesus Christ to dispose of us as He may deem best for the glory of His Father, the salvation of souls, and the good of the Church. Soon He shall be my Victim; and should not love and gratitude demand in return that I offer myself to Him to be His victim, so that He may immolate me as He permits me to immolate Him? Should I not completely abandon myself to Him as He gives Himself to me, placing myself entirely in His hands as He places Himself in mine? "Sanctissime Pater, . . . offero tibi hanc hostiam in corpus Filii tui convertendam, atque cor meum in tui amorem transformandum."[2]

In this adorable sacrifice everything has a sublime signification. All speaks to the heart of the good priest —the inclinations of the head towards the cross, especially at the conclusion of the prayers: "Per Dominum nostrum Jesum Christum," or when we give glory to God: "Gloria in excelsis Deo;" "Gloria Patri." Is not the cross the highest manifestation of the glory of the Lord, and sole cause of the efficacy of all our prayers? In like manner, the salutations of peace

---

[1] "Quando patenam cum hostiâ in manibus accipies, pones in ea cor tuum et omnium circumstantium omniumque fidelium, et ea quoque Deo offeras, hoc intentione, quod sicut panis quem offers mox convertetur in corpus Christi, ita cor tuum et omnium fidelium in ipsum Christum per amorem et imitationem transformentur."—Bona, c. v., n. 7.

[2] Tripl. Exposit.

which the priest addresses to the people, " Dominus vobiscum," either to excite their attention and piety, or to communicate to them the graces which he drew for them from the treasures of the Lord; and these tokens of respectful affection given to the altar, image of Jesus Christ, by kissing it—all are full of meaning.

II. When the priest purifies the chalice before pouring into it the wine which will soon be changed into the blood of Christ, he thinks of another vessel, a living chalice, destined also to contain the precious blood. He thinks of his own heart, and though he has already prepared it, he endeavors to purify it more and more. Whilst mixing a little water with the wine he considers the ineffable union of our nature, typified by the water, with the person of the Word, symbolized by the wine. He conceives an ardent desire to plunge, to blissfully lose himself, in the abyss of the infinite merits and per- fections of Christ. He sighs for an intimate union with the Saviour-God; and as the water when poured into the chalice immediately loses its natural properties to assume those of the wine by which it is absorbed, so he prays that his soul, stripped of all its imperfections, may assume the divine virtues and perfections of the Saviour, as He assumed our humanity.' He has taken upon Himself our transgressions, grant, O Lord, that

---

[1] " Cum misces aquam, desiderium excitabis te totum immergendi in abyssum meritorum Christi, atque ad intimam cum Deo unionem sus- pirabis."—Bona, ibid.

we may participate in His holiness; He has assumed our weakness, grant that we may be made partakers of His strength; and as this union of the divinity with the humanity in Jesus Christ shall never come to an end, grant that we may never be separated from His divine person. "Da nobis per hujus aquæ et vini mysterium, ejus Divinitatis esse consortes, qui humanitatis nostræ fieri dignatus particeps, Jesus Christus Filius tuus."

The mixing of water with wine symbolizes a three-fold union which justifies us in saying that if God in creating us raised us to a wonderful dignity—"humanæ substantiæ dignitatem mirabiliter condidisti"—He has elevated us still more marvellously in redeeming us— "mirabilius reformasti." The triple union consists in the union of the divinity with the humanity in the Incarnation, the union of man with Jesus Christ by participation in the eucharistic banquet, and the union of man with God in glory. "Ut sint consummati in unum." [1]

Cochin thus paraphrases the beautiful prayer, "Deus qui humanæ substantiæ": "O God, who hast created our nature in such an admirable manner, since Thou hast joined together two substances so essentially different—a material and destructible body to a soul spiritual, immortal, formed to Thy own image; who, moreover, hast redeemed it in a still more admirable manner through the incomprehensible union of Thy

---

[1] John xvii. 23.

nature with ours—that is, through the union of holiness and justice with weakness and the likeness of sin; hast Thou not, by this twofold prodigy, given us the right to solicit another more consoling than either?   By virtue of this mysterious mixture, grant that we may be made partakers of His divinity who out of His infinite mercy towards us vouchsafed to clothe Himself with our humanity, and whose very name declares that ineffable union.   It is Jesus, the Saviour of His people, the Christ, the image of the substance of His Father, Thy only Son and Our Lord—'Jesus Christus Filius tuus, Dominus noster.'"

We can easily understand, first, why only a very small quantity of water should be used;[1] it is, as one of the councils declared, *in order that the majesty of the blood of Jesus Christ should there superabound more than the frailty of humanity represented by the water;* secondly, why the priest blesses the water and not the wine; Jesus Christ, symbolized by the wine, is holiness itself and the source of all blessings; but humanity, typified by the water, needs purification before being incorporated with Christ.

III.   As the priest has already offered the Host, so he now offers the chalice.   He lifts it up to present it to God.   "Offerimus."[2]   When offering the bread he spoke

---

[1] " Vino aqua modicissima debet."—Eugen. IV., ad Armen.

[2] At the offering of the bread the priest, having raised his eyes towards heaven, immediately lowered them—" oculis ad Deum elevatis, et statim

only in his own name—" Suscipe ;" now he says " Offerimus"—we offer—speaking in the name of all. For the people, in whose behalf he has just prayed, and who have been blessed and represented in the chalice by the infusion of water, presently pray and unite with him in offering "calicem salutaris." [1] This cup in an instant shall be the chalice of the precious blood of Jesus Christ. It is therefore justly called the chalice of salvation. "Tuam deprecantes clementiam." An offering so holy, O Lord, cannot fail to be in itself agreeable to Thee; and it is not on its account that we

demissis " (Rub.). He was confounded at the consciousness of his own unworthiness—" quam ego indignus famulus tuus offero." Whilst offering the chalice his look is constantly turned upwards to God—" intentis ad Deum oculis " (Rub.); because the union of the people with Jesus Christ and the communication of the merits of the God·Man have inspired him with confidence and authorize him to look up to heaven.

[1] Bellarmine remarks that we do not say " calicem salutarem," but " calicem salutaris, id est, calicem Christi, qui instituit ut calix ille offerretur et consecraretur." He adds that the sense would be no less true were we to say " calicem salutarem," for these words, as well as those which accompany the offering of the bread, " immaculatam hostiam," should be referred, not to the actual state of the substances upon the altar, but to their supernatural state after consecration.

" Quamvis hoc sacrificium unicum sit duabus tamen partibus constat, corpore videlicet Christi sub speciebus panis, ejusque sanguine sub speciebus vini. Ideo, pane jam oblato seorsim, procedis ad vini oblationem. Utramque vero extendes ad omnes fines propter quos hoc sacrificium institutum fuit, qui cum sint maximi momenti, cum summo devotionis fervore hæ oblationes fieri debent, ac si tu solus esses in toto mundo sacerdos, et ab hoc sacrificio omnium hominum salus penderet."
—Bona, c. v.

The last remark of the pious and learned Cardinal is well calculated to vividly impress the soul of the celebrant and hold it under the empire of faith during the celebration of the holy mysteries.

need to implore Thy clemency in order that Thou may-est receive it as an odor of sweetness. But if the gift is always pleasing to Thee, alas, how many things must displease Thee in those who offer it! Moreover, we offer ourselves also—and what are we? Are we worthy to appear in the presence of Thy divine majesty? "Pro nostrâ et totius mundi salute." What wonderful power, then, in the sacrifice of the altar! St. Epiphanius calls it the perpetual salvation of the Church.

IV. The more the celebrant advances in the exercise of his august ministry, the more he experiences how far short he has fallen of the sanctity which so heavenly a function requires. Therefore do we now behold him with head profoundly inclined, hands joined upon the altar, in the attitude of the most humble supplicant, offering to God first of all the sacrifice of a contrite and humble heart. "In spiritu humilitatis, et in animo contrito suscipiamur a te Domine." The Church, in this instance, borrows the language of the three young captives of Babylon, who, in sight of the fiery furnace into which they were soon to be cast, so generously offered themselves as a holocaust to the glory of the Lord. "Suscipiamur." Priests and people we unite in offering ourselves also, and since we are sinners, we cannot draw down on ourselves God's merciful regard without humbling ourselves in the dust—heartily re-penting of having offended God, who should have been the sole object of our love.

The priest has hardly performed this act of humility, when he experiences the truth of these words of Scripture—"Oratio humiliantis se nubes penetrabit, . . . et non discedet donec Altissimus aspiciat." [1] He feels that he may now with confidence approach the throne of Infinite Majesty. Therefore he raises his eyes, his hands, all his desires towards the eternal hills whence he expects all aid. He invokes the Spirit, source of all sanctification, God Almighty and Eternal, to bless this sacrifice prepared for the glory of His name. "Veni, sanctificator, omnipotens, æterne Deus, et benedic hoc sacrificium, tuo sancto nomini præparatum." [2] But this sacrifice includes two offerings: one material, that is, the bread and wine; the other moral, the whole body of the faithful offering themselves to God through the priest and with the priest. For these two offerings we

---

[1] Ecclus. xxxv. 21.

[2] All is now ready and before God : the bread and wine which are to be changed into the body and blood of Christ, also our hearts, humble and contrite, which should be transformed by grace into the likeness of Jesus. The offering is complete. But the great change, the blessed transformation, can be operated only by the Holy Ghost, the Sanctifier. It is His to produce Jesus Christ upon the altar, as He formed Christ's sacred body in Mary's womb. It is His to consume the substance of the bread and that of the wine by the fire of His puissance, and to destroy all our sins or terrestrial affections by the fire of His love. (Lec.)

"Juxta sacrarum Scripturarum idiotismum, duas tantum personas, Filium et Spiritum Sanctum, invitat Ecclesia ut delebantur è cœlo. Cum vero suam dirigit orationem ad Patrem, non dicit—Veni, sed—Mitte Spiritum tuum, vel—Mitte nobis Redemptorem, mitte Agnum qui tollit peccata mundi. Quamobrem, cum oratio—Veni, Sanctificator, non possit intelligi de Filio pro quo fit deprecatio, sequitur intelligendum esse de Spiritu Sancto."—Ben. XIV., c. x., n. 21,

ask two different blessings : for the former, the blessing
of power which will operate the miracle of transubstantiation ; for the latter, the blessing of grace which may
forever unite our will to that of the Lord and consume
in us whatever is opposed to His Spirit. God alone
can perform these two transformations, both of which
procure the glory of His name—"tuo sancto nomini
præparatum."

Let us, however, again and again endeavor to acquire
perfect innocence and purity of heart. "Lavabo inter
innocentes manus meas." Our hands represent our
actions. To wash our hands means nothing else than
to purify our works.[1] But we find in this psalm a de-
tailed enumeration of the dispositions we ought to have,
the life we should lead, the virtues we should practise
to worthily and frequently celebrate the holy mysteries :
namely, delicacy of conscience and horror of every defilement, patience in trials, constancy despite persecutions, avoidance of the ways of the wicked, zeal for the
house of God, gratitude for favors already received, loving, confident recourse to the Lord, constantly renewed

---

[1] This washing of the priest's fingers is prescribed for two reasons :
one natural, the other moral. "Primo quidem, quia aliqua pretiosa
tractare non consuevimus nisi manibus ablutis ; unde indecens videtur,
quod ad tantum Sacramentum aliquis accedat manibus etiam corpo-
raliter inquinatis. Secundo, propter significationem, quia, ut Dionysius
dicit, extremitatum ablutio significat emendationem etiam a minimis
peccatis, secundum illud Joannis, c. xiii. : ' Qui lotus est, non indiget nisi
ut pedes lavet ;' et talis emendatio requiritur ab eo qui accedit ad hoc
sacramentum."—S. Thom., 3 p., q. 83, art. 5.

endeavors to become every day more and more perfect.

V. The priest has returned to the middle of the altar
after washing his hands, which will soon bear the eternal Son of God, and whose purity, according to St. John
Chrysostom, should equal that of the sun's rays. Then,
inspired by a double motive of confidence and humility,
he raises his eyes towards the cross and immediately
lowers them. He again bows low before the sovereign
majesty of the Lord, and reuniting all the constituent
parts of his oblation, viz., the bread and wine to be
changed into the body and blood of Jesus Christ; the
priest himself, and all the faithful destined to be incorporated into the divine Author of salvation, he presents to the adorable Trinity this offering of the whole
Christ—chief and members. He offers it in commemoration of the mysteries by which the Redeemer vouchsafed to accomplish His sacrifice in His natural body,
desiring that the fruits of that sacrifice should be communicated to all the members of His mystical body.

From this sacrifice, as from an inexhaustible fountain,
the Blessed Virgin, the apostles, the martyrs, all the
saints drew all the graces which made them such dear
friends of God, and assured them victory in all their
combats. At the altar the interests of heaven and those
of earth converge. There the angels find their glory,
and we our salvation. "Ut illis proficiat ad honorem,
nobis autem ad salutem." By a happy exchange of

veneration and of patronage they repay us by prayer and
intercession for the signal honor we confer on them by
associating them with the great and adorable Victim,
immolated in the Passion, glorified in the Resurrection,
raised by the Ascension to the throne of God, and presented before Him. " Suscipe, Sancta Trinitas, hanc
oblationem, quam tibi offerimus ob memoriam' Passionis,
Resurrectionis, et Ascensionis; . . . et illi pro nobis
intercedere dignentur in cœlis, quorum memoriam agimus in terris."

The great moment approaches. Very soon it will
not be question of preliminaries and preparations.
Transubstantiation is about to be operated. The Victim will soon be immolated. Hitherto, the priest has

---

[1] The following remarks of Benedict XIV. (De Sacrif. Miss., lib. ii.,
c. xi., n. 5) will enable us better to understand the meaning of the
words—" in memoriam Passionis, Resurrectionis, et Ascensionis Jesu
Christi Domini nostri ; "

" In sacrificiis Judaicis mactanda victima eligebatur, atque per ejusmodi electionem quasi sanctificata censebatur et a profano usu semota ;
humana enim electa fuit Christi natura, eaque cum natura divina hy-
postatice conjuncta, ac per eam unionem conflata fuit victima digna
quæ Deo sacrificaretur." .

" In iisdem Judæorum sacrificiis victimam sacerdos offerebat antequam mactaret ; primam itidem victimæ oblationem, ante ejus immola-
tionem, fecit Christus in momento Nativitatis suæ ; Ingrediens enim
mundum dicit: Holocaustomata pro peccato non tibi placuerunt. Tunc
dixi : Ecce venio, ut faciam, Deus, voluntatem tuam. . . .

" In sacrificiis Judaicis victima incendebatur super altare holocaus-
torum, ut quidquid in ea vitii esset flammis absumeretur, et fumus ad
cœlum tolleretur in adorem suavitatis, ut sacra Scriptura loquitur, in
nova lege consumpta fuit victima in Christi Resurrectione et Ascensione;
nam in Resurrectione absorptum fuit in Christo quod mortale est à vita,
ut ait Apostolus; absumptumque fuit quidquid inesse poterat corrupti-

been in constant communication with the people through the various desires he has expressed in their behalf, the instructions he has given them, the prayers he has been offering in their name. Now, that he prepares to enter the Holy of holies, to penetrate, like Moses, the mysterious Cloud, to converse with God alone, he, as it were, takes leave of the people, and will not again turn to them, even when saluting them, till the sacrifice is consummated. For the ministry which he is about to fulfil exalts him above humanity and entirely separates him from all that is earthly. At that awful moment he remembers that he carries within him the weaknesses of man and that he needs special aid from on high.[1] Moreover, he thinks it his duty to remind his

bile; et in Ascensione victima accepta in odorem suavitatis, et ad Patris dexteram fuit collocata.

" Denique in sacrificiis Judaicis populus partem victimæ comedebat: et in die Pentecostes populus communicavit victimæ ut Scriptores loquuntur; nam discipuli Christi Domini tunc cum eo sunt incorporati, eique tanquam membra capiti, juxta verba Apostoli, adhæserunt."

These five essential parts of the sacrifice were more clearly distinguished in this prayer as it was formerly when in general use and as it still is in the Greek Church: " Suscipe, Sancta Trinitas, hanc oblationem, quam tibi offerimus ob memoriam Incarnationis, Nativitatis, Passionis, Resurrectionis, Ascensionis Jesu Christi Domini nostri et adventus Spiritus Sancti."—V. Catech. de Montp., part. 3. sect. 2, c. vii., n. 22. Sacrifice de Jesus-Christ, tom. iii., p. 214. Idée du Sacerdoce et du Sacrifice de Jesus-Christ, p. 319.

[1] " Memor imbecillitatis tuæ, et considerans quanti momenti sit tantum sacrificium divinæ majestati offere, ad circumstantium confugiens suffragia, ipsos admones ut pro te orent. Manus autem extendis, ac si omnibus viscera pandas, et rursum jungis, quasi intra pectus receptos complectaris. Ipse vero qui alios ad orandum hortatus es, secreto quoque oras ut tuum à Deo sacrificium acceptetur."—Bona, c. v., art. 7.

brethren that though the Church prays for all, she demands of all supplication for our common wants.   He
arouses their attention and excites their fervor to the
accomplishment of this sacred duty.   " Orate, fratres."
Brethren, let us not separate; let us, on the contrary, be
more intimately united, especially on an occasion like
this, when there is question of the interests of all.   I
shall think of you; do not forget me.   I go to plead
your cause; remember the claims I have upon your
charity.   We are brethren in Jesus Christ.   Although
raised above you by the dignity of my office, I am not
exempt from your miseries.   The sacrifice which I am
about to offer is my sacrifice, and yours also—"meum
ac vestrum sacrificium."   It is mine, "meum," for,
unworthy though I am of the honor, I am its minister,
and it procures me inestimable blessings.   It is yours,
"vestrum," in a true, though less extensive sense, since
you offer it through me and in union with Jesus Christ,
the principal Priest, and since you participate in its
fruits.   We are all, therefore, deeply interested in its
being favorably received by the Father Almighty.
" Ut . . . acceptabile fiat apud Deum Patrem omnipotentem."

What will the people answer to such a salutary exhortation, to such an important invitation?   " Suscipiat
Dominus sacrificium de manibus tuis."   We will pray
and from this moment beseech the Lord to receive
favorably the offering presented at thy hands.   These

hands, already consecrated by sacerdotal unction, have often borne the " Ark of the Covenant," and have often been employed in blessing us. We beg of God that He may be pleased to sanctify them still more, that they may be efficaciously uplifted both for thee and for ourselves ; that, like the hands of Moses, they may have power to appease the anger of God and secure victory for His people. We desire that the first effect of this sacrifice should be to render to God's infinite majesty the glory of which our iniquities deprived Him. In union with the adorable Victim thou art going to immolate, we shall render to God the homage of our obedience to His law, of our confidence in His goodness, of our gratitude for His bounty—" ad laudem et gloriam nominis sui." Whilst asking that His name be praised and glorified, we shall beseech Him to show us the treasure of His mercy—" ad utilitatem quoque nostram totiusque Ecclesiæ suæ sanctæ." To the wishes thus expressed by the faithful the priest answers, " Amen." May our united petitions be favorably heard. May this sacred oblation give to God all the glory due to Him, and obtain for us the remission of our sins, an increase of justice, all the graces necessary for our salvation, and for the whole Church all the assistance she needs. " Amen." " Amen."

The Offertory, or first part of the sacrifice proper, is ended. Consecration, which is the second part, corresponds to the immolation of the victim in the ancient sacrifices. It may be divided into three parts: the Preface, or introduction to the great sacrificial action or immolation; that part of the Canon which precedes and accompanies the Consecration; that part which follows the Consecration to the "Pater Noster."

CHAPTER III.

HAVING exhorted the people to pray, the celebrant, in order that he, too, may be the better prepared to pray, is immediately absorbed in profound silence and recollection. His intercourse with God becomes more intimate. He has entered into the secret presence of the Lord. The prayer which he now offers is called by the Church "oratio secreta." What is passing between God and His minister? When he breaks this mysterious silence he seems as if he were coming out of an ecstasy. The earth, time, all created things have disappeared from his soul's sight, and his language, rising to the height of his thoughts, speaks only of things eternal. "Per omnia sæcula sæculorum." The fire of divine love has been enkindled in his heart. Such is the fruit of prayer. "Concaluit cor meum intra me; et in meditatione mea exardescet ignis" (Ps. xxxviii. 4). That fire he would fain enkindle in the hearts of all the faithful. Hence that exclamation by which he excites them to manifest their gratitude to God for His mercies, and to take part with him in what he says and does in the name of all. The people unanimously approve of the prayers which the celebrant has just secretly addressed to God.   In union with him they offer prayer, praise, and thanksgiving.   Such is the meaning of that " Amen," which is supposed to proceed from every mouth, to be the cry of every heart.   St. Jerome assures us that in the early days of Christianity, " quando Domini nostri adhuc calebat cruor et fervebat recens in credentibus fides," this response was made with wonderful fervor by the whole congregation, and that this " Amen" re-verberated through the sacred edifice like the report of a thunder-clap.   "Ad similitudinem cœlestis tonitrui reboat, Amen." [1]

What glorious emulation, what saintly harmony of pious sentiments are now manifested between the cele-brant and the faithful who are present and offer the holy sacrifice with him! [2]   When addressing the people he no longer turns towards them as before.   We may well suppose that he takes every precaution to avoid distraction, especially at a time when all the attention of which a man is capable is hardly sufficient.   But he

---

[1] Præfat. in Ep. ad Gal.

[2] " Secretis orationibus absolutis, statim clara voce dicis, Per omnia sæ-cula sæculorum, nihil sonans temporale, sed sublime et æternum.   Tum populum salutans, non te ad eum pro more convertis, quia jam debes à terrenis abductus totus Deo intentus esse; jubes autem sursum corda attolli, ac si diceres: Elevamini, omnes creaturæ, ad Deum: Emergite é fæce terræ, et quæ sursum sunt quærite."—Bona.

" Sacerdos, ante orationem, præfatione præmissa parat fratrum mentes dicendo: Sursum corda, ut dum respondet plebs: Habemus ad Dominum, admoneatur nihil aliud se quam Dominum cogitare debere."—S. Cyp., de Dominic. orat.

earnestly urges them to forget the earth and to lift up to the throne of the Almighty all their thoughts, affections, and desires. Alas, how great is our weakness! A new effort to deliver our souls from languor and to elevate us to the contemplation of heavenly things requires a new grace from the Lord. Priest and people alike need that grace. The priest requests it for the people, "Dominus vobiscum;" and the people for the priest, "et cum spiritu tuo." But the favor has been already obtained. "Sursum corda," says the priest aloud, and to this invitation all answer, What thou askest is already done—"habemus ad Dominum." If that be so, continues the celebrant, if all hearts have entered on the way of their sublime destiny by turning to God, their first beginning and last end, let us return thanks to Him from whom all blessings come. He who is our Sovereign Lord and God from all eternity made Himself *our God* in time by uniting our nature to.that of His own Son, and adopting us for His people in the person of that same well-beloved Son. "Gratias agamus Domino Deo nostro." O ye faithful! proclaim that there is nothing more just, nothing more conformable to reason, to the dignity of God and to our own. "Dignum et justum est." And thou, O priest! interpreter of the desires of all hearts, offer to the Supreme Benefactor the tribute of universal gratitude. Take up the people's refrain, repeat it in the same words, to show that this assembled multitude has but one heart and one mind when there is question of rendering to God the homage of our gratitude. Motives of interest, no less than those of fitness and of justice, demand it.

Great are the favors which we need from God's bounty. Nothing can give firmer support to our petitions and render them more efficacious than an affectionate and grateful remembrance of favors already received. The vapor of the earth ascends heavenward, but to re-descend in abundant rains. "Vere dignum et justum est, æquum et salutare." Proclaim that we should always and in all places—"semper et ubique"—return thanks to Him who always and everywhere manifests His mercy and tenderness towards us; that we should at all times and under all circumstances adore Him in whose presence all creatures are as nothing, who governs all, and disposes of all as He pleases, for all things are His. "Mea sunt omnia." We have already proclaimed it. He alone is the Lord—"tu solus Dominus." He alone is holy—"tu solus Sanctus." Yet He vouchsafed to desire that we should be called, and should be in reality, His children. "Domine Sancte, Pater omnipotens, æterne Deus." [1] God Almighty, principle and end of every created being, who contains in Himself all power and virtue! God Eternal, to whom is due an eternity of adoration, thanks-

---

[1] It has been remarked that many priests, when saying or singing the Preface, do not observe the punctuation of the missal, and consequently observe defective enunciation. They should not say, " Domine, Sancte Pater;" but, " Domine Sancte, Pater omnipotens," etc.

giving, and love. His goodness towards us could not, however—could not shine out more resplendently than in giving us His own Son to be our Mediator and Victim. It is through this Son, worthy object of His Father's complacency, that the angels praise, that the dominations adore Him. Through Him the powers that make the devil tremble, and who themselves tremble in the presence of the Almighty Lord, offer to God their homage and profoundest adoration and love. Through Him the heavens and the heavenly virtues and the blessed seraphim celebrate the glory of the Lord in unanimous transports of joy and exultation— "socia exultatione concelebrant." Through Him, also, God is pleased to accept our praises.

Offer them, therefore, to His infinite majesty in concert with the innumerable multitude of heavenly intelligences prostrate before His throne; and though you may groan under the burden of a mortal and corruptible body, though you may be confounded at the recollection of your faults, nevertheless confidently rely on the merits of a Mediator who is all-powerful with God. Join in the sublime and harmonious praise of all the angelic choirs; unite your voice to theirs in order to sing on earth the sacred canticles with which the heavens resound: "Sanctus, Sanctus, Sanctus." The four mysterious animals mentioned by St. John in his Apocalypse continually repeated the same refrain before the throne of God. " Requiem non habebant die ac nocte dicentia sanctus." Wisely, then, does the Church put this canticle on the lips of her children at a moment when the place of their assembly is about to become a real heaven through the presence of Jesus Christ. Let us imitate the angels by our fervor, and let our hearts be inflamed with the same fire which consumes theirs.

The joy that gushes forth from this hymn of triumph, as the Greeks call it, electrifies the earth. This exulting acclaim, which resounds through the mansions of eternal bliss, reaches also the place of our captivity and of our exile. Our feeble voices blend with those of the friends of God and are heard with the same complacency. Let our hearts, then, be filled with confidence. If we have not yet reached our true country, we have, at all events, been permitted a foretaste of its delights. Though we do not yet hold in our hands the palm of victory, we behold it awaiting us in the hands of God, who deigned to merit and destine it for us. In contrast to the people of God, who dared not pronounce the name of the Lord, we confidently praise and bless the Lord God of hosts. As we have become His friends and His people, He is pleased to hear us relate His wonderful works and proclaim His greatness. He is thrice holy, and we are full of sins and imperfections; yet He is full of mercy, and cannot despise the praises of an humble and grateful heart.[1]

[1] Cochin, Prones, t. v., p. 200.

This canticle, so short but so comprehensive, contains two parts which we can readily distinguish. The first part honors the sanctity of God, " Sanctus;" the second celebrates the condescendent charity of Jesus Christ, who comes to redeem us and to apply to us the merits of His superabundant redemption, " Benedictus qui venit." Both terminate with this exclamation of joy, " Hosanna in excelsis." If the heavens and the earth are filled with the glory of the Lord, is it not from a heart filled with His love these words of welcome should emanate—blessed is He who cometh in the name of the Lord? " Benedictus qui venit in nomine Domini."

The Church directs us to recite these words, taken from the one hundred and seventeenth psalm, to thereby pay our homage to the Son of God, who will soon appear in our midst as a Victim for our salvation. She considers all the blessings of which He is for the whole world the abundant source : the victory which He has obtained over death and sin; the peace which He has established between heaven and earth ; the consummated reconciliation of mankind with God; the true King put into possession of His Kingdom; idolatry banished from the world; the unjust usurper of God's glory covered with confusion by the coming and the sacrifice of Jesus, his conqueror. These are the recollections which fill the Church with joyous transports, and in order to express her gratitude therefor she calls upon all her children to unanimously sing, "Benedictus qui venit in nomine Domini. Hosanna in excelsis." Oh, that the praises of a God so good, of a Saviour so generous, were always on every tongue! that His love were in every heart! Blessed by every creature be He who comes to break our chains, comfort our sorrows, heal all our infirmities, and bring us all good! Above all, blessed be He in the manner which He prizes most—seeing us docile to His instructions, imitators of His virtues, fully submissive to the good-will of His Father! Blessed be He by our patience in trials, our moderation in success, our vigilance in temptations! Blessed be He in our bodies by chastity and mortification, in our minds by humility, in our wills by obedience! Blessed be He whilst our earthly exile lasts! Blessed be He eternally in the heavens in the assembly of the angels and saints! "Hosanna in excelsis!"

The "Sanctus" is addressed to the Most Holy Trinity, the "Benedictus" to Jesus Christ, His envoy and our saviour. The former is an act of adoration, which should be performed in an humble posture; therefore the priest, whilst performing it, makes a profound inclination. The latter is a song of triumph; hence at that time he stands erect. And as it is through the cross that Jesus Christ opened to us the treasures of His grace, the priest makes on himself that venerated sign whilst saying the words, "Benedictus," etc.

CHAPTER IV.

FIRST PART OF THE CANON;[1] THAT WHICH PRECEDES AND ACCOMPANIES THE CONSECRATION.

FROM the "Sanctus" to the Consecration, the good priest is in spirit with Jesus Christ on Calvary. He sees the executioners preparing the cross, offering to Him the wine mixed with myrrh and gall, stripping the adorable Victim of His blood-stained garments. He reflects especially on the ardent charity of Jesus, who, whilst delivering Himself up for us, conjures His Father with greater earnestness than ever to accord Him the salvation of mankind. The priest redoubles his attention. He endeavors with all possible fervor to impress upon his soul a vivid sense of the prayers which

---

[1] That part of the Mass which begins with the prayer, "Te igitur," and continues to the "Pater noster," is called Canon or Rule, because it contains the fixed rule, the invariable order to be followed in the Consecration, in what precedes and what follows it.

"Cum sancta sancté administrari conveniat, sitque hoc omnium sanctissimum sacrificium, Ecclesia Catholica, ut digné reverenterque offerretur ac perciperetur, sacrum canonem multis anté sæculis instituit, ita ab omni errore purum ut nihil in eo contineatur, quod non maxime sanctitatem et pietatem quandam redoleat, mentesque offerentium in Deum erigat. Is enim constat cum ex ipsis Domini Verbis, tum ex Apostolorum traditionibus ac sanctorum quoque Pontificum piis institutionibus."—Concil. Trid., sess. xxii., c. 4.

12

he recites and of the ceremonies which he performs. He is again absorbed in mysterious silence.

"Te igitur." From the sense of the Preface, from its joyous, exulting, elevating tone and spirit, as well as from the happy dispositions the faithful manifested by joining him in rendering to God the thanksgiving and adoration due to Him, the celebrant has been led to infer that it is time to begin the mystery of the most holy action.[1] He raises his eyes and hands appealingly to heaven, then immediately lowers them. He gives repeated tokens of his love and veneration for the altar which will soon be the throne of the King of the universe, by lovingly kissing it. With humility of heart rather than of body he implores the most merciful Father propitiously to accept and to bless the offering on the altar—"hæc dona, hæc munera."[2] Here especially every word should be deeply meditated.

I. "Te igitur, clementissime Pater." As much as our weakness would permit we have prepared ourselves for the prodigies of grace which in a moment will be operated on the altar. We have prepared our souls there-

---

[1] "Sanctissimæ actionis mysterium."—Flor., de Act. Miss. "In actione sacri mysterii."—S. Pelag. "Actio dicitur ipse Canon, quia in eo sacramenta conficiuntur dominica."—Valfrid.

[2] The difference between *rogamus* and *petimus*, between *dona* and *munera* has been aptly noted:

1. When we have no right to what we desire, we pray for it—*rogamus ;* but when we have a right to it, we demand it—*petimus.* Of himself man can only pray to God and supplicate Him, for he has no right to anything, *supplices rogamus.* But the priest at the altar as the deputy

for by instruction, prayer, and the singing of the praises of the thrice-holy God. We will, therefore—" igitur"— dare to approach nearer the majesty of the Lord. We need not now fear that we may tempt God by appearing before Him with cold hearts and empty hands. We have already offered Him the bread and wine destined to become the spotless Victim and the chalice of salvation. To this exterior matter of the sacrifice we have united the contrite and humble heart which He loves to find in sinners. Nay, on the wings of faith we have been borne beyond the confines of eternity, we have been lifted up to heaven, and borrowing from the angels their accents of burning love, we have in unison with them celebrated the glory of the infinitely holy God. But this blissful occupation, which for them is continual, must, in our present state of existence, be but of brief duration for us. How could we always sing the songs of Sion in a strange land? Therefore, " igitur," reawakened to a sense of our profound misery, though with our hearts still in heaven, towards which we long-

of the Church to which belong the merits of Jesus Christ, as representative of the Redeemer and acting in His name, has incontestable rights. Therefore he joins demand to petition, *rogamus ac petimus.*

·2. What the inferior receives from the superior, the creature from the creator, the subject from the king, etc., is called a *gift.* That which inferiors offer to their superiors or benefactors is called a *present.* The bread and wine on the altar are called gifts—*dona*—in regard to God who gave them to us. They are called presents—*munera*—in regard to men who offer them. They are called holy and unspotted sacrifices— *sancta sacrificia illibata*—by anticipation and in view of what they will become by consecration.

ingly raise our eyes, and with hands resting on this altar of the earth, where our frail nature still finds its abiding-place, we implore Thee, O Father of Mercy! "clementissime Pater"—Father of Jesus and our own! O inexhaustible Source of all blessings! if our unworthiness makes us tremble, let Thy clemency be our hope! May we not rely on it in sight of Thy holy altar and at the remembrance of Calvary? "Supplices rogamus." We beseech Thee humbly prostrate before Thy face and uniting our humility with the profoundest humiliations of Thy Son. "Ac petimus." We ask Thee, in the name and through the merits of this God-Saviour who is the personification of Thy mercy towards us—"per Jesum Christum"—to deign to accept our offering—"uti accepta habeas." Could it be otherwise than agreeable to Thee in view of what it shall soon become? Bless these material gifts, and, in Thy almighty power, transform them into a host worthy of Thee. "Et benedicas." From Thee, O Lord, we have received whatsoever we possess,—"hæc dona"—and what Thou hast given us we offer unto Thee, "hæc munera." This offering is holy—"hæc sancta." It belongs to a most pure sacrifice—"sacrificia illibata." It is holy even in its present state, for we have separated it from all that is profane by placing it on Thy altar—thus performing its first consecration. Infinitely more holy it soon will be; for, after the Consecration, in place of this bread and wine, Thou wilt behold a

Victim as pure, as holy, as adorable as Thyself, namely, Jesus Christ, Thy Son, the Image of Thy substance, the Splendor of Thy glory.[1]

But wherefore do we offer this incomparable sacrifice? Whom do we recommend to the divine clemency as proper recipients of the fruits of the Mass? First of all we offer it to Thee, O Lord, for Thy Church—" in primis, quæ tibi offerimus pro Ecclesia." Does it not deserve all Thy interest? It is Thine, O Lord!—"tua." It cost Thee dearly. It is holy—"sancta." Thou hast purified it in the blood of Thy Son, in order that it might appear in Thy sight pure and spotless. It is spread throughout the whole world—"catholica." From the rising of the sun to the going down thereof, it offers a pure oblation to the glory of Thy name. Grant it peace, O Lord, by delivering it from wars and persecutions which are the sources of so many evils! Deliver it from those scandals which desolate it and cause the loss and the ruin of so many of its children—"quam pacificare." Sustain and protect it against all the attacks

---

[1] Benedict XIV, speaking of the three signs of the cross which accompany the words—*hæc dona, hæc munera, hæc sancta sacrificia illibata*—thus explains them: " Tria crucis signa ducuntur quæ significant maximum hoc mysterium à sanctissima perfici Trinitate." He also quotes the explanation of St. Bonaventure: "Docet primum signum ad illa verba, *hæc dona*, significare primam traditionem qua Christus à Deo Patre deditus est. . . . Alterum signum ad verba, *hæc munera*, alteram innuere traditionem, qua Christus se ipse pro nobis tradidit. . . . Tertio denique signo ad ea verba, *hæc sancta sacrificia illibata*, traditionem intelligi qua Judas magistrum suum, ab omni prorsus peccato purum et integrum, in manus inimicorum ejus dedit."—De Præp. ad Miss., c. xiii., n. 28.

of its enemies, visible and invisible, so that according to Thy promise the gates of hell may not prevail against it—"custodire."   Watch over and preserve its unity, by keeping far from it, or by putting an end to, all schisms, heresies, and all those baneful divisions which should be unknown in Thy holy family—"adunare."   Govern it throughout the world by directing the minds and hearts of all who belong to it, both pastors and people.   To the former grant wisdom, meekness, charity, virtues which are so indispensable for the vicars of a God of peace; to the latter grant submission and a loving obedience towards those who direct them—"et regere digneris."

If we are anxious for the tranquillity and good government of the Church, we will not fail to solicit for its visible head an abundant effusion of heavenly gifts. We therefore pray nominally for the Sovereign Pontiff. He is the centre of Catholic unity.   To him was given the charge of leading the sheep as well as the lambs to the pastures of the Lord.   How powerful is his influence over the body of the faithful!   We pray nominally also for the prelate who by the grace of God and the appointment of the Holy See presides over the diocese within which we celebrate, "et pro antistite nostro."[1]

We recommend to God all orthodox believers and professors of the Catholic Apostolic faith; but we make

---

[1] " Non licet presbytero in aliena diœcesi missam celebranti Episcopi sui nomen in locum Episcopi illius diœcesis in qua celebrat substituere." —Pouget., t. ii., Institut. Catholic., p. 862.

particular mention of those for whom we have special reasons to pray.

II. "Memento, Domine." With God, to remember is to love, to succor. "Remember us, O Lord, in the favor of Thy people, visit us with Thy salvation." [1]

"Famulorum famularumque tuarum." The Church permits us here to apply a part of the fruits of the holy sacrifice to certain persons whom we recommend to God in a special manner, either in virtue of some agreement or through some other motive. [2]

"Et omnium circumstantium." This does not mean those only who are physically present in the holy place during the celebration of the holy sacrifice; but also all Christians—nay, all mankind. For, according to a learned and pious writer, the priest should consider himself as standing between earth and heaven, surrounded by all the inhabitants of this world, whose deputy he is to the throne of God to offer their homage and supplication. [3]

"Quorum tibi fides cognita est, et nota devotio." The

[1] Ps. cv. 4.

[2] It is before Mass, and whilst preparing for it, that the priest should form his intentions, so that a simple renewal of them may suffice in this *memento* of the living. The Rubrics give the reason—"Ne circumstantibus sit morosus."

[3] Although the word *circumstantium* should apply literally to those who assist at the sacrifice, we can hardly deny it a more comprehensive signification, since the priest, when celebrating privately, may not omit that word—though there is none present but him who serves Mass. Sacrifice de Jesus Christ, t. 3, p. 279.

Church supposes that those who assist at holy Mass do so in a religiously devout manner. But if faith and devotion are expected of those who are simply witnesses of the sacrifice, what must be expected of the celebrant himself?

"Pro quibus tibi offerimus, vel qui tibi offerunt." Prior to the tenth century, the celebrant said only, "qui tibi offerunt," because the faithful themselves offered the bread and wine. Subsequently, as many failed to bring their offerings to the church, the words, "Pro quibus tibi offerimus, vel qui tibi . . ." were added so as to include all in the same prayer. In proportion as public piety grows cold, our compassion should grow strong. O my God, those are not the greatest objects of Thy commiseration who, feeling the weight of their miseries, come to the foot of Thy altars, seeking a remedy for their ills, and uniting with us to offer Thee both their gifts and themselves. Extend also Thy mercy to those who forget Thee; for the general welfare we offer Thee our prayers.

"Pro se, suisque omnibus." Let us admire the solicitude with which the Church considers all the wants of her children, commends all their legitimate desires, teaches them what they may and should ask for, and indicates the order they should observe in presenting their petitions. It is just that in the first place we should pray for ourselves, before praying for others "pro se;" and also, that we should attend to the welfare of the soul before that of the body. Wherefore the Church wishes that the faithful should offer the holy sacrifice—"pro redemptione animarum suarum" —for the redemption of their souls; "pro spe salutis," to obtain the salvation for which they hope. Our souls are *redeemed*, that is, emancipated from all servitude, purified from every sin, freed from all penalty due to sin. They are saved only by the merits of the passion of Jesus Christ, and by the application of these merits to us. The preservation of our health —"et incolumitatis"—as far as it contributes to our sanctification, either by the gratitude it excites in our hearts, or by the works of zeal which it enables us to perform, or because of the temptations from which it preserves us, is also a very precious gift which we should ask of God through Jesus Christ.

III. "Communicantes." A ministry as God-like as ours should be exercised only by godly men. Awful and terrible even unto angels, how can it help making frail, imperfect men tremble? This conviction of our utter unworthiness, which should be vividly present to our minds during the whole celebration of Mass, becomes still profounder in the heart of the devout priest as the moment for performing the tremendous mystery approaches. It inspires him when preparing to fulfil his sublime function to unite with all that heaven contains most eminent in sanctity, in glory, and in power. "Communicantes."

We therefore unite ourselves to all the friends of God, to all who are still wayfarers, but especially to those who, having once been pilgrims like ourselves, have reached the home of the blest, and yet constitute but one body with us. Children of the same family, there exists between them and us a community of affections—this is the most consoling dogma of our holy faith. We rejoice in their triumph; they are alarmed at our dangers. We join them in their thanksgiving; they take compassion on our miseries. We honor their memory; they help us by their prayers and intercessions. For them as well as for us, there is but one sacrifice—the sacrifice of Jesus Christ. From it they derived the light, the strength, the various graces which enabled them to acquire the highest virtues. We also can, if we so choose, joyfully draw the waters of grace out of the same fountains of the Saviour.[1] As we have a right to offer it with them, we invite them to offer it with us.

"In primis gloriosæ semper Virginis Mariæ." Oh, how consoling for us the privilege of uniting our prayers, first of all to those of Mary, our worship to hers, and to have recourse to her powerful intercession whilst we recall the great things which He who is mighty has done for her! It is just that here as elsewhere she should be invoked before all the other saints, for she is their queen, and almost infinitely surpasses them in

[1] " Haurietis aquas in gaudio de fontibus salvatoris."—Is. xii. 3.

merit, in power with God, and in love for us. "Gloriosæ semper Virginis Mariæ, genetricis Dei et Domini nostri Jesu Christi." How great the glory she procured for the Holy Trinity! How great the glory she received from Him! Ever virgin Mother of God, since she is the Mother of our divine Saviour Jesus Christ, the Son of God! The Church could not pronounce on her a more magnificent eulogy in fewer words. The Church's zeal for Mary's cult—always guided by the Spirit of God —could not fail to inspire her to have frequent recourse to Mary during the celebration of so great a sacrifice. Are we not to a great extent indebted to her for our privilege of offering it? If we give Jesus Christ to the world, is it not from the Virgin Mother we received Him? Our Victim is bone of her bone, flesh of her flesh. Was not her virginal womb the source whence He derived that adorable blood which we present to God as the price of our redemption, and which He returns to us and commands us to drink as a pledge of the new covenant which He makes with us?

Next in order after the Blessed Virgin, we reverence the memory of the twelve apostles, because they are the pillars of the Church, the first sacrificers of the law of love, and because they have transmitted to us the same sacrificial power. To them we subjoin twelve other illustrious martyrs through whom we associate with the whole army of those generous athletes who returned Jesus Christ blood for blood, life for life.[1]

"Et omnium Sanctorum." Finally, we unite with the whole multitude of the blessed, with so many saintly Pontiffs, so many devout priests, so many pure souls, who so religiously celebrated the same mysteries which we celebrate, or who have themselves been consumed as holocausts in the sacred flames of charity. "Communicantes." We hope, O Lord, that in view of their merits and supplications—"quorum meritis precibusque"—Thou wilt grant us that in all things, spiritual and even temporal, we may be always defended by the help of Thy protection—"concedas ut in omnibus protectionis tuæ muniamur auxilio." That is the grace we ask of Thee through the same Jesus Christ Our Lord, who for us suffered Himself to be led to the slaughter with the meekness of a lamb. "Per eumdem Christum Dominum nostrum." So may it be, O my God! "Amen." We ask it of Thee by the charity of Thy Son, who, in order to save us, vouchsafed to be stripped of His garments, stretched upon the cross, nailed to that bloody altar, to thereon consummate His sacrifice.

IV. "Hanc igitur." When drawing nigh unto God, we feel safe and confident, having for our patrons and protectors His incomparable Mother and all those

---

[1] "Post duodecim apostolos mentio fit duodecim martyrum, quorum recentiores sunt Joannes et Paulus, qui circa dimidium quarti seculi passi sunt sub Juliano apostata."—Ben. XIV., c. xiii., n. 23.

friends of His whose will He promised to do as a reward for their fidelity in serving Him. "Voluntatem timentium se faciet."[1] This thought fortifies our soul and inspires our confidence. All leads us to hope that our gifts will be favorably received. "Hanc igitur oblationem . . . quæsumus Domine ut placatus accipias." Since we enjoy the privilege of communion with those whom Thou, O Lord, lovest, and in view of this association which renders us less unworthy of Thy paternal benevolence, be Thou propitious to us and graciously accept the oblation of our service—"oblationem servitutis nostræ." We, who are Thy honored ministers, place it on Thy altar as a mark of our entire dependence and as an homage to Thy universal sovereignty. For we do not act merely in our own name, we are the officers and agents of that great family of which Thou art the Father: "Sed et cunctæ familiæ tuæ."

Whilst reciting this prayer, we hold our hands extended over the host and chalice. This is an expressive symbol which greatly affects the devout priest's heart, and which relates to three different aspects under which the Church regards us at this moment:

First of all, as ministers of the Church and her advocates, we, if I may so express it, take full possession of Our Lord Jesus Christ, seize upon all His merits, as it were, in order that we may be able to present to God an offering worthy of Him.

---

[1] Ps. cxliv. 19.

In the second place, as priests of the Most High, and acting in His name, we accept the Victim which is offered and which is a substitute for all sinners. We unload upon that Victim all the iniquities of mankind—according to this saying of Isaias: "Posuit Dominus in eo iniquitatem omnium nostrum;"[1] and conformably to the practice of the ancient priesthood, which was but a figure of ours—"ponetque manum super caput hostiæ, et acceptabilis erit, atque in expiationem . . . proficiens."[2]

Thirdly, as members of Christ, we unite with Him and with all the faithful, whose souls, so to speak, we hold under our hands, to identify the whole mystical body of Jesus Christ with the material sacrifice, so as to form with His natural body but one and the same Victim.

Then taking advantage of an opportunity so favorable, and well understanding that in a moment like this we may obtain everything our hearts could desire, we do not hesitate to ask for every blessing. "Diesque nostros in tua pace disponas." We ask for peace, not the peace which the world gives, and which could never make us happy, but the peace of God—"in tua pace." We beg for the peace of Jesus Christ—"pacem meam do vobis"—which is the fruit of His wounds, the price of His blood, the first fruit of that reconciliation which He effected between the Father and us. We pray for

---

[1] Is. liii. 6.   [2] Levit. i. 4.

that peace which "surpasseth all understanding," which fills the heart with serene joy, which can be experienced in the midst of the bitterest afflictions. "Superabundo gaudio in omni tribulatione nostra." [1] Dispose, O Lord, our days in Thy peace, "diesque nostros in tua pace disponas." Such are our petitions for this present life, what shall we ask for the life to come? Preservation from the greatest of all evils, eternal damnation—"ab æterna damnatione nos eripi;" the possession of heaven, the happy lot of the elect—"et in electorum tuorum jubeas grege numerari, per Christum Dominum nostrum." In other words, we beseech God, through His well-beloved Son, who in a moment will be present on the altar in a state of immolation, to guard us against our enemies, to protect us from ourselves, to sustain our weakness, and to make us walk perseveringly in the way which leads to supreme felicity.

Let us here quote a beautiful remark of Father Lebrun: "No one knows the number of the elect; but it may be said that a sure mark of election is manifested by the priest who enters into the spirit of these holy prayers, wishes for nothing but the peace of God, fears nothing but eternal damnation, and earnestly prays to the Lord for grace and protection to persevere to the end."

V. "Quam oblationem tu, Deus. . . ." [2] The awful

---

[1] II. Cor. vii. 4.

[2] This prayer immediately precedes the words of Consecration and determines their signification.

moment is at hand! "Adhuc unum modicum est, et ego commovebo cœlum et terram . . . et implebo domum istam gloria."[1] For the last time the priest prays over the material gifts. In an instant Jesus Christ will be in his hands. Here, as during the whole celebration of the Mass, he is the representative both of Christ and of His Church. In the name of the Church he begins by invoking the Almighty power on the bread and wine, so that the miracle of transubstantiation may be operated; but immediately after, as minister of Jesus Christ, he no longer speaks in his own individual name, nor in the name of the Church; he uses the very words of the Saviour, and it is these words which produce the mysterious transformation. It is Jesus Christ Himself who consecrates; but He operates through the instrumentality of the priest. St. Thomas asks himself this question: "Why does the priest ask for what he positively knows he will do?" And he answers: "How many times did Jesus Christ ask for what He well knew would infallibly happen? Thus He says to His Father: 'Clarifica Filium tuum.'" "Besides," continues the holy doctor, "the priest seems to pray, not so much for the miracle of transubstantiation as for the happy fruits it may produce in our souls,"—"ut nobis fiat." "Non videtur ibi sacerdos orare ut consecratio impleatur, sed ut nobis fiat fructuosa." When we say with the prophet Isaias, " A child

[1] Agg. ii. 7.

is born to us"—"Parvulus natus est nobis"—we understand that He is born for our salvation. So also we here ask that the offering may become the body of Jesus Christ for our sanctification.[1] Vouchsafe, O Lord, we beseech Thee, that this oblation may be in all things blessed, approved, ratified, reasonable, and acceptable; that it may become for us the body and blood of Thy most beloved Son Jesus Christ Our Lord: "Quam oblationem, tu, Deus, in omnibus, quæsumus, benedictam, adscriptam, ratam, rationabilem, acceptabilemque facere

---

[1] "Fit procul dubio corpus Domini in mensa altaris semper, cum solemne illud celebratur mysterium ritu debito; sed non semper eis fit per quos fit."—Serm. de Excellentia Sanctiss. Sacrum., inter opera S. Bern.

This remark, and that of St. Thomas, relate only to the word *nobis*. The following one of Bossuet embraces the two words—*nobis fiat :*

"We say that this body and blood are made for us, in the same sense as Isaias said—"parvulus natus est nobis "—so we may understand that they are for us created in this mystery, as they were for us conceived and formed in the womb of the Blessed Virgin. We should therefore here understand a sort of production of the body and blood in the Eucharist, as real as that production which was operated in the blessed womb of Mary at the moment of the conception and incarnation of the Son of God; a production, or creation, which in a manner gives Him a new being by which He is as really on the altar as He was in the womb of the Virgin, and is now in heaven. On that account we here use the word *fiat* in order to indicate a real action which terminates by creating in this mystery a real body and a real blood, the same which were created in Mary's womb. This is what the Greeks also express in their liturgy, when they expressly pray that this bread may be made the very body, and this wine the very blood, of Jesus Christ; and they add: 'through the Holy Ghost.' As this body and blood were, in the first instance, formed by the Holy Ghost, operating in the womb of Mary, we again invoke Him to renew on our altars the same mystery, so that we may here understand a physical operation as real as that by which the Saviour's body was formed the first time."—Explicat. de quelques Difficultés sur la Messe.

13

digneris, ut nobis corpus et sanguis fiat dilectissimi Filii tui Domini nostri Jesu Christi."

Without pretending to fathom all the profound significations of this prayer, we may cite the two following, as well calculated to captivate the whole attention of the fervent priest. The first relates to the obla·tion of the bread and wine, which will soon become the body and blood of Jesus Christ; the second, to the Church who, whilst offering her adorable Spouse, offers also herself and all her members.

1. We beseech Thee, O Lord, that this oblation may be really blessed by being substantially changed into the blessed fruit of the immaculate Virgin's womb, which fruit is the source of all blessing—"in omnibus benedictam." Grant that what is yet but bread and wine may, by this salutary change, become a wholly divine Victim, perfectly adapted to the accomplishment of His design, exclusively consecrated to God—"in omnibus adscriptam." Grant that this oblation, as yet incipient, may be ratified and consummated, placed on Thy altar on high as a sacrifice in every respect perfect and accomplished—"in omnibus ratam." Grant that from terrestrial and inanimate it may be made spiritual and living, by being transformed into the glorious flesh of the Divine Word, to be the nourishment of our souls— "in omnibus rationabilem." Grant that it may become the only oblation acceptable and pleasing to Thee—that is, Jesus Christ, Thy Son, Our Lord, in whom Thou art

well pleased, and through whom alone any offering can be made acceptable to Thee—"in omnibus acceptabilem."

2. Others, with St. Thomas and St. Augustine, taking these words in the second sense, that is, applying them to the Church, to the body of the faithful, which is offered with Jesus Christ, its Head, explain them as follows: Grant, we beseech Thee, O Lord, that this oblation, which, as far as it is Jesus Christ, cannot fail to be blessed, approved, ratified, reasonable, and acceptable, may be so, too, as regards all it contains. We pray that this oblation of ourselves, united to that of Jesus Christ Our Saviour, may, in every respect, be worthy to draw down upon us Thy abundant blessing, "benedictam;" that it may attach and consecrate us entirely to the accomplishment of Thy holy will, and that through it our names may be written in the book of life, "adscriptam;" that it may be firm and irrevocable, so that we may never again separate ourselves from Thee by sin, "ratam;" that it may so spiritualize our hearts, our senses, and all that is in us, that henceforth we may render to Thee that worship in spirit and in truth which Thou expectest from Thy true adorers, "rationabilem;" and that our life, together with the lives of all the mystical members of Jesus, may become more and more acceptable to Thee through our constant endeavors to impress on our soul His image and His virtues, "acceptabilem."

"Benedictam, per quam benedicamur; adscriptam, per quam id cœlo scribamur; ratam, per quam in bono firmemur; rationabilem, per quam rationabiles efficiamur et à sensu bestiali exuamur; acceptabilem, per quam accepti et Deo grati reddamur."[1]

"Ut nobis corpus et sanguis fiat dilectissimi Filii tui Domini nostri Jesu Christi." The simplicity with which we ask for the great miracle of transubstantiation closely resembles the sublime simplicity with which Sacred Scripture describes the omnipotence of

---

[1] Tripl. Exposit.

We must here remark that the Church in applying these five terms to the Host, evidently intends to remind us of the five mysteries of Jesus Christ, which are as the five parts of the sacrifice—as we before explained. We stated that there were in every sacrifice *sanctification, oblation, immolation, consumption,* and *acceptation* of the victim.

First, the *sanctification*, which took the victim from the rank of common and profane things, in order to dedicate it to God, is represented by the words, *in omnibus benedictam*, and relates to the Incarnation by which Jesus Christ has been entirely consecrated to God.

Second, the *oblation* is signified by the word *adscriptam*, and corresponds to the offering which Jesus Christ made of Himself to His Father when he entered into this world by His nativity—an offering which He manifested by His Presentation in the temple.

Third, the *immolation* is expressed by the word *ratam*, and is accomplished by the bloody death of the Redeemer.

Fourth, the *consumption* or *clarification*, by which the victim was devoured and, so to speak, spiritualized by the fire, is expressed by the word *rationabilem;* it is accomplished in the Resurrection of Jesus Christ by which His body passed into a glorious state.

Fifth, the word *acceptabilem* designates the *acceptation* of the Victim, which took place chiefly on the Saviour's Ascension, by which He was received and joyfully welcomed by His Father.

" Quinque sunt crucis signa quæ in hoc actione fiunt; quæ quidem putant Christum significare qui secundum carnem in quinque sensibus passus est."—Ben. XIV.

God in the act of creation, "fiat lux, et facta est lux," and the equally sublime marvel of the incarnation of the Word in Mary's womb, "fiat mihi secundum verbum tuum . . . et verbum caro factum est."[1]

VI. "Qui pridie quam pateretur." It is here especially that the senses and reason rest, for now everything belongs to the domain of faith. To faith alone it belongs to pierce the clouds, to inspire us with holy fear, whilst at the same time it should fill us with the most tender and confiding love. O priest, who art going to perform a function so marvellously superhuman, how canst thou help being entirely absorbed in Jesus Christ, who uses thee as an instrument to produce His body and blood upon the altar? Thou borrowest His words; thou imitatest His action at the Last Supper; Thou actest but in His person, by the authority of His Father, and in the omnipotent virtue of His Spirit. All that He did on the eve of His death in the institution of this ineffable sacrifice thou art about to do this moment.[2] He took bread in His holy and venerable hands; thou takest it also in thine. But, alas, these hands of thine, whatever may be the care thou hast taken to preserve them pure, or to wash them in the waters of repentance

[1] " Ad illa verba : Ut nobis corpus et sanguis fiat dilectissimi Filii tui Domini nostri Jesu Christi, actualem et expressam intentionem renovabis consecrandi corpus et sanguinem Christi, per transsubstantiationem panis et vini Christi verbis conficiendam."—Bona, c. v., n. 8.

[2] Except the breaking of the Host, which takes place only a short time before communion.

—these hands, though blessed and consecrated, yet fall infinitely short of being comparable to the adorable hands of Jesus Christ, which are the only altar worthy of bearing so holy a Victim! " Accepit panem."

Like Christ, thou lookest up to heaven, to Him who can do all things. That look is a prayer of entreaty by which thou implorest Him to manifest again His power and love. Thou enterest, so to speak, into the very bosom of God, to seek His Word, who " was from the beginning and by whom all things were made," that He may Himself come and derogate from the laws of nature which He has established, and substitute Himself for these material gifts. " Et elevatis oculis in cœlum ad te Deum Patrem suum omnipotentem." [1] The essential object of the Eucharist, as indicated by its name, is thanksgiving. Immediately before instituting it, Jesus gives thanks to His Father for all the favors He deigned to bestow upon man, from the creation until that day when, having given them His Son for their Saviour, He gives them the flesh of that same beloved Son for their food and His blood for their drink. To that Father, who always hears Him, He returns thanks for having prepared for Him and for all His true disciples, as a

---

[1] This circumstance and many words found here are not related by the Evangelists in the history of the Last Supper. The Church derived them from tradition. It was customary with Our Lord to raise His eyes to His Father when He was going to perform some great prodigy, in order to show that He acted in union with the Father, and by the same power.

magnificent recompense for brief humiliations and sufferings, an immense amount of glory. He thanks the
Father because the power of darkness which will soon
triumph shall find its confusion and defeat in its very
victory; and because the sting of death which will soon
wound the Author of life shall be turned against death
itself to its destruction. "Ero mors tua, O mors!" [1]
Finally, He thanks His Father for all the effects of the
sacrifice of the cross and of the altar—"tibi gratias
agens." [2]   And thou, O priest, who art the medium of
universal gratitude's outpouring, who hast received so
large a share of the divine bounty, thou also returnest
thanks with Jesus Christ.   He blesses and you bless,
"benedixit," and that benediction, which operates what
it signifies, after having been pronounced at the altar by
so many priests successively for over eighteen hundred
years, shall have as much virtue and efficacy on your
lips as on those of the Saviour Himself.   The bread is
broken, "fregit," to teach us that it is the will of the
heavenly Father that all the children of His family
may partake of ·it, and receive at His table the pledge
of a blessed immortality.   "Deditque discipulis suis."

---

[1] Osee xiii. 14.

[2] Sacred writers never mention the thanksgivings of Jesus Christ but
in connection with some signal miracle, such as the multiplication of the
loaves and the resurrection of Lazarus. Whilst ingratitude is a burning
wind which dries up the channels of grace, our gratitude provokes the
liberality of the Lord, and induces Him to pour down new blessings
upon us.

"Dedit." Behold the use He makes of what is most precious in heaven and on earth! His Father had given Him all things—"omnia dedit ei Pater in manus." Now He takes into His hands all that the Father had given Him, all that He has of goods, riches, graces, merits, holiness, and perfections. In what manner and in whose favor will He dispose of this magnificent treasure? Will He return it to His Father? No; He gives it to His disciples. "Deditque discipulis suis, dicens: Accipite." "Take," He says to them, "this is My body; this is My blood; it is My soul, it is My divinity, My whole self, all that I have, all that I am. Take, all that I have is yours. Be not satisfied with keeping Me in a sanctuary in your midst, where I shall be ever ready to hear your prayers and console you in your troubles; be not content with exposing Me as an immolated Victim before the eyes of My Father, to appease His justice and to assure you of His bounty; but receive Me into your mouths, nourish yourselves with My substance, incorporate yourselves with Me, your Saviour and your God, 'manducate.'" But, O Lord, we are not all equally pure, equally innocent and fervent! True; but if you are all My disciples, if you are already united to Me by faith and charity, unite yourselves more intimately to Me by partaking of the sacrament of My love. I Myself will augment your innocence and fervor, I will consummate the work of your sanctification. Eat ye all of this Living Bread.

I give, bequeath, and devise it to you—"manducate ex hoc omnes."

Oh, what mortal could ever have foreseen or imagined such an excess of charity? Oh, how elevated are the thoughts of Jesus above ours! How generous His heart! How vast His designs! How precious and magnificent His gifts! O priest, with such a treasure, how rich thou art! Enjoying as thou dost the delights of this table, thou mayest well despise all the vain pleasures of the world. What dost thou experience in the great and solemn moment that thou pronouncest[1] the words of consecration? Art thou not enraptured? Art thou not taken up to heaven, or does not heaven descend to earth for thy sake? "An putas te adhuc cum hominibus et in terra esse? An non potius in cœlo translatus? . . . O miraculum! O Dei benignitatem!"[2] Bend the knee; adore Jesus Christ, God and man sitting at the right hand of the Father, and at the same time in thy hands! Annihilate thyself, as it were, be-

---

[1] The rubric which prescribes the reading of the whole canon secretly—*secreto*—recommends it again here, for the mental application wherewith these dread words are pronounced would naturally excite us to raise our voice if we were not warned to check it. As to the manner of pronouncing the two sacramental formulas, we find the following wise directions in a missal of Grenoble, printed in 1522: "Cum summa attentione, reverentia et veneratione, integre, distincteque sunt proferenda, quoniam illa sacerdos quasi ore Christi eloquitur. . . . Debentque proferri tractim, uno spiritu, ne se immisceat alia cogitatio : nec dividenda est forma illa cujus tota virtus dependet ab ultimo verbo, quod in persona Christi dicitur."

[2] S. Chrys., de Sacerd., i., 3.

neath the weight of His most sacred Majesty! "Adoro te supplex, latens Deitas." Be the first to render Him homage together with the angels prostrate around thee; and then present Him for the adoration of the faithful by elevating the sacred Host, being careful, however, to keep thy eyes intently fixed on it.' Offer Him to His Father as the ransom of mankind and the Victim for our sins. Offer at the same time thy own self and the whole Church, that all may be made one sacrifice with Him. Abandon thy heart to all the emotions with which a lively faith and an ardent charity would have inspired it if thou hadst stood on Calvary beside the disconsolate Mother and the beloved disciple; if thou hadst been permitted to kiss the cross or the feet of Jesus expiring, to witness His cruel agony, to hear His last words, to feel the redeeming blood trickling from His wounds upon your head.

"Nusquam in toto missæ decursu debet sacerdos tam devotus et attentus adesse, quantum in hoc parte, in qua operatur divinissimum mysterium, in qua aperiuntur

---

¹ Three things are intended by the elevation of the sacred Host:

First, to expose Jesus Christ, now present on the altar, to the adoration of the faithful; second, to represent the elevation of Jesus Christ's body on the cross, so that everything may remind us of that great mystery when it is being renewed ; third, to offer to God in silence this unique Victim of our salvation, as the priests of the Old Law offered Him their typical victims by elevating them.

In the Latin Church, till the beginning of the twelfth century, the priests did not elevate the consecrated Host and chalice till the end of the canon, at the words, " omnis honor et gloria." It is now called the "little elevation." Later on, however, as errors against the *Real Presence*

cœli et ima summis conjunguntur. Trementes assistunt angeli, laudantes Dei bonitatem et misericordiam ejus in sæculum sæculi; horrescunt angelicæ virtutes, videntes Dominum suum traditum in manus peccatorum; mirantur Cherubim ac Seraphim, quoniam cui incessanter proclamant: Sanctus, sanctus, sanctus, ad vocem miseri sacerdotes quasi obediens, descendit super altare immolandus. Væ ergo sacerdotibus insipientibus! Væ tepidis! Væ imparatis! Nam propter negligentiam terribile cum eis judicium fiet, . . . si non ea qua par est reverentia talia sacramenta tractaverint." [1]

"Simili modo." The same power which has changed the bread into the body of Jesus Christ will now change the wine into His blood. In imitation of our divine Redeemer, we also take in our hands the excellent chalice—"accipiens et hunc præclarum calicem," symbolized by that of the Royal Prophet which inebriated him so delightfully—"calix meus inebrians quam præclarus est!" [2] Like Jesus, we bless this chalice of veritable thanksgiving [3] which substitutes reality for

began to spread, the solemn elevation now practised was instituted in order to encourage the faithful to more openly profess the truths attacked by heresy. At the sound of the little bell the faithful prostrated themselves, and the greater number remained thus prostrate till after the consecration of the chalice, or even to the end of the "Pater." A large bell was also tolled to announce the consecration to the absent, and to invite them to join in adoration.

[1] Tripl. Exposit.

[2] Ps. xxii. 5.

[3] St. Luke, chap. xx. distinctly mentions two cups. The first, which was drunk at the beginning of the legal repast, had not been consecrated.

figures, and then we hear the Adorable Priest saying to us as to His first representatives, " Accipite, et bibite ex eo omnes." This is the chalice of My blood! This is the blood of the new and eternal covenant ' which I make with you. Drink ye all of it. Oh, how much does this covenant excel that which was the glory of God's former people! How original in its form, in its effects, in its extent! The Jewish covenant was but for a time; the Christian will endure for eternity. The former was confirmed by the blood of animals; the latter was sealed by the blood of the Son of God. To us sinners how consoling it is to remember that for our sakes, for the remission of our sins, that blood was poured out on Calvary, and that for us also it is now offered on the altar "in remissionem peccatorum."

Not without a profound reason is this cup, which contains such riches, called the mystery of faith—"mysterium fidei;" for within a commonplace exterior it contains the most magnificent, though hidden, treas-

The second, which was drunk at the end of the supper, according to the Jewish rite, was called the cup of thanksgiving, and of it the father of the family, after having thanked God for the deliverance of the Israelites from Egyptian captivity, partook first, and after him all the assembly. It is this cup that Jesus Christ, in order to consummate the figures by the substitution of the reality, changed into His precious blood. He thereby made it the veritable eucharistic cup, or chalice of thanksgiving.

¹ "Novi et æterni testamenti." The word testament has in Scripture two different meanings. One is, that a testament is the last will which a person makes before his death ; the other, that it is an alliance, a treaty. These two significations are here realized in the most admirable manner.

ures. The greatest of mysteries, or rather the mystery of all religion, consists in this, that the blood of a God was to be shed for the salvation of man, and that God loved man to such an excess as to be willing to shed His blood for man's salvation. Therein are the sum and relations of all our holy dogmas, the whole order of God's designs in the great work of our redemption, the incomprehensible evil of sin which for full atonement required the immolation of such a Victim, the infinite wisdom of the Lord in devising such wonderful means, His dread justice pursuing man's sin to the very person of His own Son, but, above all, the excessive charity of Jesus Christ, who for our sakes transforms into a chalice of ineffable blessings the bitter cup which He had received full of the indignation of His outraged Father. Finally, we have on the altar, which is the representation and continuation of Calvary, the whole secret of our sanctification, all the science of salvation. There, above all other places, we are inspired with that salutary fear which deters us from sin, the sovereign evil, and with that love which unites us to God, the Sovereign Good. This sacrifice is an ineffable union of severity which frightens and of goodness which touches the heart; an abyss of justice when considered in regard to God, who ordered it; an abyss of charity considered in the Incarnate Word, who there immolates Himself.

"Hæc quotiescumque feceritis." Behold the most admirable power ever given to man. "Hæc." What did Jesus Christ just do? What has become of the material substances which He had before Him? What does He now hold in His holy and venerable hands? The prodigy which He has just operated, the priest also will operate in the same manner with the same words, not only once, but every day until the consummation of the world.

"In mei memoriam facietis." [1] We have already remarked what a touching recommendation this is. Should not this remembrance, which Jesus considered an infallible means of securing for Him complete possession of our hearts, be to us an easy and welcome task, at least at this part of the holy sacrifice, when the great event of Calvary is represented to us in so realistic and striking a manner?

This investiture with the most astounding of all powers; this twofold commandment of the Son of God to His ministers to do what He Himself had just done, and to do it in commemoration of Him, will be for holy priests in heaven the subject and the cause of an eternal ecstasy. On earth they love to meditate on these words, and in order to contribute to their piety, we here reproduce the following beautiful and solid reflections:

The words, "do this in commemoration of Me," embody a duty which must be extremely important, since

---

[1] It is an error to say the words, " Hæc quotiescumque . . ." during, or after, the elevation of the chalice. They ought to be said immediately after the consecration of the wine, whilst the chalice is being placed on the altar.—Mgr. Gousset.

it is the only one signalized at this solemn moment. It consists in remembering Jesus Christ and all He has done for us; and this comprehends the mysteries of His life and especially those of His sufferings and death. But, O Lord, is that all Thou requirest of those whom Thou hast delivered from iniquity, whom Thou hast saved from hell, from eternal death, from irrevocable malediction, from an avenging justice, the weight of which would have crushed them forever? What claims hast Thou not on our life? What sacrifices canst Thou not demand of those for whom Thou didst not refuse to die on the cross? Why dost Thou not require of us a like immolation? Does not justice exact that we should die as Thou didst in the midst of sorrows and ignominies? Should we not be greatly honored in being permitted to follow Thee? And can there be anything difficult or painful in Thy commandments, when Thou Thyself hast given us the example of obedience even unto the death of the cross?

But what shall be the nature, the extent, the evidence of this remembrance which Thou commandest us to make of Thee? It would seem, dear Lord, that all Thou demandest is love and gratitude. But was a commandment necessary thereto? Is it not for us a glory as well as a duty to offer as a sacrifice of thanksgiving that which Thou didst offer as a sacrifice of reconciliation? What ingratitude could be more criminal than ours, if, at the very moment that we immolate Thee and fill our chalice with Thy precious blood, we should forget the shedding of that blood on the cross?   The very ceremonies of the holy sacrifice, which are intended to vividly represent Thy bloody immolation, would be our reproach and condemnation.   And how could we forget the mystery of Thy death when the separate consecration of Thy body and blood strikingly represents, and in a very sensible manner marks, the violent separation of Thy soul from Thy body, and perpetuates the remembrance thereof?   Could it be said, O my God, that I have memory and understanding, if, at the awful moment when, at my command, Thou comest down from heaven upon the altar, and Thy divine Spirit, as a heavenly flame, transforms the material gifts into Thy body and blood, and I elevate both towards heaven and before the throne of Thy Father, I should so far forget myself as not to know what I am doing?   Were I capable of such forgetfulness, I would richly deserve that my right hand, which so irreverently operates such tremendous mysteries, should forget its cunning, and that my tongue, which utters without recollection or intelligence words full of spirit and of life, should cleave to the roof of my mouth.   "Oblivioni detur dextera mea. Adhæreat lingua mea faucibus meis, si non meminero tui." [1]

"How easily can the priest, standing at Thy altar, absorbed in the profoundest silence, surrounded by de-

[1] Ps. cxxxvi. 5, 6.

vout worshippers, guided and aided by the prayers and directions of sacred liturgy, recall the remembrance of Thy death and of Thy incomprehensible charity in suffering for sinners who knew Thee not and dishonored Thy sacrifice by their blasphemies! In the midst of their tumultuous cries, reproaches, and curses Thou rememberest us. Not an instant didst Thou lose sight of our wants, notwithstanding the torments, insults, and contumelies they heaped upon Thee. From Thy cross on high Thou lookedst down on me through the long vista of future centuries, and on me in particular Thou shedst Thy tears and Thy blood, long before I had begun to resist. Could I now forget such kindness and mercy? How can I, whilst receiving or offering the Victim which reconciled me to Thy Father, not recognize Thee, or received it blindly and with an ungrateful heart?" [1]

However, let us not forget that this remembrance—"memoriam"—which seems to sum up all the acknowledgment the Saviour requires of us, should not be confined to a few simple thoughts or transient sentiments of tenderness. If it is really engraven on our hearts, it will there produce what St. Paul calls its inseparable effects. After citing the words, "This do ye for a commemoration of Me," the Apostle adds: "For as often as you shall eat this bread and drink this chalice, you

[1] Explication du mystère de la passion de Notre Seigneur Jesus-Christ, t. iv., p. 668.

14

shall show the death of the Lord, until He come."[1] The intention of St. Paul—as some estimable interpreters remark—was to give us to understand that by assisting at the holy sacrifice, and especially by offering it, we take upon ourselves the obligation to announce, that is, to show by our conduct that we are one with Jesus Christ, who died and was buried for us, and who, being now risen, dies no more, "but in that He liveth, He liveth unto God."[2]

[1] I. Cor. xi. 26. [2] Rom. vi. 10.

CHAPTER V.

THE Victim is immolated. Who will reap the abundant fruits of His immolation? They arc divided between God, to whom the sacrifice is offered, and man, for whom and through whom it is offered.

I. First of all, God "partakes with the altar," [1] as St. Paul expresses it. We have no right to our share of the treasures of grace acquired by the adorable Victim until it has first been offered to the Lord and He has, so to speak, communicated by receiving the glory which accrues to Him from its immolation. Hence, we who are Thy servants—"nos servi tui"—and with us the whole Christian family—"sed et plebs tua sancta"—cheerfully complying with the affectionate recommendation just addressed to us by our Saviour—"in mei memoriam facietis"—and with souls wholly filled with grateful remembrance of Him—"unde et memores"—offer to Thy Supreme Majesty—"offerimus præclaræ majestati tuæ"—a pure Host, a holy and unspotted Host.[2]

---

[1] I Cor. ix. 13.

[2] By these three qualities attributed to the Victim, the Church not

A pure Host—"Hostiam puram"—for it was formed by the operation of the Holy Ghost in the chaste womb of Mary; "Hostiam sanctam"—a holy Host, since it is substantially united to the Divinity, who is holiness itself; "Hostiam immaculatam"—a wholly unspotted Host, since it could never contract the least defilement, and by its glorification it has been delivered from even that semblance of sin which in its mortal state it had assumed. This Victim is a living bread, and for us the principle of such a life as we desire—a life exempt from old age and decay—"panem sanctum vitæ æternæ," a delicious chalice of eternal salvation—"Calicem salutis perpetuæ."

Hence, again, we make another special mention of the three mysteries of Jesus Christ which procured most glory for God, being, as we have already observed, the essential parts of His Son's sacrifice. They are *His Passion*—"tam beatæ passionis"—so dolorous for Him, so salutary for us, for it delivered us from all real evil and merited for us all true good; *His Resurrection*, in which all the divine attributes, but especially power, justice, wisdom, and goodness, shine forth so resplendently; *His glorious Ascension*, which so fittingly crowned the work of the redemption of mankind.

only extols its excellence above the victims of the Old Law, but she also reminds us that in this sacrifice we find the perfect accomplishment of the celebrated prophecy: "In omni loco sacrificatur, et offertur nomini meo oblatio munda."—Malach. i. 11.

This latter mystery was the necessary corollary of the Resurrection, and the consummation of the sacrifice of His whole existence which Jesus Christ had made to His Father. By rising from the dead He enters an immortal, impassable, and all-glorious life, but He does not immediately enter into possession of His glory. It is by His Ascension He takes possession thereof, sits at the right hand of His Father, and receives the final reward due to His most sublime and generous devotedness. In heaven also He consummates His sacrifice, there continually offering Himself for us.

But wherefore these many signs of the cross? The priest makes no fewer than five during this short prayer. The Church desires that during the sacrifice we should have no thought but of Calvary; or, at least, that after the consecration, Jesus Christ crucified and dying should be ever present to our mind and the object of all our affections.

Besides, we must remember that the signs of the cross which follow the consecration have a signification quite different from those which precede or accompany it. These latter are made to draw the blessings of God on the gifts, or to signify that His grace was expected as the effect of the merits of the crucified Saviour; but those which follow till the communion are destined to strongly impress our minds with the conviction that the Victim which we behold is the same which was immolated on the cross, and that the sacrifice of the altar is the same as that of Calvary.[1]

II. "Supra quæ propitio ac sereno vultu respicere

[1] "Nihil Ecclesia prætermittit quo in animis imprimat sacerdotum et adstantium idem esse sacrificium altaris cum sacrificio crucis. Et sane cuperet ut, præsertim sacerdotes, sibi ipsi post consecrationem Christum Jesum objicerent animo immolatum in cruce, ut ait Apostolus ad Galatas, qui post ejus prædicationem Christum crucifixum ab oculos semper habebant : Ante quorum oculos Jesus Christus præscriptus est in vobis crucifixus. Atque ut ejusmodi oriatur effectus, vult Ecclesia omne verbum quod exprimat corpus et sanguinem Domini, cum signo crucis proferri, quo declaratur hostiam et quod continetur in calice idem esse corpus quod cruci fuit affixum, et ipsum sanguinem qui in cruce effusus est."—Ben. XIV., l. ii., c. xvi., n. 6.

Speaking of sacerdotal dignity, it is sometimes said that the priest who offers the holy sacrifice enjoys the extraordinary honor of blessing Jesus Christ, who, being under the form of a victim in the sacred species, is in a manner inferior to His minister. That reflection is more specious than solid. After the consecration we no longer *bless* the sacred gifts; we offer them, and pray God to accept them.

"Sacerdos post consecrationem non utitur crucesignatione ad benedicendum, sed solum ad commemorandum virtutem crucis."—S. Thom. iii. p., q. 83, art. 5. Or, if it be said that we do bless them, Bossuet will tell us in what sense : "The word *bless* in general is a good expression—*benedicere*. Thus we bless God when we celebrate His praises, and there is no doubt that Jesus Christ may be blessed in that manner. But here there is no question of that kind of blessing; there is question of the blessing wherewith the faithful are blessed, when we pray over them, and wherewith we operate or confer the sacraments. This is ordinarily accompanied by the sign of the cross, to acknowledge that through the cross of Jesus Christ every spiritual blessing descends upon us. In this sense we bless the faithful and confer the sacraments. But let it be remembered that the blessings with which the sacraments are operated or conferred are more extensive, since the sacraments are intended for the sole purpose of blessing, consecrating, or sanctifying those who receive them. Therefore sacramental blessing has two effects : one regards the sacrament itself ; the other, him who receives it. This being understood, all difficulty disappears. For when we bless the gifts, that is, the bread and wine, before the conse-

digneris.[1] Can the Lord refuse to look down with a propitious countenance upon—nay, to behold and accept with infinite delight, a Victim as great and as holy as Himself? Undoubtedly not, but He may perceive, and often does perceive, in the priest and in the faithful imperfections and faults which contrast sadly with the sanctity of a religious action so perfect in itself, and which prevent Him pouring down upon us His graces as abundantly as He would desire.

Our gifts are pleasing to Thee, O God, and nothing that we can offer is better calculated to touch Thy heart. But, alas! it is sinful men who offer them; therefore we implore Thee not to distinguish between our offering and ourselves. Thine eyes lovingly behold it; in consideration of it mercifully look down upon us.

Moreover, the Church, after offering to God, by the preceding prayer, the natural body of Jesus Christ, now offers His mystical body, whose members, being still liable to sin, too often displease Him by their trans-

cration, this blessing has its twofold effect: the one regards the sacrament which is to be operated; the other relates to man, who is to be sanctified through the sacrament. But after the consecration, the blessing which has already had its effect as regards the sacrament is repeated for the benefit of man, who is to be sanctified by participation in the mystery."—Explic. de la Messe.

The five signs of the cross which the priest here makes over the Host and chalice represent the five wounds of Our Lord.—Ben. XIV., l. ii., c. xvi., a. 6.

[1] Our unworthiness and miseries solicit the Lord's propitious regard; the complacency He finds in the Victim, and the glory which it procures to Him.

gressions.   For these two evils we seek a remedy in His bounty.   We beseech Him to favorably regard us both as offerers and as components of the offering.

Therefore, concentrating, as it were, in ourselves all the religion of past ages, we remind the Lord of those ancient sacrifices from which He derived most glory and satisfaction, either because of their resemblance to that of His Son, or of the eminent virtues and elevated sentiments of those who offered them.   How great was the innocence of Abel, whose bloody death was caused by the envy of his brother, just as the innocent Jesus was immolated on account of the jealousy of the scribes and Pharisees!   How magnanimous the faith, how heroic the obedience of Abraham, who on account of his sacrifice merited the title of "Father of the Faithful," as Jesus by His became the Head of all believers! What disengagement from all earthly affections, what holiness, what close resemblance to the Saviour of men, in Melchisedech, that prince of justice and peace, who, as St. Leo remarks, offered, not Jewish hosts, but the species which Our Redeemer consecrated by changing them into His body and blood. Hence Melchisedech's sacrifice is called "sanctum sacrificium, immaculatam Hostiam."[1]   If the shadow and the figure were pleasing

[1] Opinions are divided as to whether these four words—"sanctum sacrificium, immaculatam Hostiam"—should be understood as relating to the sacrifice of Melchisedech, or to that of our altars. Several authors have thought it more natural to refer them to the sacrifice of the Mass which is being actually celebrated. Father Lebrun is of a different

to Thee, O Lord, how much more acceptable must be the reality which we offer Thee! May we, through our good dispositions, be always pleasing to Thee, as we are sure to please Thee through Christ Jesus, Thy Son, Our Lord!

III. "Supplices te rogamus." For the third time we offer to the Lord the Victim He vouchsafed to give us. But whilst in the two preceding prayers we applied the sacrifice to its primary end—the glory of God, to whom it is offered—here we consider the interests of those for whom we offer it, or who offer it with us.

For the first eight centuries no attempt was made to fathom the mysterious signification of this admirable prayer, and those who first attempted it do not pretend to have succeeded. Florus, deacon of the Church of

opinion. He thinks this addition was made in order to raise Melchisedech's sacrifice above all other sacrifices which were offered under the Old Law, as being a more perfect figure of Jesus Christ's. And he adds that if these words designated the sacrifice of Christ, the sign of the cross would certainly be prescribed whilst pronouncing them, as it is every time after the Consecration there is mention of the body and blood of Jesus; for instance, at the words, "Hostiam puram, Hostiam sanctam, Hostiam immaculatam," of the preceding prayer.

Benedict XIV. does not pronounce on the question, but contents himself with saying: "Suarez æque in utramque sententiam se ostendit propensum ; cujus nos vestigia sectantes, dicimus, utrumvis intelliges, bonum iis verbis sensum contineri."—L. ii., c. xvi., n. 17.

"It is evident," says Bossuet, " that there is no intention to compare gift with gift, but persons with persons. On that account, only the holiest of men are nominally mentioned : Abel, the first of the just ; Abraham, the common father of the faithful ; and lastly, Melchisedech, who was greater than Abraham, since the latter offered him the tithe of his spoils, and received from him in return bread and wine—a foretaste of the Eucharist."—Explic. de la Messe.

Lyons, wrote in the ninth century: "Who can comprehend words so profound, so admirable, so marvellous? Or who can adequately explain them? Veneration and fear would avail more than discussion to impress their meaning on our minds." Innocent III. says nearly the same thing: "Tantæ sunt profunditatis verba hæc, ut intellectus humanus vix ea sufficiat penetrare."[1]

The explanation adopted by Father Lebrun seems to us the most approved. We here substantially reproduce it.

Prostrate before God as behooves humble *supplicants*, and convinced that these most sacred gifts on the altar are nothing else than the body and blood of Jesus Christ,

---

[1] The reader may consult on this difficult passage the various opinions cited by Benedict XIV. in the chapter which we have quoted—n. 24 and 25.

St. Thomas, and with him the greater number of theologians, see Jesus Christ Himself in the person of the angel here mentioned. Bellarm., vol. iii. of his Controversies. Lib. vi., de Miss., c. 24.—Suarez in iii. part, vol. iii., q. 83.

Bossuet manifests a great unwillingness to accept that opinion. He thinks that "the angel, who here appears to offer the prayers, is of the same nature as the others whom St. John in his Apocalypse represents as acting everywhere; of the same nature as the seven angels of whom the evangelist speaks in the eighth chapter, wherein mention is made of the angel of prayer, who also for this reason is called simply *another angel*, of no higher nature than the others.

"But in order fully to understand this prayer and clear up the difficulties connected with it, we should always bear in mind that *these things* —' jube hæc '—are in reality the body and blood of Jesus Christ; but that they also include us, our vows and prayers, which, united to the body and blood of Christ, constitute but one oblation. This oblation we desire to render in every respect pleasing to God, both as regards Christ, the Victim offered, and those who offer Him, and offer themselves with Him. With that design, what better could be done than again to so-

which cannot be worthily offered but by Jesus Christ Himself, we express a desire that they may be so offered, in order that everything connected with our oblation may be pleasing to God—both the gifts and the hand which presents them.   O Lord, who art Almighty, command, we beseech Thee—"supplices te rogamus, jube." But whom command?   Reverence does not permit us to say, Command Jesus Christ, Thy Son.   We therefore simply say, Command that this divine oblation be carried by the hands of Thy holy angel, the Angel of the great Council, the Angel of the Testament, Thy chosen Envoy, He who came into our midst to restore Thy glory and to save us; that it be taken to Thy altar on high,[1] to heaven, the throne of Thy adorable majesty.

licit the society of the holy angel who presides at prayer, together with that of all the holy companions of his beatitude, in order that our oblation may promptly and more acceptably ascend to that altar on high when presented by that blessed company ? It may not be amiss to remark that whilst our Canon speaks of only one angel, that called the Ambrosian includes all the angels, to explain the holy union of all the blessed spirits, who all do by consent what each does by operation and by virtue of a particular destiny."—Explic. de la Messe.

[1] According to the author of "Idée du Sacerdoce de Jesus-Christ," and many other interpreters, this *sublime altar*—"sublime altare"—is nothing less than the very person of the Word.   The true temple of God, wherein this altar is placed, is the bosom of the Father, or, as St. Augustine says, "the infinite abyss and the impenetrable secret" of the Divinity.   Consequently the veritable altar of God, that of which all others are but figures, is the Divine Word, who sustains, vivifies, and sanctifies God's Victim, that is, the humanity of Jesus Christ.   "Altare quod sanctificat donum" (Matt. xxiii.).   That altar being infinitely greater than the Victim, it is from it that the latter receives its sanctification and excellence.   We can also take in this elevated sense what we say at the beginning of the Mass—"Introibo ad altare Dei "—I will go

In this explanation the word " perferri" should be taken in a metaphorical sense. As Jesus Christ does not leave heaven, He cannot be carried thither anew. This is an allusion to the ancient sacrifices, in which the victim was consumed by fire, so as to be carried, in a manner, from earth to heaven by the smoke which ascended from the altar. It is also intended to remind us that Christ has really fulfilled that figure by His Ascension, in presenting His glorified humanity before the throne of His Father. Now, what is it that will not be obtained by Jesus Victim offered by Jesus Pontiff, who, as St. Paul says, "appears now in the presence of God for us"? [1] It is not too much to ask that in consideration of such a sacrifice we, who eat the flesh and drink the blood of this august Victim, may be filled with every heavenly blessing and grace. " Ut quotquot ex hac altaris [2] participatione sacrosanctum Filii tui corpus et sanguinem sumpserimus, omni benedictione cœlesti et gratia repleamur." It is not at all surprising that the Church in her prayers makes special men-

unto the altar of God ; "ad Deum," to that altar which is God and the Son of God, who, in renewing me by His grace, replenishes my heart with the joy of His Spirit.

[1] Heb. ix. 24.

[2] Here we have two altars clearly indicated : the invisible high altar which is in heaven, and the visible altar on earth. St. Augustine clearly distinguishes them when he says that both the good and the wicked approach the visible altar on earth, but that the wicked are invisibly repulsed from the invisible altar in heaven, whilst the just alone approach it, and receive therefrom heavenly blessings.

tion of the faithful who with her ministers partake of the eucharistic banquet. As they partake more than others with the visible altar of earth, they ought also partake more than others with the invisible altar of heaven.

Though the *Holy Angel* may really signify Jesus Christ, and the word "hæc" designate the gifts on the altar, that is, the body and blood of the Saviour, Innocent III., fearing lest we might be dazzled by the greatness of the mystery, remarks: "Passing over the mysterious sense of the sublime expression, we may with greater simplicity and assurance understand these words thus: 'Jube hæc,' command that these things, that is, the vows, supplications, and prayers of the faithful, be carried by the hands of Thy Holy Angel, through the ministry of the blessed spirits, to Thy altar on high, in sight of Thy divine majesty, as the angel Raphael offered to God the prayers and tears of Tobias."

By uniting the two interpretations, the sense of the prayer would be: Vouchsafe, O Lord, to grant us that this pure and spotless Victim, this body and blood of Thy divine Son, which we are unworthy to offer Thee, may be presented to Thee by Thy Son Himself, so that in our sacrifice everything may be pleasing to Thee, and that there may be no obstacle to the abundant fruits we hope to receive from it. Grant, also, that the holy angels may offer Thy divine majesty our vows and prayers, ourselves, who have the honor to be offered in union with Jesus Christ as members of His mystical body, so that in receiving His natural body by holy communion we may be filled with every heavenly blessing and grace.

IV. " Memento etiam Domine."[1] The Church thinks of all. Her maternal solicitude extends to all her children, wherever they may be and whatever may be their state. Could she, at a moment when she can wipe away so many tears, forget those who weep in the flames of purgatory—temporarily banished from the presence of their God? She calls upon us to implore in their behalf the mercy of God, so that in her great family charity may link together all hearts, and, despite all diversities of condition, unify our interests. The Church on earth offers herself with Jesus Christ, unique Victim for all sin, and in union, also, with her members already glorified in heaven, to do, as it were, violence to God in behalf of her members suffering in purgatory, who are all the more to be pitied because they cannot of themselves either alleviate or abbreviate their sufferings. These souls are holy, it is true, since they left this world

---

[1] As Jesus Christ is present on the altar during this second " memento," the priest lowers his eyes, not only for the purpose of recollection, but in order to keep them fixed on the Blessed Sacrament whilst he mentally prays for the souls of the departed.

The Church has never offered the holy sacrifice without praying for the relief and deliverance of the souls in purgatory. " We pray," says St. Cyril of Jerusalem, " for all those who left this world in our communion, believing that their souls receive great relief from the prayers offered for them in the holy and dread sacrifice."

with the sign of faith; they had also practised good works, and now they "sleep the sleep of peace."[1] Yet they need to be purified still more before they can be admitted into that kingdom of glory where nothing defiled ever enters.

God Himself inspires us with this commiseration for those poor souls whom He paternally chastises, but tenderly loves. They are His children and our brethren. Can He turn a deaf ear to petitions so unselfish and charitable, especially when presented in the voice of the blood of His immolated Son? But what do we ask for those afflicted souls? Three things, which correspond to the three kinds of sufferings they endure: "locum refrigerii, lucis et pacis."

Imagine a sick man tormented by excessive thirst, consumed by devouring heat, with flaming eyes and open mouth, madly rushing to seize a delicious cup which cruelly eludes his eager grasp. You have an imperfect picture of the state of the soul deprived of God, whom she loves vehemently and towards whom she is drawn by an inexpressible desire. In heaven, says a learned Cardinal, there is an eternal circulation of love and of joy. Love produces joy, and joy inflames love. But

---

[1] "Dormiunt in somno pacis." Holy Writ represents the death of the just under the sweet image of *sleep*, because they are soon to awaken and arise to life everlasting. Hence the name *cemetery* or *dormitory* given to the burial-place of the faithful.

The Church calls their death a sleep of *peace*, not to signify that they are free from suffering, but because they left the world in the peace and friendship of the Lord.

in purgatory, on the contrary, love continually produces and augments pain. The more the soul desires, the more she suffers; and the more she suffers, the more she desires—dolorous desires, truly, because they are accompanied by privation—privation continuous, since the pain which it causes ever excites new desires. Besides, this is only one of the pains of purgatory—the pain of loss. To it must be added the pain of sense. Let us remember that the fire which rages there is probably the same as that of hell;[1] that those souls deprived of the beatific vision for which they were destined are immersed in an ocean of sorrow and darkness; that nothing on earth can be compared with the trouble and anguish in which they are involved by such a violent state, and we shall understand how much they need "refreshment, light, and peace." Though some of these suffering souls might be special objects of our compassionate remembrance, none should be excluded from our prayers. They are all members of our family, and dying in the peace of Christ entitles them to participation in the fruits of His immolation.[2]

V. "Nobis quoque peccatoribus." Finally, if

---

[1] "Eodem igne torquetur damnatus et purgatur electus."—S. Aug.

[2] "Orat sacerdos pro animabus omnibus quæ detinentur in purgatorio, ut verba illa indicant: 'Ipsis, Domine,' id est pro quibus præcipue oravit, 'et omnibus in Christi quiescentibus,' iis scilicet omnibus qui in purgatorio igne expiuntur. Pro omnibus autem postulat 'locum refrigerii,' quod respicit ignem illum quo cremantur; 'locum lucis,' quod spectat ad eas tenebras in quibus versantur; 'locum pacis,' quod ad illam pertinet mentis anxietatem qua conflictantur; quo triplici pœnarum

heaven, earth, and purgatory derive so many and such precious advantages from our august sacrifice; if God, to whom it is offered, receives therefrom so much glory; the faithful, living and departed, so much aid, consolation, and comfort, what abundant blessings may not we, who have the signal happiness of offering it, hope to receive? If we know how to turn it to profit, this rich talent should suffice to realize all our legitimate desires. Indeed, it seems that at the altar God says to us as formerly to His own people: Multiply your desires, let them be as limitless as you will, I will satisfy them. "Dilata os tuum, et implebo illud."[1]

We have just besought Almighty God, through the merits of Jesus Christ Our Lord—"per Christum Dominum nostrum"—to grant the suffering souls of purgatory the cessation of their torments and a participation in the joys of the Church triumphant. But may we not also desire for ourselves, may we not also beg for ourselves, that sojourn of eternal light, that beautiful heaven, that ravishing society of the elect, which we have asked for our brethren? "Nobis quoque." We are indeed unworthy of so great a favor, since we are sinners—"peccatoribus." Therefore, whilst we pray

genere miseræ illæ animæ à divina expiantur justitia."—Ben. XIV., c. xvii., n. 3.

"In Memento mortuorum orabis, primo pro consanguineis ; tum pro his qui tibi causa fuerunt alicujus crucis, seu molestiæ ; deinde pro benefactoribus ; postea pro aliquo specialiter commendato ; demum pro iis qui neminem habent cujus suffragiis nominatim juventur."—Bona, c. v.

[1] Ps. lxxx. 11.

for it, we strike our breast, and, with the humility of the Gospel publican, acknowledge our sinfulness. We have no hope, O Lord, but in Thy boundless and manifold mercies. "De multitudine miserationum tuarum sperantibus."

Whilst pronouncing the first words of that prayer, we elevate the voice a little, so that the faithful present may hear us, may unite and humble themselves with us, and with us obtain from the goodness of God some share —"partem aliquam donare digneris"—in the blessed lot of His faithful servants who have fought the good fight, and whose victory has been crowned with never-ending glory.

Before the Consecration we entered into communication with the saints—"communicantes"—in order to offer the universal sacrifice in the name of the universal Church. Here we again unite with them to earnestly demand the fruits we have a right to expect through the powerful efficacy of this sacrifice, that is, ultimate participation in their happiness. We name some martyrs of the various conditions which go to make up the Church: St. John the Baptist,[1] prophet; St. Stephen, deacon; St. Matthias, apostle; St. Barnabas, disciple; St.

[1] "Quidam opinantur quod Joannes ille non sit Baptista sed Apostolus; at immerito, quia nullus sanctorum qui in oratione 'Communicantes' fuerunt nominati, nec ipsa Virgo Maria, in hac iterum nominantur. Propterea genuinus sensus illorum verborum est : societatem donare digneris cum tuis sanctis apostolis et martyribus jam supra commemoratis, et insuper cum Joanne Baptista, Stephano, etc."—Tripl. Exposit.

Ignatius, bishop; St. Alexander, Pope; St. Marcellinus, priest; St. Peter, exorcist; SS. Perpetua and Felicitas, of the married state; St. Agatha, St. Lucy, St. Agnes, St. Cecily, and St. Anastasia, virgins,[1] to remind us that the road to heaven is open to all, that we may go that way if we choose, as did others who bore the weight of the same infirmities under which we groan. Only martyrs are expressly mentioned, because through the effusion of their blood in testimony of the truth they more perfectly represented the sacrifice of Jesus Christ.

[1] It may be remarked that all the saints named in this prayer, like those whose names are contained in the "Communicantes," suffered at Rome, or in places subject to the Roman patriarchate ; because, since Charlemagne, the whole West has adopted the Canon of the Mass such as it was then used in Rome.

It should be remembered that there were three catalogues or diptychs, all or part of the names on which were read out during the Canon of the Mass: the catalogue of the saints, that of the faithful and of the benefactors living, that of the faithful and of benefactors departed. "Asseres quidem erant diptyca, divisi in partes tres, ita sibi juncti ut complicari possent ; in quorum primum quorumdam sanctorum et præsertim B. Virginis, apostolorum et martyrum. In alterum fidelium nomina referebantur qui viverent et dignitate essent illustres, vel de Ecclesia essent optime meriti : inter eos Romanus Pontifex, patriarcha, episcopus et alii ex clero primi ponebantur ; deinde imperator, vivi principes, etc. Tertius asser habebat nomina defunctorum qui in fidelium communione essent mortui."—Ben. XIV., c. xiii., n. 26.

Formerly, the principal saints, whose names were written in the diptychs of the diocese, were in each diocesan church mentioned with the others on the general Canon, and this practice was continued till the eleventh century. Hence, as every one knows, came the word *canonize*. When with the common consent of a church they wished to proclaim any one a saint, the whole ceremony consisted in inscribing his name in the Canon of the Mass, that is, in the diptych of saints. Excommunication consisted in effacing the name of the sinner from the catalogue of the living. *Vide* Sacrifice de Jesus-Christ, vol. iii., p. 288.

But all the saints sacrificed themselves each in his own way. They all constituted but one and the same victim with Jesus Christ—" et omnibus sanctis tuis."

We ask not of Thee, O Lord, to grant us a reward equal to that of Thy holy apostles and martyrs, those magnanimous heroes of our faith, whose example, alas! we are far from imitating. We ask not to be raised to the rank they occupy in the place "where Thy glory dwelleth." That were too much above our deserts. We simply desire to participate in their happiness in whatever degree Thy justice may determine. Yet we beseech Thee to grant us a part and fellowship with those who, through the effusion of their blood, were so perfectly united to Thy sacrifice, as we ourselves desire like union by the destruction of our sins and the immolation of our whole selves. For to sit in Thy Kingdom, were it even in the last place, we must drink the chalice which Thou first didst drain; and if we are not called upon to sacrifice our life for love of Thee, we should at least live a life of sacrifice. Grant us, O Lord, a share in the happiness of all, not in consideration of our merits— for we have none, but by freely pardoning our offences. It is not a debt which we call upon Thy justice to pay, but a grace which we solicit from Thy mercy. " Non æstimator meriti, sed veniæ, quæsimus, largitor admitte."

The Church lets pass no occasion to impress on our souls this sentiment of profound humility which constitutes the Christian's strength, and with which Daniel, the prophet, was penetrated when he declared to God in the name of all the just of his day: "Neque enim in justificationibus nostris prosternimus preces ante faciem tuam, sed in miserationibus tuis multis."[1]

It may be readily observed that, if our mind is attentive and our heart well-disposed during the celebration of holy Mass, we may at any moment produce acts of the most excellent virtues. Now, they may be acts of religious fear and adoration, when, together with the angel charged to present Him our gifts, our homages and supplications, we bow down or genuflect before His Sovereign Majesty; now, acts of charity towards our neighbor by praying, by offering the holy sacrifice, for him as well as for ourselves; now, acts of humility when striking our breast as befits sinners; now, acts of confidence and love, casting ourselves into the arms of God, as children into the arms of their father, hoping all from His mercy, expecting all from His goodness— even the bliss of the saints, our brethren, who served Him so much better than we do.

How august this sacrifice! In it God is everything and acknowledged as the Author of all good. How insignificant man here becomes even in his own eyes, and how easily he makes a solemn avowal of his nothingness! How readily he confesses that he can do nothing in order of nature, or of grace, or of glory except through Jesus Christ, Source of all our blessings. "'Per quem

---

[1] Dan. ix. 18.

hæc omnia, Domine, semper bona' (panem scilicet et vinum) 'creas,' quia per ipsum omnia facta sunt; 'sanctificas,' cum in prima oblatione sacrificio sunt destinata; 'vivificas,' mediante transsubstantiatione; 'benedicis,' quia per hæc sacramenta copiosam acquirimus gratiam; 'et præstas nobis,' in cibum et redemptionem."[1]   The several signs of the cross which we make teach us that it is by His death and the application of its merits the Saviour sanctifies these gifts, and through the gifts ourselves—"sanctificas;" that it is by His death He animates them, changes them into His body and blood, and makes them for us fruitful germs of blessed and immortal life—"vivificas;" that it is by His death and its merits He makes of this Living Bread a sacrifice of praise to His Father and an inexhaustible source of graces and blessings to the whole Church—"benedicis;" and, finally, that after we have offered it to God as a sacrifice, He gives it to us as a sacrament to be the nourishment and support of our souls—"et præstas nobis."   We do not make the sign of the cross when we pronounce the word "creas," because all things were created by Jesus Christ as the Word and Wisdom of the Father, but not as incarnate and immolated. The blessing of creation is anterior to that of redemption; but the Church is instant in teaching that it is through the cross, or through Jesus Christ crucified—"per ipsum, cum ipso"—all glory is given to God, the

---

[1] Bona, c. v., n. 9.

Father Almighty, in the unity of the Holy Ghost, world without end.

Herein are clearly indicated the three degrees of our union with Jesus Christ, our Mediator, our Brother, the Head of a body whose members we are.

"Per ipsum." Through Him, through His mediation, we have access to God. He presents us to His Father, and on His account the Father hears us favorably, forgives and loves us.

"Cum ipso." He has—if I may dare so express it—made His and our interests identical. *With Him* we are children of God through the adoption which He merited for us, and, as a consequence, we are his co-heirs. As long as God sees us in fellowship with His Son, wearing His livery, clothed with His merits, uniting our thoughts to His thoughts, our affections to His affections, we are sure to please Him.

"In ipso." This is the last and most perfect degree of that union. Between Him and us there is but one and the same life—a divine life which flows from the Head to the members. He is in us, and we are in Him—"in ipso." Our nothingness, our sins, our miseries are, as it were, absorbed and disappear in the abyss of His greatness, His sovereign sanctity, His infinite perfections.

"Per ipsum." We follow Him as clients whose advocate and patron He is; "cum ipso," we are at His side as brothers of whom He is the eldest; "in ipso," we are in Him, we constitute but one same body, one same Christ, with Him.

At the words, "omnis honor et gloria," we elevate the Host and chalice a little,[1] as if to restore unto the hands of God this sacrifice which we owe to His liberality, and to proclaim that through Jesus Christ alone, with Jesus Christ, and in Jesus Christ do we pretend to acquit ourselves of our duties towards God as religion prescribes—adoration, praise, and thanksgiving. "Omnis honor et gloria." Oh, if these words and the simultaneous elevation of the sacred gifts were always accompanied with a lifting up of the soul and with sentiments of divine love issuing from our hearts, as heat escapes from a furnace, what delicious perfume, what odor of sweetness would ascend to God, not only from the Victim which is ever pleasing to Him, but also from the celebrant! How sad to think that, at the very moment when the divine Victim is being consumed in the flames of charity, the priest who beholds, touches, and prepares for a most intimate union with Him should be inattentive, lukewarm, and languid! "O amor et desiderium cordis! O hostia Deo Patri odorifera, cur non sum conversus totus in tuum amorem? Cur ego non sum illaqueatus et captus?

---

[1] Before the twelfth century this was the only elevation of the Host during Mass. But then it was more solemn than now. The priest raised the sacred species high enough to be seen and adored by the congregation.

Undique me circumdat amor tuus, et nescio quid sit amor."[1]

This is the end of the Canon, or unchangeable rule of the sacrifice of Jesus Christ.[2] We pronounce aloud the words which terminate it, "per omnia sæcula sæculorum," and which are connected with the preceding words—"omnis honor et gloria"—in order that the faithful, by answering "Amen," may assent to all that we said and asked in their name, whilst we prayed in a low voice. We will now treat of the third and last part of the holy sacrifice, that is, the Communion.

[1] Bonav., Stimul. Amor., p. 2, c. 2.
We fully indorse the sad reflections which an esteemed writer has made on this subject. " After what has been said regarding the profound sense of this last prayer of the Canon, what is to be thought of priests who, whilst holding in their hands the body of Jesus Christ, and pronouncing words worthy of so much respect, make some vague, indefinable motions of the hand over the sacred gifts, instead of well-defined signs of the cross, and flutter the sacred Host above and before the chalice in so disrespectful and precipitate a manner as to resemble a play or sleight-of-hand trick more than a mysterious action which terminates the most holy of all the prayers of the Church ?"—Sacrifice de Jesus-Christ, vol. iii., p. 415.

[2] "Orationem dominicalem sunt qui putant partem Canonis conficere ; verior est tamen contraria opinio, quæ statuit Canonem ad sextam orationem terminari . . . Canon igitur expleto, in hac missæ parte sacerdos propius se ad communionem parat."—Ben. XIV., c. xix., n. 1.

CHAPTER VI.

AFTER the Consecration, which put the adorable Victim into our hands, our first duty was to offer it to God as a magnificent homage to His sovereignty, to His justice, His goodness, and all His infinite perfections; and next to apply the fruits of our sacrifice to all those for whom and by whom it was offered. Not, however, for the sole purpose of being our Victim did Christ deliver Himself to us. When He gave us His body and blood He said, "manducate et bibite;" just as He had foretold when promising this mystery of incomprehensible love: "Caro mea vere est cibus et sanguis meus vere est potus."[1] Henceforth, all our thoughts shall be concentrated on the sacred banquet, to which the Church invites all her children, and the honors of which she desires her ministers to do, when they have first partaken for themselves. "O sacrum convivium!" The Lord's Prayer begins the proximate preparation therefor.

I. The celebrant recites it aloud and in the name of all the faithful. During the silence which accompanied

[1] John vi. 56.

the tremendous action of consecration, each one offered his particular prayers in secret communication with his God. The " Pater" is the common prayer of all. God loves in His children harmony of sentiments and union of hearts. Here, then, we have the whole family in concert addressing their Father.

The priest says, " Oremus"—Let us pray. Thereby the attention of the assembly is aroused, and fervor receives a new impulse. In every heart there is one predominant desire—that of praying well.

In order better to dispose the people thereto, the priest exhorts them in a short preface to consider attentively what they are going to do. He endeavors to form them to the conception of an exalted and adequate idea of the admirable supplication which they are to address to the Lord. In fact, this prayer establishes between us an intercourse so intimate and glorious, " Pater noster;" it so fully comprehends all that we may ask; everything in it breathes such a filial confidence; in a word, it is so perfect, so far above our intelligence, that before we presume to say it we feel the need of recalling to mind the salutary commandment we received concerning it, and the adorable Master who taught us to pray in this manner. " Præceptis salutaribus moniti, et divina institutione formati, audemus dicere."

What treasures of light, what transcendent truth, what sweetness in this sublime supplication offered to the

Lord and dictated by the Lord Himself! Faith discovers therein almost all religion summed up in a few words. A God infinitely above us, since He is in heaven, yet, out of His pure bounty, holding such intimate relations with us as to authorize us to call Him Our Father; a God whose name is holy and terrible, but also sweet to whomsoever reverently invokes and glorifies it; a God whose power extends over all creation and calls even nothingness into being; but who, in exercising His power over us, makes us find our happiness in obedience to His laws; a God who, shrouded in His own glory, seemed accessible to angels only, but who deigns to associate us with them in serving Him, and who desires us to imitate on earth the loving docility with which they accomplish His holy will in heaven.

The three first petitions regard God immediately—His greatness, His goodness, His sovereign authority; the four others concern man—his wants, his miseries, his duties. We ask for our *bread*, that is, for everything necessary for our twofold life. That of the body should concern us less than that of the soul. O my God! give its *bread* to this poor soul that has no hope but in Thee. Give it whatever it needs to live before Thee a full and perfect life. Permit it not to fall into a languor which might lead unto death—"ne nos inducas in tentationem." If it is sad, comfort it with Thy promises; if weak, strengthen it with Thy all-powerful aid; if it thirsts after holiness and justice, fill it with Thy grace;

but, above all, never refuse it that *Living Bread* which came down from heaven, and which alone is worth all Thy other gifts. We ask for bread only, that is, for the one thing necessary. We ask it for the day only, because we have no real wants but those of the present day. "Da nobis hodie." Insolvent, hopeless debtors that we are, what would become of us if Thou shouldst treat us according to Thy inexorable justice? But Thou hast promised to show mercy to the merciful, to remit unto those who would remit unto others. Therefore, O merciful God, forgive our trespasses, for we forget, we forgive from our hearts all our neighbors' trespasses against us. "Dimitte nobis debita nostra, sicut et nos dimittimus debitoribus nostris." May Thy paternal eye be ever on us in our dangers. If we waver, sustain us; if we fall, raise us up.

Now, at what moment do we address to heaven this divine prayer, whose every petition—independently of the grace which it solicits for us—contains an instructive lesson, and deposits a pious sentiment in our heart? Powerful as it is in itself, it derives new efficacy from the circumstances under which we offer it to the Lord. The moment could not be more favorable. We have just offered to the Lord a Victim which infinitely pleases Him—a Victim which, by transmitting its merits to us, gives us a right to be always heard. God sees His Son immolated for His glory as well as for our salvation, and that Son's state of profound humiliation on the altar is in itself a touching prayer. How, then, could He turn a deaf ear to our petitions for the sanctification of His name, the reign of His grace over us to prepare us for His heavenly kingdom, the accomplishment of His adorable will, all the succor we need, the remission of our sins, peace with our brethren, victory over our passions and over the spirits of darkness, and, finally, deliverance from all that is evil—"libera nos a malo"?

II. The priest, as organ and mediator for the faithful, says the Lord's Prayer aloud so as to be heard by the people, who in turn, to proclaim their participation in his supplications, repeat aloud the last petition, which is also as the vivid expression of their sorrows and sufferings—"sed libera nos a malo." They feel the weight of their miseries; they bewail them and ask to be delivered from them. "Amen," replies the priest—so be it, O my God. In my name, and in that of all my brethren, I beseech Thee, deliver us from evil. Deliver us from all evils. "Libera nos quæsumus Domine ab omnibus malis."

It would seem that this dolorous cry—"libera nos"— escaping from every heart, has excited the compassion of him who ought to bear the infirmities of his people. The priest, then, takes up this plaintive supplication which so touched his heart, and adds thereto another which is but its continuation. O Lord, he continues, since Thou art so good a Father, deliver us from all evils, past, present, and to come.   The many sins which we have certainly committed, but for which our repentance is unfortunately so doubtful; the sad consequences of them which still abide with us; the punishments which they entail—these are the evils which cause us anxiety for the past—"præteritis."   Our wicked inclinations, many exterior enemies ever bent upon our destruction and whose assaults we must parry, our own cowardice, lukewarmness, and languor are but a part of the evils which afflict us in the present—"præsentibus." Finally, in the future we foresee new tempests, new dangers, new obstacles to our happiness—"et futuris."

Yet we can sum up all these evils in one—sin, because it entails all the others,[1] especially divisions and troubles.   O Lord, deliver us from sin!   Deliver us from it in such a manner that being freed from its cruel and shameful tyranny, we may enjoy the liberty of Thy children.   Give us peace—"da propitius pacem"—such peace as will preserve us from all baneful agitations; from agitations of the heart, when we have been unfaithful to Thy law; agitations of the mind, when we are enveloped in darkness, and the light of faith has grown dim; agitations in families through dissensions

---

[1] "Nulla" nobis "nocebit adversitas, si nulla" nobis "dominetur iniquitas," oratio super populum, Feria sexta post cineres.

"In oratione : Libera nos, sacerdos Dominum precatur ut nos liberet ab omnibus malis præteritis, quæ sunt peccata ; præsentibus, quæ sunt variæ tentationes quibus ad peccatum impellimur ; futuris, quæ sunt pœnæ peccatis debitæ, sine temporales sint, sine æternæ."—Ben. XIV., ibid., n. 7.

and discords, in states by internecine wars.   But, above all, give peace to Thy Church when the spirit of error and of schism strives to foment trouble therein, and to excite the children to rebellion against their mother. Deliver us from sin and we shall be sheltered from these deplorable disturbances.   "Ut a peccato simus semper liberi, et ab omni perturbatione securi."   In this prayer which we address to Thee, O Lord, we regard only Thy mercy; in it alone we put our trust—"ope misericordiæ tuæ adjuti"—and in the infinite merits of Jesus Christ, Thy Son, Our Lord.   "Per eumdem Dominum nostrum Jesum Christum."

In order the more surely to obtain this twofold grace of lasting innocence and peace, we beseech the Blessed Virgin Mary, Mother of Jesus and our own, to present and second our supplications—"intercedente beata et gloriosa semper Virgine Dei genetrice Maria, . . . et omnibus sanctis."

From this moment until the Communion, we shall persist in demanding almost exclusively the blessing of peace.   We wish it to the faithful when, holding in our hand a particle of the sacred Host which has reconciled heaven with the earth, and making three times over the chalice, with the body of Jesus Christ, the sign of that cross [1]—sacred instrument of veritable peace, we say to

---

[1] In these three signs of the cross we may see three kinds of peace which Jesus Christ bestows upon men, or the three kinds of persons to whom He grants peace.

First, His blessed soul, by going down into limbo, brought the peace

them: "Pax Domini sit semper vobiscum"—May the peace of the Lord be and abide always with you. The people, on their part, reciprocate our good wishes towards them: "Et cum spiritu tuo." O priest! O faithful! above all, ask for that delightful peace which we shall enjoy when, after the struggles of this life are over, we shall enter into the joy of the Lord and shall live of His eternal, blissful life. "Hæc commixtio et consecratio[1]

of eternal beatitude to all the saints who expected His coming. This same peace He gives to His elect, whom He glorifies and will glorify in heaven.

Secondly, He gives peace to the just, who, still on earth, live in the grace and friendship of God.

Thirdly, He offers it to sinners by inviting them to repentance and pardon.

We may also understand these three signs of the cross to signify the triple peace which He merited for us by His death—" Pax gratiæ cum Deo, pax interna in corde cum seipso, et pax fraterna cum proximis nostris."—Tripl. Exposit.

[1] The words, "consecration of the body and blood," signify the body and blood consecrated. St. Laurence said to Pope St. Sixtus: " Prove the minister to whom thou hast confided the consecration of the blood of the Lord;" instead of—" to whom thou hast confided the consecrated blood of Jesus Christ"—as it was the deacon who distributed it at communion. (De Offic., l. i., c. 41.)

Other interpreters explain these words somewhat differently. They observe that the mixture in question here is connected with the Consecration; that it symbolizes the resurrection of the Saviour, as the Consecration represents His death ; and that these two mysteries complete the work of our redemption, according to the declaration of St. Paul: " Traditus est propter delicta nostra, et resurrexit propter justificationem nostram."—Rom. iv. 25. In their opinion it amounts to saying : " May the glorious resurrection, represented by this mixture which I make and the divine death figured by the Consecration already performed, be to us, who are going to receive the body and blood of Christ, the principle and pledge of eternal life ; and as they have merited for us the joys and glories of heaven, may they put us in blissful possession thereof."

16

corporis et sanguinis Domini nostri Jesu Christi, fiat accipientibus nobis in vitam æternam." This part of the liturgy is full of mystery; let us stop a moment and consider it.

Whilst pronouncing the words, "per eumdem Dominum," etc., which are the conclusion of the prayer "Libera nos," the priest breaks the Host and thereby represents, in a more sensible manner than hitherto, the separation between the soul and body of Jesus Christ— that is, His death. It is tantamount to saying: Grant us peace, O Lord. Preserve us from sin and from all trouble which might be its cause or effect. This grace we ask through the merits of Jesus Christ, Thy Son, dying on the cross; through the sufferings He endured at the last awful moment when He expired.

But if the death of Christ is well represented by the breaking of the Host, as it had already been symbolized, especially by the separate consecration of the two species; nothing so striking represents His Resurrection as the union of these species, when the priest puts the particle of the sacred Host into the precious blood in the chalice.

Thus far the Church in her ceremonies has clearly expressed only the Passion of the Son of God. Now, as the Sacrament of the Altar is the renewal and the representation together with the reality of all the mysteries by which He worked out our salvation, His Resurrection and His glorious return to His Father on the day of His Ascension, must necessarily be represented as well as His death. The Church does it at this part of the holy sacrifice. For the species of wine, by penetrating that of the bread, admirably expresses the reunion of the body and blood of Christ at the Resurrection, and the divine glory wherewith His humanity was entirely penetrated.[1] Wherefore, do we say whilst

[1] "Actio hæc particulum hostiæ immittendi in calicem est plena mysterii. In missa usque ad hanc de qua loquimur partem, Jesu Christi passio et mors representatur per consecrationem corporis et sanguinis separatim factam, vi consecrationis sub speciem panis corpore Christi, et sub vini speciem sanguine subeunte ; et quamvis separatio hæc tantammodo mystica sit, neque enim seipsa corpus est sine sanguine, nec sanguis vicissim sine corpore, tamen mystica hoc separatione corporis à sanguine, et sanguis à corpore, expresse Christi passio et mors nobis representatur. Reliquum erat ut gloriosa exprimeretur Christi resurrectio ; neque id concinnius fieri poterat, quam si hostiæ particula immitteretur in calicem, atque ita corpus iterum conjungeretur in sanguine."—Ben. XIV., ibid., n. 17.

Lecourtier develops this explanation as follows : " It is certain, as the Council of Trent declares, that by virtue of the sacramental words pronounced over the bread, it alone becomes the body of Christ, and that by virtue of the sacramental words pronounced over the chalice, the wine alone is changed into His blood. Yet it is of faith that this separation is only mystical, and that in reality the body is not without the blood, nor the blood without the body, since the body of Jesus Christ is a living and glorified body. Now, it is important that in the sacrifice the death of Christ and His subsequent glorious life should be represented, because the Mass is the renewal and continuation of the sacrifice He offered on the cross and which He, though living in heaven, still continues to offer. The separate consecration of the bread into His body and of the wine into His blood is the sign of His death. The breaking of the sacred Host is another very expressive representation thereof. The body and blood reunited are symbolical of the life He resumed by His Resurrection ; for the species of wine penetrating the species of bread vividly represents to us that the body and blood are reunited as in a living body. Though sacred liturgy does not remind us of the Resurrection till the prayer of the post-communion, and repre-

commingling the body and blood of Christ, " Pax Domini sit semper vobiscum"—thus recalling the peace salutation which He addressed to His apostles, when He appeared to them after His resurrection. It was indeed by this mystery that He established on a sure and permanent basis our peace and reconciliation with God. "He was delivered up for our sins," says St. Paul, "and rose again for our justification." [1] In dying He combated for us, and in rising from the dead He overcame and triumphed for us. Henceforth, there shall be no combat without victory for him who fights under the standard of Christ; and every victory shall be the pledge of eternal peace to him who always adheres to Christ. [2]

Another mystery symbolized by this mixture is the union and incorporation about to take place between Jesus Christ and man through sacramental communion. Therein the soul is wholly penetrated by Jesus, His spirit and life, in the same manner as the species of bread is penetrated by the species of wine. And as

sents to us the hearts of the priest and of the faithful who communicate as the grave in which the body of Christ is deposited, it is fitting that this representation of a living and risen God should precede the communion, since Christians receive at Mass the body of Jesus Christ both immolated and glorified, which communicates to them the grace to die to sin and to lead a new life according to justice and holiness."—Expl. de la Messe, p. 481.   [1] Rom. iv. 25.

[2] In the first ages of Christianity the Church permitted priests to break off two particles of the Host, and send one in sign of communion to whomsoever distance or danger of persecution prevented assisting at the celebration of the holy mysteries. In this sign of communion and

this transitory union of Christ with us in the eucharistic communion is destined to produce another more excellent and lasting, this mixture, in the third place, represents the union of the whole body of the elect with God, through the perfect eternal communion of the Head with the members—after which God shall be all in all—" ut sit Deus omnia in omnibus."[1]   Then, at last, the elect shall be fully consecrated and perfected, body and soul, in the unity and peace of God.   Such are the wonderful effects of sacramental communion which the Church desires for her children when she prays : " May this mixture and consecration of the body and blood of our Lord Jesus Christ be to us who receive it effectual to life everlasting.   Amen."

III. " Agnus Dei."   All the prayers we have said from the beginning of the Canon to the present were addressed to God the Father through His Son, whom we have all along considered as Victim and in a state of death.   Those which follow till the Communion are addressed to Jesus Christ, whom we henceforth consider

charity the faithful found the source of great confidence.   It encouraged the timorous, strengthened the weak, filled the just with fervor.   They fancied they heard the Pontiff, or rather Jesus Christ Himself, say to them :   " May the peace of the Lord be, and always abide, with you." " Pax Domini sit semper vobiscum." " May it comfort you in times of terror when your lives or your goods are in danger.   Let not your hearts be troubled.   You believe in Me.   I am with you, and the exchange which I propose to you of life eternal for a perishable one, and of never-fading glory for contemptible riches, should sustain your hearts in submission and patience."—Cochin. Prônes., l. v., p. 361.

[1] I. Cor. xv. 28.

as risen from the grave, since by the mixture and union of the two sacramental species we represented the mystery of His resurrection.   As we are soon to be united to Him by eucharistic communion, we consider Him as full of life and clothed with the glory of His resurrection, to which He unites the goodness and meekness of His mortal life.

Humbly bowed down, and with eyes tenderly intent on the holy Victim, we say to Him in language full of respect, confidence, and love : " Lamb of God, who takest away the sins of the world, have mercy on us."   Whilst saying the last words, we strike our breasts; for we consider that our sins and the sorrow which we have for them are the most powerful motives of commiseration we could offer Jesus Christ, who died for sinners.

" Agnus Dei."   To Jesus we give the meek name of Lamb.   It was by that name He desired to be called by the prophets and by His precursor.   " Ego quasi Agnus, qui portatur ad victimam."[1]   " Ecce Agnus Dei."[2] Thou art both the Lamb and the Pastor.   We are the sheep of Thy fold, and the ravishing wolf always goeth about the flock seeking to devour them.   Save us from that cruel enemy who hates us all the more for Thy blessings.   O Lamb who hast redeemed the sheep!— " Agnus redemit oves"—O Paschal Lamb, whose blood is not applied exteriorly to the doors of our dwellings as was that of the paschal lamb of old to the door-posts of

[1] Jer. xi. 19.   [2] John i. 29.

the Hebrews to signify their deliverance from temporal servitude, but courses through our veins and hearts to carry salvation to our inner self, mark our souls with the seal of redemption, and deliver us from eternal slavery! True Lamb of God, alone capable of appeasing His anger, Victim of the Lord, excelling all others, have mercy on us!

"Qui tollis peccata mundi." Yes, Thou takest away, takest on Thyself, effacest, not only our sins, but also those of the whole world. One tear of Thine would suffice to expiate the crimes of a thousand worlds, if they existed, and behold, Thou wilt have us dispose of all Thy tears and of all Thy blood! How, then, can we be other than confident when we say, "miserere nobis"?

For the glory of Thy name, to insure the fruits of Thy death, to manifest the efficacy of Thy precious blood, that Thy enemy and ours may not boast of having prevailed against us, that he may not contemptuously ask us where is our God, where are the evidences of God's love for us—*have mercy on us;* on us who are Thy people, Thy members, Thy brethren, the co-heirs of Thy kingdom, the children of Thy Church. Show us now that compassion which made Thee ardently desire the baptism of Thy blood, and drink so patiently the chalice of Thy suffering and humiliations.

"Dona nobis pacem." Peace again! Do the treasures of God's mercy contain anything more desirable? Though we have already so often solicited it, we ask for it with renewed fervor in the first of the three beautiful prayers which immediately precede communion and which are the proximate preparation therefor. We are about to become the living temples of Him who dwelleth not with agitation and trouble—"non in commotione Dominus,"[1]—but who loveth to abide in the soul basking in the sunshine of calm and peace—"in pace locus ejus."[2]

IV. "Domine Jesu Christe." In order to become one body and one spirit with the Saviour and with all His members, we need peace with God, with our neighbor and ourselves. This great blessing we fervently solicit, holding our hands joined on the altar and our eyes constantly fixed on the adorable sacrament. We remind Our Lord Jesus Christ that when on the eve of His death He bestowed upon His apostles the most affecting proofs of His love, He said to them: "Pacem relinquo vobis, pacem meam do vobis." It is precisely what we ask for ourselves and for the Church. We ask not merely for the peace which *He leaves*, and which the apostles already enjoyed, since they were clean— "vos mundi estis;" but we require also the peace which *He gives*,[3] His peace—"pacem meam"—a peace which is

---

[1] III. Reg. xix. 11.   [2] Ps. lxxv. 3.

[3] St. Augustine distinguishes between these two kinds of peace. The former is the beginning of interior tranquillity which comes from a good conscience and from the joy which it procures. This peace does not exempt us from having to combat still, or from being obliged often to say to God, "Forgive us our trespasses." The latter excludes all

lasting and unalterable, which He Himself enjoys, and which He destines for His elect.   This peace is consequently one according to His will—"secundum voluntatem tuam"—since He wishes to reunite us all with Him in the bosom of His Father, there to participate in His eternal happiness.

But how can I promise myself, or how can I hope to obtain for my brethren, a peace so desirable, since I am a sinner?   O Jesus, consider not, I beseech Thee, the multitude and enormity of my sins!   "Ne respicias peccata mea."   Or if the very object of Thy sacrifice necessarily reminds Thee of the iniquities which Thou camest down from heaven to expiate, remember that these iniquities are ours no longer, since Thou hast condescended to take them on Thyself—"Iniquitates eorum ipse portabit."[1]   Remember that Thou hast given us the right to say to Thy Father, "Ne respicias."   Turn away Thine eyes, O Lord!   Regard not our disobedience, our ingratitude, our repeated violations of Thy law.   Remember only Thy well-beloved Son who made Himself obedient unto death, even the death of the cross.   Remember also Thy Church, who by her faith appropriates to herself the merits of her divine Spouse to clothe her children therewith, and hide them from the eyes of Thy justice.   "Ne respicias peccata mea, sed

trouble.   It is eternal peace, the peace enjoyed by the Saviour Himself, and which on that account He calls His peace—"pacem meam."

[1] Is. liii. 11.

fidem ecclesiæ tuæ." Vouchsafe to give her peace with Thee—"pacificare." Vouchsafe to establish and maintain union between all her members—"adunare."

V. In this first prayer we continued our supplications for the Church and for ourselves. We besought for ourselves the pardon of our sins, and for the Church peace with God and union of hearts between all her children. In the two prayers which follow we beg for ourselves only. The moment of communion is at hand. Every other interest dwindles into comparative insignificance before the immense importance of well performing so solemn and sacred an action. These two prayers are the proximate preparation for it. They have been adopted by the Church, inspired by the Spirit of God, who is her guide, and are the best preparatory prayers that can be offered for a worthy communion.[1]

First prayer.—" Domine Jesu Christe, Fili Dei vivi." Lord Jesus Christ, Son of the living God, who by Thy death hast given life to the world, I this moment behold, and am about to incorporate myself with, Thy

[1] In the early ages of the Church no special prayer was designated as a preparation for communion, because those which preceded seemed sufficient. But many devout priests, seized with reverence and fear at the approach of the dread moment of communion, were prompted to beg anew for the remission of their sins, and for the salutary fruits of a fervent communion. Of the many prayers which such sentiments inspired and introduced into this part of the Mass, the Church has chosen two which for six or seven hundred years have been regarded as handed down by a sacred tradition.

This point has not been disputed by any liturgical writer. " Scribit Micrologus, non ex antiqua summorum pontificum institutione tres in

sacred humanity, the instrument of our redemption. Through this same divine body and this adorable blood, listen to my humble prayer—"per hoc sacrosanctum corpus et sanguinem tuum." Deliver me from all my iniquities and from all evils—"ab omnibus iniquitatibus meis et universis malis." And since Thy goodness excites my confidence, grant me another grace which will be the consummation of all Thy graces: eternize the union I am about to contract with Thee, by attaching me so firmly to Thy law that nothing can ever separate me from Thy love. "Fac me tuis semper inhærere mandatis, et à te numquam separari permittas." But as this prayer is of the utmost importance both in itself and because of the time in which we offer it, we must fully explain the sentiments it expresses.

The first of these is admiration. "Domine, Jesu Christe!" "The first disposition of a heart which desires to love," says Bossuet, "is a certain admiration for the object which is already loved from the very fact that it is desired." This is the first wound which divine love inflicts on the heart. All that the soul does,

missa recitari orationes ante communionem, sed piorum et religiosorum hominum traditione. Micrologo assentiuntur Bellarminus, Azorius, Gavantus, etc.—Ben. XIV., c. xx., n. 20. Lebrun, p. 479, Le Sacrifice de Jesus-Christ, t. iii., p. 477. Origines et raison de la liturgie Catholique, p. 395.—"Ex his liquet has orationes, non simul et semel, sed sensim fuisse inductas in liturgiam Romanam. . . . Unde inferri potest quod lex de nihil addendo vel minuendo in celebratione missarum, non ità stricte ligaret ut jam post decretum Pii V. Ex ore religiosorum paulatim transierunt in libros liturgicos, donec tandem sub seculo xiii. partem fecerint liturgiæ nostræ."—Romsée, t. iv., p. 329.

whilst under the influence of this blessed admiration, is to let itself be attracted by the charms of Jesus and to respond to the attraction by only an exclamation of admiration: O Jesus! O Jesus! O Jesus!

"Fili Dei vivi." The Church wishes us to consider our Redeemer in the aspect of Son of God as the most proper to interest heaven in our behalf, and the best calculated to excite respect and confidence in our own souls. *Son of God*, equal to the Father in goodness, in power, in wisdom; eternal as the Father though born in time of the Immaculate Virgin, and every day undergoing a new nativity through the ministry of His priests; immense as the Father, though wholly contained in the Host before us; glorious as the Father, though veiled under lowly appearances and reduced to the most abject state for our sake. *Son of the living God*, of God who is the principle of life and communicates it to His Son, with full power to communicate it to whomsoever He pleases. "Sicut Pater habet vitam in semetipso, sic dedit et Filio habere vitam in semetipso. Et Filius quos vult vivificat." [1] O my soul, let us go to this fountain of life to sate the thirst for happiness which devours us!

"Ex voluntate Patris." Though the Son of God is in all things equal to the Father, He made Himself for our sake the humblest and most obedient of servants. His Father's will determined the time, the place, the

[1] John v. 26, 21.

circumstances of the Incarnation. The same divine will regulated all His journeys, inspired all His discourses, commanded all His miracles, as well as the kind, the duration of His sufferings and humiliations. The actual oblation of Himself on the altar, the gift He will soon offer us of His body for our food and of His blood for our drink, are the effect of His submission to the will of the Father as well as of His wonderful love for us. And as the will of God—who is not only Christ's Father, but ours, also—is ever merciful and inspired by charity towards us, the Holy Ghost, the Spirit of love, could not fail to take an active part in the mysteries of our redemption—"cooperante Spiritu Sancto."

By His divine operation, He formed the body of our Victim in the womb of the most pure Virgin, and He every day reproduces it through our ministry. He is the flame which consumes our holocaust, and the sacrifice which we offer on the altar perpetuates that of the cross on which Jesus Christ by His death gave life to the world—"per mortem tuam mundum vivificasti." What a prodigy is this! A God dies, and mankind, which was dead, arises as it were from the grave! O Death, where, then, is thy victory? And lest thou shouldst forget thy defeat, every day and on thousands of altars, the same sacrifice is renewed and produces the same results. Every day, in virtue of this sacrifice, arise again to life thousands of unfortunate victims of sin and of the death which it brings to the soul. "God willeth not the death of the sinner, but rather that he should be converted and live,"[1] and this will of God is being continually realized on the altar. The Son, ever obedient, always immolates Himself; the Holy Ghost, ever sanctifying, always applies to men the fruits of this continually renewed immolation.

At the altar, surely, I may, I must have confidence, especially as I am to be incorporated with the Author of my salvation! Have I not the most powerful motive to cry out, Deliver me, O Lord?—" Libera me." Deliver me from all my iniquities! Pardon, blot out more and more the sins which I have committed! Repair the injury they have done me, and save me from the misfortune of ever falling back into them! This favor I crave, O my God, by these sacred pledges of Thy excessive love, by this body and blood which I now behold and adore! Protect me from the evil inclinations which tempt me to violate Thy law. What shall I fear, what can injure me, when I possess my Almighty Saviour in my bosom? "Ab omnibus iniquitatibus meis, et universis malis." O Jesus, is it not time that I should henceforth and forever adhere to Thy divine precepts? Thy grace can make the observance of them so easy and agreeable! Engrave them indelibly upon my heart. Grant that I may esteem them above every other good—even life itself. " Fac me tuis semper inhærere mandatis." All Thy commandments are

---

[1] Ezech. xxxiii. 11.

summed up in this one—to love Thee. Grant me, O Lord, to do what Thou commandest. Am I not going to draw from the perennial fountain of divine love? Is not Thy heart the furnace whence issued the flames which fired the hearts of all the saints, of all apostolic men? In a moment that Sacred Heart shall be my treasure. Grant me to love Thee, as Thou first hast loved me; if necessary, even to sacrifice, to immolate myself for Thee. Grant me also to love my neighbor as Thou commandest, since that is the essence of Thy law. It is true, then, that I am going to be united to Thee, O Lord! "He that eateth my flesh and drinketh my blood abideth in Me and I in him."[1] How it fills my heart with the liveliest joy! O holy, O ineffable union! O my God, make it eternal! Unite me to Thee with the bonds of a love stronger than death! Enable me to despise hell and its fury, the world and its allurements, affliction and its bitterness, honors the highest, humiliations the deepest, and all created things that would separate me from Thee. "Et a te nunquam separari permittas."

Second Prayer.—"Perceptio corporis," etc. When we meditate on the different prayers which dispose the celebrant for holy communion, we perceive that the Church desires sincere humility to be the chief foundation of his dispositions. A moment ago she inspired him with fear, lest his sins might be an obstacle to the

[1] John vi. 57.

mercies of God upon him and his people—" ne respicias peccata mea."   In the preceding prayer, she directed that, penetrated with a lively sense of his weakness, he should beseech Jesus Christ never to permit him to be separated from Him.   Now she reminds him in more energetic language of his unworthiness.   She obliges him to reflect seriously on it.   What is he going to do? Is it not presumptuous on his part to dare receive the body of His Lord and God?   "Quod ego indignus sumere præsumo."   Should he not be terrified at the thought that he may find his judgment and condemnation in the most holy of all actions unless he performs it with due holiness?   O Lord, permit it not!   "Non mihi proveniat in judicium et condemnationem." When I consider Thy goodness towards me and the prodigal love wherewith Thou givest Thyself to me, I take confidence.   I come to Thee, and I hope to derive immense advantages from the visit Thou condescendest to make me.   "Pro tua pietate prosit mihi."   Thou shalt be my refuge when alarmed at the thought of Thy Father's justice—"ad tutamentum."   Thou shalt be my rampart and defence against all my untiring enemies, interior and exterior.   I am every day buffeted by new temptations, afflicted by repeated infidelities; every day also Thou wilt come in Thy sacrament to renew my strength, to heal my wounds and weaknesses. Thy adorable flesh shall be to me both a preservative and a remedy.   It will impart light and firmness to my soul, and my very bones will cry out in their own language—Lord, who is like unto Thee? Thy body will produce in mine a principle of strength and purity which will enable me to triumph over concupiscence. " Ad tutamentum mentis et corporis, et ad medelam percipiendam." If, from necessary intercourse with the world, I contract some defilement; if, from constantly hearing the language of its passions, my own are aroused; if I should unfortunately participate in its malice and corruption—I will go promptly and cleanse my soul in the blood of the Lamb and in my tears; and Thou, O charitable Physician, wilt come in the sacrament of Thy love, to complete the healing of my soul!—"ad medelam." If oppressed by toil or sadness; if greatly discouraged at the fruitlessness of my labors in Thy vineyard; whatever may be my sufferings or sorrows— in Thee shall I find the remedy—"ad medelam percipiendam."

17

CHAPTER VII.

I. EVERYTHING is ready for the consummation of the sacrifice and for partaking of the heavenly banquet, the Victim is immolated, the table is laid, Jesus Christ is impatient to give Himself to those whom He loves. "Desiderio desideravi hoc pascha manducare vobiscum."[1] The priest falls on his knees and profoundly adores Him who vouchsafes to become his food. But encouraged by the infinite condescension of a God who so tenderly inclines to him, he rises up full of saintly ardor and exclaims with the eagerness of a famished person—I will take the bread which alone can satiate all my desires, the heavenly bread which gives a foretaste of blessedness to those who receive it—"Panem cœlestem accipiam"—and in the joy of my soul I will call upon the name of the Lord—"et nomen Domini invocabo." These last words, according to St. Augustine, may be considered as an expression of ardent desires. For to invoke the Lord is to invite Him to come in us to be our strength, our light, and our life. "Quid est invocare, nisi in se vocare." We may

[1] Luke xxii. 15.

also give them another meaning.   To invoke the Lord is to adore and thank Him—to render Him, in a word, all the duties of religion.   That I can never do more perfectly that when I am become one with Christ Himself.   But the body of the Saviour is already in the hands of His minister, whence it will pass into his heart, uniting itself to his being, as bread to the body which it sustains.   With this thought a new feeling of terror seizes the soul of even the most fervent priest.   What is he to do?   What wonder if fear and confidence succeed each other with such rapidity when he is about to perform an action which, in the judgment of the Church, may be the cause of death or the source of life.   " Mors est malis, vita bonis."   Therefore will I humble myself, dearest Lord!   I will acknowledge my utter unworthiness, and in the language of the centurion whose faith Thou didst commend, I shall say to Thee whilst I penitently strike my breast, " Domine, non sum dignus." Who am I that Thou shouldst come to dwell in my house?   What can there be in common between the Lord of lords and a vile creature, between the Holy of holies and a sinner?   It is a God whom I am about to receive.   The heavens cannot contain Him, and the earth with its vast expanse is but His footstool.   He is God, and He Himself declares to me that He is a jealous God, that He abominates iniquity, that the justices of His people are in His sight like soiled linen.   How, then, can I dare to appear before Him?   " Domine, non sum dignus." Were I to take counsel of my unworthiness only I should say to Thee as did the prince of the apostles—" Exi a me, quia homo peccator sum."[1] But I consider also Thy goodness, Thy desire, Thy express intention to give me Thyself. I have recourse to Thy mercy, that abyss in which all our miseries are swallowed up. I reflect on Thy almighty power, which spoke and all things sprang into existence. I beseech Thee to speak that word which produces all it expresses. Say that word of clemency which filled with consolation the soul of the penitent Magdalen, that word of compassionating regard which so powerfully moved and changed the heart of Peter. Pronounce that consoling word, and all my iniquities shall be healed. " Sed tantum dic verbo, et sanabitur anima mea."[2]

At last the moment has come. With an act of loving, boundless confidence the priest abandons himself unreservedly to a Friend so generous and faithful. He casts himself into the arms and reclines upon the bosom of the Lord Jesus Christ. He delivers his soul into the keeping of that sacred body immolated for his salvation. May that adorable body be to it a mysterious

---

[1] Luke v. 8.

[2] Origen, cited by Benedict XIV., c. xxi, n. 1, mentions the practice which always existed of repeating these words before communion : " Quando sanctum cibum illudque incorruptum accipis epulum, quando vitæ pane et poculo frueris, manducas et bibis corpus et sanguinem Domini ; tunc Dominus sub tectum ingreditur. Et tu ergo humilias teipsum, imitare hunc centurionem et dicito : Domine, non sum dignus ut intres sub tectum meum."

salt to preserve it from all corruption! May it impress upon his soul the seal of a glorious immortality! "Corpus Domini nostri Jesu Christi custodiat animam meam in vitam æternam. Amen." Then he plunges into that ocean of tenderness and love, and the holy union is consummated.[1]

The good priest immediately shuts himself up with Jesus Christ in the sanctuary of his soul. He beholds angels prostrate around him, celebrating his happiness, participating in his joy. He hears them say to him: "Exulta et lauda, habitatio Sion, quia magnus in medio tui Sanctus Israel."[2] Reverently he gathers up the particles of the sacred Host, and already full of gratitude—"quid retribuam Domino"—he superadds another motive therefor by taking the chalice of salvation—"calicem salutaris accipiam." Behold the heart of God! It loves to enrich us with its gifts and to receive as acknowledgment of its favors the stretching out of our hand to receive more. "Calicem salutaris accipiam, et

---

[1] "Then the priest, all his desires now accomplished, unites himself heart to heart with his God, and during the brief time required to take up the sacred species is absorbed in meditation and in interior conversation with God—conversing as friend with friend. But these precious moments must be of short duration, for the Mass is essentially an *action* made up of something to be done or said.

"Therefore, as if reluctantly, he comes out of that ecstasy of admiration and love. He lifts up that head which reposed so lovingly on the breast of Jesus in this other cenacle. He opens his eyes as if surprised to find himself still on earth, and his heart, like an overflowing fountain, pours forth a stream of gratitude. In the burning accents of the prophet he exclaims: 'What shall I render to the Lord for all He has rendered unto me?'"—M. Lecourtier.

[2] Is. xii. 6.

nomen Domini invocabo." Yes, I will again call upon Him. I will invite Him in me. I will invoke the Lord by singing His praises—"laudans invocabo Dominum." He shall be Himself the homage of my gratitude. He shall be my Protector and my Saviour. With Him I shall be sheltered from all the attacks of my enemies—"et ab inimicis meis salvus ero." With what lively faith, hope, and love the fervent priest drinks the blood of Jesus Christ! He fancies he sees it flowing from the sacred wounds! It pervades his whole being. Irrigated by this heavenly dew, bring forth fruits, O my soul, and let thy fruits remain! May this divine blood heal thy wounds, render thee henceforth invulnerable, and preserve thee unto life everlasting. "Sanguis Domini nostri Jesu Christi custodiat animam meam in vitam æternam."

II. After so great a blessing, thanksgiving cannot begin too soon or be continued too long. The pious priest begins to acquit himself of that duty before leaving the altar. He enters into the spirit of the Church by devoutly reciting the prayers which end the Mass, and whose principal object is to keep the soul intimately united with Christ and filled with an ardent desire to profit by His visit.

"Quod ore sumpsimus, Domine, pura mente capiamus." To excite our vigilance during these precious moments the Church distinguishes between communion of the tongue and communion of the soul—"ore . . .

mente." Alas, there is too much reason for the distinction. He alone, says St. Augustine, is really sated at the table of the Lord, who communicates spiritually by imitating Him, as he communicates corporally by eating His flesh. "Ille satuartur qui imitatur." Now, there are unfortunately a great number of Christians, and of priests too, who receive Jesus Christ on their tongue and yet are not spiritually nourished of Him. They communicate with His body, but not, or but little, with His spirit and affections. Yet it is by partaking of His spirit, His truth, His holiness—in a word, by intercommunion of souls—"mente"—that the heavenly gifts bestowed on us in time may heal our souls of all evil in this world and be available for eternity. "Et de munere temporali fiat nobis remedium sempiternum."

When we possess the Lord Jesus Christ, only one thing more is desirable—to possess Him forever, to keep Him in the inmost recesses of our souls. That is what we ask for in the prayer—"Corpus tuum, Domine, quod sumpsi, et sanguis quem potavi, adhæreat visceribus meis." The food which we eat must be retained in the stomach to be digested and to generate fluids which, distributing themselves through all parts of the body, impart vigor and vitality. The same is to be said of the body and blood of Christ, which really are our spiritual sustenance only in so far as they penetrate to the inmost parts of our souls to entertain and strengthen therein the life of grace through transfusion of the spirit of the Redeemer. " Qui manducat me, et ipse vivet propter me." [1]

Having purified and covered the chalice, the priest, still absorbed in silent adoration of Him who dwells in his heart, goes to the Epistle side of the altar, and reads the antiphon called Communion, because it is generally taken from a psalm which was formerly sung during the communion of the faithful.[2] St. Cyril of Jerusalem relates that in his day the church at the communion resounded with the chant of the Psalmist's words: " Gustate et videte quoniam suavis est Dominus." Then come the last prayers, by which the Church makes us offer God public thanksgiving before doing it privately. When these prayers are said, the missal is closed, and Mass is over. The priest now says to the faithful, " Ite, missa est." Go in peace. The mysteries are accomplished. You have been associated in the oblation of the sacrifice of Jesus Christ. You have been sprinkled with His precious blood. To this they reply—we have therefore a great duty to perform—" Deo gratias." This prayer is so short, yet so comprehensive, so per-

---

[1] John vi. 58.

[2] " Antiphona idcirco communio dicitur, quia, ut observat Gavantus, canebatur interea dum populo eucharistia distribuebatur. Hæc missæ pais, in qua communio et postcommunio recitantur, olim vocabatur gratiarum actio, ut ait Rupertus de divinis officiis, l. ii., c. 18; 'Cantus quem communionem dicimus, quem post cibum salutarem canimus, gratiarum actio est ;' quod multo antea dixerat Augustinus, Epist. 149 : 'Participato tanto sacramento, gratiarum actio concludit.' "—Ben. XIV., c. xxiv, n. 2.

fect, so conformable to the proper sentiments of a soul which has just received from heaven an inestimable favor, that the Mass could not be more happily ended. "Hoc nec dici brevius, nec audivi lætius, nec intelligi grandius, nec agi fructuosius potest." [1]   It was thus that the disciples, after receiving the last blessing of Jesus Christ ascending into heaven, returned full of joy to Jerusalem, praising and thanking the Lord.

In the first Christian ages, after the celebrant had thus dismissed the congregation, he kissed the altar and immediately withdrew.   But since the eleventh century, the piety of the priests and of the faithful has led to the introduction of three additions, namely, the prayer, " Placeat," the blessing, and the reading of the Gospel according to St. John.

This prayer—" Placeat tibi, Sancta Trinitas"—which is well calculated to enkindle devotion in the priest's heart, is somewhat of a recapitulation of all that he said to God during the great action which he has just consummated, a *résumé* of all the holy aspirations which he has produced and which he now fervently renews.   It is a supreme effort by which he supplicates the Most Holy Trinity to accept agreeably the sacrifice offered through his unworthy ministry, to receive it as an ardor of sweetness in the sight of His divine majesty, and to communicate the salutary effects thereof to him and to all those for whom it was offered.   " Mihique et omnibus pro

---

[1] St. Augustine.

quibus illud obtuli, sit, te miserante, propitiabile." This petition, as all others, he offers through the mediation of Jesus Christ—"per Christum Dominum nostrum."[1]

The faithful, however, remain in the holy place, though they have been told to retire and return to their ordinary occupations. O priest, understand their desires. They will not leave till you have blessed them. Once more, then, press your lips to the altar as if to draw grace from the Source of all graces, and with heart, and hands, and lips distilling benedictions, bless them in the name of God Almighty the Father, the Son, and the Holy Ghost. Bless the just and the sinful. Bless your own people, bless all men, and they shall be blessed by Him from whom all blessings flow, and who now abides in you. "Benedicat vos omnipotens Deus."

You are now about to leave the altar at which you have performed such astounding things and received such immense blessings. But before you go, contemplate a moment the Eternal Word in the bosom of the Father and in yours. Meditate on the words, "In ipso vita erat;" and also on these others, "Lux in tenebris lucet." Tremble lest it be said of you: "Tenebræ eum non comprehenderunt." Deplore, but have no

---

[1] "Ad orationem: Placeat tibi, rursum offeres sacrificium purissima intentione, et cum omni desiderio triumphantis ac militantis Ecclesiæ, prout ipsa verba sonant. Deinde populo benedicens uberem à Deo omnibus fidelibus benedictionem, omniumque cœlestium gratiarum abundantiam ex animo precaberis, ut nunc in via, postea in patria, sanctissimam Trinitatem omnes glorificent."—Bona, c. v.

share in, the blindness of a world through which He passed doing good, but which knew Him not. " In mundo erat, . . . et mundus eum non cognovit. In propria venit, et sui eum non receperunt." Adore the greatness of the Word who was from the beginning, who was with God, who was God, and through whom all things were made. But fail not to adore the unspeakable humiliations which love impelled Him to undergo. The Word made flesh dwelleth within you. He is full of grace and truth; full of truth to enlighten you, full of grace to sanctify you and enable you to sanctify your brethren. Abide with Him in your heart, and when you come down from the holy mountain, as your eyes beheld the Saviour of men, keep them closed to earthly things. To Him alone now listen, for now is the time to taste and see how sweet the Lord is, and by your gratitude insure your happiness.

CHAPTER VIII.

St. John the Evangelist says of the traitor Judas: "Cum accepissit buccellam, exivit continuo. Erat autem nox."[1] There are some unfortunate priests who aim at following his example. Hardly have they come down from the altar and entered the vestry, than they hastily pull off the sacred vestments, throwing them away as carelessly as they would worthless garments. They are ready at once to converse with any person who will speak to them, except to Jesus Christ, who would have so many things to say to them, and so much good to do them. After a short prayer, which they inattentively repeat, they escape hurriedly from the church, as prisoners from their prison. Carrying in their heart their adorable Guest, they go at once and busy themselves with profane affairs, or engage in frivolous conversations, completely forgetting Him, as the dead man is forgotten in his grave. "Oblivioni datus sum, tanquam mortuus a corde."[2] Where is our faith? What deplorable blindness! Let us reflect on the following words of St. John Chrysostom:

[1] John xiii. 30. [2] Ps. xxx. 13.

"Audiamus et sacerdotes et subditi: ante gratiarum actionem resilire domumque redire, non mediocrem contemptum habet. . . . Vultis dicam cujusnam opus perficiant illi, qui, cœna absoluta, gratiarum actionis hymnos non offerunt? Durum fortasse videbitur quod sum dicturus, sed necesse est tamen ut ob plerorumque negligentiam dicatur. Quando ultimæ cœnæ communicavit Judas nocte illa postrema, cæteris omnibus recumbentibus, ipse se proripiens excessit; illum imitantur et isti, qui ante gratiarum actionem discedunt. Hæc igitur mente versemur, hæc apud nos cogitemus, et huic propositam sceleri damnationem reformidemus. Ipse suam tibi carnem largitur; at tu, ne verbis quidem remuneraris, neque pro eis quæ accepisti gratias agis. Atqui dum hoc corporeo vesceris cibo, post mensam ad orationem te convertis; dum vero spiritualis, et omnem creaturam tum visibilem, tum invisibilem superantis, fis particeps, tametsi homo sis et vilis naturæ, non expectas ut gratias agas et verbis et factis? Quid est aliud quam extremo supplicio sese obnoxium reddere?"—Homil. de Bapt. Christi, in fine.

Before receiving the heavenly gift, which contains all good, you had exhorted the faithful to gratitude—"gratias agamus Domino Deo nostro." You had proclaimed before the world that "it is truly meet and just, right and salutary, that we should always, and in all places, give thanks to God," and now you yourself are the first to fail in that duty at the very moment it becomes a most urgent obligation. You have hardly come out of the cloud wherewith the majesty of the God of Israel surrounded you; a ray of His glory seems to linger still upon your brow, and you already employ in idle conversation that tongue empurpled by His sacred blood! It is but a moment since you declared three times in succession, and apparently with feelings of the profoundest conviction, that you were not worthy to become the dwelling of a God so holy—" Domine, non sum dignus." But no sooner does He, with a condescension which throws the Church into astonishment and consternation, give Himself to you—" O res mirabilis! manducat Dominum"—than you think of Him no more, you turn your back upon Him! You have nothing to say to Him, no homage to offer Him; no grace to ask of Him! Are you not afraid that you may change His love into wrath, when you are so grievously wanting in reverence to the first and most dreadful of all majesties?

Let us once more cite for you the learned and pious Cardinal Bona:

" Quia finis honorum debet esse gratiarum actio, ab altari post sacrum discessurus canticum incipis trium puerorum, quo ad gratias pro tanto beneficio Deo agendas omnes creaturas invitas. Ipsum itaque recitabis dum pergis in sacristiam, dum te sacris vestibus exius, omni possibili devotione atque ardentissimo affectu Deum benedicendi et superexaltandi propter ipsius infinitam bonitatem. Quo absoluto in persona Ecclesiæ, quæ illo concludi sacrificium præcipit, in locum te recipies ab omni strepitu et distractione remotum, in quo clauso ostio cordis tui, cæterisque cogitationibus exclusis, soli Deo vacabis, nec ab eo recedas donec benedixerit tibi. . . . Nullum certe pietatis sensum habere convincitur, qui non libenter cum Deo manet. Nec valent prætextus negotiorum vel studii, quibus se tepidi excusant : quod enim gravius et utilius negotium quam de animæ salute cum Deo tractare? Vel quid possunt docens libri quod non Deus præsens melius doceat?" [1]

St. Liguori recommends that after Mass at least half an hour be spent in thanksgiving. If on account of our occupations, not to say our tepidity, we should find that too long, the saintly theologian would accept a quarter of an hour's entertainment with Jesus Christ. We can, however, easily conclude from his mode of expression that he greatly regrets his inability to exact more. "*A quarter of an hour,*" he says, "*is very little, too little.*" [2]

It is much to be desired that no priest should find it necessary to have recourse to any prescribed method to pass holily and profitably the time of after-Mass thanksgiving. We should avail ourselves of it only when the Spirit of God says nothing to our hearts. To contemplate, to listen to Jesus Christ, to hold sweet converse with Him—therein consists the *proximate* thanksgiving. That which may be termed the *remote* consists in con-

---

[1] Bona, c. vi.   [2] Selva, ii. part, inst. 1.

serving the remembrance of what transpired between Our Saviour and ourselves during the time of Holy Mass, in recalling the sentiments with which He inspired us and the promises which we made Him.

The real presence of Jesus Christ in us when we have consummated the sacrifice by the reception of holy communion; the state of immolation and annihilation in which He therein abides, and which is so well calculated to move the heart of His Father and profoundly touch ourselves; the generous and merciful dispositions of His loving heart towards us especially at that favorable moment,—all conspire in rendering the first instants after the celebration of the holy mysteries the most precious time of our life. We know, according to St. Teresa, that there is no other time when we can so easily enrich our soul with virtues, or so rapidly advance to a high degree of perfection.

Here imagination is not brought into requisition. There is no need to endeavor to fancy what does not exist. Not only the divinity of Jesus Christ is present in your bosom, but His humanity also, both abiding there as long as the substances of bread and wine would remain had they not been destroyed by the miracle of transubstantiation. Before Mass, you adored the Son of God in heaven and in the holy tabernacle; during Mass, you adored Him on the altar and in your hands; now, you possess Him in your heart. " In me manet et ego in eo." What a blessed moment when the priest can apply his lips to the open side of his Redeemer and satiate the thirst of his soul at the Source of all graces and of all consolations ! What a happiness is yours !

It is the opinion of many profound theologians that the acts of virtue produced immediately after communion have a special merit and value—because emanating from a soul substantially united to the Son of God. During these precious moments, all that you do through the inspiration of Him who becomes the Life of your life, the Soul of your soul, Christ does in union with you. You adore, and He adores. You return thanks, and He returns thanks. Your acts, like His, with which they are united, are in a manner theandric, or divinely human. Hence it is that the Lord regards you then with such complacency.

Let everything else vanish, let everything else be silent in the presence of a Majesty so great, yet so amiable. "Dominus in templo sancto suo; sileat a facie ejus omnis terra." [1] Entering with Jesus into the sanctuary of your heart, abide with Him as long as you can in silent reverence and admiration. In His adorable presence, suspend all the operations of your soul. Allow His divine substance to penetrate and transform all your powers, to substitute His divine life for your human life. "Qui manducat me, . . . vivet propter me." [2] There is no manner of adoration more befitting His sovereign greatness, or more becoming our nothingness,

---

[1] Habac. ii. 20. [2] John vi. 58.

18

than this momentary cessation of all action, of all thought, and, to a certain extent, of all personal life in His presence. Thereby, we best acknowledge that He is far above all that we can think or say of Him; and thereby, too, we render to His infinite Being the homage of our own. Then pour forth your soul in hymns of joy and thanksgiving. Let all your senses, all your faculties, say to Jesus, " Lord, who is like to Thee? " [1] in goodness, in condescendence, in inventions of love? Adore, give thanks, love, offer, pray.

I.—*Adore* Jesus Christ dwelling in your soul. Adore Him the more profoundly that He is the more humiliated for love of you. Summon into His divine presence all the powers of your soul and all the senses of your body, and say to them : " Venite, adoremus, et procidamus, . . . ante Dominum" [2]—just like a man who, preparing to receive a prince, would invite his relatives and neighbors to come and honor his royal guest. Offer your adoration, gratitude, and love in union with those of the Holy Virgin when she received the same Son of God in her virginal womb, to those of the angels now prostrate around you as around the tabernacle. Invite the whole heavenly hierarchy to adore Him in you and with you. " Adorate eum, omnes angeli ejus." [3]

II.—*Thank Him* all the more lovingly, the less you deserve so precious a favor. What more can you desire? Jesus Christ is yours! He is all yours. The

[1] Ps. xxxiv. 10.   [2] Ps. xciv. 6.   [3] Ps. xcvi. 7.

Father gave Him to you. He gave Himself to you without restriction and without reserve. He gave His humanity, His divinity, all that He has, all that He is. "Dilexit me, et tradidit semetipsum pro me." [1] For me He gave Himself, not only to be my Ransom, but also my Consoler, my Support, my Physician, my Guide, my Advocate, my Saviour. "Benedic, anima mea, Domino; et omnia quæ intra me sunt nomini sancto ejus." [2] O heavens!—"intra me!" What do I behold within my breast at this blessed moment? "Gratias Deo super inenarrabili dono ejus." [3] "Te Deum laudamus. . . . Magnificat anima mea Dominum."

III.—*Love Him.* What shall you ever do with your heart if you bestow it not on Him who employs means so powerful to attract and possess it? Will you resist all the attractions of His goodness? It was His love which induced Him to give Himself to you. Let love also impel you to give yourself to Him. Yes, give yourself up unreservedly to such a magnanimous Friend, abandon yourself entirely to His care, cast all your solicitude on Him, confide to Him all your interests both for time and eternity, have no anxiety but to please Him, suffering Him to act and live in you as in a dwelling which He owns, of which He is the absolute Master, and wherein He alone shall be obeyed and loved. Say with St. Philip Neri, adoring Him on the altar: "Behold my Love! Behold my Love! Behold

---

[1] Gal. ii. 20.   [2] Ps. cii. 1.   [3] II. Cor. ix. 15.

my only Love!" Say to him with St. Paulin: "Let the rich possess their riches, let the kings possess their kingdoms; as for me, Thou alone, O my Jesus, art my riches and my kingdom!" [1]

IV.—*Offer*, first yourself to Jesus Christ, and then Jesus to His Father. The following prayer of St. Ignatius will answer admirably for the first offering, especially if you add to it whatever your ardent love for God will suggest: "Suscipe, Domine, universam meam libertatem; accipe memoriam, intellectum atque voluntatem omnem. Quidquid habeo vel possideo, mihi largitus es; id tibi totum restituo, ac tuæ prorsus voluntati trado gubernandum. Amorem tui solum cum gratia tua mihi dones, et dives sum satis, nec aliud quidquam ultra posco."

"Lord of all things, gentlest Ruler of those who love Thee, accept the offering of my whole being. Accept my memory, and engrave thereon the ineffaceable remembrance of all Thy benefits; accept my intelligence, and let its most cherished occupation be to think of Thee and meditate on Thy law; accept my will, which I forever subject to Thine. All that I am, all that I have, interiorly, exteriorly, Thou hast bestowed on me. To Thee I offer them all. Direct my thoughts, purify all my intentions, regulate all my actions. Dispose of me according to Thy good will and pleasure, and the inter-

---

[1] Sibi habeant divitias suas divites, regna sua reges, mihi Christus gloria et regnum est.

ests of Thy glory. Let health and sickness, successes and reverses, joys and sorrows, life and death—all be disposed according to Thy divine will. I am no longer mine. I am Thine. Henceforth my sole ambition shall be to be able to say with Thy Apostle: " Vivit in me Christus. . . . Mihi vivere Christus est." Only give me Thy love and grace. Grant that I may love Thee and be loved by Thee. Root out of my heart whatever may be displeasing to Thee, and implant therein whatever may be agreeable in Thy sight. I know well that, to be pleasing to Thee, I must continually increase in Thy love. That is therefore my heart's highest desire. Grant me that one grace, and I shall be sufficiently rich, and shall have nothing more to ask of Thee."

But, since Jesus is yours, take advantage of your privilege and avail yourself of His divine presence in you according to the designs of God and His own. Make use of His inexhaustible treasures to pay all your debts, and offer all His merits to His Father for that intention. Are you not in duty bound to adore His greatness, to acknowledge His favors, to satisfy His justice? Were you deprived of His presence, you might justly be troubled at the thought of your extreme indigence; but when you possess Him, you are rich indeed. He has been given you to supplement your shortcomings. What have you, then, to fear? Your homages, adorations, thanksgivings, considered as coming from yourself, are totally disproportionate to the majesty of the

Almighty. But contemplate within yourself the Son of God, consubstantial with the Father and equal to Him in all things. There He is, as it were, annihilated, and, by His voluntary annihilation, He most perfectly honors God's greatness. A God disappearing in the presence of God, placing Himself, so to say, under His feet, renders Him infinite honor, an honor as great as God is great. That is precisely what Jesus Christ does within you at this moment. Unite yourself to this adoring God and to all the acts of religion which He offers His Father. By virtue of such union you appropriate to yourself the acts of the Son of God, and the Almighty is glorified by you as much as He deserves.

Are you disturbed at the recollection of your sins, alarmed at the imperfection of your penitence, terrified at the thought of the dread judgment? Offer to God the penance which Christ, your Redeemer, performed for your sake from the moment of His Incarnation to that in which He expired on the cross. Offer up the sorrows of His heart, the sadness of His soul, the sufferings of His body, the holiness of His life, the priceless value of all His actions, to atone for the sinfulness and the unprofitableness of yours. Offer His humility to atone for your pride, His ardent charity for your tepidity, the infinite merits of His death for the innumerable sins of your life.

We know that, according to St. Paul, " it is a dreadful thing to fall into the hands of the living God," [1] that is, for those who appear before Him with empty hands, and souls defiled by sin. But it must be a blissful thing to fall into His hands in company with our divine Lord, intimately united to Him, hating sin as He hates it, offering our heart's contrition in unison with the sorrows of His life, and the whole of our penance with the infinite treasure of His.

Finally, implore the complacent regard of the Father, not only on the past sacrifice of His adorable Son, but also to that which He still offers Him within you. You may not be aware of it, yet it is none the less true, that after your communion angels surround you and contemplate in silent adoration the unspeakable prodigies which are being operated within you. By the alteration which the species of bread and wine undergo, Jesus Christ gradually loses His sacramental being in your bosom. On your heart, therefore, as upon a living altar, He sacrifices Himself at this moment for the glory of His Father, the welfare of the world in general and your own in particular. By this actual sacrifice, which has no other witnesses than the holy angels, He continues to render infinite glory to God, and to procure for mankind the immense merits of His bloody immolation on Calvary. Unite yourself to this God Sacrificer and Sacrificed; for on your heart, as on the altar, or on the cross, Jesus is ever both Priest and Victim. Praise,

[1] Heb. x. 31.

glorify, thank God through Jesus Christ and with Jesus Christ, who is the praise, the glory, the delight, the eternal joy of the Father.

V.—*Pray.* All power has been given you in heaven and on earth, and that power you exercise through prayer. To you may be applied at this moment what the holy doctors have said of Mary's unlimited power— "Omni potentia supplex." Meditate, according to the method of St. Ignatius which we have already explained, on the touching words of Christ after the Last Supper: "Pater, venit hora, clarifica Filium tuum, ut Filius tuus clarificet te." [1] How admirable is this prayer on the tongue of the priest who has just celebrated and whose lips are yet empurpled with the blood of Jesus Christ! It contains all that will insure the success of our petitions and all that we ought to pray for.

"Pater." First of all consider attentively and try to relish the full import of that blessed word. Let it be, like the sweet name of Jesus, honey to your mouth, a melody to your ears, a joy to your heart. Repeat it with respectful familiarity, and fear not lest you dwell too long upon it. "Pater!" Yes, my Father, for such Thou art, O Lord! That I feel and understand better now than ever before. Who would dare to question my right to call Thee by this sweet name? The duty of a father is to nourish his children, and what can I say of the divine nourishment Thou hast just given me?

[1] John xvii. 1.

"Pater." Thou art indeed my Father, since I am one with Thy well-beloved Son. His blood circulates in my veins. His heart beats against mine. When Thou beholdest me, Thou beholdest Him in me. "In me manet et ego in eo." O my God, how I love to think that Thou hast for me the affection of a father! What wilt Thou not do for the happiness of Thy child!

"Venit hora." The favorable hour has come for the accomplishment of all Thy designs on me and on the souls Thou hast confided to my care. Can it be possible for Thee, O best of fathers, to refuse me any favor? "Pater, venit hora." Now or never Thou wilt grant me all the graces, all the blessings, I desire or ought to desire. Now or never Thou wilt lavish them upon me beyond all I can wish or hope for; because Thy Son, who is in me and prays with me and for me, merits infinitely more than I can desire or demand. The hour has come—"venit hora"—to attach myself to Thee in eternal bonds. The hour has come for Thee to bless my labors, to save my people.

O my God, my Father! hearest Thou not Thy Son who, present in my heart, with me and in my behalf, addresses to Thee the prayer which He offered on the eve of His death: "Pater Sancte, serva eos in nomine tuo, quos dedisti mihi." [1] He thus pleaded in behalf of all those who through the preaching of His ministers would believe in Him, and especially in be-

[1] John xvii. 11.

half of the ministers themselves. "Sanctify them, O Father," said He to Thee, but with that veritable sanctity which consists in imitating Me and living My life. "Sanctifica eas in veritate." Behold what need they have of great and solid virtues for the important mission which I give them, for the sublime office which I confide to them. I promised to be always with them, aiding them by My personal co-operation, till the consummation of the world. My word is not a vain word, for it is Thine. It is truth itself. "Sermo tuus veritas est." I sacrifice Myself to secure their sanctification and to let My sanctity flow into them together with my blood. "Pro eis ego sanctifico [1] meipsum, ut sint et ipsi sanctificati." Thus will they accomplish the views of My mercy in the sanctification of souls and enable Me to reward themselves according to the full measure of My desires. For I will, O My Father, that where I am they also may be whom Thou hast given Me, that they may see the glory I enjoy, that they may share in My happiness and in My glory. "Pater, quos dedisti mihi, volo ut ubi sum ego et illi sint mecum, ut videant claritatem meam quam dedisti mihi." [2]

Hear, then, His prayer. O Father of Jesus and mine ! It is a God, Thy own Son and Victim, immolated this very moment upon the altar of my heart, who addresses

---

[1] In the two texts : "Sanctifica eas," etc., "Ego sanctifico meipsum," the word "sanctificare" has two different significations. In the first it means to make holy ; in the second, "to immolate one's self as a holy victim."   [2] John xvii. 24.

it to Thee in behalf of all Thy priests, but particularly of him towards whom He manifests so much love by giving Himself to him. Does not this Adorable Suppliant deserve to be heard, especially when to His prayers He adds His tears, His blood, the wounds which cover His body, and the abysmal humiliations which He undergoes?

"Clarifica Filium tuum." He sought to promote Thy glory, be Thou solicitous for His. In His other mysteries Thou glorifiest Him in proportion to His humiliations and annihilations. In His incarnation Thou gavest Him, in the chaste womb of Mary, the purest, the holiest, the most august temple this world could offer. At His birth in the stable Thou didst send shepherds, kings, and angels to adore Him. Wilt Thou suffer Him to remain unhonored in His eucharistic state—the humblest, because the most hidden, of all His mysteries? O my God, glorify Him by imparting to me the virtues, the perfections of His incomparable Mother at the moment of the incarnation, since the incarnation has now been renewed, and the Word made flesh dwelleth within me! Grant me the faith, the fervor, the simplicity of the adoring shepherds, for my heart is as rich as the stable of Bethlehem at the moment of my Saviour's birth. Grant me the courage, the fidelity of the Wise Men prostrate before His crib, since my heart is the manger wherein He reposes. May I also enjoy the happiness and delight of the angels, as I am more con-

cerned than they in the new nativity which He has undergone on the altar and in my heart.   " Clarifica Filium
tuum."

But what further glory wilt Thou, O Lord, give Him
at this moment?   Grant Him that glory which He most
desires.   The glory of a charitable rich man is to help
the indigent; the glory of a physician is to heal the
sick, the infirm; the glory of a Saviour is to save.
Grant Him that glory.   Suffer it not to be said that
Thy Son Jesus came to visit a sick man whom He
healed not, a blind man to whom He gave not sight, a
man in the most abject misery whom He succored not,
a repenting sinner casting himself into the arms of His
mercy whom He did not sanctify and save.   O my God,
give Him the glory of having at last transformed or van-
quished all my bad passions, eradicated all my vices,
repaired all my misfortunes, adorned my soul with all
priestly virtues which will render me less unworthy to
represent Him and to gain souls for Him.

"Ut Filius tuus clarificet te."   O my Father, if
Thou wilt grant me what I ask—and how canst Thou refuse anything to the merits and prayers of Thy Son?—
Thou shalt then be glorified, not indeed by me, for of
myself I can procure no glory to Thy Majesty; but
Thou shalt be glorified by Thy Son present in me.   He
shall inflame my heart with holy desires, inspire my
mind with holy thoughts, move my lips to praise and
bless Thee, and infinitely enhance the value of all my

works. He shall be on my lips when I declare Thy law, and what light and force will He not impart to my words! How powerful and efficacious Thy sacred Word will be when proclaimed more by Jesus Christ than by myself! He shall be with me in all my ministrations and in all my labors, to make them fruitful by the abundant blessings He will draw down upon them. Sinners will be converted, tepid souls will be reawakened to earnestness and zeal, the just will advance in the ways of divine perfection, and to Thee shall be given all the glory.

After you have thus spoken to God and have offered Him the rich present you received from Him, after you have made your acts of adoration, thanksgiving, and supplication, you may, if you feel so disposed, request your kind, compassionate Redeemer to consider the various infirmities of your soul, showing Him each of your interior faculties in succession with its peculiar weaknesses; just as is done in a general hospital, where the physician is led successively from one patient to another. Finally, when you have made all your requests, both in your own behalf as well as for those for whom you are particularly bound to pray, repose lovingly upon His adorable heart, uniting yourself intimately with Him in all that He does in you for the glory of His Father. Cease to act yourself in order to let Him alone act in you. Cease to live your own life in order to live of His life.

As, according to the author of the " Imitation," it is useful to vary methods in exercises of piety in order to avoid routine and to excite devotion, we may sometimes use the formula of thanksgiving which we find in one of the works of Father Bernardine de Picquigny.

To understand it well we should distinguish three different ways of glorifying God, which elevate us, as it were, by degrees to the plenitude of His infinite Being, and enable us to render Him all the honor He deserves. The first is founded on the natural order, and consists in inviting all creatures to praise and bless the Lord. Thus the Royal Prophet often ascribes life and sentiment to inanimate creatures in order to make them partake of his joy and gratitude. The second is in the order of grace and of the hypostatic union. We glorify God in this manner when in union with Jesus Christ we praise God in Him, with Him, and through Him, offering to the Sovereign Lord the glory which Christ and all the saints, the head of the Church and all her members, render Him in heaven and on earth. The third is in the divine order. It consists in uniting ourselves to God by perfect charity in and with Jesus Christ; taking delight in the contemplation of His infinite Being, the centre and source of all beauty, of all greatness, of all good, of all perfection; rejoicing because of the superabundant happiness and glory inherent in His nature which exalt Him infinitely beyond the praise of every created being, and, under the influence of this joy, offering Him the glory which in Himself and from Himself He possesses eternally.

The first of these three kinds of homage which we render to God is finite, as are also the creatures that praise and bless Him. The second is infinite, as far as it relates to the divine nature of Jesus Christ; but as to His human nature, which, though the most perfect of all creatures, yet continues to be a creature, this homage does not adequately honor the greatness of God, which is in every respect infinite. As to the third method of glorifying the divine Majesty, as it consists in offering God to God, it is perfectly worthy of Him. God alone, in fact, can bestow on Himself adequate praise, hence we terminate all our magnificent canticles to His honor by repeating the doxology, which sums up and completes them all: "Gloria Patri. . . . Sicut erat," etc. May God be glorified with that glory which was His before all creation, which He now enjoys, and which He will possess eternally independently of every creature. We thereby declare that all the praises of men and of angels fall infinitely short of adequately honoring a majesty so great, and that to have it worthily praised and glorified it must be its own praise, benediction, and glory. Having premised these explanations, we now come to the practical deductions.

As soon as you have read the Gospel of St. John— "In principio"—and heard the last "Deo gratias" of the faithful, reminding you of the important duty of returning thanks, descend the altar steps with the air of one coming down from heaven who has seen God and carries God in his bosom. Suffer nothing to distract your mind from the contemplation of the profound mysteries which are being accomplished in you. Be blind, deaf, dumb, to all that concerns creatures. Be to all things earthly as one deprived of senses. When, if not at this moment, shall you belong wholly to God and to the things of eternity? Whilst returning to the vestry and disrobing with becoming gravity and recollection, glorify God according to the first manner we have indicated, inviting the heavens, the earth, the sea, and all that they contain, also all angels and men, nay, all irrational and inanimate things, to participate in your joy, to praise and bless the Lord with you. For this purpose the Church directs us to recite the canticle of the three young Hebrews—"Benedicite, omnia opera Domini, Domino." To a lukewarm soul their language is but an empty sound; but how feelingly it expresses the sentiments of the fervid soul which after communion relishes the gift of God and breaks forth in holy transports of gratitude and love! If we do not experience such feelings of heavenly joy and exultation, let us therefore humble ourselves all the more, and let us not forget that the prayers which the Church recommends or commands are intended not only to express, but also to excite, sentiments of devotion. Having thus glorified the Lord according to the first method, proceed to the second.

Contemplate the Son of God really and substantially present in you. Unite yourself heart and affection to Him in all that He does in the temple of your soul. Christ is there not only in a state of humiliation, but also in that of annihilation, in order the more perfectly to adore the Father. Annihilate yourself also in the presence of this God annihilated in you and for you. Adore this adoring God. The more He humbles Himself for your sake, the more does He deserve that you should endeavor to compensate for His humiliations by your adorations. "Adoro te devote, latens Deitas. Jesu, quem velatum nunc aspicio. Ave verum." When you have received holy communion, it may most truly be said of Jesus that He is "totus in usus nostros expensus." Appropriate to yourself Christ whole and entire with all His greatness, humiliations, merits, thoughts, affections, His present state of immolation in you, that you may be able in Him and through Him to thank and bless God in a godlike manner, and acquit yourself most perfectly of all the duties of religion. With this object in view you might say:

"1. I am quite incapable, O my God, of honoring Thee by myself. For, besides that, my homages would be but the homages of nothingness; the darkness of my intelligence, the vagaries of my imagination, do not allow me a thought worthy of Thee. But I offer Thee the divine thought of Jesus Christ, the infinite praises which the Spirit of Thy well-beloved Son now offers

19

Thee within my heart and will continue to render Thee in heaven for all eternity. The coldness of my heart towards Thee saddens and afflicts me; but I offer Thee the Sacred Heart of Jesus Christ with all its burning love. Through this loving heart I love Thee. It is mine, for Thou hast given it to me. Oh, do not put to me the question which so troubled and saddened the heart of Peter: 'Diligis me?' For I would answer with equal confidence: 'Tu scis quia amo te.' Thou shouldst be content with my love when, as now, it is the emanation of a heart substantially united to the heart of Thy adorable Son."

" 2. Personally laden with Thy blessings and deputed ambassador of the Church and the universe, I am in duty bound to offer Thee due gratitude, not only for all the graces which I have received from Thee, for the eternal love wherewith Thou hast loved me, but also for all the blessings which Thou pourest down upon all living creatures, for all that the elect and the reprobate have received of Thee."

" Gratitude should be proportionate to the favor. By approaching the altar, I accepted the charge of returning Thee adequate thanks in behalf of mankind in general for all Thou hast done for it, and particularly for the inhabitants of that heavenly country. Who can say what they owe to Thee, O bountiful and merciful God? What shall you return to the Lord, O apostles, martyrs, confessors, virgins, and thou above all, Mary, the most privileged and grateful of creatures? You invite me to glorify Him with you. 'Magnificate Dominum mecum.' That I do. I thank Him for you and for myself. Thanks to His unspeakable mercy towards me, I can cancel your debts as well as my own, however immense they may be. He has given me His Son, the image of His substance, another Himself. It is His own Son whom I offer Him in return, His Son who praises and thanks Him in me and in the name of the whole Church, of which He is the adorable Head. Oh, how consoling for me to acquire claims to the gratitude of the saints and the Queen of saints by enabling them to offer to God a thanksgiving proportionate to the favors which they received!"

" 3. O my God, my life hitherto has been but a continual series of prevarications! I even still offend Thee every moment, and such is Thy sanctity that Thou canst not regard anything defiled by sin. ' Respicere ad iniquitatem non potens.' Behold Thy Christ, the great Restorer of Thy glory! To efface my numberless iniquities, and those of my brethren, sinners like myself. I offer Thee the rigorous expiation of Gethsemani, of the Prætorium, and of Calvary. It should suffice, however countless and enormous may be my crimes and those of the whole world. When I find myself united to this Victim of propitiation, when I blend the voice of my supplications with the voice of His blood, my soul is filled with hope in imploring pardon for myself and for all sinners. Canst Thou forgiveness refuse when the sorrow, the tears, the death of a penitent God demand it?"

"4. I have implored Thy clemency and satisfied Thy justice; but my confidence in Thy goodness increases with every new evidence of Thy love. I therefore unite my prayer to the prayer of Him whom I possess within me, and whom Thou always hearest. I address myself to Thee as to the tenderest and most generous of fathers. I come to pour forth my soul into Thy bosom and to crave new blessings. Thou knowest, O Lord, what are the wants of my soul. My desires also are known to Thee. ' Domine, ante te omne desiderium meum.' I have now no other desires but those of Thy Son. At least they are the only ones I acknowledge and beg of Thee to consider. To my prayer and His grant that my union with Him, and through Him my union with Thee, may become unalterable, eternal, and daily more perfect. As to the details of the particular graces which my weakness, my inclinations, my dangers, my ministry and its grave obligations imperatively require, I leave all to the love of my Saviour for me, and content myself with simply indorsing all His petitions. I only beseech Thee, O my God, to extend Thy mercy and blessings to all those for whom I am bound to pray, for whom I would presently pray were their wants or desires known to me; and to those for whose welfare Thy beloved Son Himself desires that I should pray."

Finally, soaring above all things earthly, above all ages and all time, above everything which is not God, you will come to the greatest glory of God, and that is—God Himself. He was from all eternity infinitely happy, infinitely glorious. In Himself He possessed all. He was His own heaven, His own happiness. His attributes, His perfections were His glory, and that glory was essential, absolute, immutable, inseparable from His infinitely perfect Being. Rejoicing in this glory, you practise the love of complacency. Of all love this is the purest, the freest from all selfish interest, and consequently the most pleasing to God. Rejoice that the wicked with all their criminal machinations can never detract from this glory of your Sovereign Lord and loving Father,—nay, can but give to it additional lustre. Rejoice that He has no need of your praise, or of the praises of any created being, or even of the external glory which accrues to Him from the Incarnation of His Word. Intoxicated, lost in this ocean of infinite glory and felicity, say the " Gloria Patri" with all the fervor of which you are capable. Glory be to the Father, to the Son, and to the Holy Ghost—a glory independent of all but Himself, a glory which He had before all ages, which He now has, and shall have for ever and ever. " Sicut erat in principio, et nunc et semper et in sæcula sæculorum. Amen."

We know good priests who derive much spiritual

consolation and profit from the following manner of thanksgiving:

As soon as they have taken off the sacred vestments and recited the psalm " Benedicite," shutting themselves up with Jesus Christ in their hearts, in profound silence and recollection, they adore with Mary the Word who became incarnate in her womb, and who now dwells within them, where He immolates and annihilates Himself in His sacramental state. They contemplate and admire the wonders which He works in them by transforming them into Himself and communicating to them His divine life. They listen to what He says, to what He desires for them, in order that they should respond to His love. Then, whilst continuing to meditate, they recite the form of prayer called Chaplet or Crown of Our Lord, because its object is to honor the mysteries of His nativity, life, death, and resurrection.[1]

The fervent priest who has just received at the altar so affecting a pledge of the love of Jesus Christ is impatient to repay that love by laboring with Him for the glory of His Father and the salvation of souls. The

---

[1] This Crown is composed of three decades of Paters, each decade being preceded by one Ave Maria ; of three other Paters, to complete thirty-three, corresponding to the years of Our Lord's natural life, preceded and followed by one Ave Maria. The five Ave Marias of the Crown are said in honor of the five wounds of Jesus Christ. The Chaplet ends with the Credo, in which are resumed the mysteries of the Saviour.

Many indulgences are attached to this devotion.— *Vide* Raccolta, Chaplet of Our Lord.

effect of a well-said Mass is to fire us with sacred zeal. We are ready to suffer everything for God—labor, fatigue, apparent uselessness of our ministry, humiliation, ennui, contradiction of all kinds which are so often inseparable from our labors. We are ready to die for Him whose death we have just been meditating on, whose merits have been applied to our souls, and, if necessary, to declare with Him the great and supreme "Consummatum est." A life of prayer, good works, self-immolation should be our continual thanksgiving after the celebration of the holy sacrifice. "Vita sic canta," says St. Augustine, "ut nunquam sileas."

PRINTED BY BENZIGER BROTHERS, NEW YORK

STANDARD CATHOLIC BOOKS

PUBLISHED BY

BENZIGER BROTHERS,

CINCINNATI:
843 Main St.

NEW YORK:
86 & 38 BARCLAY ST.

CHICAGO:
178 Monroe St.

ABANDONMENT ; or, Absolute Surrender of Self to Divine Providence. By Rev. J. P. CAUSSADE, S.J. 32mo, *net*, o 40

ANALYSIS OF THE GOSPELS of the Sundays of the Year. By Rev. L. A. LAMBERT, LL.D. 12mo, *net*, 1 25

ART OF PROFITING BY OUR FAULTS, according to St. Francis de Sales. By Rev. J. TISSOT. 32mo, *net*, o 40

BIBLE, THE HOLY. With Annotations, References, and an Historical and Chronological Index. 12mo, cloth, 1 25
Also in finer bindings.

BIRTHDAY SOUVENIR, OR DIARY. With a Subject of Meditation for Every Day. By Mrs. A. E. BUCHANAN. 32mo, o 50

BLESSED ONES OF 1888. By ELIZA A. DONNELLY. 16mo, illustrated, o 50

BLIND FRIEND OF THE POOR : Reminiscences of the Life and Works of Mgr. de SEGUR. 16mo, o 50

BROWNSON, ORESTES A., Literary, Scientific, and Political Views of. Selected from his works, by H. F. BROWNSON. 12mo, *net*, 1 25

BUGG, LELIA HARDIN. The Correct Thing for Catholics. 16mo, o 75

—— A Lady. Manners and Social Usages. 16mo, 1 00

CANONICAL PROCEDURE in Disciplinary and Criminal Cases of Clerics. By the Rev. FRANCIS DROSTE. Edited by the Right Rev. SEBASTIAN G. MESSMER, D.D. 12mo, *net*, 1 50

CATECHISM OF FAMILIAR THINGS. Their History and the Events which led to their Discovery. 12mo, illustrated, 1 00

CATHOLIC BELIEF ; or, A Short and Simple Exposition of Catholic Doctrine. By the Very Rev. JOSEPH FAÀ DI BRUNO, D.D. Author's American edition edited by Rev. LOUIS A LAMBERT. 200th Thousand. 16mo.
Paper, 0.25 ; 25 copies, 4.25 ; 50 copies, 7.50 ; 100 copies, 12 50
Cloth, 0.50; 25 copies, 8.50; 50 copies, 15.00; 100 copies, 25 00

"When a book supplies, as does this one, a demand that necessitates the printing of one hundred thousand [now two hundred thousand] copies, its merits need no eulogizing."—*Ave Maria.*

"The amount of good accomplished by it can never be told."—*Catholic Union and Times.*

CATHOLIC FAMILY LIBRARY. Composed of "The Christian Father," "The Christian Mother," "Sure Way to a Happy Marriage," "Instructions on the Commandments and Sacraments," and "Stories for First Communicants." 5 volumes in box. 2 00

CATHOLIC HOME ANNUAL. A Charming Annual for Catholics. 0 25

CATHOLIC HOME LIBRARY. 10 volumes. 12mo, each, 0 50
Per set, 3 00

CATHOLIC MEMOIRS OF VERMONT AND NEW HAMPSHIRE. 12mo, cloth, 1.00 ; paper, 0 50

CATHOLIC WORSHIP. The Sacraments, Ceremonies, and Festivals of the Church explained. BRENNAN. Paper, 0.15 ; per 100, 9.00. Cloth, 0.25 ; per 100, 15 00

CATHOLIC YOUNC MAN OF THE PRESENT DAY. By Right Rev. AUGUSTINE EGGER, D.D. 32mo. paper, 0.15 ; per 100, 9.00. Cloth, 0.25 ; per 100, 15 00

CHARITY THE ORIGIN OF EVERY BLESSING. 16mo, 0 75

CHRIST IN TYPE AND PROPHECY. By Rev. A. J. MAAS, S.J. 2 vols., 12mo, *net*, 4 00
"By far the most serviceable manual that has hitherto appeared in the English language on a most important subject."—*London Tablet.*

CHRISTIAN ANTHROPOLOGY. By Rev. J. THEIN. 8vo, *net*, 2 50

CHRISTIAN FATHER, THE : what he should be, and what he should do. Paper, 0.25 ; per 100, 12.50. Cloth, 0.35 ; per 100, 21 00

CHRISTIAN MOTHER, THE : the Education of her Children and her Prayer. Paper, 0.25 ; per 100, 12.50. Cloth, 0.35 ; per 100, 21 00

CIRCUS–RIDER'S DAUGHTER, THE. A novel. By F. v. BRACKEL. 12mo, 1 25

CLARKE, REV. RICHARD F., S.J. The Devout Year. Short Meditations. 24mo, *net*, 0 60

COCHEM'S EXPLANATION OF THE MASS. With Preface by Rt. Rev. C. P. MAES, D.D. 12mo, cloth, 1 25

COMEDY OF ENGLISH PROTESTANTISM, THE. Edited by A. F. MARSHALL, B.A. Oxon. 12mo, *net*, 0 50

COMPENDIUM SACRAE LITURGIAE Juxta Ritum Romanum una cum Appendice De Jure Ecclesiastico Particulari in America Foederata Sept. vigente scripsit P. WAPELHORST, O.S.F. 8vo, *net*, 2 50

CONNOR D'ARCY'S STRUGGLES. A novel. By Mrs. W. M. BERTHOLDS. 12mo,   1 25

COUNSELS OF A CATHOLIC MOTHER to Her Daughter, 16mo,   0 50

CROWN OF THORNS, THE ; or, The Little Breviary of the Holy Face. 32mo,   0 50

DATA OF MODERN ETHICS EXAMINED, THE. By Rev. JOHN J. MING, S.J. 12mo,   *net*, 2 00

DE GOESBRIAND, RIGHT REV. L. Christ on the Altar. Instructions for the Sundays and Festivals of the Year. Quarto cloth, richly illustrated, gilt edges,   6 00

—————— Jesus the Good Shepherd. 16mo,   *net*, 0 75

—————— The Labors of the Apostles: Their Teaching of the Nations. 12mo,   *net*, 1 00

—————— History of Confession; or, The Dogma of Confession Vindicated. 16mo,   *net*, 0 75

EGAN, MAURICE F. The Vocation of Edward Conway. A novel. 12mo,   1 25

—————— The Flower of the Flock, and the Badgers of Belmont. 12mo,   1 00

—————— How They Worked Their Way, and Other Stories,   1 00

—————— A Gentleman. 16mo,   0 75

ENGLISH READER. Edited by Rev. EDWARD CONNOLLY, S.J. 12mo,   1 25

EUCHARISTIC GEMS. A Thought about the Most Blessed Sacrament for Every Day. By Rev. L. C. COELENBIER. 16mo, 0 75

EXAMINATION OF CONSCIENCE for the use of Priests who are making a Retreat. By GADUEL. 32mo,   *net*, 0 30

EXPLANATION OF THE BALTIMORE CATECHISM of Christian Doctrine. By Rev. THOMAS L. KINKEAD. 12mo, *net*, 1 00

EXPLANATION OF THE GOSPELS of the Sundays and Holydays. From the Italian, by Rev. L. A. LAMBERT, LL.D. With An Explanation of Catholic Worship. From the German, by Rev. RICHARD BRENNAN, LL.D. 24mo, illustrated.
Paper, 0.25; 25 copies, 4.25; 50 copies, 7.50; 100 copies,   12 50
Cloth, 0.50; 25 copies, 8.50; 50 copies, 15.00; 100 copies,   25 00

"It is with pleasure I recommend the 'Explanation of the Gospels and of Catholic Worship' to the clergy and the laity. It should have a very extensive sale; lucid explanation, clear style, solid matter, beautiful illustrations. Everybody will learn from this little book."—ARCHBISHOP JANSSENS.

FABIOLA ; or, The Church of the Catacombs. By CARDINAL WISEMAN. Illustrated Edition. 12mo,   1 25
Edition de luxe,   6 00

FINN, REV. FRANCIS J., S.J. Percy Wynn ; or, Making a Boy
    of Him. 12mo,   0 85
—— Tom Playfair; or, Making a Start. 12mo,   0 85
—— Harry Dee; or, Working it Out. 12mo,   0 85
—— Claude Lightfoot ; or, How the Problem was Solved.
    12mo,   0 85
—— Ethelred Preston; or, The Adventures of a Newcomer.
    12mo,   0 85
—— Mostly Boys. 16mo,   0 85

    Father Finn's books are, in the opinion of the best critics, standard works in modern English literature ; they are full of fascinating interest, replete with stirring and amusing incidents of college life, and admirably adapted to the wants of our boys.

FIVE O'CLOCK STORIES ; or, The Old Tales Told Again.
    16mo,   0 75

FLOWERS OF THE PASSION. Thoughts of St. Paul of the Cross.
    By Rev. LOUIS TH. DE JÉSUS-AGONISANT. 32mo,   0 50

FOLLOWING OF CHRIST, THE. By THOMAS À KEMPIS.
    With reflections. Small 32mo, cloth,   0 50
    Without reflections. Small 32mo, cloth,   0 45
    Edition de luxe. Illustrated,   from 1 50 up.

FRANCIS DE SALES, ST. Guide for Confession and Com-
    munion. Translated by Mrs. BENNETT-GLADSTONE. 32mo, 0 60
—— Maxims and Counsels for Every Day. 32mo,   0 50
—— New Year Greetings. 32mo, flexible cloth, 15 cents ; per
    100,   10 00

GENERAL PRINCIPLES OF THE RELIGIOUS LIFE. By
    Very Rev. BONIFACE F. VERHEYEN, O.S.B. 32mo,   *net*, 0 30

GLORIES OF DIVINE GRACE. From the German of Dr. M.
    Jos. SCHEEBEN, by a BENEDICTINE MONK. 12mo,   *net*, 1 50

GOD KNOWABLE AND KNOWN. RONAYNE. 12mo, *net*, 1 25

GOFFINE'S DEVOUT INSTRUCTIONS on the Epistles and
    Gospels. With Preface by His Eminence Cardinal GIBBONS.
    Illustrated edition. 8vo, cloth, 1.00; 10 copies, 7.50 ; 25 copies,
    17.50; 50 copies,   33 50
    This is the best, the cheapest, and the most popular illustrated edition of Goffine's Instructions.

"GOLDEN SANDS," Books by the Author of :
    Golden Sands. Third, Fourth, Fifth Series. 32mo, each, 0 60
    Book of the Professed. 32mo.
        Vol. I.   )   (*net*, 0 75
        Vol. II.   } Each with a steel-plate Frontispiece. { *net*, 0 60
        Vol. III.)   (*net*, 0 60
    Prayer. 32mo,   *net*, 0 40
    The Little Book of Superiors. 32mo,   *net*, 0 60
    Spiritual Direction. 32mo,   *net*, 0 60
    Little Month of May. 32mo, flexible cloth,   0 25
    Little Month of the Poor Souls. 32mo, flexible cloth,   0 25

GREETINGS TO THE CHRIST-CHILD.   A Collection of Christmas Poems for the Young.   16mo, illustrated,   o 50

GROU, REV. J., S.J.   The Characteristics of True Devotion. Translated from the French by the Rev. ALEXANDER CLINTON, S.J.   A new edition, by Rev. SAMUEL H. FRISBEE, S.J. 16mo,   *net*, o 75

———— The Interior of Jesus and Mary.   Edited by Rev. SAMUEL H. FRISBEE, S.J.   16mo, 2 vols.,   *net*, 2 oo

HAMON'S MEDITATIONS.   See under MEDITATIONS.   5 vols. 16mo,   *net*, 5 oo

HANDBOOK FOR ALTAR SOCIETIES, and Guide for Sacristans and others having charge of the Altar and Sanctuary. 16mo,   *net*, o 75

HANDBOOK OF THE CHRISTIAN RELIGION.   For the use of Advanced Students and the Educated Laity.   By Rev. W. WILMERS, S.J.   From the German.   Edited by Rev. JAMES CONWAY, S.J.   12mo,   *net*, 1 50

HAPPY YEAR, A; or, The Year Sanctified by Meditating on the Maxims and Sayings of the Saints.   By ABBÉ LASAUSSE. 12mo,   *net*, 1 oo

HEART, THE, OF ST. JANE FRANCES DE CHANTAL. Thoughts and Prayers.   32mo,   *net*, o 40

HIDDEN TREASURE; or, The Value and Excellence of the Holy Mass.   By ST. LEONARD OF PORT-MAURICE.   32mo,   o 50

HISTORY OF THE CATHOLIC CHURCH.   By Dr. H. BRUECK. With Additions from the Writings of His Eminence Cardinal Hergenröther.   Translated by Rev. E. PRUENTE.   2 vols., 8vo,   *net*, 3 oo

HISTORY OF THE CATHOLIC CHURCH.   Adapted by Rev. RICHARD BRENNAN, LL.D.   With a History of the Church in America, by JOHN GILMARY SHEA, LL.D.   With 90 Illustrations. 8vo,   2 oo

HISTORY OF THE MASS and its Ceremonies in the Eastern and Western Church.   By Rev. JOHN O'BRIEN, A.M.   12mo, *net*, 1 25

HOLY FACE OF JESUS, THE.   A Series of Meditations on the Litany of the Holy Face.   32mo,   o 50

HOURS BEFORE THE ALTAR; or, Meditations on the Holy Eucharist.   By Mgr. DE LA BOUILLERIE.   32mo,   o 50

HOW TO GET ON.   By Rev. BERNARD FEENEY.   12mo, paper, o 50; cloth,   1 oo

HUNOLT'S SERMONS.   Sermons by the Rev. FRANCIS HUNOLT. Priest of the Society of Jesus and Preacher in the Cathedral of

Treves. Translated from the original German edition of Cologne, 1740, by the Rev. J. ALLEN, D.D.   12 vols., 8vo, 30 00
Per set of 2 vols.,   *net*, 5 00
Vols. 1, 2.   The Christian State of Life.
Vols. 3, 4.   The Bad Christian.
Vols. 5, 6.   The Penitent Christian.
Vols. 7, 8.   The Good Christian.
Vols. 9, 10.   The Christian's Last End.
Vols. 11, 12.   The Christian's Model.

His Eminence Cardinal Satolli, Pro-Delegate Apostolic: " . . . I believe that in it is found realized the desire of the Holy Father, who not long ago in an encyclical urged so strongly the return to the simple, unaffected, but earnest and eloquent preaching of the word of God. . . ."

His Eminence Cardinal Gibbons, Archbishop of Baltimore: . . . "Contain a fund of solid doctrine, presented in a clear and forcible style. These sermons should find a place in the library of every priest. . . ."

His Eminence Cardinal Vaughan, Archbishop of Westminster: " . . . I cannot praise it too highly, and I think it might find a place in every priest's library."

His Eminence Cardinal Logue, Archbishop of Armagh, Primate of all Ireland: " . . . What is of real service is some work in which the preacher can find sound, solid matter. I believe Father Hunolt's Sermons furnishes an inexhaustible treasure of such matter. . . ."

IDOLS; or, The Secret of the Rue Chaussée d'Antin. A novel. By RAOUL DE NAVERY. 12mo,   1 25

INSTRUCTIONS ON THE COMMANDMENTS and the Sacraments. By ST. LIGUORI. 32mo. Paper, 0.25 ; per 100, 12 50
Cloth, 0.35 ; per 100,   21 00

KONINGS, THEOLOGIA MORALIS. Novissimi Ecclesiæ Doctoris S. Alphonsi. In Compendium Redacta, et Usui Venerabilis Cleri Americani Accommodata, Auctore A. KONINGS, C.SS.R. Editio septima, auctior, et novis curis expolitior, curante HENRICO KUPER, C.SS.R. The two vols. in one, half morocco, *net*, 4 00

LEGENDS AND STORIES OF THE HOLY CHILD JESUS from Many Lands. Collected by A. FOWLER LUTZ. 16mo, 0 75

LEPER QUEEN, THE. A Story of the Thirteenth Century. 16mo,   0 50

LIBRARY OF THE RELIGIOUS LIFE. Composed of "Book of the Professed," by the author of "Golden Sands," 3 vols. ; "Spiritual Direction," by the author of "Golden Sands" ; and "Souvenir of the Novitiate." 5 vols., 32mo, in case,   3 25

LIFE AND ACTS OF LEO XIII. By Rev. JOSEPH E. KELLER, S.J. Fully and beautifully illustrated. 8vo,   2 00

LIFE OF ST. ALOYSIUS GONZAGA. From the Italian of Rev. Father CEPARI, S.J. Edited by Rev. F. GOLDIE, S.J. Edition de luxe, richly illustrated. 8vo,   *net*, 2 50

LIFE OF THE EVER-BLESSED VIRGIN. From Her Conception to Her Assumption. 12mo, imitation cloth,   0 30

LIFE OF FATHER CHARLES SIRE. By his brother, Rev. VITAL SIRE. 12mo,   *net*, 1 00

LIFE OF ST. CLARE OF MONTEFALCO. By Rev. JOSEPH A. LOCKE, O.S.A. 12mo,   *net*, 0 75

LIFE OF THE VEN. MARY CRESCENTIA HÖSS.
  12mo, *net*, 1 25
LIFE OF REV. MOTHER ST. JOHN FONTBONNE. By
  Abbé Rivaux. 12mo, *net*, 1 25
LIFE OF ST. FRANCIS SOLANUS, APOSTLE OF PERU.
  16mo, *net*, 0 50
LIFE OF ST. GERMAINE COUSIN. 16mo, 0 50
LIFE OF ST. IGNATIUS OF LOYOLA. By Father Genelli.
  12mo, *net*, 1 25
LIFE OF ST. CHANTAL. See under St. Chantal. *net*, 4 00
(LIFE OF) MOST REV. JOHN HUGHES, First Archbishop of
  New York. By Rev. H. A. Brann, D.D. 12mo, *net*, 0 75
LIFE OF FATHER JOGUES. By Father Felix Martin, S.J.
  From the French by John Gilmary Shea. 12mo, *net*, 0 75
LIFE OF MLLE. LE GRAS. 12mo, *net*, 1 25
LIFE OF MARY FOR CHILDREN. By Anne R. Bennett, née
  Gladstone. 24mo, illustrated, *net*, 0 50
LIFE OF RIGHT REV. JOHN N. NEUMANN, D.D. By Rev.
  E. Grimm, C.SS.R. 12mo, *net*, 1 25
LIFE OF OUR LORD AND SAVIOUR JESUS CHRIST and of
  His blessed Mother. Adapted by Rev. Richard Brennan,
  LL.D. With nearly 600 illustrations. No. 1. Roan back, gold
  title, plain cloth sides, sprinkled edges, *net*, 5 00
  No. 3. Morocco back and corners, cloth sides with gold stamp,
  gilt edges, *net*, 7 00
  No. 4. Full morocco, richly gilt back, with large figure of Our
  Lord in gold on side, gilt edges, *net*, 9 00
  No. 5. Full morocco, block-paneled sides, superbly gilt, gilt
  edges, *net*, 10 00
LIFE OF OUR BLESSED LORD. His Life, Death, Resurrec-
  tion. 12mo, imitation cloth, 0 30
LIFE, POPULAR, OF ST. TERESA OF JESUS. By L'Abbé
  Marie-Joseph. 12mo, *net*, 0 75
LIGUORI, ST. ALPHONSUS DE. Complete Ascetical Works of.
  Centenary Edition. Edited by Rev. Eugene Grimm, C.SS.R.
  Price, per volume, *net*, 1 25

  Each book is complete in itself, and any volume will be sold separately.
  Volumes 1 to 22 are now ready.

Preparation for Death.	True Spouse of Christ, 2 vols.
Way of Salvation and of Perfection.	Dignity and Duties of the Priest.
Great Means of Salvation and Perfection.	The Holy Mass.
	The Divine Office.
Incarnation, Birth, and Infancy of Christ.	Preaching.
	Abridged Sermons for all the Sundays.
The Passion and Death of Christ.	Miscellany.
The Holy Eucharist.	Letters, 4 vols.
The Glories of Mary, 2 vols.	Letters and General Index.
Victories of the Martyrs.	Life of St. Alphonsus, 2 vols.

LINKED LIVES. A novel. By Lady GERTRUDE DOUGLAS. 8vo,   1 50

LITTLE COMPLIMENTS OF THE SEASON. Simple Verses for Namedays, Birthdays, Christmas, New Year, and other festive and social occasions. By ELEANOR C. DONNELLY. 12mo, *net*, 0 50

LITTLE MANUAL OF ST. ANTHONY. Illustrated. 32mo, cloth,   0 60

LITTLE MANUAL OF THE SODALITY OF THE CHILD JESUS. 32mo,   0 20

LITTLE PICTORIAL LIVES OF THE SAINTS. With Reflections for Every Day in the Year. Edited by JOHN GILMARY SHEA, LL.D. With nearly 400 illustrations. 12mo, cloth, ink and gold side,   1 00
10 copies, 6.25; 25 copies, 15.00; 50 copies, 27.50; 100 copies, 50 00
The book has received the approbation of the following prelates: Archbishop Kenrick, Archbishop Grace, Archbishop Hennessy, Archbishop Salpointe, Archbishop Ryan, Archbishop Gross, Archbishop Duhamel, Archbishop Kain, Archbishop O'Brien, Archbishop Katzer, Bishop McCloskey, Bishop Grandin, Bishop O'Hara, Bishop Mullen, Bishop Marty, Bishop Ryan, of Buffalo; Bishop Fink, Bishop Seidenbush, Bishop Moreau, Bishop Racine, Bishop Spalding, Bishop Vertin, Bishop Junger, Bishop Naughten, Bishop Richter, Bishop Rademacher, Bishop Cosgrove, Bishop Curtis, and Bishop Glorieux.

LITTLE PRAYER BOOK OF THE SACRED HEART. Prayers and Practices of Blessed Margaret Mary. Sm. 32mo, cloth, 0 40
Also in finer bindings.

LITTLE SAINT OF NINE YEARS. From the French of Mgr. DE SEGUR, by MARY McMAHON. 16mo,   0 50

LIVES, SHORT, OF THE SAINTS; or, Our Birthday Bouquet. By ELEANOR C. DONNELLY. 16mo.   1 00

LOURDES. Its Inhabitants, Its Pilgrims, Its Miracles. By R. F. CLARKE, S.J. 16mo, illustrated,   0 75

LUTHER'S OWN STATEMENTS Concerning his Teachings and its Results. By HENRY O'CONNOR, S.J. 12mo, paper,   0 15

MANIFESTATION OF CONSCIENCE. Confessions and Communions in Religious Communities. By Rev. PIE DE LANGOGNE, O.M.Cap. 32mo,   *net*, 0 50

MANUAL OF THE HOLY FAMILY. Prayers and Instructions for Catholic Parents. 32mo, cloth,   0 60
Also in finer bindings.

MANUAL OF INDULGENCED PRAYERS. A Complete Prayer Book. Arranged and disposed for daily use by Rev. BONAVENTURE HAMMER, O.S.F. Small 32mo, cloth,   0 40
Also in finer bindings.

MARCELLA GRACE. A novel. By ROSA MULHOLLAND. With illustrations after original drawings. 12mo,   1 25

MARRIAGE. By Very Rev. PÈRE MONSABRÉ, O.P. From the French, by M. HOPPER. 12mo,   *net*, 1 00

MARRIAGE, Popular Instructions On. By Very Rev. F. GIRARDEY, C.SS.R. 32mo, paper, 0.25; per 100, 12.50; cloth, 0.35; per 100,   21 00

The instructions treat of the great dignity of matrimony, its indissolubility, the obstacles to it, the evils of mixed marriage, the manner of getting married, and the duties it imposes on the married between each other and in reference to their offspring.

MEANS OF GRACE, THE. A Complete Exposition of the Seven Sacraments, of the Sacramentals, and of Prayer, with a Comprehensive Explanation of the "Lord's Prayer" and the "Hail Mary." By Rev. RICHARD BRENNAN, LL.D. • With 180 full-page and other illustrations. 8vo, cloth, 2.50; gilt edges, 3.00; Library edition, half levant,   3 50

"The best book for family use out."—BISHOP MULLEN.
"A work worthy of unstinted praise and heartiest commendation."—BISHOP RYAN, of Buffalo.
"The wealth of matter, the admirable arrangement, and the simplicity of language of this work will make it a valuable addition to the household library." —BISHOP BRADLEY.

MEDITATIONS (BAXTER) for Every Day in the Year. By Rev. ROGER BAXTER, S.J. Republished by Rev. P. NEALE, S.J. Small 12mo,   *net*, 1 25

MEDITATIONS (HAMON'S) FOR ALL THE DAYS OF THE YEAR. For the use of Priests, Religious, and the Laity. By Rev. M. HAMON, SS., Pastor of St. Sulpice, Paris. From the French, by Mrs. ANNE R. BENNETT-GLADSTONE. With Alphabetic Index. 5 vols., 16mo, cloth, gilt top, each with a Steel Engraving,   *net*, 5 00

"The five handsome volumes will form a very useful addition to the devotional library of every ecclesiastic."—HIS EMINENCE CARDINAL LOGUE.
"Hamon's doctrine is the unadulterated word of God, presented with unction, exquisite taste, and freed from that exaggerated and sickly sentimentalism which disgusts when it does not mislead."—MOST REV. P. L. CHAPELLE, D.D.
"We are using them daily, and are delighted with them."—MOTHER M. BLANCHE, Mother House Sisters of Charity, Mt. St. Joseph, O.
"Having examined the 'Meditations' by M. Hamon, SS., we are pleased to recommend them not only as useful and practicable for religious, but also for those who in the world desire by means of mental prayer to advance in the spiritual life."—SISTERS OF ST. JOSEPH, Flushing, L. I.

MEDITATIONS (PERINALDO) on the Sufferings of Jesus Christ. From the Italian of Rev. FRANCIS DA PERINALDO, O.S.F. 12mo,   *net*, 0 75

MEDITATIONS (VERCRUYSSE), for Every Day in the Year, on the Life of Our Lord Jesus Christ. By the Rev. Father BRUNO VERCRUYSSE, S.J. 2 vols.,   4 00

MEDITATIONS ON THE PASSION OF OUR LORD. By a PASSIONIST FATHER. 32mo,   0 40

MISTRESS OF NOVICES, The, Instructed in her Duties. From the French of the ABBÉ LEGUAY, by Rev. IGNATIUS SISK. 12mo, cloth,   *net*, 0 75

MOMENTS BEFORE THE TABERNACLE. By Rev. MATTHEW RUSSELL, S.J. 24mo,   *net*, 0 40

MONK'S PARDON. A Historical Romance of the Time of Philip IV. of Spain. By RAOUL DE NAVERY. 12mo,   '1 25

MONTH OF THE DEAD. 32mo,   0 75

MONTH OF MAY. From the French of Father DEBUSSI, S.J., by ELLA MCMAHON. 32mo,   0 50

MONTH, NEW, OF MARY, St. Francis de Sales.   32mo,   0 40

MONTH, NEW, OF THE SACRED HEART, St. Francis de Sales. 32mo, • 0 40

MONTH, NEW, OF ST. JOSEPH, St. Francis de Sales. 32mo, 0 40

MONTH, NEW, OF THE HOLY ANGELS, St. Francis de Sales. 32mo,   0 40

MR. BILLY BUTTONS. A novel. By Walter Lecky. 12mo, 1 25

MÜLLER, REV. MICHAEL, C.SS.R. God the Teacher or Mankind. A plain, comprehensive Explanation of Christian Doctrine. 9 vols., crown 8vo. Per set,   *net*, 9 50
The Church and Her Enemies.   *net*, 1 10
The Apostles' Creed.   *net*, 1 10
The First and Greatest Commandment.   *net*, 1 40
Explanation of the Commandments, continued. Precepts of the Church.   *net*, 1 10
Dignity, Authority, and Duties of Parents, Ecclesiastical and Civil Powers. Their Enemies.   *net*, 1 40
Grace and the Sacraments.   *net*, 1 25
Holy Mass.   *net*, 1 25
Eucharist and Penance.   *net*, 1 10
Sacramentals—Prayer, etc.   *net*, 1 00

—— Familiar Explanation of Catholic Doctrine. 12mo,   1 00

—— The Prodigal Son; or, The Sinner's Return to God. 8vo,   *net*, 1 00

—— The Devotion of the Holy Rosary and the Five Scapulars. 8vo,   *net*, 0 75

——- The Catholic Priesthood. 2 vols., 8vo,   *net*, 3 00

MY FIRST COMMUNION: The Happiest Day of My Life BRENNAN. 16mo, illustrated,   0 75

NAMES THAT LIVE IN CATHOLIC HEARTS. Cardinal Ximenes—Michael Angelo—Samuel de Champlain—Archbishop Plunkett—Charles Carroll—Henry Larochejacquelein—Simon de Montfort. By ANNA T. SADLIER. 12mo,   1 00

NATALIE NARISCHKIN, Sister of Charity of St. Vincent of Paul. By Lady G. FULLERTON. 12mo,   *net*, 0 75

NEW TESTAMENT, THE. 32mo. Limp cloth, *net*, 0.20 ; levant, *net*, 1.00 · French calf, red edges,   *net*, 1 60

OFFICE, COMPLETE, OF HOLY WEEK, according to the
Roman Missal and Breviary, in Latin and English. New
edition, revised and enlarged. 24mo, cloth, 0.50 ; cloth, limp,
gilt edges, 1 00
Also in finer bindings.

O'GRADY, ELEANOR. Aids to Correct and Effective Elocution.
12mo, 1 25
———— Select Recitations for Schools and Academies. 12mo, 1 00
———— Readings and Recitations for Juniors. 16mo, *net*, 0 50
———— Elocution Class. A Simplification of the Laws and Prin-
ciples of Expression. 16mo, *net*, 0 50

ON CHRISTIAN ART. By EDITH HEALY. 16mo, 0 50

ON THE ROAD TO ROME, and How Two Brothers Got There.
By WILLIAM RICHARDS. 16mo, *net*, 0 75

ONE AND THIRTY DAYS WITH BLESSED MARGARET
MARY. 32mo, flexible cloth, 0 25

ONE ANGEL MORE IN HEAVEN. With Letters of Condo-
lence by St. Francis de Sales and others. White mar., 0 50

OUR BIRTHDAY BOUQUET. Culled from the Shrines of Saints
and the Gardens of Poets. By E. C. DONNELLY. 16mo, 1 00

OUR LADY OF GOOD COUNSEL IN GENAZZANO. By
ANNE R. BENNETT, née GLADSTONE. 32mo, 0 75

OUR OWN WILL, and How to Detect it in Our Actions. By the
Rev. JOHN ALLEN, D.D. 16mo, *net*, 0 75

OUR YOUNG FOLKS' LIBRARY. 10 volumes. 12mo. Each,
0 50 ; per set, 3 00

OUTLAW OF CAMARGUE, THE. A novel. By A. DE LAMOTHE.
12mo, 1 25

OUTLINES OF DOGMATIC THEOLOGY. By Rev. SYLVESTER
J. HUNTER, S.J. 3 vols., 12mo, *net*, 4 50

PARADISE ON EARTH OPENED TO ALL ; or, A Religious
Vocation the Surest Way in Life. 32mo, *net*, 0 40

PEARLS FROM FABER. Selected and arranged by MARION J.
BRUNOWE. 32mo, 0 50

PETRONILLA, and other Stories. By E. C. DONNELLY. 12mo, 1 00

PHILOSOPHY, ENGLISH MANUALS OF CATHOLIC.
Logic. By RICHARD F. CLARKE, S.J. 12mo, *net*, 1 25
First Principles of Knowledge. By JOHN RICKABY, S.J.
12mo, *net*, 1 25
Moral Philosophy (Ethics and Natural Law). By JOSEPH
RICKABY, S.J. 12mo, *net*, 1 25
Natural Theology. By BERNARD BOEDDER, S.J. 12mo, *net*, 1 50
Psychology. By MICHAEL MAHER, S.J. 12mo, *net*, 1 50
General Metaphysics. By JOHN RICKABY, S.J. 12mo, *net*, 1 25
A Manual of Political Economy. By C. S. DEVAS, Esq., M.A.
12mo, *net*, 1 50

PICTORIAL LIVES OF THE SAINTS. With Reflections for Every Day in the Year. Edited by JOHN GILMARY SHEA, LL.D. 50th Thousand. 8vo,   2 00
5 copies, 6.65 ; 10 copies, 12.50 ; 25 copies, 27.50 ; 50 copies, 50 00

PRAYER-BOOK FOR LENT. Meditations and Prayers for Lent. 32mo, cloth,   0 50
Also in finer bindings.

PRAXIS SYNODALIS. Manuale Synodi Diocesanæ ac Provincialis Celebrandæ. 12mo,   *net*, 0 60

PRIEST IN THE PULPIT, THE. A Manual of Homiletics and Catechetics. Adapted from the German of Rev. I. SCHUECH, O.S.B., by Rev. B. LUEBBERMANN. 8vo,   *net*, 1 50

PRIMER FOR CONVERTS, A. By Rev. J. T. DURWARD. 32mo, flexible cloth,   0 25

PRINCIPLES OF ANTHROPOLOGY AND BIOLOGY. By Rev. THOMAS HUGHES, S.J. 16mo,   *net*, 0 75

REASONABLENESS OF CATHOLIC CEREMONIES AND PRACTICES. By Rev. J. J. BURKE. 12mo, flexible cloth, 0 35

RELIGIOUS STATE, THE. With a Short Treatise on Vocation to the Priesthood. By ST. ALPHONSUS DE LIGUORI. 32mo, 0 50

REMINISCENCES OF RT. REV. EDGAR P. WADHAMS, D.D., First Bishop of Ogdensburg. By Rev. C. A. WALWORTH. 12mo, illustrated,   *net*, 1 00

RIGHTS OF OUR LITTLE ONES ; or, First Principles on Education in Catechetical Form. By Rev. JAMES CONWAY, S.J. 32mo, paper, 0.15 ; per 100, 9.00 ; cloth, 0.25 ; per 100,   15 00

ROSARY, THE MOST HOLY, in Thirty-one Meditations, Prayers, and Examples. By Rev. EUGENE GRIMM, C.SS.R. 32mo, 0 50

RUSSO, N., S.J.—De Philosophia Morali Prælectiones in Collegio Georgiopolitano Soc. Jes. Anno 1889-90 Habitae, a Patre NICOLAO RUSSO. Editio altera. 8vo, half leather,   *net*, 2 00

ST. CHANTAL AND THE FOUNDATION OF THE VISITATION. By Monseigneur BOUGAUD. 2 vols., 8vo,   *net*, 4 00

ST. JOSEPH, THE ADVOCATE OF HOPELESS CASES. From the French of Rev. Father HUGUET. 24mo,   1 00

SACRAMENTALS OF THE HOLY CATHOLIC CHURCH, THE. By Rev. A. A. LAMBING, LL.D. Large Edition, 12mo,   *net*, 1 25
Popular Edition, illustrated, 24mo.
Paper, 0.25 ; 25 copies, 4.25 ; 50 copies, 7.50 ; 100 copies,   12 50
Cloth, 0.50 ; 25 copies, 8.50 ; 50 copies, 15.00 ; 100 copies,   25 00
"Am glad you have issued so practical a work, in a shape in which it ought to reach every Catholic family."—CARDINAL SATOLLI, Delegate Apostolic.

SACRED HEART, BOOKS ON THE.

    Devotions to the Sacred Heart for the First Friday of Every Month. By P. HUGUET. 32mo,   0 40
    213. Imitation Levant, limp, gilt centre, round corners, edges red under gold,   1 35
    Imitation of the Sacred Heart of Jesus. By Rev. F. ARNOUDT, S.J. From the Latin by Rev. J. M. FASTRE, S.J. 16mo, cloth,   1 25
    Month of the Sacred Heart of Jesus. From the French of Rev. Father HUGUET. 32mo,   •   0 75
    New Month of the Sacred Heart, St. Francis de Sales. 32mo, 0 40
    One and Thirty Days with Blessed Margaret Mary. From the French by a Visitandine of Baltimore. 32mo, flexible cloth,   0 25
    Pearls from the Casket of the Sacred Heart of Jesus. A Collection of the Letters, Maxims, and Practices of the Blessed Margaret Mary Alacoque. Edited by ELEANOR C. DONNELLY. 32mo,   0 50
    Month of the Sacred Heart for the Young Christian. By BROTHER PHILIPPE. From the French by E. A. MULLIGAN. 32mo,   0 50
    Sacred Heart Studied in the Sacred Scriptures. By Rev. H. SAINTRAIN, C.SS.R. 8vo,   *net*, 2 00
    Revelations of the Sacred Heart to Blessed Margaret Mary; and the History of her Life. By Monseigneur BOUGAUD. 8vo,   *net*, 1 50
    Six Sermons on Devotion to the Sacred Heart of Jesus. From the German of Rev. Dr. E. BIERBAUM, by ELLA McMAHON. 16mo,   *net*, 0 60
    Year of the Sacred Heart. Drawn from the works of PÈRE DE LA COLOMBIÈRE, of Blessed Margaret Mary, and of others. 32mo,   0 50

SAINTS, THE NEW, OF 1888. By Rev. FRANCIS GOLDIE, S.J., and Rev. Father SCOLA, S.J. 16mo, illustrated,   0 50

SECRET OF SANCTITY, THE. According to ST. FRANCIS DE SALES and Father CRASSET, S.J. 12mo,   *net*, 1 00

SERAPHIC GUIDE. A Manual for the Members of the Third Order of St. Francis.   0 60
    Roan, red edges,   0 75
        The same in German at the same prices.

SERMONS, HUNOLT. See under HUNOLT.

SERMONS ON THE BLESSED VIRGIN. By Very Rev. D. I. McDERMOTT. 16mo,   *net*, 0 75

SERMONS for the Sundays and Chief Festivals of the Ecclesiastical Year. With Two Courses of Lenten Sermons and a Triduum for the Forty Hours. By Rev. JULIUS POTTGEISSER, S.J. From the German by Rev. JAMES CONWAY, S.J. 2 vols., 8vo, *net*, 2 50

SERMONS, SHORT, FOR LOW MASSES. A complete, brief course of instruction on Christian Doctrine. By Rev. F. X. SCHOUPPE, S.J. 12mo, *net*, 1 25

SERMONS, SIX, on Devotion to the Sacred Heart of Jesus. From the German of Rev. Dr. E. BIERBAUM, by ELLA McMAHON, 16mo, *net*, 0 60

SHORT CONFERENCES ON THE LITTLE OFFICE OF THE IMMACULATE CONCEPTION. By Very Rev. JOSEPH RAINER. With Prayers. 32mo, 0 50

SHORT STORIES ON CHRISTIAN DOCTRINE: A Collection of Examples illustrating the Catechism. From the French by MARY McMAHON. 12mo, illustrated, *net*, 0 75

SMITH, Rev. S. B., D.D. Elements of Ecclesiastical Law.
    Vol. I. Ecclesiastical Persons. 8vo, *net*, 2 50
    Vol. II. Ecclesiastical Trials. 8vo, *net*, 2 50
    Vol. III. Ecclesiastical Punishments. 8vo, *net*, 2 50
—— Compendium Juris Canonici, ad usum Cleri et Seminariorum hujus regionis accommodatum. 8vo, *net*, 2 00
—— The Marriage Process in the United States. 8vo, *net*, 2 50

SODALISTS' VADE MECUM. A Manual, Prayer Book, and Hymnal. 32mo, cloth, 0 50
Also in finer bindings.

SOUVENIR OF THE NOVITIATE. From the French by Rev. EDWARD I. TAYLOR. 32mo, *net*, 0 60

SPIRITUAL CRUMBS FOR HUNGRY LITTLE SOULS. To which are added Stories from the Bible. By MARY E. RICHARDSON. 16mo, 0 50

STORIES FOR FIRST COMMUNICANTS, for the Time before and after First Communion. By Rev. J. A. KELLER, D.D. 32mo, 0 50

STORY OF JESUS SIMPLY TOLD FOR THE YOUNG. By ROSA MULHOLLAND. 24mo, illustrated, 0 50

SURE WAY TO A HAPPY MARRIAGE. A Book of Instructions for those Betrothed and for Married People. From the German by Rev. EDWARD I. TAYLOR. Paper, 0.25; per 100, 12.50; cloth, 0.35; per 100, 21 00

TALES AND LEGENDS OF THE MIDDLE AGES. From the Spanish of F. DE P. CAPELLA. By HENRY WILSON. 16mo, 0 75

THINK WELL ON'T; or, Reflections on the Great Truths of the Christian Religion. By the Right Rev. R. CHALLONER D.D. 32mo, flexible cloth, 0 20

THOUGHT FROM ST. ALPHONSUS, for Every Day of the Year. 32mo, 0 50

THOUGHT FROM BENEDICTINE SAINTS. 32mo, 0 50

THOUGHT FROM DOMINICAN SAINTS. 32mo,   o 50

THOUGHT FROM ST. FRANCIS ASSISI and his Saints. 32mo,   o 50

THOUGHT FROM ST. IGNATIUS. 32mo,   o 50

THOUGHT FROM ST. TERESA. 32mo,   o 50

THOUGHT FROM ST. VINCENT DE PAUL. 32mo,   o 50

TRUE SPOUSE OF CHRIST. By St. Alphonsus Liguori. 2 vols., 12mo, *net*, 2.50 ; 1 vol., 12mo,   1 50

TRUTHS OF SALVATION. By Rev. J. Pergmayr, S.J. From the German by a Father of the same Society. 16mo, *net*, o 75

TWELVE VIRTUES, THE, of a Good Teacher. For Mothers, Instructors, etc. By Rev. H. Pottier, S.J. 32mo, *net*, o 30

VISIT TO EUROPE AND THE HOLY LAND. By Rev. H. F. Fairbanks. 12mo, illustrated,   1 50

VISITS TO THE MOST HOLY SACRAMENT and to the Blessed Virgin Mary. For Every Day of the Month. By St. Alphonsus de Liguori. Edited by Rev. Eugene Grimm. 32mo,   o 50

WARD, REV. THOMAS F. Fifty-two Instructions on the Principal Truths of Our Holy Religion. 12mo, *net*, o 75
—— Thirty-two Instructions for the Month of May and for the Feasts of the Blessed Virgin. 12mo, *net*, o 75
—— Month of May at Mary's Altar. 12mo, *net*, o 75

WAY OF INTERIOR PEACE. By Rev. Father De Lehen, S.J. From the German Version of Rev. J. Brucker, S.J. 12mo, *net*, 1 25

WENINGER'S SERMONS.
Original Short and Practical Sermons for Every Sunday of the Year. Three Sermons for every Sunday. 8vo, *net*, 2 00
Sermons for Every Feast of the Ecclesiastical Year. Three Sermons for Every Feast. 8vo, *net*, 2 00
Conferences specially addressed to Married and Unmarried Men. 8vo, *net*, 2 00

WHAT CATHOLICS HAVE DONE FOR SCIENCE, with Sketches of the Great Catholic Scientists. By Rev. Martin S. Brennan. 12mo,   1 00

WOMEN OF CATHOLICITY: Margaret O'Carroll—Isabella of Castile—Margaret Roper—Marie de l'Incarnation—Margaret Bourgeoys—Ethan Allen's Daughter. By Anna T. Sadlier. 12mo,   1 00

WORDS OF JESUS CHRIST DURING HIS PASSION, explained in their Literal and Moral Sense. By Rev. F. X. Schouppe, S.J. Flexible cloth,   o 25

WORDS OF WISDOM. A Concordance of the Sapiential Books. 12mo, *net*, 1 25

ZEAL IN THE WORK OF THE MINISTRY; or, The Means by which every Priest may render his Ministry Honorable and Fruitful. From the French of L'Abbé Dubois. 8vo, *net*, 1 50